The Wolverton Demons

VJ Nash

ISBN-13: 978-1-7395539-5-1 (digital)

ISBN-13: 978-1-7395539-6-8 (print)

10 9 8 7 6 5 4 3 2 1

Book cover design by ebooklaunch.com

Also by

The Bermuda Covenant

Jack Kidd and Annie Ingels' happy life in New York is shattered by the sudden death of his estranged father in England. Now they are dragged into the brutal darkness of Jack's past – a past he'd so carefully buried. The reading of the will sets Jack and Annie in direct conflict with his sisters - Rosalind and Veronica. They're rich, devastatingly attractive and have an other-worldly power over men... except their brother. And they hate him for it.

As Jack and Annie are plunged into a murderous nightmare, they uncover the disturbing truth that a mythical evil is at work and will stop at nothing to destroy them and those they love. From England to the Italian alps, to the rich playground of the Hamptons, Jack and Annie must fight for survival as they are drawn inexorably to a final confrontation in the place it all began... Bermuda - the Isle of Devils.

Malevolent

Detective Inspector Ray Ennis doesn't believe in evil. He certainly doesn't believe the claim of a serial killer that all his victims were members of an evil cult and that an abomination lurks beneath the glittering skyscrapers of the City of London, but...

...when a dismembered torso with evidence of ritual sacrifice washes up in the Thames, Ray quickly finds his professional and personal lives unravelling. Elizabeth Russell, a 'Regulator' from the Treasury, seems intent on blocking his investigations, while his daughter, Chloe, is plagued by screaming nightmares that are seeping into reality. And who is the old man in the trench coat, who always seems to be nearby, watching Ray's family and seething with hate?

With the emerging truth challenging his beliefs and his sanity, can Ray put the pieces together before darkness and chaos overwhelm his family? Is there something truly malevolent in the heart of London? And if there is, how can he confront it?

About the author

As someone who is Canadian by birth, Hungarian/Yorkshire by blood and brought up in the south of England, it's fair to say I've never quite fitted in. I didn't help my already slim chances of fitting in by becoming a DeadHead in 1983. Nobody knew who the Grateful Dead were in rural Surrey in the 1980s, so I had to follow that obsession all alone. I have always had a love of horror and spent much of my childhood terrifying myself by reading books and watching films that I really shouldn't have. It probably didn't help that my grandparents' ancient house (it pre-dates the founding of the United States by 200 years) was undoubtedly haunted. Neither did the fact that all the sensible adults in my life had stories to tell of bizarre, unexplained happenings they'd experienced. One of my Hungarian aunts – a reasonable and intelligent person – was even convinced that werewolves and vampires actually existed back in 'the old country'. So, it's hardly surprising I'm writing horror. Also, maybe like you, I often wonder what's out there in the dark, just beyond the bounds of human knowledge.

Preface

While this is purely a work of fiction, a lot of research has gone into its creation and there are certain aspects of it that are based in what we laughingly call 'reality'. The towns named do exist (or have done in the past). The Isle of Wight is an incredible place to experience and well worth an extended visit. It is not only beautiful, but it is also unlike any other part of England. Its history, while partly shared with the rest of the country, also has much that is unique. It was, after all, the last pagan stronghold in England. It is a place steeped in magic and folklore – the Swaailen really is a thing - and its numerous local scarecrow festivals are certainly something to see to be believed.

Meanwhile, The Key of Solomon, referenced here, is an important magical text. Whether you believe it can work or not, its importance in the history of magic is undeniable. It is a good example of how, in previous times, ceremonial magic was not something that anyone could do as a distraction on a wet Saturday afternoon. It took planning, rare materials, discomfort, effort, language skills, academic research and more. Today, certain websites claim that you don't need to fast, ritually cleanse yourself or do anything that involves dedication or hard work in order to conjure a demon. Apparently, you just have to really believe and concentrate hard, then hey presto, you'll have a demon arrive to do your bidding. Really?

I personally would never recommend trying to conjure anything. Either it's all nonsense and you'll just be wasting your time, or something might come to you from out there in the unknown. And once you've invited it in, what then?

Contents

Chapter One

The Iron In The Fire

Elizabeth Russell had hoped that the second rum and coke would improve her mood. It didn't. She looked out of the window at the Atlantic passing by far below her and sipped at the drink glumly. It was indicative of her problem with planes, because even the best ones couldn't provide passengers with a single decent ale. Her violet eyes narrowed as she thought of her litany of complaints about flying, which anti-terrorist and anti-Covid measures had made much, much longer. And she wasn't even slumming it. She was travelling in the highest class and had all the comforts, from a seat that turned into a bed, to full access to the exclusive lounge. Yet she still felt out of place - literally. She agreed with the old Arabic saying that the soul travels at the pace of a camel. All this gadding about the planet at five hundred miles an hour left the soul quite discombobulated. But was that the real problem? She ran a hand through her white hair and sighed. No, the real problem was that she resented the plane for taking her away from the man she'd fallen in love with, and straight towards a job that would be messy at best.

Yesterday morning had started so well, too. She'd woken up spooning her boyfriend, Andy Harper, in the bed of his flat near Southwark Park and had luxuriated in the simple pleasure of sleepily cuddling him until the alarm went off. When she'd arrived at the office, nothing serious had happened during the night, which was a bonus. As The Regulator for His Majesty's Treasury, her job was to defend Britain from all supernatural threats – annoyingly, the forces of evil and chaos did have a penchant for wreaking havoc at night - but yesterday morning had revealed no evil machinations. It'd had all the hallmarks of a slow day right up to ten fifteen when the phone had rung and her executive assistant had answered it,

"Hello, Office of the Regulator, Oliver Fernsby speaking... ah, good morning, Bishop FitzOsbern..."

At the sound of that name, Elizabeth Russell shot straight out of her chair and was across her office and standing in the connecting doorway with Oliver's,

"Is The Regulator here?" Oliver said looking at his boss, who made a sour face, then reluctantly nodded her head,

"Yes, she is..." and then Oliver listened. The frosted skylight above him gave the room an odd underwater feel and made the juxtaposition of his olive complexion, youthful good looks and shock of white hair look rather uncanny. She watched his features, trying to glean what was being said, until he finally replied,

"Can she come and see you within the hour?"

She grimaced at the prospect of seeing Bishop FitzOsbern,

"Let me just check her schedule..." and Oliver noisily shifted some papers around on his desk to make it sound like he was doing something. He looked up at her. She rolled her eyes but nodded again,

"Yes, she can come over to your office..." and then Oliver had to suppress a laugh as she mimed hanging herself,

"Yes, with you by eleven fifteen. Thank you, Bishop, goodbye," and he replaced the earpiece of the 1930's candlestick style phone back in its cradle.

"You're really naughty sometimes!" he chided.

"Oh, come on, he must know we take the piss out of him every time he calls."

"But it's clearly important, because he's making the call himself," Oliver said looking up at her seriously.

"Yeah, I s'pose," Elizabeth Russell replied petulantly.

"And I don't want to accidentally laugh down the phone at a bishop," Oliver added.

"Now, that is a good point," she conceded, "Got to be careful around bishops. One minute they're all please and thank you, and the next they're trying to have you burnt at the stake."

Oliver nodded. It was sage advice.

"He's probably read the report on the Krowos operation and wants to try to haul me over the coals for it... better have the car brought round in ten minutes," and she turned to go back into her office, but paused,

"And Oliver, do something about your hair – it's freaking me out."

"Do something? Like what? It's not my fault it went white. Anyway, your hair's white and you don't hear anyone complaining,"

"That's because I make it look good," she replied.

Oliver looked up at her – the white hair, styled with a pixie cut, perfectly framed her angular features and high cheek bones. And even though she was clearly in her late twenties, her white hair also suited her very pale skin and her glittering violet eyes. Combined with the scarlet trouser suit, black shirt and the heavy silver rings on all her fingers, it gave her a remarkable presence.

"Okay, I'll do something about the hair," Oliver conceded.

"Just don't shave it all off – I don't want a slap-head for an assistant."

"Anything else about my personal grooming you want to have a go at?" Oliver asked with exaggerated tiredness.

"No, that's it. See you in a bit," she smiled sweetly and went back to her office.

At eleven-thirty, Elizabeth Russell was sitting in an ornately decorated first-floor salon with a view across the central garden of Hyde Park Square. Sitting in an armchair opposite her was a fat man of about fifty with deep-set eyes and unruly hair. His clerical collar, purple shirt and large cross worn outside the shirt indicated to those in the know that he was a bishop. However, the Right Reverend Peter FitzOsbern was no ordinary bishop. He was The Bishop Without Portfolio of the Church of England, overseeing Deliverance ministry across the country. In short, he was the country's chief exorcist. He was also the Church's liaison with the Office of the Regulator. Having been speaking for the last ten minutes, he was concluding the tragic tale of a British citizen in America who was the possible victim of demonic possession,

"...Then, two weeks later, at the funeral of her husband, she trapped her son-in-law in the vestry and raped him."

"And this Aggie Thompson is a seventy-four-year-old?" Elizabeth Russell asked.

"Yes. The son-in-law, Richard Turner, is under forty and is an active serviceman, but she was able to overpower him. Broke three of his ribs into the bargain. Since the incident, she has been in the secure ward of a psychiatric hospital..."

Elizabeth Russell nodded - yes, that was probably the safest thing to do, given the circumstances, then she said,

"And the medical tests?"

FitzOsbern's fat fingers flicked through the report on the table between them,

"No tumours or any other abnormalities," he replied.

"Did she come back to her senses?"

"Yes, for about three days. Then she started screaming at the staff and tried to sexually assault them. The following day, she was back to normal and telling them how it wasn't her, but a being that was inside her. Over time, the periods of lucidity have diminished and now she is almost permanently in a state of violent disorder."

"And the Americans won't do anything?"

"No, they say that as a British citizen, she's our responsibility. And since she's a regular Anglican churchgoer, that makes her my responsibility."

FitzOsbern slumped back into his armchair.

"Have you checked her out?" Elizabeth Russell asked, though she found it unlikely. He looked too rested to have been over the Atlantic and back.

"Not personally, but one of my team paid her a visit."

"And?"

"Let's just say he got quite the floorshow."

"So, does he think she's possessed or just off her rocker?"

"Not sure. She talked a lot of gibberish which might be a language she couldn't possibly know, but might just be nonsense. May I?" and FitzOsbern indicated an old-fashioned tape recorder that was sitting on the delicately carved table between them. Elizabeth Russell nodded her assent and the bishop pressed 'play' and sat back. The sounds that came out of the small speaker were unearthly and alternated between angry and beguiling. After about twenty seconds, she said

"I've heard enough. You can turn it off."

FitzOsbern did so.

"Yeah, she's possessed. What we were listening to right there was a member of the Tzitzimimeh,"

At the bishop's blank expression, she explained,

"They're Aztec fertility deities. In their natural form, they look like skeletons. For some inexplicable reason it has latched onto this poor woman and is now trying to satisfy its desire for sex. And it's more than a little pissed off that people are trying to stop it."

"She was speaking Aztec?"

"An archaic version of Nahuatl. If the Americans had taken an interest in this case, they'd've probably spotted that quickly."

"Why?" FitzOsbern asked coldly. He didn't like the inference that his team were somehow inferior to the Americans, whom he still occasionally referred to as 'the colonists'.

"Because they've done a lot of academic work on the language - but the fact is, nobody's spoken like that in the Americas for at least five hundred years. No way this woman's been learning it on the sly. So, there you go – confirmation that the sweet old dear has been possessed. What are you going to do now?"

This was the moment FitzOsbern had been dreading. He looked across at Elizabeth Russell – this arrogant young woman in her sharp suit wielded far too much power for his liking. After reading the Krowos report, he had wanted to make a formal complaint to the archbishop about her and her working methods – twenty-one people dead in a week was unacceptable.

Annoyingly, this possession business had landed in his lap before he'd been able to make his move. Now he needed her help and it infuriated him,

"Those are the three vicars who have tried to deliver her," he said, turning the page of the file and pushing it towards her.

She looked at the photographs of three men, all of whom had been badly beaten and were recovering in hospital with various limbs in casts.

"Wafers and holy oil not cutting it, eh?" she said.

"No," FitzOsbern admitted painfully, "His Grace the Archbishop wondered if you might do the honours?"

"Of course," she smiled, "I'm always very happy to accommodate his Grace."

"Thank you. When will you be able to..."

"I'll leave tomorrow."

"Really? You don't need more time to prepare?" FitzOsbern found the arrogance of the woman startling.

"No, I can organise everything I'll need this afternoon."

"Well, that is good news," he said. She really was a piece of work! It was this sort of swaggering attitude that had caused all those deaths during her last case.

"If that's everything, I'd better get my skates on," Elizabeth Russell said, standing up.

"Of course, and you can keep that file – I have a copy," Bishop FitzOsbern stood and walked with her towards the door. He knew that he should try to keep her sweet in order to get the job done, but there was something about the Krowos case that was annoying him,

"There was one other thing," he said, just before he opened the door, "I was reading the Krowos report..."

"Yes?"

"That deal you made with the druids... you've given no details at all," his enquiry was perfectly polite.

"No," she gave it as a statement of fact.

"Why not?" his tone was still very polite.

"Because I made a promise to the chief druid that only he and I would know the details."

Infuriating woman!

"So, we're going to have to simply trust you on this?"

"Yes."

"Even though druids are known to commit atrocities during their pagan rites, including human sacrifice?"

"Yes," Elizabeth Russell wished they wouldn't, but unfortunately some of their gods were essential to the spiritual safety of the planet. And if those gods required sacrifices, then sometimes sacrifices had to be made.

"Right, well, I suppose that's cleared that up, then," FitzOsbern's tone made it plain that he felt it wasn't cleared up at all,

"Good luck," he added, opening the door for her.

"Thanks," she said and then he closed the door quietly behind her.

Bishop FitzOsbern stood and listened to the heavy tread of the silver clock on the mantlepiece. Yes, the Krowos report was the first timber of the gallows he would build to hang her.

***

Sitting in the comfy seat of the plane and draining the last of her rum and coke, Elizabeth Russell wondered what Bishop FitzOsbern would do if he realised she could hear his thoughts. Why did he dislike her so much? She'd never been anything but polite and cooperative with him, but he had thought ill of her from their first meeting and in every subsequent meeting since. Had he been dropped on his head by a witch when he'd been a child? So far, she hadn't had the opportunity or inclination to go delving into his mind to find out his exact motives. Whatever they were, she found his hostility wearing. When she got back from America, she'd have to do something about him. But right now, she had to get ready for a difficult confrontation. She called over a member of the cabin crew, ordered another rum and coke, and relaxed into her seat. When her drink arrived, she sipped at it gratefully. Yes, that finally hit the spot. It would be the last alcohol she'd be able to have for the next few days, because she would purify herself before the attempted exorcism. She thought about Aggie Thompson. Why should an elderly woman living a quiet life by the beach in Delaware suddenly be possessed by a Mexican fertility deity? It didn't make sense. She lived fifteen hundred miles from Mexico and, according to her file, she'd never been there and had no links to it. And why would a fertility deity want to possess a woman in her mid-seventies? That was odd. They were usually only interested in attacking children, or women of child-bearing age. Of course, that had been lengthened by the advent of IVF, but still, seventy-plus was way outside their usual range. Surely there was something else at work here? What could have pushed Aggie Thompson into the path of the Tzitzimitl? And why had it latched onto her? Why not her daughter? Or her grandchildren? According to the file, her daughter, Mary, had witnessed the first outward signs of possession, and her kids had been in the house at the time. Surely the Tzitzimitl would have gone for one of them instead?

Elizabeth Russell took a pull at her drink and looked out of the window. Forty thousand feet seemed a long way up – practically skimming the stratosphere. It was a bloody long way to fall if something went wrong. She shuddered – not at the thought of the height, but at the technology that made it possible. It made witchcraft and magic seem very tame! And yet all the technology in the world could do nothing for Aggie Thompson. She opened Aggie's file and looked at it. Even though she'd married an American, she hadn't become one. Interesting or irrelevant to the case? Hard to tell. So, she was originally from the Isle of Wight and had met her husband when his ship, the USS Nimitz, had been moored outside Portsmouth Harbour back in 1980. They'd met in a pub in Portsmouth – Elizabeth Russell thought about the vast number of pubs in the town, but particularly of the Still & West next to the mouth of the harbour. Yes, you could while away a sunny afternoon watching the boats go by over a few pints of Fuller's ESB...

"Focus, Bess!" she said out loud and got her mind back on the job.

So, Aggie and Tom had met and hit it off sufficiently that he was able to lure her away from 'The Island', as the Isle of Wight was commonly known in the local vicinity... and London, where so many of The Island's second-home owners lived. So, she'd left The Island and lived the life of a Navy wife, first in Norfolk, Virginia, and then over on the west coast near Seattle. When Tom retired from the Navy, they went back to his hometown in Delaware. They'd lived in Bowers, where he ran his own electrician's business until he was seventy. Then they'd moved to the other side of the Muderkill River, to a beach house in South Bowers. Aside from the baffling name of the river, there was nothing to suggest anything out of the ordinary in the file. Yes, they attended church, but that would only come into play if the entity they were dealing with had some Middle Eastern connection. No, Bess was sure there was definitely some other element at work here. What? It wasn't clear. She thought about how she would tackle the Tzitzimitl. Normally, with someone young, she'd just go at the invading entity head-on, but Aggie was no spring chicken. Bess didn't want to save her from the Tzitzimitl, only to have the old dear expire from the strain. She'd have to play this one very carefully... she thought for a moment how annoyed Bishop FitzOsbern had been about having to bring her in on the case. He was lucky. If she did the job right, he'd look good for properly delegating the case to her; if it all went south, she'd look bad and he could place all the blame on her. For him, this was a win-win. For her? Well, she'd find out soon enough.

Chapter Two

The Murderkill Mystery

A month earlier, Aggie Thompson was sitting on her back porch, sipping her morning coffee and enjoying the view across the white sand to the glittering sea beyond. It was early, but already heating up nicely. It would be another glorious early August day, and when her grandchildren arrived for lunch, she'd be able to simply release them onto the beach and let them play until chow time. She shielded her eyes against the low sun as she looked east across the Atlantic and took a long, deep breath. The clean air filled her with pleasure. Was there anything better than this? She couldn't think of anything. Once, she'd have immediately said 'Sex, duh!', but seventy-four years on the planet had turned sex into a test of what still worked, rather than an exquisite expression of love and desire. Her husband Tom's discovery of Viagra had helped, but they still needed to check nothing was broken or had fallen off after they'd done the dirty deed. She looked down at her hand holding the coffee mug. Whose hand was that? It was all wrinkled and liver spotted. Was it really hers? And how come it looked so old? She harrumphed quietly to herself,

"Blummin' old age! Creeps up on you and next thing you know, you look like a little old lady and you're wondering where you left your teeth. Still, it's better than the alternative!"

Her voice had a burr to it that was not native to South Bowers, Delaware. No, you'd need to travel about three and a half thousand miles east to find the origin of that accent. As a little girl, looking out west from the beach at Chale on the Isle of Wight, Aggie had always hoped to get away from England and head off into the setting sun. Now she was on that western shore and, after a life of wandering, that was where she would stay. She got up and walked across the wooden boards of the open porch and stopped at the top of the steps that led straight down onto the beach. Her nose crinkled at the feel of sand on the boards under her bare feet. She'd have to sweep it all off after breakfast. That was the problem with living in a beach house, you always got a lot of beach in the darned house. She leant on the wooden railing that ran around the porch, and looked to her right. Theirs was the last of the houses that straggled along the shore of the beach at South Bowers, so she had an uninterrupted view of the sand and the wild, scraggy marshland behind it. On the other side of the beach road, the Murderkill river meandered about the marshes before heading off inland towards its birthplace. Looking southward, the view of untamed marshland and windswept beach reminded her of the opening chapter of Great Expectations. She always half-expected a great brute of a man with a leg iron round his ankle to come hobbling out of the reeds like Magwitch. Then, in spite of the heat, she shivered.

Odd. She sipped her coffee, but the hot liquid could not dispel the chill. It was as if she knew in her heart that something was coming. Would it wait until night and then come lurching up out of the marsh towards her back door? No! What? What nonsense was this?

"Come on, Aggie, don't get old and chuckleheaded now!" she said, trying to shake off the unsettling suspicion that something horrible was about to happen. The best thing to do was to get moving and then she'd forget all about it. Even though it was only just seven, she wanted to start preparing things for lunch. These days she couldn't move as fast as she once had, so she made up for that with better organisation. She padded over to the screen door, brushed the sand off her feet on the mat and went inside. The back door led straight into the sitting room, with its big picture windows that perfectly framed the Atlantic. There was nothing she and Tom liked more than snuggling up on the couch on a windy winter's afternoon and watching the waves crashing on the beach from the warmth of the little nest they'd created.

The house itself was unremarkable – mid twentieth century, clad in white clapboard and raised on stilts like all the other beachfront properties – but it was Aggie and Tom's final haven. As she walked through the sitting room filled with memorabilia from Tom's life in the navy, Aggie smiled at the softball-sized rock on the sideboard. It was port-coloured with a bubbly texture and was a lava bomb from Santorini in the Mediterranean. Before the kids, she and Tom had had a *wild* time there.

"Phew!" she murmured, shaking her head at the memories – they had been hopelessly in lust and didn't always wait until they'd got back to their hotel room before...

"You're up early," yawned Tom, coming down the corridor by the side of the stairs. He was wearing baggy shorts and a T shirt with a picture of the USS Nimitz and 'Been There Done That' emblazoned across it. Although Tom was a little broader than he'd been in his prime, he hadn't run to fat and still cut a pretty good figure. His deep tan contrasted with a head of fine white hair, which Aggie still loved to run her fingers through. He intercepted her before she got to the kitchen and they kissed.

"I was feeling restless, so I thought I'd may as well get up and enjoy the morning. It's proper pretty out there," Aggie smiled.

"After you," Tom said, wafting a hand towards the door of the kitchen/diner.

"Thank you, sir," Aggie said with a little curtsy, then walked over to the pot of coffee on the stove,

"Want some?"

"You know it!" Tom exclaimed. Truth be told, he was a little thick-headed after one too many rums while out star gazing on the beach the previous night. He slumped into the banquette behind the old oak table in the far corner of the kitchen and awaited his coffee.

"So, this restless feeling... is it your guts again?" Aggie had had diverticulitis two years earlier and ever since he'd worried that it would come back. He'd never seen her so ill, so he'd become hyper-vigilant for anything that might indicate its return.

"No," Aggie sighed, bringing the coffee and taking the chair opposite him, "Just... restless. Kinda prickly all over, but not prickly heat. Unsettled. I dunno. I'd say it was coming up to my time of the month, but those days are long gone."

"Weird. Well, if you're feeling washed out, I can always fire up the barbecue – save you a ton of work."

On the face of it, this sounded like a good offer, but the reality was very different. Tom had been a brilliant nuclear electrician's mate for thirty years on ships including the Nimitz. He'd kept the power flowing and been the go-to troubleshooter. He could do anything... except barbecue. 'Cremations' was how Aggie described the times Tom had tried to barbecue and, although in recent years he'd got better, it was still hit and miss. Mainly miss. Aggie couldn't put the family through that. And besides, it only gave ammunition to their son-in-law Richard. He was a lovely guy, a great husband and father, but he was in the Air Force. And he was a barbecue king. The back and forth about which service was better – Navy or Air Force – was one where Tom could hold his own, but as soon as he started cremating good meat, that was the end of it. Richard would wipe the floor with him:

"Hey gramps, whaddya use to cook these burgers – a nuclear reactor?"

"Tommy, you're supposed to cook 'em, not nuke 'em!"

"Hey kids, remember to duck and cover when gramps is cooking!"

And although Tom took it in good humour, he would always be a bit down the next day. Aggie would spare him – and them – all that.

"I'm very happy cooking," Aggie said with a smile, "But if you want to help, you're very welcome."

After breakfast, Tom mucked in with Aggie, acting as her assistant as they prepared the feast that would feed them and their daughter Mary's family of five. While Aggie prepared the centrepiece roast of pork, Tom set to work getting the potatoes on for the potato salad.

"You starting the roast already?" Tom asked as he cleaned the potatoes.

"It's gonna be too hot today to have this straight out of the oven. I'll cook it now and we can slice it up when they arrive and have it cold with the rest."

"Yeah, that'll be tasty. So, you'll be wanting pickles sliced into the potato salad, right?"

Aggie nodded, then opened the hot oven, waiting a moment to let the wave of heat escape, before bending down to put the pork in. Over the next hour and a half, they prepared all the side dishes, chatting merrily, making mental notes about what to get on their next trip to the store and setting the table. Between the hot sun outside and the roasting pork in the oven, the temperature in the kitchen was stifling by half-ten.

"Goddam it's hot!" Tom muttered, wiping sweat from his brow to avoid it dripping into the tomato and avocado salad he was making. He'd swapped his bedtime shorts and T shirt for a daytime shorts and T shirt combo (this time the Nimitz T shirt had the legends 'Old Salt' and 'Teamwork A Tradition' printed on it). Even with the windows open, he was sweating like a good 'un.

"Yes, I know – it's my own fault for not getting air-con," he added before Aggie could launch into her well-rehearsed gripe about the lack of air-con,

"What was it you said?" and she pretended to think hard to recall it, even though they both knew what she was going to say off by heart,

"Oh yes – 'Don't worry, the sea breezes will keep us cool. It's a waste of money' – that was it, wasn't it?" and she gave him a smug smile that made it clear that they both knew it was precisely what he'd said.

"Yeah, yeah," he laughed, waving away her know-it-all attitude.

Aggie smiled and got on with washing the lettuce, but the strange thing was, she wasn't feeling hot at all. Chilled. That was how she was feeling. Something right in the core of her had got chilled. Maybe she was coming down with something? Anything but Covid! She couldn't stand the thought of getting it again. 2020 had been miserable! Although neither of them had ended up in hospital or anything like that, she had suffered months of brain fog afterwards, which had been very worrying. It hadn't helped that she'd just turned seventy and had been feeling paranoid about getting old and the rapidly approaching possibilities of Alzheimer's or dementia. As she rinsed the leaves and put them into the lettuce spinner, she assessed her symptoms. No headache, no feeling like she'd been punched in the back of the eyeballs, no aching bones, no scratchy throat or cough, tummy all right. Well, that was all good, but she couldn't shake off that feeling of internal cold! And there was that niggling sense of dread. What the hell was that about? As someone with a naturally sunny disposition, this feeling was very odd. She gave the lettuce an especially vigorous spinning in the hope that the action would warm her up. Yes, that was a little better.

Soon it was midday and then came the sound of Mary and Richard's car pulling onto the driveway. Tom looked at the clock – bang on twelve. As a Navy man, Tom had always been a stickler for punctuality and he'd used that to put his Air Force son-in-law in his place. Early on in Richard's courtship of his daughter, Tom had ribbed him for his typical airman's lax attitude to time keeping. Although this had always been a joke, it had got under Richard's skin sufficiently for him to make a point of arriving bang on the agreed time for any visit or event. Tom smiled – yes, he had his son-in-law on a string. They went to the door and were instantly overwhelmed by their grandchildren,

"Gramma! Gramps!" they cried as they hugged and kissed their venerable grandparents. Tom and Aggie had to hold fast so they weren't knocked over by the three kids who were an excited jumble of sun-browned limbs and sandy-coloured hair. Meanwhile, Mary and Richard were unloading the nonsensical beach clutter that Zak, Zoe and Zaza had insisted on bringing.

Tom held out his hand for Zak to shake. Now the boy was thirteen, Tom felt that a degree of manly decorum was in order. Zak was a skinny kid, but tried his best to give his Gramps a bone-crushing handshake.

"Nice try!" Tom laughed, "You're getting better. Now c'mon, bring it in!" and he opened his arms and Zak hugged him. To him, Gramps was the best. He was happy, kind and had never once raised his voice to him – unlike his own dad, who could be a real grouch sometimes.

"Iced tea and lemonade on the back porch, go help yourselves," Aggie said to the kids, and loved the fact that they were still young enough to get excited at such a prospect as they ran noisily through the house. By next year, Zak would probably be unimpressed by the offer of cold drinks, but Zoe was only ten and Zaza eight, so they still had a few Wonder Years left.

"Hey, mom," Mary said, giving Aggie a kiss on the cheek,

"You okay?"

"Merry as a mallard!" Aggie smiled.

"Been cooking all morning?"

"Had to – it was that or let your dad barbecue."

'Thank you!' Mary mouthed with a roll of her eyes, then she said,

"The kids insisted we bring their favourite ice cream; I hope that's okay?" Mary didn't want her mom to think she was encroaching on her territory.

"That's fine, just pop it in the ice box," Aggie said. Then, as Mary headed into the house and Richard stepped forward to give her a kiss, Aggie had the strangest sensation. Richard was in good shape and not yet forty, and when she looked up at him in the bright sunshine, her heart skipped a beat - even though he looked faintly ridiculous laden down with buckets, spades and various beach toys. And when he planted a perfectly innocent peck on her cheek, she felt a thrill run through her.

"How're ya doin, Aggie?"

"Me? Oh... er, I'm fine, thanks for asking. Um... how are you?" she flustered like a high school girl who's just been noticed by the captain of the football team.

"I'll be better when I've dumped all this craperoo round the back," he said, "Don't worry, I won't go through the house."

"I don't mind," Aggie replied and then, before she knew it, she was fixing him with a very flirtatious look and saying,

"You can do whatever you want."

"Er..." Richard was nonplussed, then found a reply, "Great. I'll see you out back."

It was only a moment that had passed between them, but as soon as Richard started walking away, Aggie felt a wave of deep embarrassment. What just happened? Where did that come from? And why was she feeling that insistent tugging sensation between her legs? Having felt chilled all morning, she was suddenly hot with a flush that radiated across her breasts. What... the... hell?

"I'd better give him a hand or God knows where he'll put that stuff," Tom muttered and he walked through the house oblivious to what had just happened, leaving Aggie disoriented and feeling somehow ashamed. She stood at the bottom of the front steps for a full minute trying to figure out what was going on. Was she coming down with something? Only if desire was an illness, because – make no mistake – she was feeling desire. She hadn't felt that insistent ache for over twenty years and having it again was unsettling and inappropriate. Especially when the object of that desire was her son-in-law.

"Keep it together, Aggie!" she whispered, then she gave herself a shake and took a good look around. Ahead of her was the beach road with the wetlands and river stretching out beyond it to a distant treeline. The sun glared off the other beach houses and there was a hot, southerly breeze. It all seemed perfectly normal. Real. Nothing out of the ordinary.

"Okay, Aggie, hold onto that. It's all good..."

But was it?

Lunch was a success. The kids got themselves good and hungry playing on the beach and when it came to eating, everyone got stuck in. The conversation – and a certain amount of beer – flowed, so that the afternoon passed in relaxed conviviality... for everyone but Aggie. As the others talked about their week, joked and told stories, Aggie felt as if she was slowly but surely being dragged away from them. It was like she was going backwards down a tunnel. The daylight and the sights and sounds of her family enjoying themselves were getting smaller and more distant, as impenetrable darkness filled the void around them. Of course, neither Tom nor Richard noticed, and the kids were in a world of their own. Only Mary clocked her mom's growing reticence and distracted look. So, when they were together clearing up in the kitchen while the rest were walking off the lunch down the beach, Mary took her chance to find out what was going on,

"You all right, mom? You seem kinda quiet."

Aggie wanted to say 'No, I'm not all right, everything is very strange', but her throat seemed constricted and her mouth was apparently no longer connected to her brain, because at the other end of the dark tunnel, she distinctly heard her voice say,

"I'm fine. I just wanna know – does Richard satisfy you?"

Mary looked at her mother in bewilderment. Did she just ask...?

"Sorry, what?" Mary must've misheard.

To Aggie's horror, she heard her own voice reply,

"When he fucks you, are you satisfied?"

Mary's mouth dropped open.

"He looks fit," Aggie said and her usually smiley demeanour was replaced with a sly, lascivious look,

"I bet he could go all night. Does he? Does he go all night?"

Mary was lost for words. There were so many things she wanted to say, but she couldn't catch any of them and she was still trying to articulate her thoughts as Aggie continued,

"I've been watching him. I can tell he's got a big, fat cock and I bet he gives it to you hard. Does he? Does he give it to you hard? Oh, I bet he does..." and Aggie's hands slid down to her crotch as she seemed to picture her son-in-law giving it hard to her daughter.

"Jesus! What the fuck, mom!" Mary finally found her voice and it was shrill with shock and disgust.

"What?" Aggie pasted an innocent look on her face, but there was something in her eyes that was devious.

"What are you...? Why are you talking like this? Are you alright?"

From the depths of the tunnel, Aggie desperately tried to call out to her daughter. Mary must know that she'd never say anything like this. This wasn't her!

Instead, she heard her voice reply,

"A mother needs to know that her daughter is in good hands. So, does he stretch you open and fuck your..."

The slap was instinctive. Mary had delivered it before she'd even realised what her mother was saying. Aggie reeled from the blow and Mary had to reach forward and stop her falling.

"I'm sorry! Fuck! I'm so sorry," Mary spluttered.

"It's okay," Aggie gasped. The slap had brought her instantly from the depths of the dark tunnel and back into the world of light.

"I don't... I don't know what I was saying," and her voice was broken and confused.

Mary held her mom by the shoulders as Aggie took in great gulps of air and then collapsed into her daughter's arms in a fit of tears.

"Hey, it's all right," Mary soothed, stroking her mom's hair as she rocked her gently back and forth, "You're all right now," but she wasn't sure she believed it. What had she just witnessed?

"I... I could hear myself saying those horrible things, but I swear it wasn't me saying them," Aggie choked though her tears.

"Come on, let's sit down," Mary said and she helped her mom to a chair,

"I'll put the kettle on and make some tea."

"Oh God, yes!" Aggie groaned. Yes, tea would settle her nerves.

While the tea brewed, Aggie told Mary about what had happened and how she'd felt like she'd had no control over herself.

"Oh my God, mom, why didn't you say something earlier?" Mary said, clutching her mom's hands in hers.

"Because the further down the tunnel I went, the less control I had."

"If it happens again, you gotta say something!" Mary insisted.

"If I can, I will, but once it started, it was like my body was being taken over. Like someone else was in here with me and they're stronger than me."

Mary's look of confusion prompted Aggie to explain,

"It's like I could almost hear another person's thoughts, but that person was here," and she pointed to her head,

"And they aren't nice thoughts. They're filthy. Seriously, me and your pop were no angels, but what this other thing wants to do... it's disgusting!"

Mary was struggling to compute what she was hearing.

"I know it sounds crazy, but you've gotta believe me – I'm not crazy," and Aggie's eyes urgently sought her daughter's faith in her. She needed to see that Mary believed her, in part because she wasn't sure she could believe it herself.

"No, mom, you're not crazy, but whatever this is, it's serious. You're gonna have to see Dr Bennet first thing Monday," Mary didn't want to say it out loud, but she was thinking that it could be some kind of brain tumour. Didn't they sometimes cause personality changes?

"But what's he going to do? He'll think I'm just another old biddy who's gone crackers."

"No, mom. He's a good doctor and he'll take it seriously. I'll come with you..."

"Oh, you don't want to be wasting your time with me – and anyway, who'll look after the kids?"

"Zak's over at Tommy's Monday; Zoe's at an art day; and I can get Laura to watch Zaza for a coupl'a hours. Seriously, we need to do this right away."

"Really?" now Aggie had calmed down and drunk some tea, the incident seemed as unreal as a dream.

"Yes, really," Mary insisted.

"But I feel fine now. Maybe it was just lack of sleep getting the better of me..."

"What about feeling the other presence in your head?"

"I don't feel that way now. And you know what?"

"What?"

"I don't feel cold inside anymore," and it was true. All those un-Aggie-like feelings of cold and dread had dissipated like the mist over the marshes under the sun.

"All the same, we've gotta get you seen," Mary insisted and Aggie knew she wouldn't take 'no' for an answer,

"Okay," she agreed.

"Are you gonna tell pops?"

"What good would it do? He'd only worry. Let's keep this strictly between us," and Aggie looked at Mary hopefully.

"Okay, but if there's anything going on, we tell him immediately," and Mary fixed her mom with the serious look she used on her kids.

"You got it," Aggie nodded.

"C'mere!" Mary sighed, opening her arms and giving Aggie a cuddle.

"This feels good," Aggie whispered into her daughter's ear, and in spite of the kernel of fear deep within her, she took comfort in being able to trust Mary with the responsibility of looking after her.

Chapter Three

Unholy Communion

Sunday dawned bright and warm, so that by the time Aggie and Tom were in their Chrysler Pacifica heading to an Episcopal Church in Dover, they already needed the air-con blowing. Aggie was refreshed by a good night's sleep and felt more and more as if the previous afternoon had been some weird dream. The drive to Dover gave her plenty of time for reflection, because they had to follow the road around the edge of the marshes before they could take the highway. Yeah, that was one thing they hadn't thought through when they'd decided to get the house in South Bowers, Aggie thought. The mouth of the Murderkill River split Bowers from the houses just to the south and there was no bridge. This meant that unless they could get someone to ferry them the seventy or so yards across the river, they faced a thirteen-mile detour via Little Heaven just to get to Bowers. In fact, every journey began with the detour around the wetlands, but that morning, with the reeds waving in the light breeze and the sun shimmering off the river, it was a perfect example of the ineffable beauty of God's creation.

Within an hour, they were thanking God for that creation within the walls of the red brick church. Aggie and Tom weren't the most religious people – they had discussed the fact that neither of them had ever felt the presence of God – but they both took comfort from attending church... especially now they were getting uncomfortably close to meeting their maker! Aggie had been brought up in the Church of England and, after she and Tom had started going out seriously, she'd coaxed him away from the Presbyterians to the tradition and tolerant solidity of Anglicanism. Tom took to the old-fashioned feel of the Anglican church and from then on, wherever they were in the world, they would find the local Anglican church for their worship. For Aggie, each service was like a comfy old pair of slippers. Sure, they were nothing exciting, but the way they made her feel was just lovely. The singing, responses, prayers and moments of silent contemplation soothed her soul. And that sunny Sunday morning was no different.

When the time came to take Communion, Aggie was smiley and relaxed. She followed the other parishioners to kneel before the altar with the unshakeable sense that God was in his heaven, everything was calm and the events of the previous afternoon were dispelled. It didn't even hurt that much to kneel, which was a nice change because her left knee had been giving her gyp on and off since March. After a few moments, the vicar stood in front of her,

"The body of Christ keep you in eternal life,"

Aggie tried to give the response, but nothing beyond a mumble came out. The vicar paused for a moment, then placed the wafer on her tongue. Ugh! It tasted like cigarette ash! Aggie took it into her mouth, but that taste and the horrible feeling of ash crushing between her teeth was excruciating! Her first instinct was to spit it out. Knowing she couldn't do anything of the sort, she swallowed hard. Wow! That was unpleasant! And she still had that grinding ash feeling between her molars... Aggie sneaked a look at Tom, who took his wafer without a flicker, and no one else down the line seemed to have had any trouble either. Well, the wine would be with her soon, so that would take the ashy residue and the taste away. Then things would be better... they weren't. The wine was like having a heavy swig of vinegar and it took Aggie's breath away. Swallowing it was physically painful and it burned her throat. Again, she glanced around her, but no one else seemed to be affected. Urgh! This was horrible!

She was glad to get up and shuffle back to her seat, but by the time she got there, she was feeling distinctly queasy. Aggie watched Tom return to the pew looking rather dapper in his Sunday best. As he approached, she tried to catch his eye, but he missed her cues. Typical man! He took his seat, unaware anything was wrong... until she gave him a light dig in the ribs. He turned to look at her. She made a gesture he couldn't understand, but he now picked up on the fact that she looked unwell. Having been a sailor for most of his life, he could spot the first signs of nausea a mile away. As the Communion drew to its quiet close, Aggie and Tom silently conveyed their thoughts to each other with somewhat haphazard hand signals. Aggie made it clear she was sick and wanted to leave, Tom gesticulated that it was only about ten minutes to go, Aggie shook her head slowly and tried to convey the fact that she would hurl long before that. Tom shrugged and shifted out of her way so she could exit the pew. And now Aggie was on the move. She could feel saliva suddenly gathering and knew she had to hurry to avoid vomiting in the church. However, she was equally aware that moving too fast would result in instant vomit. So, as the vicar led the congregation in saying,

"Almighty God, we thank you for feeding us with the body and blood of your Son Jesus Christ,"

Aggie was awkwardly hurrying but not hurrying towards the back of the church, while trying not to imagine bodies or blood, and thinking,

Come on, Aggie, don't be sick,

"Through him we offer you our souls and bodies..."

Please don't make a projectile offering,

"To be a living sacrifice. Send us out..."

Yes, please send me out,

"In the power of your Spirit, to live and work..."

And NOT vomit,

"To your praise and glory..."

Thank Christ! I'm out...

Then Aggie accompanied the congregation's final,

"Amen,"

with an unpleasant spewing of the body and blood of Christ down the side of the steps leading up to the church door. She shook as she steadied herself against the handrail, then heaved again to add half-digested eggs, toast, bacon, fried tomato and coffee to the mess in the once neat flowerbed by the side of the steps.

Now she was very shaky, and her legs were starting to buckle when a gentle hand with the uplifting touch of an angel took her elbow and held her safe. She turned and it was Tom, who was looking concerned,

"Got any more in there?" he asked softly.

Aggie gave an unpleasant tasting burp and shook her head. No, that was it. Her entire stomach contents had comprehensively drowned the dahlias.

"Can we go before they finish?" she said in a small voice, while she pulled a tissue from her sleeve and wiped around her mouth.

"C'mon, we know how the service ends," Tom replied with a sympathetic smile, and he helped her down the steps and over to the car. After gallantly opening her door, he got in and started the engine.

"I'll drive us round the corner so we're out of the way, then I'll stop until you're sure you're okay."

Aggie nodded gently and thought, as he carefully pulled out, what an excellent nurse he could have been. He was so calm and patient and focussed on her comfort. She was lucky to have him.

Tom drove slowly to the next block and eased the car to a halt next to a small park. There were children playing and a few early picnickers setting up their stuff on the grass. Aggie was glad it was peaceful. They sat in silence for a few minutes. Aggie was lost in her own thoughts, while Tom tried not to overtly ogle a couple of twenty-something girls who were playing frisbee while wearing far too little for a Sunday morning. There were two things he regularly thanked God for – Daisy Dukes and lycra jogging pants – and he was about to repeat his silent praise to the Almighty, when he stopped himself. Would he get smited for thanking God for Daisy Dukes and lycra on a Sunday? Possibly. So, he quietly enjoyed the view a bit longer, then turned to Aggie and said,

"How're ya doing?"

"Okay," she replied and she sounded perfectly well.

"So, what happened?"

Aggie explained her problem with the wafer and wine.

"Nasty," Tom said.

"And a bit terrifying. I'd've never lived it down if I'd thrown up in the font."

Tom couldn't help but guffaw – the thought of it!

"Strange thing is, I feel totally fine now."

Tom looked across at her and there was no doubt that she was transformed from the sick puppy she'd been about ten minutes earlier.

"You look pretty good."

"And now I'm starving!" she exclaimed, "Can we go and get barbecue? I have a yen for meat."

"Wouldn't be the first time," Tom grinned, nudging her and winking.

"You've got a filthy mind, Tom Thompson!" Aggie laughed.

"Sure you're feeling good enough?"

"Yeah! C'mon, take me to that barbecue place uptown."

"Or we could head home and I could barbecue..." Tom began, but stopped under Aggie's withering gaze,

"Okay, I'll just drive the car."

The rest of the day was just a normal August Sunday. Aggie ate a good lunch and the incident of the morning was dumped into the trashcan of history. Then it was home, a few chores, reading on the back porch, a walk down the beach, beer and sandwiches for dinner and then bed. All perfectly normal. Monday's trip with Mary to see Dr Bennet was unremarkable. He was a slight man in his mid-fifties with very dark hair, which smacked of Just For Men. Sitting in his airy office, he listened with interest to the two women as they described the incident from Saturday and the nausea from Sunday, but was unsure what exactly he could do. In the end, he decided on some blood tests with a possibility of an MRI scan if there was a recurrence. The tunnel vision sounded like it might have been some sort of migraine, but he'd never heard of anyone changing personality because of one. Again, the sudden onset of vomiting could be migraine related, but then it had dissipated just as quickly. Very peculiar. Aggie and Mary were, at least, comforted by the visit to the doctor. After that, the week was distinctly ordinary – just another sunny week in retirement... until Friday.

It had been a hot, windless day and, rather than sitting around the house melting and cursing Tom's stupidity for not putting in air-con, they spent much of the afternoon bobbing about in the sea. They had a strategy for days like that. Cool off in the sea, then come back to their loungers on the sand up by their house and dry off in the sun before shading themselves with their big beach umbrellas. This was interspersed with trips back into the house for cold drinks and comfort breaks. Usually, that was all they needed, but Aggie was feeling strangely restless – like she wasn't quite comfortable in her own skin. By five-o-clock, Tom reckoned she'd spent more time going back and forth to the house than she had in the sea.

"You okay?" he asked her as she returned to the loungers from the house for the nth time.

Aggie looked distracted as she replied,

"Yeah, I'm feeling..." and then she trailed off, staring straight out to sea.

"What?" Tom asked, "You're feeling what?" Tom got up from his lounger and looked hard at her.

Outwardly, Aggie was standing there looking at the sea with calm eyes, but inwardly things were going terribly wrong. Previously, her feeling of being in a tunnel and watching the world become smaller and smaller had taken all afternoon before it was bad. This time, it was different. She had just got down the steps, felt the warm sand under her feet and walked towards Tom when he'd asked her how she was. She'd started to reply and then suddenly she was falling backwards down the tunnel, with Tom and the world rapidly disappearing. She was trying to scream, but the darkness all around her muffled her attempted cries. And yet she could hear everything so clearly – the surf, the birds, Tom's question about what she was feeling and then the unsettling sound of her voice saying,

"Horny!"

Tom did a double-take and said,

"Did I hear that right?"

Aggie marched straight to him with a predatory look on her face and pushed herself up close to him as her right hand went to his crotch,

"I'm horny and I want this right now," and she squeezed his dick, which slowly started to awake from its usual state of torpor.

"Wow! Aggie..." Tom began, but she silenced him with an intense kiss, then released him and looked into his eyes. There was a fire which he didn't recognise, but which touched something deep inside him. And now he was feeling a level of desire he hadn't felt since...

"Come!" Aggie ordered, taking his hand and leading him towards the house.

The elderly, sensible part of him kicked in and he said,

"But what about the beach stuff?"

Aggie stopped and looked at him, then said with total seriousness,

"Do you want to use the beach stuff to fuck me?"

"Er... well... no..." Tom stammered.

"Then leave it," Aggie said firmly and pulled him into the house.

At the bottom of the well of darkness inside her, Aggie watched the distant round window into the real world. She could feel the other presence inside her and that it was in complete control. All Aggie could do was watch. She couldn't even scream to Tom to warn him that this wasn't her, that she was a prisoner and that whatever had taken over wasn't good. Yes, she could feel that. Whatever had taken control of her was bad and only out for itself. And now it was stripping her husband right there in their sitting room and forcing him back onto the couch. It was expertly using Aggie's hands and mouth to get him hard and then it was riding him and screaming like a vixen in heat. Aggie couldn't stand the way it was using her body. This wasn't lovemaking, it was rough fucking. Aggie stared as one of her hands held both of Tom's down above his head, while the other went to his throat and started to choke him.

"Jesus! Please, sweet Jesus, deliver us from evil," Aggie prayed in the darkness. She was terrified. She suddenly knew that whatever had taken over her body wouldn't stop until Tom was dead.

Tom was caught in the firestorm of passion and couldn't even take a moment to think about what was happening. Somehow, Aggie's strength was far greater than his and, as she pounded herself up and down on his cock, there was nothing he could do to stop her. It was incredible. Like nothing he'd ever known. Her energy and strength... her desperation! They were intoxicating. Tom tried to keep up with her, but there was no way and now that familiar building up of pressure in his balls would need to be released.

"I'm coming," he gasped, his heart beating twenty to the dozen. Aggie screamed in ecstasy, her face twisted with lust and that desperate need for sex. Tom bucked as he came, but Aggie wasn't stopping. She kept on riding him and he was trying to catch his breath,

"Aggie, please!"

She let go of his throat and slapped his face hard.

"Aggie! Stop!" and there was an edge of fear in his voice. She had him pinned and there was nothing he could do to stop her. He looked up into her face, but although it was Aggie, somehow it wasn't. The features were hers, but the wanton intent and devious curl of her lip were not Aggie at all. And the profanities spewing from her mouth were like nothing he'd ever heard.

"Aggie, I..." but Tom was silenced by Aggie forcing all the fingers of her right hand into his mouth.

Now a deep sense of self-preservation was triggered and he bucked and writhed, desperately trying to throw her off. God! How could she be so strong! It just wasn't possible! How could this small woman who weighed less than a hundred and twenty pounds hold him down? Everything was a blur and the fingers in his mouth were making him gag.

"Yeah! Take it, bitch!" Aggie screamed, grinding down hard on him and pushing her fingers in and out of his mouth.

Tom was struggling for breath and a sudden sweat broke out across his face. He tried to cry out, tried to turn his head for a moment's respite, but Aggie's fingers were wedged into his mouth. His attempts to throw her off only served to push him deeper into her and redouble her carnal frenzy. As she drove herself down on him and ground herself against his pubic bone, her face just above his was warped by lust and greed. He couldn't breathe, things were blurring and now she was screaming in a language he didn't understand, but which had a very clear meaning. She was screaming into his face, exhorting him to fuck harder, spurring him on, demanding that he use all his strength... then there was the sharp pain in the back of his neck, a sudden tightening across his chest and a golden sunburst of agony like he'd never known. His struggling became weaker as his straining heart failed to pump, his face crumpled with pain and then he stopped, even as Aggie hammered down onto his rapidly softening cock.

"No! Don't stop!" she screamed in frustration and started beating his chest in the hope of bringing him back. She gave an angry growl, then tilted her head back and screamed to the sky.

Watching the horror unfold from the darkness, Aggie was in anguish. Her beautiful Tom! What had the thing done to him? Aggie strained to see whether he'd passed out, or... No! She couldn't think of the alternative. All she could see was that he was still, and then there was that scream from the thing that had taken over her body. God! It was shrill and loud and soul-piercing. And then the small circle of light was hurtling towards her. Suddenly, Aggie was plunged back into her body and she gasped and gulped for air as if she'd fallen into freezing water. She was kneeling astride Tom on the sofa and she immediately felt for his pulse. Oh God! Nothing. She felt another point on his neck, then another, then another, but there was nothing.

"No, Tom! No, please no! I'm sorry! Please don't go!" but as Aggie looked at his face, she knew that the vital spark had been smothered. Tom was gone. Aggie fell across the body of the only man she had ever truly loved and wept until she had no more tears to shed.

She came to an hour later, still flung in grief across Tom's dead body. Tom stared sightlessly up at her with the pain and fear of his final moments carved into his features. Dear God, why couldn't it have all been some horrible dream? Aggie pushed herself up from his chest which had that strange solidity of a lifeless body. Her mind reeled at the thought that Tom was really gone, and she gave a great shiver. She was cold. Cold to the core. She eased herself off her dearest friend and felt shame and disgust that she was sticky and wet from his last ejaculation. She wasn't usually squeamish about that sort of thing, but this was different. Although her body had done this to Tom, Aggie knew that it hadn't been *her* doing it. *She* hadn't caused him to come, it had been the thing that had taken her over. It was as if the mess was caused by some other lover, but she was having to clear it up and it was in her body. Aggie felt violated, but as she looked down at Tom, she realised that part of him was still alive. Still alive and swimming around inside her, on a hopeless journey to find a non-existent egg to couple with. God, what a nightmare! What should she do now? Surely, she should clean him up and arrange him so that it looked like he'd had a heart attack while taking a nap? Yes, that's what she'd do, then she'd call the paramedics and clean herself up while they drove over. When they arrived, she'd give them a story that he'd napped on the sofa, while she was reading in their room and that she'd found him like that when she came to make dinner.

She put her plan into action and by the time the ambulance arrived, she'd got Tom's shorts back on with some difficulty and arranged him to fit her story. The paramedics were very kind and explained that he'd probably died peacefully in his sleep – although one look at the expression on his face told them that his last moments were far from pleasant. Aggie didn't have to work hard to appear frightened and confused. She had no idea what was happening to her and she was terrified by thoughts of what might happen next.

"Do you have anyone we can call who can come and look after you?" asked one of the paramedics.

"My daughter, Mary."

"What's her number?"

Aggie told him and he called Mary from the landline. As Aggie watched, she was relieved that she wasn't having to tell Mary the news. But what about later? Mary would come over with a thousand questions and what then? Should Aggie really tell her that her possessed body had screwed her dad to death? How could she do that? But there was something inside her and it was evil. What if it turned on Mary or, God forbid, the kids! Aggie would never be able to forgive herself if this thing in her caused any more harm to those she loved. It would be a hard conversation, but she had to have it. The paramedics waited until Mary arrived and then, amid tears, they loaded Tom into the ambulance and drove away. As Aggie watched the ambulance disappear, she had an overwhelming feeling of sadness, but it was mingled with relief. The paramedics hadn't even vaguely suspected the truth. Well, who would?

Chapter Four

The Beach House

As the black Cadillac CT5 slipped onto the Chesapeake Bay bridge, Elizabeth Russell couldn't help but smile. It was a glorious afternoon and the sight of the bridge curving ahead of them across the bay was spectacular. Things only got prettier after they'd crossed the bridge, and soon they were on the 404, cutting through picturesque farmland under a deep blue sky interspersed with cotton wool clouds. The car and driver were being provided by the Church and were at her disposal for the whole trip. This was good, because Bess didn't enjoy driving at the best of times, let alone in a foreign country on her way to a difficult exorcism. Her driver, Gustavo, was the sort of chauffeur who seemed to have a perfect intuition about how much to talk to his passengers. With some, he was chatty, with others he was as silent as the Sphinx. Today he had a quiet one, so he decided to keep his counsel until spoken to. Yes, she was a quiet one but striking. When he'd seen the tall woman in a purple trouser suit wheeling her case out of passport control, he'd somehow known that she was his passenger and that they wouldn't be chewing the fat all the way to their destination. Now, after a protracted silence, Elizabeth Russell said,

"It's flatter than I'd expected," as a daughter of the Yorkshire town of Sheffield, she found anywhere without hills slightly disconcerting.

Gustavo chuckled and looked at her in the rear-view,

"You know, you're the first person I ever drove here who said that."

"Nice to be a trend-setter," she smiled back at him. He had friendly brown eyes and an easy smile under his bushy black moustache.

"I never really thought about it, but I guess you're right – it *is* kinda flat," he said.

"Pretty, though," Elizabeth Russell liked a bit of countryside.

"I guess," Gustavo replied with a shrug of his big shoulders, "Me, I prefer the city – things going on, people to see – y'know? But the countryside... it's just trees and grass."

She couldn't help but laugh out loud. In a split second, he'd reduced the wonders of nature and the human relationship with it to 'just trees and grass'.

"That's certainly one way of looking at it," she said, and they smiled at each other via the rear-view.

"May I ask you a question?" he said, hoping she wasn't going to make some smart-assed response about how that in itself was a question.

"Shoot," Elizabeth Russell replied, passing his asshole test with flying colours,

"How come you ain't staying at the Church residence in Dover? Reverend Davies was looking forward to meeting you."

"Ah... that," she'd wondered whether her choice of accommodation had put any noses out of joint – clearly it had.

Before she replied, she needed more information. She said,

"Do you work for the Church, or..."

"Exclusively for the Church," he replied, "I mainly drive the bishop and senior members of the clergy. Some of the things they gotta discuss can be..." and he searched for the right way of putting it, "...sensitive. They can't risk anything getting out by using third party drivers."

"And do you know why I'm here?"

"The old lady in Dover?"

"Aye. So, I need to purify my body and spirit over the next couple of days and focus all my mental, emotional and spiritual energy on the job," as she spoke, Gustavo was nodding along,

"But I'm not going to be able to do that if I spend the next two days glad-handing VIPs and getting chummy with her vicar..."

"And that's why I'm taking you to the back of beyond," Gustavo concluded for her.

"Exactly."

And when they arrived at Big Stone Beach, a few miles down the coast from Bowers, it really did seem like the back of beyond. Once they'd turned off the main road and onto Big Stone Beach Road, they immediately left the farmland behind and were driving with woodland on their left and reedy wetlands on their right. It didn't take long before the trees thinned too, leaving them with flat wetlands all around, interspersed with the occasional scrubby copse. The road curved slightly, then ran arrow straight. As Elizabeth Russell looked ahead, it seemed as though the road stretched straight into the blue. Surely that couldn't be right? But as they kept going, it looked more and more like they were heading off the land.

Gustavo slowed as he realized that the road literally ran into the beach. The three red diamond signs set across the road and the large orange sign in the middle with 'Dead End' written on it, seemed a bit superfluous, given the fact that the sand covered the end of the road and the sea was thirty yards beyond it.

"Guess it's down here," Gustavo said, taking the sharp turn down the dirt track to their right.

There were clapboard houses on stilts just like Aggie's strung out along the narrow track, with some on the seaward side and others on the landward. The house they wanted was on the seaward side and, as Gustavo pulled up in front of it, a middle-aged woman in raggedy jean shorts and a Grand Funk Railroad T-shirt got up out of a chair on the front porch.

"You Elizabeth Russell?" the woman called in a nasal voice that seemed to be caught between a southern drawl and northern gabble,

"Yes, how are you doing?" Bess replied, walking up to the porch and extending her hand. The woman took it reluctantly and briefly,

"Marcy Walker," then she eyed her new 'guest' suspiciously from under her fringe of frizzy brown hair,

"Where're you from?" the woman asked.

"England. I just flew in," Bess smiled.

"New England?"

"No, old England. You know, with the King and all."

"Oh," Marcy Walker drew out the sound as the penny dropped, "Didn't know you was gonna be no foreigner."

"Is that a problem?" Elizabeth Russell's voice and demeanour were at their most unthreatening.

"I guess not. You've already paid in full, so the place is yours," and she held out the keys, which Bess took and examined briefly.

"They're all clearly marked – two for the front door, two for the back – but truth to tell, nobody here locks their doors."

"Nice to know it's safe."

"I don't know about safe, it's just there's only one road in and out, we're a tight little community, we all look out for each other, and we all got guns," Marcy pitied anyone who tried to fuck with them,

"Come on in, I'll show you around," and without waiting, Marcy walked through the front door. Elizabeth Russell followed, indicating to Gustavo that he should leave her case on the front porch.

Inside, the house was clean, light and airy. The décor was neutral, with a few pictures on the walls of seascapes and beach scenes. There were no ornaments, aside from a large wooden bowl of pretty shells on the coffee table in the sitting room. It was clearly set up as a holiday rental with as little for clumsy tourists to break as possible.

"Kitchen in here," Marcy led the way into the kitchen/diner, which seemed to have everything one might need for a week or two by the beach.

"Cooker's electric, dishwasher under here and the fridge stocked as requested," and Marcy opened the big, stainless-steel fridge to reveal every shelf and the inside of the door stocked with mineral water,

"Still mineral water in glass bottles. You got twenty in there and thirty in the store cupboard," then she went over to a narrow door in the wall and opened it to reveal a shallow cupboard with three boxes of water bottles stacked on the floor.

The tour of the rest of the house didn't take long and Bess was pleased to see that the bath was well-proportioned and deep.

"Ten freshly laundered white bathrobes as requested," Marcy said with a slightly aggrieved look as she indicated a stack of robes on the laundry basket behind the door. She'd never had a guest give her such specific instructions before, but the extra payment for the service had sweetened the bitter pill.

"It's perfect, thank you," Bess smiled as they left the bathroom and came down the stairs into the front hall.

"You're welcome. So, you got it for the next two weeks. Any problems, you got my cell, but I live next door to the left, so you can shout or knock on the door any time from seven a.m. to midnight."

"Great," Elizabeth Russell beamed.

"Have a good stay," Marcy said, looking the woman in the purple suit up and down. Weird and a foreigner to boot! She hoped she wouldn't end up regretting taking the rental,

"Bye," she said and left, passing Gustavo, who was leaning on the wooden rail of the porch.

"Come on in," Bess beckoned and he joined her in the front hall,

"Okay, so I won't be needing you tomorrow or Sunday," she began and she could see a look of relief on his face,

"But I do want to go to the house in Bowers first thing Monday morning. Depending on what I find there, I may or may not need to go and see Aggie Thompson. Do you know where she's being cared for?"

"Yeah, it's outside Dover."

"Ah, good. Nice and close. Right then, you're off the hook for the weekend!"

"Am I?" Gustavo said with a wry smile, "Not driving you means I'm gonna end up trailing round the designer stores in the outlet at Rehoboth Beach watching my daughters spend my money," and he gave an exaggerated shudder. Elizabeth Russell laughed,

"See you Monday morning at seven," she said and he nodded, then walked out to the car and drove off into the evening.

Elizabeth Russell wasted no time settling in, and she was unpacked within ten minutes. She changed into some yoga pants and a t-shirt, then went out onto the back porch. The sun was starting to set, but it was still warm and she went down the steps and straight onto the sandy beach. The sand was fine between her toes and she thought it must have been glaringly white in the sun earlier in the day. At that moment, with the sun getting low behind her, it had taken on a pinkish hue. The fluffy clouds from earlier had been blown away and now there was an endless blue of sea and sky before her. She walked down to the shore and let the wavelets lap over her feet. Yes, this was the perfect way to start her preparations. She loved standing on a beach, looking out into the distance and fancying that she could actually see the curvature of the earth where the sky touched the sea. The air smelt of salt with a vaguely fishy undertone and she held a deep breath of it as long as she could before finally exhaling slowly. Stifling a yawn, she checked her watch – around six. That would make it eleven at night in England. Normally, she didn't tire so early, but she'd been up most of the previous night making preparations for the trip. Yawning again, she turned and walked back to the house - she wanted to get moving with her first purification before she got too tired to fully concentrate.

Twenty minutes later, she turned off the taps for the first of her purifying baths. Over the next two days, she would take five such baths. This one would be a classic from the great occult book The Key of Solomon. As she took off her white bathrobe, she recited psalm twenty-seven,

"The Lord is my light and my salvation; whom shall I fear...?"

Although she didn't believe in the god as described by the Abrahamic faiths, she was able to say the words with conviction, because she had absolute faith in the power of goodness and light. She had seen The Truth at the heart of existence, seen the chaos and insanity, seen pure good and pure evil in their eternal struggle. She knew that certain rituals of all faiths were able to tap into the universal power of good, and she would use whatever one was most appropriate for her goals. Right here and now, a psalm was what she needed and once she'd recited it, she eased into the hot water, then said the words of the prayer to exorcise the water. After this, she washed herself thoroughly, reciting a list of magical words which included Adonai, Tetragrammaton and some of the other names of God. Once she was clean, she got out of the bath, sprinkled water from it on herself and recited a prayer. Then, as she put the bathrobe on, she recited a selection of psalms, followed by a prayer over the bath. Bess picked up a glass jar of Tibetan rock salt, prayed over it, then recited psalm one hundred and three before adding some of the salt to the bath. As she disrobed again, she spoke more words of power, then got back into the bath and recited psalms one hundred and fifteen, and psalm eighty-one.

When she finally got out of the bath and let it drain, she dried off, put on a fresh, white linen kaftan and went down to the kitchen for a glass of water. Officially, the sun had now set, but there was still plenty of light to see outside, so she went out onto the back porch. If it had been any normal day, she'd have got herself a beer and maybe some tortilla chips. Annoyingly, this wasn't a normal day, so she had to make do with the large glass of mineral water and the sounds of her stomach wondering where dinner was. She was pleased to see that one of the chairs on the porch was a rocker. She sat down and rocked gently as the dusk settled, thickened and darkened until the stars started coming out over the sea. The light breeze was still warm and brought with it the vague sounds of next door's TV. Elizabeth Russell closed her mind to them and thought about her adversary, the Tzitzimitl. It was apt that her thoughts turned to it as the stars came out, because the Tzitizimimeh were creatures of the stars in Aztec myths. According to legend, they attacked the sun during eclipses and wanted nothing more than to descend to earth and destroy mankind. It was no wonder the Aztecs created ceremonies to keep them at bay. She guessed that the Aztecs had been wrong about all that, because it was a couple of hundred years since anyone had performed such a ceremony and the Tzitizimimeh still hadn't overrun the planet.

Aztec superstition aside, a peeved Tzitzimitl was not a cheery prospect. They were strong and dangerous – especially to women. As fertility deities, they could wreak havoc with a female opponent. Under normal circumstances, Bess might have been tempted to send one of her male colleagues to sort this one out, but Oliver didn't have enough experience and the three most powerful men she had were still unavailable. So, it was down to her to find a way of sending it back to the Great Beyond. She certainly wasn't out to destroy it. The Tzitizimimeh weren't necessarily evil, or even hostile - they could help women just as easily as harm them. This one just happened to be out of place... out of place... maybe that was the key to the whole thing? It had appeared out of nowhere and was angry about it. Why? If it wanted to be here, why was it so pissed off? And *there* was the answer. Maybe it didn't want to be here? Maybe it had been forced to come into the human world? But who could have done that? And why? Why would anyone be so reckless as to unleash one of the Tzitizimimeh? There was always the possibility that this was accidental. Idiots kept on trying to conjure entities from the Great Beyond... but any entity worth its salt would invariably take out its anger on whichever idiot conjured it.

Elizabeth Russell had long held the belief that attempting to bring anything from the Great Beyond into this world was very, very stupid. There was almost no way to control an 'experiment' as they were called in the Key of Solomon. Vanishingly few people had the power, knowledge or discipline to conjure the entity they wanted and fewer still were able to protect themselves from whatever manifested. And yet people continually insisted on risking their lives and souls for some desired gain. A sardonic smile played around her lips as she thought about the book that contained the ceremony she'd just performed. The Key of Solomon was claimed to have been dictated by King Solomon of Israel and gave the reader a handbook for the conjuring and controlling of demons. God had apparently revealed this truth to Solomon in a vision. The book was very precise on how and when things needed to be done, based on the positions of the seven planets. Each planet held sway over a different day of the week and different times of each day. So, the preparations for an 'experiment' might need to be done on a day ruled by Saturn – Saturday – during an hour ruled by Mars (on Saturdays, those would be the first, eighth, fifteenth and twenty-second hours of the day) during a period when the moon was waxing. Then the actual 'experiment' itself would need to be performed under the auspices of a particular planet, which meant choosing the correct day and hour for that, too. This therefore took a lot of thought, because there are only so many Saturdays during the year when the moon is waxing. Weather conditions also played a part, so wind or rain could scupper all your best laid plans. And all of this used to be done hundreds of years before Excel spreadsheets. It made her brain ache just thinking about it.

However, what had brought that sardonic smile to her lips was the fact that the Key of Solomon, one of the greatest handbooks for those wishing to summon demons, was horribly inaccurate. The slight snag was that God clearly hadn't informed the wise Solomon about how the solar system worked, because two of the 'planets' were the sun and the moon. Meanwhile, Uranus and Neptune had been left out totally. The result was that the days and hours as laid out in the original book were simply wrong. Such a glaring error also revealed the truth about the book itself – that it wasn't the product of Divine dictation but had been written by a man (probably in the fourteenth century). It was a hotch-potch of collected magic from Europe and the Middle East, which used the invented connection to God and Solomon as medieval advertising hyperbole. Although some aspects of it, such as the purification ritual she'd just performed, were spot on, the overall result of the astronomical inaccuracy was that anyone following the book to the letter was doomed to some sort of failure. However, there were a few situations where the variables weren't affected by the misplacement of the planets. The fact that by sheer luck The Key of Solomon did occasionally work, meant that it had gone down in history as a great work of magic. Any 'experiments' that didn't work were blamed on the failure of the practitioners, the weather, or some other problem rather than the inaccuracies of the book itself.

Naturally, a few true followers of magic who understood the problems with the book had reworked it in the light of the confirmed existence of Uranus in 1781 and Neptune in 1846. Elizabeth Russell could still remember with perfect clarity the night in 1857 when she had joined her then husband and occult scholar Count Hermes D'ambrisio in putting his newly re-calculated Key of Solomon to the test. They, with three others, had conjured and controlled the demon Belial to do their bidding. After the successful 'experiment', she had had to reveal her true identity and impound the book as a threat to the security of Britain. Yes, her husband hadn't taken that very well at all. What had enraged him wasn't so much that she had turned out to be the Treasury Regulator and had only married him to break up his demonic cult, but the fact that she'd taken away the fruits of ten years of his labour. And then put him in prison. But that was another story... what concerned her in the here and now was the conjuration of a Tzitzimitl. Could someone have used a re-calculated version of the Key of Solomon to conjure this entity and somehow put it in the path of Aggie Thompson? The more Bess thought about it, the more convinced she became that this possession was no mere accident. She needed to do some investigating to make sure all the working copies of the Key of Solomon were accounted for and weren't being used by a third party. The problem was, she couldn't do anything while purifying herself.

Elizabeth Russell got up from the rocking chair, took a deep breath of the delicious sea air, then went back inside. She went over to the landline phone, which was on a table at the end of the sofa. She reluctantly picked it up, perched herself on the edge of the sofa, steeled herself for the unpleasant experience of phone use, then dialled a number. She waited, holding the earpiece as far away from her head as possible until she heard it connect,

"Oliver!" she said it as a statement of fact, because no one else could answer his phone.

"I'm listening," Oliver's muffled voice replied.

"I need you to check that our Key of Solomon is safe,"

"Yes, will do."

"And I need Andy to investigate the whereabouts of the other copies. Do you have everything ready for him to start?"

"Yes," Oliver replied.

"Good. I'll send him to you. Help him in any way you can."

"Of course," Oliver said, "Anything else?"

"No," she replied.

"Goodbye," Oliver rang off.

Bess quickly put down the phone and shivered. Urgh! They made her feel prickly all over. However, she was very happy with Oliver. He'd answered the phone quickly, even though it was after midnight back in England. Also, he hadn't indulged in the usual telephone pleasantries, or asked any other guff about her flight or what the beach house was like. He'd allowed her to say what she needed to, then let her get off. Yes, she had trained him well. However, her next call would be more tricky. First, because the person she was phoning hadn't been trained in the way she liked to communicate on the phone, and second, because it was someone who might upset her purification process. She had to be pure in body, mind and spirit. This included any kind of sexual contact or thought. The problem was, the man she had to phone really turned her on. She looked at the phone like it was the enemy, twisted her head to the side to unclick the tension that was already building, then picked up the receiver and dialled.

"Hello?" Andy Harper's voice sounded distant.

"Hello, handsome," even though she wasn't supposed to have any impure thoughts, Elizabeth Russell couldn't help but react to the sound of him.

"All right? How was your flight?" Andy's voice was raised to cut through the ambient noise of wherever he was,

"Horrible. Are you in the pub?" her annoyance at not being there herself was clear to Andy even from across the Atlantic.

"Yeah. It's open late, but don't worry, it's not a Fuller's."

Well, that softened the blow slightly. Even though she loathed talking on the phone, Bess found herself wanting to ask him what he was drinking, what he'd done earlier in the day, what he was going to do tomorrow,

"So, what's up?" Andy asked and Bess focussed herself on the task at hand,

"There's some information I need quickly - can you check something out for me?"

"Yeah, 'course," Andy replied and he listened carefully as she gave him the names and addresses of three people who owned working copies of the Key of Solomon.

"And what do you need me to do?"

"I want to know if anyone other than the owners have laid eyes on those books in the past three years, and that they are still in possession of their copies."

"No problem."

"Go to my office tomorrow and Oliver will give you everything you need."

"Can I go after I've seen Ray and Chloe?" Andy asked. He was due to visit his former boss and his daughter in Surrey.

"Aye, that's fine. If you could get to my office for three..."

"Three. Got it. Anything else I need to know?"

"Only to be careful. The people you'll be dealing with are dangerous."

"I'm always careful. How else do you think I've stayed so pretty," Andy replied and Bess could imagine the gleam in his eye as he said it,

"What are you doing?" he asked. Andy had no idea why she'd gone to America, only that she'd had to go suddenly,

"I'm fasting and purifying myself ahead of an exorcism," she replied simply.

"Sounds like fun."

"It's dreadful. I'm not even allowed to have impure thoughts," she said glumly.

"Well in that case, I won't tell you what I'm wearing," he replied.

Bess laughed, but could feel herself being drawn towards thoughts of him,

"Right, I've got to go. Good luck and I'll give you a call early next week, okay?"

"Can't wait," he was already missing her more than he'd expected.

"And... thanks," she said, then rang off before he could reply and fill her head with impure thoughts. So, that was that. It was time for her to focus on the task ahead. She leant down and unplugged the phone, then walked through to the kitchen to get more water.

Chapter Five

The Obsidian Butterfly

By seven-o-clock on Monday morning, Elizabeth Russell was as pure as she was ever going to be. Having purged herself on Saturday, she'd spent Sunday meditating, fasting and performing the last of her rituals. And yet she didn't feel hungry as she stood in the morning sunshine outside the front of the house. No, she felt serene. Ready. When Gustavo arrived to pick her up, he thought that her relaxed demeanour was at odds with her scarlet trouser suit, which seemed to say 'Bring it on!'.

"I have news," he said after they'd exchanged pleasantries about the weekend.

"Yes?" Bess said, buckling herself into the back seat.

"Aggie Thompson has escaped," Gustavo watched her face via the rearview – not a flicker,

"She knocked out a couple of guards yesterday evening and jumped the fence of the psychiatric hospital. We'd've told you, but your phone was dead and you said you didn't want to be disturbed."

"That's fine," she replied and still Gustavo could see no emotion at the news.

"They've got the police looking for her, but so far nothing."

And now Elizabeth Russell smiled,

"I thought she might do this... Okay, let's get over to her house before she does."

"You think that's where she's headed?" Gustavo said, turning the car and heading back to the main road.

"Yes. I have a hunch that there's something she needs in that house."

"Like what?"

"Don't know exactly, but I think whatever it is, it's the reason Aggie's been possessed. Will the daughter be there as I requested?"

"Yeah," Gustavo nodded,

"Good. I might need her."

The journey took them through the dappled sunlight of woodland, through open fields glistening with dew and finally across the reedy marshland behind South Bowers. Bess hoped that Aggie hadn't got there first. That would be annoying. It was only fifteen miles direct from the psychiatric hospital to the house, but that was cross country and, if she was staying off the roads, she'd have to swim two rivers. That would be hard for someone of her age – even when possessed. Although possessing entities could imbue their victims with incredible strength, they were ultimately constrained by the body they were in. So, if the Tzitzimitl pushed Aggie's ageing body too hard, the body could die, potentially leaving the entity with a problem. Dead bodies were harder to control, took more energy and would eventually have to be abandoned in favour of a live host. No, Elizabeth Russell was sure the Tzitzimitl would be looking after Aggie until it found whatever was in that house. After that, all bets were off.

When they arrived at Aggie's beach house, there was no one else there. Elizabeth Russell stood outside letting the wind blow through her hair as she looked out at the dazzling sand and sea. This was a good place... but... there was something. She walked to the front porch and touched the timbers. The house had a positive energy. It had been a place of laughter and love but...

She walked down the side of the house, touching the clapboard every now and then. Yes, love and laughter... but...

When she got to the back of the house, she could sense that it had been a focal point for the family. So many good times... but...

She walked up the back steps onto the porch and opened the screen door, which made that unmistakeable light, springy squeak. Elizabeth Russell turned the handle of the back door and immediately felt a thrill. Something with evil intent was in that house. She stepped inside without making a sound, closed the door softly, stopped and listened. The house was still, but not silent. There was the background wash of the sea, which gave the stillness of the house a constant shimmer. She slowly scanned the room, taking in the friendly jumble collected from Tom and Aggie's life together. It all seemed very... nice. Elizabeth Russell didn't uncoil, moving through the room with a hunter's careful tread. She looked in at the kitchen – no, there was nothing untoward in there, but she was closing in on something that didn't want to be found. She could feel it trying to blend in with everything else in the house, but the more it tried, the more it failed. Why? Because nothing else in the house was *trying to be* anything, they simply were. All she had to do was keep homing in on the thing trying not to be noticed.

Elizabeth Russell moved with sudden speed and stealth down the passage towards the front of the house and slipped into the master bedroom. All very neat. She suspected the daughter had been in to tidy up since her mother had been committed. And now Bess knew the thing she was looking for was in the room with her. It was the old feeling of playing hide and seek, entering a room and being able to sense someone holding their breath in the cupboard. One side of the bed was distinctly male, with naval history books on the bedside table and, of all things, a Corby trouser press. Probably picked up in England. The other side of the bed was Aggie's, and Bess was drawn to it. Not the bedside table, but the old-style dressing table under the window. It had a glass top and slim legs with three drawers on either side of the space where the lady of the house could sit and prepare her look for the day. Yes, on the left side, second drawer. Elizabeth Russell almost laughed out loud. Whatever this thing was, it was worse at hide and seek than a toddler who's standing behind a curtain with their feet showing at the bottom. There was darkness seeping out of the front of the drawer and sinking towards the floor like whisps of black mist. She approached with the care of someone trying to catch a cobra – whatever was in the drawer probably wasn't alive, but she wasn't taking any chances.

She stood slightly to the side of the drawer, muttered an incantation under her breath and gently pulled it open. The sudden squeal and flash of black leaping out made her recoil with her hand up to protect her face, but the thing didn't attack. Escape was its goal and there was a thump as something black and heavy hit the floor, then scuttled on thin legs for the door.

"No!" Elizabeth Russell yelled and the bedroom door slammed shut, blocking the escape route. The black, spider-like thing skittered to a halt, pulsed up and down on its legs as if it was weighing up options and then pelted back towards the bed.

"Oh no you don't!" and Bess grabbed the edge of the bed and heaved it up onto its side. The thing stopped and turned towards the window, flexed its legs and leapt, but Bess was lightning fast, pulling down hard on the cord to close the curtains. There was a muffled thump as the curtain softened the impact on the window, then a thud as the thing hit the floor. Bess tore one half of the curtain off its hooks and threw it at where she thought the thing had landed.

"Sod it!" she cursed as it made a break for the other side of the room and scampered behind the upturned bed.

Bess drew her sleeve across her sweating brow and picked up the fallen curtain, then pushed the end of the bed so she could be sure it was pressed fully against the wall. She rounded the end of the bed with the curtain held before her like a net. Yes, there was the little bugger in the corner by the bedside table. She approached cautiously. This thing was quick and when cornered it might go for the throat like a rat. It was gently pulsing up and down on its spindly black legs. It was definitely going to leap, but the question was would it be at her or over the bed? She stopped about five feet from the thing and looked at it. There was a rounded, thick body without a discernible head, and the legs seemed to be nothing more than whisps of smoke emanating from its body. Her breaths were short and her heart was hammering as the seconds stretched out. It was about to leap... any... second... now!

In the moment it flexed its legs to jump, Bess threw the curtain over it. The stifled squeal sounded angry, but now Bess was on it and wrestling the lump wrapped in the curtain. God, it was strong! It was thrashing wildly but she had it trapped and was shouting the words of an incantation. The struggling within the material lessened, then stopped when she repeated the incantation, loading each word with as much power as she could. She leant her full weight down on it and could feel that all the fight was gone. Bess lay on top of it in the corner of the wrecked bedroom until she got her breath back. Finally, she pulled out a handkerchief, wiped the sweat off her face and neck, and slowly unwrapped the thing, while keeping a firm grip on it through the cloth. To her surprise, what she revealed was a polished piece of obsidian. One face had been carved with the shape of a butterfly. As tendrils of black mist slowly reached up towards her, she waved her hand to scatter them, then plucked the obsidian butterfly from the curtain and held it in a firm grip.

"Well, aren't you a nasty piece of work!" she said out loud, examining the exquisitely carved piece of volcanic glass. It was painfully cold, so she swapped it between her hands as she looked at it. She left the bedroom, closing the door behind her, and carried the obsidian butterfly through to the kitchen, where she spoke the words of another incantation and placed the thing on the table. It lay perfectly still, held in place by the spell, and she sat down in the corner banquette to consider it. As it lay on the table, threads of darkness seeped out until they reached the table's edge and sank to floor. Elizabeth Russell had never seen anything like it. The workmanship was mind-blowing. Not just the carving of the butterfly but the magic that had gone into making it...

"Wow!" she said, "Just wow!" and she stared at it for a couple of minutes in silence. Finally, inexplicably, she started to smile, and then to laugh,

"Bloody hell... it bloody is! I don't believe it... that is incredible... Oh yes... that's a good one!"

Elizabeth Russell was still smiling to herself a few minutes later when the front door opened,

"Hello?"

It was a woman's voice.

"Kitchen," Elizabeth Russell called back, easing herself out of the banquette. She didn't think it would be polite to look like she was lounging in someone else's kitchen.

"Mary?" she said, as a worried-looking woman in her late thirties appeared in the doorway.

"Are you...?" the woman looked confused.

"Elizabeth Russell. I'm here to help your mother."

"Oh... I... I wasn't expecting you to look... oh, I don't know what I was expecting," Mary stammered, stepping forward to shake hands.

"Did you think I'd look like a nun?" Bess asked.

"Kinda," Mary nodded, "The vicar said the Church was sending a woman who was a specialist, so I just assumed..."

"It's all right, I get that a lot," Bess smiled and then she became serious, "Would you mind if we got straight down to brass tacks?"

"Oh... okay..." Mary said.

"Shall we sit?" Bess indicated the table.

"Sure... oh, what's that doing out here?" Mary asked, noticing the obsidian butterfly on the table.

"I took it out of the drawer in your mother's dressing table – I hope you don't mind. I was just admiring the workmanship."

Mary sat on a chair and replied,

"No, that's fine," although she wasn't sure this stranger should be going through her mom's things without permission.

"Is this an old family heirloom?" Bess asked as the butterfly continued to emit black tendrils of heavy smoke.

"No, it's new," Mary replied, oblivious to the smoke. All she saw was a black rock with a butterfly carved into one face,

"I bought it as a present for mom."

"Oh, really? Where from? Somewhere local?" Elizabeth Russell hoped it wasn't from some flea market, because tracing it would be nigh-on impossible.

"No, I picked it up in England earlier this summer."

"England?"

"Yeah, mom's from the Isle of Wight, so I thought it would be fun for the kids to see where Gramma grew up. We – Richard, my husband, and our three kids – went in July for two weeks. I found this in a shop in a little place called Shanklin. D'ya know it?"

"I've been a few of times," Elizabeth Russell replied with a frown, then she pulled a small pad and a pen out of her pocket,

"Can you remember the name of the shop?"

"Er... yeah, it was The Crystal Guy,"

"The Crystal Guy in Shanklin?"

"Yeah, but I don't see..."

"I'm going to have to have a serious word with the Crystal Guy."

"Why?"

"Because he sold you something cursed."

Mary wasn't sure what to say to that, so she simply looked at the innocuous trinket, then up into Elizabeth Russell's mesmerizing violet eyes.

"Cursed?"

"Aye. This contains one of the most powerful examples of black magic I've ever come across."

"My God..." Mary shivered in spite of the heat in the kitchen.

"It's also a fiendishly clever piece of work," and there was some admiration in Bess's voice, "You see, someone conjured an Aztec demon out of the Great Beyond and trapped it in this carving."

"Aztec demon?" Mary whispered. This was getting weird and unsettling.

"Well, a Tzitzimitl is a fertility deity really, but the conquistadores labelled them as demons. Now, to summon a spirit like that and trap it in an artefact takes incredible power. What makes this clever is that the spell allowed the demon to leave the artefact, and when it did, it possessed your mother."

"Fuck..." Mary was shellshocked, "So she really is..." she could hardly bring herself to say it out loud, it sounded so ridiculous, "...possessed..."

"Yes. Sad to say, but yes," and Elizabeth Russell could see the sudden feeling of displacement in Mary's face. The surety of her world view had opened up like a trapdoor beneath her and the plunge into a new reality made her feel like her stomach was left behind.

"But what makes this fiendishly clever," Bess continued, "Is that it didn't simply release the demon. It released it for a short period of time, then pulled it back into the artefact. Then, after a while, it released it into your mother again and allowed it to possess her for a longer period before dragging it back into the artefact."

Mary looked bewildered.

"Did you notice how the periods between your mother's strange behaviour got shorter and shorter, while the length of each possession got longer?" Elizabeth Russell asked.

Mary thought about it and nodded. Yes, the periods of madness were coming more often and lasting longer.

"This thing," and Bess nudged the obsidian butterfly, "Was basically fitted with a slow-release mechanism. I've never seen anything like that, and I've been doing this job a very long time."

Mary looked at the young woman sitting opposite her. White hair aside, she didn't even look thirty. Surely, she couldn't have more than ten years' experience doing her job?

"So, what can we do?"

"Find your mother and help the spirit get back to where it belongs."

"Help it? It raped my husband at my dad's funeral," Mary's anger flared in her chest.

"Yes, that is terrible..." Bess wasn't about to share her theory that the Tzitzimitl had undoubtedly killed her father,

"But you've got to understand that this spirit didn't choose to do any of this. It was forced into the artefact against its will. Whoever did that knew it would be angry when it was released and that it would lash out. Not only that, but that each time it got released then dragged back to the artefact, its anger would only increase. Whoever created this is the real enemy, not the Tzitzimitl... although I do still need to exorcise it."

Mary was shaking her head. It was too bizarre! Demons? Exorcists? Cursed artefacts? It was all nonsense! But what other explanation was there? The alternative was that her mom had gone insane and turned into... Christ, she didn't even know *what* she'd turned into. While Mary processed, Elizabeth Russell was thinking about next moves. Her hunch was that the Tzitzimitl was coming to the house with one thing in mind – to destroy the obsidian butterfly. That was the only way it could be free. The only problem was that if it was successful, it would still be in possession of Aggie Thompson. And it would be on the loose. That wasn't acceptable. Unfortunately, the likelihood of reasoning with the Tzitzimitl and getting it to go back to its own dimension was pretty much zero. They didn't see humans as equals, but as lesser beings, so it wouldn't listen to her and it certainly wouldn't trust her. No, she'd probably have to do this the hard way.

"Now you understand the situation and have told me all I need to know, I think it would be safer if you left," Elizabeth Russell said at last.

"But if mom comes here, maybe I can talk to her..." Mary began,

"No," Elizabeth Russell cut her off, "Whatever arrives here won't be your mother anymore. Sure, she'll be in there somewhere, but the Tzitzimitl will be running the show and it can't be reasoned with. Besides, exorcisms are hard to watch – even more so when it's someone you love. It would be better if you weren't here for that."

The sound of a car horn being sounded repeatedly, broke in before Mary could protest.

"Speak of the devil..." Bess muttered and then she was up and sweeping the artefact into her jacket pocket before heading quickly to the front door with Mary on her heels.

Outside, Gustavo was standing next to the Cadillac, with one arm through the open window pressing on the horn.

"Where?" Bess called and Gustavo stopped sounding the horn and pointed out into the marsh.

Bess and Mary looked out from the front porch and there, lurching through the high reeds towards them was Aggie. She was a ghastly sight. The regulation issue white gown from the psychiatric hospital was a muddy, soaking mess, clinging to her frail body. She struggled through the mud, then stumbled and fell face-first into the marsh.

"Mom!" Mary cried out, starting forward to help her,

"No!" Bess ordered, holding her back,

"Get off me!" Mary struggled to loose the strong grip,

"Right now, that is not your mother. Don't go near her," and Elizabeth Russell's powerful voice quelled Mary's need to help,

"Stay there!" the order was delivered over her shoulder as Bess leapt down the front steps, and the force of the words made Mary step back.

Aggie rose up out of the marsh, pale as death with her hair plastered across her face by the stinking water. As Bess swiftly crossed the driveway, she could see that Aggie's body was nearly spent and that it was taking all the Tzitzimitl's strength to keep her moving.

"Great and powerful goddess, I welcome you and beseech you to hear my words," Elizabeth Russell held onto the old-fashioned notion that politeness costs nothing.

Aggie growled, yanking at a part of her gown that was caught in the reeds, then spat,

"Get you gone, sorceress! I have business here,"

Sorceress! Bess liked that. What she didn't like was the way the Tzitzimitl was looking at her. She could feel those eyes like hands all over her. Aggie squelched out of the reeds and onto the drier grass of the verge on the far side of the road.

"Noble goddess, I know that you have been greatly wronged, but these people are not the ones who have wronged you. Allow me to help you return to your home and I vow to avenge you."

"I have no need of your aid. I shall break the spell on me and stay here on this earth to take my revenge as I please."

Elizabeth Russell was afraid that would be its attitude, and that the final 'as I please' was thin code for 'indiscriminately'. Well, they couldn't have that, now, could they?

"I know you have my prison. Give it to me!" Aggie rasped, holding out a hand. Her eyeballs were turned upwards so far that only the whites of her eyes were showing.

"Run!" Elizabeth Russell shouted, turning to dash into the house. As she went, she was glad to see Gustavo making a break for the houses down the road. Mary, on the other hand, was rooted to the spot on the front porch. She couldn't believe what she was seeing. Her mom was giving chase on all fours and, after springing across the road, had got to the house in three great bounds.

"Run!" Bess yelled as she sprinted past Mary and through the front door, but the idiot just stood there staring! Why couldn't she do as she was told?

And now the Tzitzimitl was prowling up the front steps, looking first at Mary and then through the front door to where Bess had run.

"Mom?" Mary's voice was constricted with fear, which rose as her mother turned at the top of the steps to face her. She was still on all fours, looking up at Mary with those white eyes that stared out of the deathly-pale face.

"The crone is almost spent," the voice was inhuman, "But you look strong..." and the sly grin that warped her mother's face curdled Mary's stomach. She felt the need to run, but couldn't move and now it was creeping towards her across the porch.

"Shit!" Elizabeth Russell hissed as she stood in the back room, watching Aggie turn towards her daughter. That was not what she wanted. She needed to get the Tzitzimitl inside so she could contain it. Running to the front door, she took the freezing obsidian butterfly out of her pocket,

"Hey!" she shouted at the Tzitzimitl, "You want this?"

Aggie's head turned and she growled at Bess over her shoulder.

"It's right here," and Bess held the artefact in front of her to tempt the Tzitzimitl away from Mary. Wrestling the demon while it was inside Aggie would be bad enough, but if it got into Mary, it would be stronger.

The Tzitzimitl looked from one woman to the other, clearly going through the same calculations, then it suddenly leapt at Bess. Even with all her experience and skill, Bess was caught out by the sheer speed of the attack and was thrown backwards into the corridor. She skidded on her back along the wooden floor, with Aggie clawing at her face and throat. Now everything was a chaos of screaming, punching and biting as Bess fought to keep Aggie's hands from the artefact. The stench of stagnant mud and marsh water was stifling amidst the kaleidoscope of violence, then Aggie's twisted face reared up, with teeth bared in a snarl. It was the first opening Bess had been offered and she took it, headbutting the old woman in the face.

The crack of Aggie's breaking nose gave Elizabeth Russell a pang of guilt, but with the demon momentarily dazed, it was the perfect chance to put some distance between them. Before it could recover, Bess kicked the demon off her and scrambled into the sitting room. She'd barely made it when Aggie regained her feet and bounded on all fours down the corridor. Bess began the incantation to send the demon from Aggie back into the obsidian butterfly.

"Your words can't stop me, bitch!" Aggie's guttural tone was laden with menace,

"And you have more to lose than you think,"

Bess tried to block out what the creature was saying and concentrate on the words of power as it slowly circled around the edge of the room.

"You don't know, do you?"

Don't listen to it. Concentrate!

"Let me stay and I'll let her live!" Aggie rasped in the demon's voice.

"How can she live when you're possessing her?" Bess demanded, then began the next part of the incantation.

"Not this old woman – the girl inside you."

No! It's just lies. Keep weaving the spell.

"I can sense her growing. She's so small, so fragile, so easily smothered..."

Don't listen!

Still Bess delivered the incantation, but now the Tzitzimitl's tone became silkily threatening,

"Give me the old hag and you can keep the life growing inside you. That's a fair exchange. What is this one to you, anyway?"

The words cut through and Elizabeth Russell faltered momentarily. The demon leapt at her, grabbing for the artefact. The hand missed its mark but caught Bess's wrist. Aggie's other hand reached for Bess's midriff. She fended off the hand, which was seeking the area just above her pubic bone. Bess was trying to finish the incantation, while attempting to catch the hand before it could touch her. She wished she could use more force, but she couldn't risk hurting Aggie. The whole point of this was to save her body and soul. But what if the Tzitzimitl was right? What if she was carrying life? She knew that this entity could snuff it out in a moment. Or was it just a typical diversionary tactic – do anything to put the exorcist off their stride? She couldn't take the risk. She tried to push Aggie away, but the demonic grip on her wrist made it impossible. And all the while, the obsidian butterfly was freezing her hand so that white pain was flashing up to her shoulder. She *had* to hold on! The incantation was almost finished, but she was trying to do too many things at once.

Aggie's free hand was slippery, fast and cunning, and it was only a matter of time before...

The grin on the distorted face of the possessed woman was triumphant,

"Wither!"

The palm pressed against her belly was a twisting knife and Bess screamed in agony. Even as she doubled over, the demon's hands were scrabbling for the obsidian butterfly, wrenching and tearing at the hand that held it. Elizabeth Russell choked in anguish and pain but wasn't about to lose the life inside her *and* the artefact. Her free hand wrenched back Aggie's hair, so that she was dragged over backwards and her fingers lost grip on the hand that held the artefact. Bess thrust Aggie away with all her strength and, before the demon could renew its attack, she finished the words of the incantation. Aggie instantly convulsed as the demon was thrown out of her and back into the obsidian butterfly. Without the presence of the demon giving her strength, Aggie collapsed in a heap. In Bess's hand, the obsidian butterfly was fizzing with blue flashes of electricity. Her eyes glanced around the room for something to... yes, that would do! She ran to the sideboard and picked up the lava bomb from Santorini. Elizabeth Russell placed the obsidian butterfly on the sideboard and put her face up close to it,

"Even if you hide in the furthest reaches of eternal darkness, I will seek you out and fucking destroy you!" and the hatred in her voice cut through to the gnashing demon trapped within the artefact.

Elizabeth Russell smashed the lava bomb down on the obsidian butterfly with all her strength as she screamed the words of power that would banish the demon back to its own space. The force of the blow split the block of obsidian into three.

"Fucker!" she screamed at it, and the power of her fury shook the entire house, shattering the windows. Then she doubled over in pain as the searing cold of the demon's touch radiated through her pelvis and back. Falling against the wall, she slid along it to the door, worked her way through it and edged along the corridor. She had to get out! The freezing pain in her womb wasn't dissipating and she could still feel the outline of the hand that had pushed against her. She stumbled out of the front door, lurched to the rail of the porch and vomited blood. She attempted to stand upright, wiped the blood off her chin with her sleeve, tried to walk and collapsed onto the front steps.

Mary was still rooted to the spot, but seeing the English woman collapse galvanised her. She rushed forward and put a hand on Elizabeth Russell's shoulder,

"Are you okay?"

Bess looked up at her and although she was clearly in pain, she replied,

"Fine. Go to your mother. She needs your help. Try to get a blanket over her and get her moving,"

Mary stared back at her,

"Go!" Bess ordered and finally Mary ran into the house. Why the hell did some people have to be told things more than once? Dammit! She shifted herself so that she was sitting on the top step and leaning against the end of the balustrade. The freezing sensation was beginning to ease, but she was feeling twisted and sour inside. She put her face in her hands and slipped into the cocoon of darkness.

So, she'd conceived and now the embodiment of her love for Andy was dead. The fact that she hadn't known she was pregnant until just now didn't soften the blow. The tiny life inside her had been deliberately murdered and now the flame of her anger exploded into a storm. She would hold good to her vow and hunt the Tzitzimitl across time, space and the dimensions in between. But she wouldn't simply kill it. That would be too much of a let off. No, she would slowly unravel the consciousness of that demon bitch and scatter its essence into different dimensions, so that it could never be reabsorbed into the Great Darkness at the heart of existence. It would be total destruction from the cosmic to the quantum. That thought cheered her up. She took her hands away from her face and blinked at the brightness. She should get back to work... Bess tried to stand, but her legs were jelly and she slumped down onto the step. Everything had gone swirly. Another couple of minutes and she'd be fine... she thought of Andy. He was the first man she'd fallen for in a long, long time and she wished he was there to hold her. Then the tears came.

Chapter Six

New Beginnings

"Cheer up!" Ray Ennis smiled with a gleam in his eye, "I'll be back at work and bossing you about again in no time – no hospital can hold me!" and he shook his fist in mock ferocity at the minimalist sanitorium behind him.

"Yeah, you'll be back in no time," Andy Harper smiled with all the cheer he could muster.

They made an incongruous pair. Andy was a pasty-looking brute in his early forties, with untidy brown hair and an ill-fitting blue suit. Ray was mid-thirties and, even in white hospital pyjamas and sitting in a wheelchair, looked lithe and quick of eye with deep brown skin and a perfectly shaved head. They were sitting on the terrace of the Woodlands Centre, a high-security psychiatric hospital nestled in the green belt between South London and the great ring-road of the M25. The terrace was bathed in the golden sunshine that September offers to the English as a demonstration of what might have been during the summer. The tranquil gardens beyond the terrace sloped down towards a valley of fields and woodland.

"Don't get me wrong," Ray continued cheerily, "It's a great place and it's got a lovely view," and he waved vaguely towards the valley, "But it's not like being back in the thick of it."

"No," Andy replied, struggling to smile with any enthusiasm. Ray was lucky. He couldn't remember what had happened. He didn't even realise that being 'in the thick of it' had resulted in the loss of both his legs above the knees and the brutal murder of his wife, Vicky. Ray was blissfully unaware of his reality.

"Yeah, you and me'll be out there catching killers by next week!"

As a Detective Inspector with one of the best conviction rates in the Met, he was happy at the prospect of getting back in the saddle.

"Well, they won't catch themselves," Andy replied, shifting his bulk in the ornate, cast aluminium chair. Truth be told, his heart was breaking. He'd been Ray's Detective Sergeant and had witnessed first-hand what great police work looked like. Ray Ennis had been the best, but now... Andy quickly reached into his pocket for his handkerchief and feigned sneezing, hiding behind the cloth as he choked back tears.

"You all right, Andy?"

"Yeah, fine – touch of hay fever," Andy said hoarsely, "All these bloody trees."

Ray laughed,

"You East Enders! Take you out of the grime and smoke, and you start falling apart in ten minutes."

"Yeah, speaking of, I'd better get back to town," Andy was struggling. His emotions were churning inside him and he wasn't sure how much longer he could hold them back.

"I was going to sling you out anyway," Ray grinned, "Vicky should be here any minute and I'm feeling love is in the air."

That was the last straw. Andy couldn't control his emotions anymore,

"All right, I'll see you soon," he said abruptly, turning away and hurrying towards the sliding door that led to the rec room.

"Bright and early Monday morning!" Ray called after him, "And don't go solving anything without me, right?"

Andy said nothing, but waved without turning as he hurried into the building.

He marched across the rec room, his great chest heaving as he tried and failed to hold back the sobs. Why wasn't this getting any easier? This was the fourth time he'd visited Ray, but seeing him like that... it was as raw as ever. Why couldn't he keep it together? He stumbled through the double-doors and into the corridor beyond only to find Ray's daughter,

Chloe, standing there waiting for him. Andy went down on one knee and immediately enveloped the girl in a big hug. Now his tears came in a flood and he was telling her he was so very sorry and what a brave, brave girl she was.

"It's okay... it's okay," she soothed with an assured tone far beyond her seven years.

Andy released her from his embrace and half-sobbed, half-laughed as he looked at her,

"I should be comforting you," he said, sniffling and reaching for his handkerchief again.

"You are," she said, and there was so much calmness in her blue eyes that he couldn't help but smile.

"Really? Then why am I always the one crying on your shoulder?"

"Seeing how much Ray means to you is the comfort," she said, laying a hand on his arm, "And how much Vicky meant to you."

Andy smiled again – Chloe had always referred to her parents by their names, not as 'mum' or 'dad', and it had always made him laugh.

"I'm sorry I couldn't..." he began, but Chloe said,

"You were half-dead in the hospital. There was nothing you could have done. What happened... happened."

Although Andy nodded, he couldn't shake the thought of what he'd been told about the scene – they'd gutted Vicky and strung her up from the ceiling like a pig carcass. How could Chloe be so composed?

"For him," she said nodding her head in the direction of the terrace.

Andy found it disconcerting that she could read his thoughts.

"Sorry," she said quickly, "I shouldn't have done that," and she looked worried that she'd offended him.

"It's okay. I know you're still learning. It must be hard to control."

Chloe looked relieved as she said,

"It is! Sometimes it just happens by accident."

"It's going to take a bit of getting used to for both of us," Andy sighed, standing up. Their eyes met and they acknowledged a mutual understanding of the strangeness of what had happened and what was happening still.

"Our world has turned upside down. It's not easy," she said, looking up at the giant towering over her.

"And who's looking after you?" he asked, gazing down at the little girl. She had always carried herself differently to other children, as if she was seeing an alternate reality to everyone else, but since the dreadful events of the summer, she'd assumed an unnaturally mature poise.

"The nurses mostly. I keep Ray happy and they keep me happy. And there's you, Elizabeth Russell, and her special friends. And Vicky. She's in a good place now."

At the thought of Vicky, Andy felt a pang of such sadness he was afraid he'd start crying again.

"You're talking to her?" he said, giving himself a little shake,

"Yes. She's still angry about what happened to her, but she's happy where she is," Chloe said it in a matter-of-fact way, as if she'd been casually chatting to her on the phone. Andy shook his head – he was in a new world and constantly felt out of his depth.

"I know how weird that sounds, but that's life – and death," Chloe said, reaching out her hand and gently touching the back of his. Her hand looked amusingly small next to it.

"I'd best be off," he said, looking back through the glass window of the double-doors and catching a view of Ray sitting happily in the sunshine,

"And you're sure you two will be okay?"

"Yes," she smiled, "And say hi to Bess for me."

"No trouble. I'll see you two next week," he bent down, gave her a kiss on the cheek and started down the corridor,

"Who knows," he said, turning and walking backwards as he continued, "Maybe next time I won't cry like a baby?"

"I'll believe it when I see it!" Chloe laughed and then she turned and went to join Ray in the sunshine.

As Andy drove back to town through the narrow country lanes, he thought of how his world had changed irrevocably since the summer. Before, he'd been an ordinary copper who'd been promoted as far as he was likely to go. He was forty-two and he'd more or less accepted that his chance of making Detective Inspector had passed. He'd been doing interesting work and occasionally putting bad people away – it had been all right. His world had been 'normal'. Now, there was no 'normal'. It wasn't 'normal' that Ray had been mutilated by a hideous freak from another dimension, or that his daughter's psychic powers were the only thing keeping him happy and stopping him from falling into screaming insanity. It wasn't 'normal' that Andy was leaving the Metropolitan Police to go and work for his new girlfriend, Elizabeth Russell, who ran a secret department within the Treasury. And it certainly wasn't 'normal' that Elizabeth Russell was a powerful witch, that magic and devilry and nameless evil forces were real, and that he was now part of that infinitely greater universe. But least 'normal' of all was the fact that he was hopelessly in love with a woman thirteen years his junior and who for some bizarre reason, loved him back!

He pulled over into a lay-by to allow a car to pass, flipped down the sun visor and looked at himself in the little mirror. His face was puffy and the blue of his eyes seemed dull from crying,

"What've you got yourself into, mate?" he said, then banged the car into gear and took off. Even the area he was driving through wasn't 'normal'. Here he was, barrelling down ridiculously narrow country roads with names like Skid Hill Lane and Saltbox Hill, all overhung by ancient trees around which the roads were forced to wind, and yet he was less than fifteen miles from the centre of London. These roads were as wild and woolly as any in the heart of Cornwall, and at night they felt as far away from civilisation as you could get. He slowed for a tight turn which, in spite of the glorious sunshine, was dark because of the canopy of oak branches overhead. The woodland either side of the road seemed impenetrable, but as soon as he was around the turn, he was instantly in suburbia. Suddenly, there were white, pebble-dashed 1930's semi-detached houses with tile-hung bay windows, built-in garages and neat little front gardens. He passed a side-road with its well-ordered houses, closely trimmed grass verges and elegant silver birches set at pleasing intervals, and realised that this had been his life. Before the summer, he'd been living in a cosy world, oblivious to the wilds beyond his garden fence. Even though he'd been living in the rough, tough side of that world, everything he'd seen was nothing next to what lay beyond. Now he was out there in it, and it was deeply unsettling.

By three in the afternoon, Andy was walking up the steps of His Majesty's Treasury. The imposing building, built at the height of Britain's imperial power, glared white in the afternoon sun. As he walked into the reception area, Andy had to blink to help his eyes adjust to the transition from the outside. He approached the reception desk and went through the rigamarole of signing in, then stood waiting for the Regulator's personal assistant, Oliver Fernsby, to arrive. Andy felt that fluttering he always got before an interview or an exam. Well, this was his first day at the new job, so some nerves were natural. After a few minutes, a man in an immaculate grey suit approached him,

"Andrew Harper?"

"Andy,"

"Hi, Andy, good to meet you, I'm Oliver Fernsby," he said, holding out his hand. The firmness of his handshake matched his athletic bearing,

"Follow me," he said and Andy did so, wondering to himself why a young, good-looking man should have such incongruous white hair. It jarred.

Andy was soon clanking his way up an iron spiral staircase that led to a single office on the sixth floor. When they got to the final gantry that led from the top of the stairs to the solitary door, Andy had to stop and catch his breath. He looked over the guardrail at the long drop, which got dimmer towards the ground, because the sole light source seemed to be from the dome of frosted glass in the ceiling.

"Am I going to be working up here?" Andy asked.

"No, I'm afraid it's just me and Ms Russell up here," Oliver said apologetically.

"Good!" Andy said - doing this on a regular basis would have ended up putting a strain on his relationship as well as his heart.

"Come on in," said Oliver and led the way to the door, which Andy noted was carved in an array of occult symbols. The words 'Office of The Regulator' were painted on the door in gold leaf.

"Tea? Coffee?" Oliver asked once they were inside.

"Coffee please," said Andy, and Oliver got the machine going, then went over to the antique desk inset with red leather across the top.

"Okay, so here we have your ID card," and he handed a laminated card in a neat leather holder to Andy, who looked at his likeness on the card and grimaced,

"And that also serves as your dongle for any Government building. One of the perks of working for the Regulator is that your card gives you access to everything - even the Prime Minister's private office."

"Should I be impressed or worried?" Andy replied, looking at the card with newfound respect.

"Don't worry, after a couple of weeks you'll get used to all this. This is your company credit card. Use it for everything you need when you're on the clock,"

"Nice!" Andy thought it was a bit like Christmas.

"And here are your calling cards," and Oliver passed him a silver card holder along with a box of two hundred cream-coloured cards. Andy looked at one, which read,

Andrew Harper
Investigator
HM Treasury
1 Horse Guards Road
London
SW1A 2HQ

"So, that's my title – Investigator?"

"Yes," Oliver smiled, "You'll find these cards probably get you into more places than your dongle. Almost no one has the balls to shut the door on an Investigator from the Treasury."

Andy smiled back. He was warming to Oliver Fernsby. Beneath that rather stuck-up veneer, he was relaxed and quite funny. Although that white hair... did he really think it suited him?

"You also get one of these," Oliver continued, reaching into the desk and producing a Glock 26, a shoulder holster and three clips of ammunition.

"Woah, hang on!" Andy didn't like the smell of this, "Is that legal?"

"Yes. As soon as you made the transfer here, you gained the legal right to carry any concealed or unconcealed weapon under a special Act of Parliament from 1707. You also get one of these," and Oliver handed him a black-handled folding knife.

"A flick knife?" Andy pressed the button on the side and a silver blade instantly clicked into place. Andy drew his breath slowly between his teeth, then sighed,

"When in Rome..."

"And you get one of these,"

Andy took the silver knuckle-duster, which had various religious symbols etched into the face,

"That's just a stopgap until..." but then Oliver reigned himself in, "Sorry, has she told you any details about joining us here?"

"Like what?" Andy said warily, placing the knuckle-duster into his pocket.

"Like..." Oliver wasn't sure how much to say, but then decided that if Andy was spooked by what he might say, then he wasn't the right man for the job anyway,

"Like the fact that all our operatives have religious symbols etched into their knuckles and other bones."

Andy looked back at Oliver and gave a 'Hmmph!'.

"No, Bess didn't mention that. Is it done under anaesthetic, or is it a weird initiation test?"

"Under anaesthetic," Oliver said with an amused look.

Andy shrugged,

"Fine by me. I guess it's some sort of protective thing?"

"Yes. Once you've had it done, you'll pack a punch if you ever get into a fight with the sort of things we deal with."

"Will I have to have tattoos on my knuckles like Bess?"

"Oh no. Once we developed the laser etching onto the bones, there was no longer any need for the tattoos."

"Good, because my dear old mum would rather die than see me get a tattoo. She thinks it's common," then a thought occurred,

"So presumably the laser thing is new?"

"Not really... why do you ask?" Oliver wondered where this was going,

"Bess has all those knuckle tattoos. She must've been annoyed when they became obsolete so quickly."

"Maybe. I've never discussed it with her," Oliver didn't want to say any more on the subject, because the question of how long she'd been The Regulator was something for her to discuss with Andy.

"Hang on, are these silver bullets?" Andy's attention had been drawn back to the gun and ammunition clips.

"Yes. Sadly necessary in this department."

Andy laughed dryly,

"Be honest, Oliver, am I mad getting into this?"

Oliver looked up at him. Andy certainly had a bunch of city miles on him, but there was something indefatigable about him and an intelligence in those eyes...

"You're already in it. The question you need to ask yourself is 'do I want to be in this big, dangerous new world with the knowledge and tools to defend myself and others... or not?'. You already know what my choice was," he replied, drawing back his jacket to reveal the gun nestled in the holster under his arm.

"Good point," Andy picked up the Glock 26 to gauge its weight,

"Lighter than what I'm used to... and you're saying that I have full license to carry and use this?"

"Yes."

"And this card gives me access to anywhere including Ten Downing Street?"

"Yes."

"Bit iffy without a psychiatric test, innit? What if I try to off the PM?" Andy could become a folk hero overnight.

"The Regulator has assessed you as zero risk. That's all you need."

A deep silence followed Oliver's pronouncement as it sunk in.

"Right... and if I'm out investigating and things go sideways?" without the police force behind him, Andy wondered what backup he had.

"Dial 333 on any phone and give the codeword Jackdaw. Help will come."

"333 Jackdaw," Andy repeated.

"Want that coffee now?" Oliver smiled.

"I think I'd better."

On the other side of the room, four club chairs were arranged around a well-polished table. Andy took a seat while Oliver sorted out the coffee. When it came, it was strong.

"Just the way Bess likes it," Andy said, but he noticed a flicker across Oliver's face.

"You find it odd when I call her Bess, don't you?"

"A bit," Oliver admitted.

"All right... from now on I'll refer to her as Ms Russell or The Regulator while I'm at work. Okay?"

"Fine... but I really wasn't..." Oliver began, but Andy held up his hand to stop him,

"I get it. It's better if I keep my relationship at home," then he met Oliver's gaze,

"Is it going to be a problem that I'm only here because of her?"

Oliver looked back at him and replied,

"No. One thing I've learned over the last seven years is to trust her judgement. Even if her decisions might seem odd or driven by some whim, they almost always work out – and they are always done for the good of the country."

Andy wasn't sure whether his appointment fell into the 'odd' or 'whim' category. Probably both. Oliver took a sip of his coffee and continued,

"I know you're not here to take my job. You're here because your knowledge and skills will fill a gap. How you got here and what your relationship is with her... well, that's irrelevant. We're all here to help each other do our best. The fight is out there, not in here. It's as simple as that."

They sat in silence for a couple of minutes, drinking their coffee until finally Oliver drained his cup and set it on the table,

"Now, if you're done, I'll show you to your office."

Andy knocked back the last of his coffee and followed Oliver across the room to one of the bookcases near his desk.

"This is not the main way you'll access your office. You've got your own staircase on the other side of the building."

"No lift?"

"No, sorry," Oliver pressed a concealed button and part of the bookcase swung open to reveal a bright passageway beyond,

"Follow me," and Oliver walked through with Andy in his wake. After a yard, the passage turned ninety degrees to the right, then stretched away for at least fifty yards ahead of them. The walls, floor and ceiling were white and it was brilliantly lit. Andy shielded his eyes from the glare and once they were half way along it, he was able to see that every surface was covered in occult drawings and words in languages he didn't recognise.

"What's with the designs?"

"Oh yes, so..." Oliver thought about where he should start, "Basically, this is a safe space. If either your office or our office is compromised, we can escape in here and the forces of darkness can't follow us in. These," and he indicated the designs all around them, "Are all powerful protections. It's a bit like a nuclear bunker. But it's also a handy way of getting from the offices of the active operatives to ours."

"Do any normal Treasury staff know about this?"

"No. These are all secret rooms. They don't even appear on the blueprints. All the main access points to our parts of the building can only be opened with our cards, so there's no chance of anyone accidentally blundering in on us... right, here we are..." said Oliver, turning the corner at the end of the passageway, before pressing a red button on the wall and opening another hidden door.

They emerged into a room very much like Oliver's office. It had the same diffused light from the skylight above the antique desk, the same bookshelves, club chairs, table and area for making tea and coffee, but there was one big difference – this room smelled of expensive perfume.

"So, this is Hester's office – she is the assistant to our operatives. Unfortunately, she isn't here today – personal day – but she'll be in tomorrow. You are through here," and he opened the door in the left wall. The large room beyond was an open-plan workspace for four, with antique desks laid out across each corner of the room. Three of them were empty, but the fourth, on the far side of the room, had an iMac on it. Although there were no windows, there was plenty of light from skylights above them. Floor to ceiling bookshelves lined the walls and overall, Andy thought it was just like the study he'd seen on a visit to a stately home.

"Your desk is the one with the computer – are you okay with a Mac?"

"Yeah, fine," his home computer was a Mac.

Oliver walked across the room to a door on the far side, which he opened,

"Changing room and bathroom. Your locker is number four. I recommend you stash a couple of changes of clothes in here. We do have to work some all-nighters, so it's good to be able to change. Also, working here can sometimes be very messy."

Oliver closed the door once Andy had taken a look inside.

"And that's about it," Oliver said, going over to Andy's desk,

"There's a standard orientation pack about the rest of the building here, and this," he picked up a slim, brown folder, "Is a file with background information on the people you'll be investigating over the next few days. Have a read, and if you've got any questions, let me know," he handed the file to Andy.

"Now, then," Oliver said, "What else...?"

"Who are the other three and where are they now?" Andy indicated the empty desks.

"Bob Jones is in hospital, but should be back inside a month,"

"What happened to him?"

Oliver puffed out his cheeks,

"Er... his last target didn't want to go back where it belonged and there was an explosion. Could have been worse. Jed Smith is out of the country on a job and Alan Brown is currently missing, but we think it's part of his deep cover," Oliver didn't seem disconcerted by any of this,

"Smith, Jones and Brown?" Andy was sceptical about whether any of the names were real.

Oliver laughed,

"I know – they sound totally fake, but those are their actual names. It's just a fluke. Anything else?"

"No, I'm good," Andy replied, although 'overwhelmed' would have been more accurate.

"Right, I'll leave you to it, then," Oliver said, walking back to the entrance, "Anything, anything at all, just come over... There's no restriction on coming to see us, but if you could warn us you're coming, that would be handy. There's a green intercom button on Hester's desk, though usually she's here to send you through. Aside from that, I highly recommend reading all the books," Oliver smiled, "That door leads to your access staircase, and you'll need this for your car," he said, taking out a keyless fob on a keyring with the number 5 drawn on it in permanent marker.

"Is it an Aston Martin?" Andy asked.

Oliver smiled,

"No. Golf GTE. See you, and good hunting!" and Oliver gave a cheery wave as he went back through the door in the bookcase, which clicked shut behind him.

Andy stood and took in his new surrounding for a minute.

"Mate, what have you got yourself into?"

Chapter Seven

The Joke

Four days later, Oliver was prodding at the pieces of obsidian that had been laid on his desk,

"An obsidian butterfly..." he mused, then he looked up at Elizabeth Russell with a smile of understanding,

"Oh, I get it..." and he chuckled, "Yes, that's a good one."

Bess nodded and gave him a wink.

"I must be missing something," said Andy, leaning over the pieces to take a closer look,

"I can see it's a butterfly carved into obsidian, but what's the joke?"

"Tell him, Oliver," Bess said, stepping away from the desk and leaning on one of the bookcases.

"Yes, so the creature that was trapped in this object was an Aztec fertility spirit called a Tzitzimitl," and he looked at Andy to check he was following so far. Yes, he was,

"And the queen of the Tzitzimimeh is a death goddess called Itzpapalotl, who is often represented as an obsidian butterfly. Trapping a Tzitzimitl in an obsidian butterfly is a bit of dark humour."

"So, someone did this as a joke?"

"That's about it," said Bess, "One man dead, another raped, an elderly woman's health shattered and a family traumatised, all for a piss-poor pun."

She didn't add the loss of her own developing foetus to the list. For now, that was hers alone.

"And it came from the Isle of Wight?" Oliver shook his head – he found this the most unlikely part of the story.

Andy flashed Bess a quizzical look and she said,

"We haven't had anything serious to deal with on the Isle of Wight for the best part of a decade. We've got some good people down there, so whoever did this is very clever..."

"And powerful," Oliver chimed in, "To trap an entity like a Tzitzimitl would take immense power and a deep knowledge of how to conjure spirits."

"And there's the slow-release mechanism to cause maximum terror for the victim and designed to anger the spirit," Bess said,

"Every time it gets dragged back into the artefact, it's like putting a hornet in a matchbox and giving it a good old shake. The next time it gets released, it's going to sting someone."

"So, what we're looking for is a conjuror of immense skill, power and a bleak sense of humour, who's living on the Isle of Wight?" Oliver ventured.

"Not necessarily," she replied, "Maybe our conjuror made the item somewhere else and took it to the Isle of Wight."

"Or maybe not," Andy said, taking a notebook out of his jacket pocket.

The other two turned their attention to him as he flipped through the pages,

"So, I did as you asked and spoke to the three parties who own working copies of the Key of Solomon – interesting book, by the way..."

"You've read it?" Bess was surprised.

"Yeah, that creepy fella, Armand Hetherington, allowed me to stay overnight at his house on the Wrekin. I guess you both know him," the looks of vague disgust on their faces confirmed it,

"So, you'll know he doesn't have a telly or the urge to talk about anything other than black magic."

The others both nodded, yes that was an accurate assessment,

"In his horror museum of a study and under his watchful eye, I spent the night reading the book. And you're saying that it actually works?"

"Follow the instructions in that book and you could conjure any spiritual entity you like," Bess smiled.

"Great," Andy would take that on advisement, "Just as well it's never left his sight since he acquired it, then."

"*Never* left his sight?" Oliver asked.

"Keeps it about his person at all times – even when he's having a dump or, presumably, a very rare wash," yes, Andy's nostrils had had a challenging eighteen hours in Hetherington's company.

"For some reason, he only washes when he's purifying before a ritual," Oliver replied.

"Thinks that not washing connects him to the earth somehow," Bess added, "He's a bit weird even in the circles we move in. How about the others?"

"I then went to see the Order of the New Dawn," Andy had expected them to be based in East Grinstead like so many other cults, but was tickled by the fact that their headquarters was an ordinary tower block at Elephant and Castle,

"The High Priestess says their copy hasn't left their temple in twenty years. And since their security is..." Andy searched for the right word,

"Terrifying?" Oliver suggested.

"Yeah, that. It's terrifying and the book is kept in a locked room on the twentieth floor. That book's about as secure as anything could ever be."

"So that just leaves Bunny and Chop," Bess said.

"Yeah," Andy's mouth turned down at the names. He couldn't quite understand the penchant of the English upper class to give each other ridiculous nicknames,

"I drove down to West Sussex and met with Lord and Lady Ardingly..."

"Lovely, aren't they?" Oliver couldn't help but say it out loud.

Bess nodded and, although they were a bit whiffly and eccentric for his taste, Andy had to admit that he liked them, too,

"So, their copy is safe, but I did find out one thing – it went missing for a morning last year."

"But they found it again and it's definitely the same copy?" Elizabeth Russell asked,

"Yeah," Andy replied, "It's got an unmistakeable binding..."

"Skin purportedly flayed from the back of the demon Haagenti over five hundred years ago," Oliver interjected.

"Exactly. Impossible to fake," Andy continued, "But last year they took their copy away from their house to perform a ritual. Can you guess where?"

"Isle of Wight," Bess said.

"Yep. They were staying in the Four Gates Hotel near Seagrove Bay and they mislaid the book for three hours one morning."

"Mislaid how?"

"Lady Ardingly said that when they awoke, it wasn't where she'd left it. They thoroughly searched the room, but still couldn't find it, so they extended their search to the rest of the hotel and grounds. No luck. But when they went back to their room, they found it had fallen behind a dresser. Lord Ardingly swore that he'd checked there, but his wife couldn't be sure. At the time, they put it down to their being too focussed on the ritual they were going to perform..."

Too bloody scatterbrained, more like! Bess thought to herself.

"They checked over the book and everything seemed fine," Andy continued, "Their ritual was a success, then they went home and put it down to one of those things."

"Hmmph! Three hours!" Bess said and she looked over to Oliver, who shook his head,

"It would take superhuman speed and accuracy to copy it in three hours," he said.

"Took me six hours just to read it," Andy admitted.

"But still... it was missing for three hours. Long enough for certain superhuman creatures to nick it and bang out a copy?" Bess suggested.

"Pff!" Oliver snorted, "Not during daylight hours they couldn't!"

"Fair point," she conceded, "But it's too much of a coincidence. An object containing a conjured demon turns up on the Isle of Wight within a year of a copy of The Key of Solomon going walkabout on the very same island? Smells wrong to me."

They thought in silence. At last, Elizabeth Russell said,

"We've got to go to The Island to see the Crystal Guy anyway. So, we'll stay at the Four Gates and check out Bunny's story while we're at it."

"We?" Andy said.

"I can't go off investigating without my official Investigator, can I?"

"Fair enough," Andy conceded.

"I deserve some time off after that exorcism, so we can look on it like a mini break. It'll be fun."

Andy nodded, although he wasn't sure his idea of fun included tracking down people who could conjure demons and trap them in holiday souvenirs.

"You'll be okay here holding the fort, right?" she said to Oliver,

"Of course."

"Then that's settled!" Bess said excitedly, "It'll be our first trip away together," and she gave Andy a wink that made his heart skip a beat. Okay, maybe her idea of fun did overlap with his in certain respects after all.

"We'll go home and pack, then get off immediately," she added.

"Don't we need to book a ferry or something?" Andy hadn't been to the Isle of Wight, but he was sure there was a ferry involved.

"Not for us. We've got a boat moored in Portsmouth. I'll drive the boat if you drive us down there in one of the company cars."

"All right. Is there anything special we need to take?" having never been involved in anything like this, Andy wondered if they needed to stock up on holy water, or something similar.

"Not really... oh, hang on! There is one thing, come on!"

Elizabeth Russell led Andy out of Oliver's understated workspace and into her enormous office with its huge round window overlooking St James' Park. Easy chairs and a coffee table were placed with a view out of the window, while the opposite wall was plastered with maps and charts. Below them, a long table was covered in intriguing objects including an antique astrolabe. In the corner near the door, there was a round table covered in green baize with eight high-backed chairs around it. On the other side of the room, her large desk was empty, save for a thin folder on it and in the corner between the desk and the window there was a big, leather-covered day bed. Oliver hadn't followed them in, and Bess said in a low voice,

"And now you work here, we can christen the bed... and the desk... and those chairs... and the séance table."

"Is that very professional?"

"No, but it'll be fun," and her violet eyes glittered.

Andy looked at the desk and imagined...

"Yeah, just like that," she said, then laughed at his reaction,

"Sorry, I shouldn't have read your mind, but I wanted to know we were on the same wavelength."

"It's okay," he smiled. He was getting used to it, although since they'd been dating, she had promised not to.

"Or, we could try this..." and she projected her fantasy into Andy's mind.

"Oh yeah..." he said, bringing her close and looking down into her eyes, "We can do that whenever you like."

She kissed the end of his nose, then led him to the wall behind her desk,

"Anyway, what we need's in here," and she opened a hidden door by pressing the marker for Sheffield on a map of Britain on the wall.

The door opened onto a large dressing room with sage coloured walls and a patterned maroon carpet. Opposite the door, a three-foot high apothecary cabinet ran almost the length of the wall. Above it, there was a large selection of weaponry and what Andy now recognised as magical equipment such as sickles. Since Bess had told him who she was, he'd been taking a crash-course in magic, lore and witchcraft. She walked across to the wall and picked a black walking cane from its holders.

"This should do nicely for you," she said, handing it to him.

"Am I looking that old?"

"No, for protection."

"What, and this won't work?" and he drew back his jacket to reveal his holstered Glock 26.

"Not as well. You see, this is special," and she took back the stick, twisted the handle and drew the sword hidden within. The blade gleamed as she gave it a couple of deft swishes.

"Yeah, I can see that will come in handy if I get transported back to the eighteenth century and challenged to a duel. I thought visiting the Isle of Wight was supposed to be like going back to the nineteen-fifties, not the seventeen-fifties," he smirked.

"Oh, you can laugh..."

"And I will!"

"But you're visiting the last pagan stronghold in Britain. They converted to Christianity much later than everyone else and they had a much higher proportion of Jutes living there, so you need something suffused with their magic. Look..." and she showed him the flat of the blade. Silver runes were inlaid all along its length.

"It's a spell, written in Elder Futhark runes. And in case that isn't enough..." then she turned to blade over to reveal inlaid Latin writing.

"Et lux per tenebras secabit," Andy read.

"And the light will cut through the darkness," Bess translated, "Have a feel," and she gave the sword back to him.

Andy wasn't sure whether he felt anything magical or not, but he gave it a couple of good swishes,

"Feels alright. I've never used a sword before."

"When we get back, I'll get you enrolled in our defence programme. All our field operatives do it. Using swords is one of the skills."

"And it's really better than a gun?" Andy looked unconvinced as he put the sword back into the walking cane and clicked it into place.

"Sometimes you've got to hack things off," and she looked at the ugly meat-cleaver of an axe hanging on the wall.

"And what about you?" Andy asked, "You taking any of these?"

"No, I'm fine. If I need anything, I'll borrow it off you. Right, let's go," and she swept out of her office and across Oliver's, opening the outer door and holding it for Andy to go first,

"By the way, well done with the hair, Oliver. It no longer freaks me out," she said.

Oliver ran his hand through his newly dyed dark brown locks and said, "Thanks... happy trails!"

Chapter Eight

Country Roads

An hour and a half later, Andy was easing the vintage Jaguar Mark II out of Forest Hill and south towards New Addington. As he listened to the sound of the engine, he couldn't help but grin,

"Makes me feel like a villain in an old episode of The Sweeney."

"I thought you'd appreciate it. I don't know much about cars, but I like Jaguars – take the next left."

Andy did so and, with Bess directing him, they were quickly through the suburbs and into the countryside.

"We're coming up to Ray's hospital soon," Andy said as he negotiated his way down the narrow country lanes.

"Aye, I'm just chatting to Chloe now – she says 'hi'."

"Send her my love," he replied. Would he ever get used to people being able to connect purely with their minds?

Within another ten minutes, they were crossing under the M25.

"And you're sure you don't want to take the motorway?" Andy asked.

"This way's much prettier, the driving's more fun and there's a Fuller's pub in Petworth right by the road. We can have lunch and a pint on the way."

"And you say you're not reading my mind!" Andy smiled, glancing over at her. She had a way of lounging that was effortlessly sexy and when she looked back into his eyes, she made him feel like no one ever had before. It was more than just physical attraction; it was a deep connection he couldn't articulate. In some ways, it was the only thing that seemed real to him.

Everything else was upside down and weird, except the way he felt when he was with her. But the strangest thing of all was why *she* was with him. He couldn't figure it out. She could have her pick of anybody, but here she was in a car with him driving through the gorgeous English countryside under the golden September sun.

"Got something you want to ask me?" she didn't need to read his mind to know that he had questions – the sort of questions that aren't easy to ask someone you've only been dating a few weeks.

He thought for a moment. So far, he'd been trusting his luck. Why overthink things now and potentially wreck everything? But he knew that if he didn't ask that one question, the not knowing might start the rot of doubt that could wreck everything,

"What does a successful, incredible young woman like you see in me? I'm not young, I'm not suave, I'm not that good looking, I've under-achieved in my career... according to my business card, I'm supposed to be an Investigator, but it's got me baffled."

Elizabeth Russell smiled. Yes, that was the question she'd expected and feared. He feared that not knowing the answer would ruin their relationship over time, but she feared the truth might ruin it faster. All of a sudden, she felt strangely fluttery,

"It's a fair question, because obviously I am amazing," she smiled and she was glad to see he did, too,

"But it only seems baffling because you don't know the truth about me."

"What, beyond you being a witch? Or beyond you running a secret department that keeps the country safe from evils that most people can't imagine?"

"That's only part of it. I'm very complicated. You see..."

Wait! Should you say it?

"You see..."

Take the plunge! Andy will get it. Deep down you know it.

"I'm not as young as I look..."

"What, so you're mid-thirties?"

"Older than that."

"Come on, you can't be over forty!" Andy couldn't believe that.

Elizabeth Russell's face had a slightly pained expression as she indicated that he should be thinking higher.

"You're not older than me!" it was a statement of obvious fact.

"Well..." she replied and her voice sounded strained and less assured than usual...

Tell him!

"Put it this way, my birthday's on November the sixth and if you want to treat me, you're going to have to buy me a cake big enough to fit three hundred and fifty eight candles."

The bomb was dropped. No going back now.

Andy looked at the traffic ahead, saw it was clear, then looked over at her. Oh! She had the look of someone who's finally told the truth and left themselves open and vulnerable. He looked back at the road.

"You're serious."

"Aye... I was going to tell you, but it's not something you can slip into a post shag conversation – 'that were amazing, love, oh, and by the way, when I was your age, Queen Anne was on the throne'," and she watched Andy's face with concern. Sure, she could read his mind if she wanted to, but she needed to let this happen naturally.

Seconds passed. Then, to her relief, Andy started to smile. The smile became a chuckle and the chuckle became a laugh. Was this a good laugh, or one of those kneejerk hysterical laughs that end in anger?

"I can't believe that ever since we started going out, I've been worrying about being a cradle snatcher. While you..." and now he was trying to get the words out through the laughter,

"...were dating someone three hundred and sixteen years younger than you. That must be a record!"

"Possibly," she said, but she was still unsure of how he was with it.

"That is brilliant!" and he reached across, took her hand, brought it to his lips and kissed it with a big smackeroo,

"So, all this time we've both been worrying about whether we're too old for each other?" Andy laughed.

"Looks that way."

"It's priceless! Oh God, that's a relief."

"Why a relief?"

"Because the only thing I've worried about between us is me being older than you," Andy said.

"You really don't care how old I am?" Bess searched his face for the truth,

"Nah..." but then he became serious, "Unless you're going to suddenly age all in one go like that bloke in Indiana Jones and the Last Crusade?"

Bess laughed,

"Don't worry, that can't happen."

"Good, 'cos that would be horrible. Although you're ageing much better than me – sure that's not a problem?"

"Quite sure," she said, smiling in a way that made him feel warm all over.

As Elizabeth Russell had expected, Andy had some follow-up questions and, since he seemed comfortable with the situation, she felt able to answer them openly.

"So, how does it work? Do you not age, or what?"

"I do age, but only one year per century."

"Bugger me... How? Magic?"

"No. Not magic. More like an industrial accident," she replied.

"Well, now you've got to explain that don't you?"

"Okay, so I was born in 1666..."

"The year of the Great Fire of London,"

"Indeed, and I was the sixth child, born on the sixth of November. Somehow the stars aligned and I was born with The Gift. Trouble was, in those days you could get hanged for being a witch. It was only a matter of time before something went wrong. Anyway, long story short, I was sentenced to be burned at the stake."

"Burned at the stake? Who did you kill?" Andy had a love of history and knew that in England, unlike many other places, witches were hanged, not burned. However, if a woman committed petty treason – an offence which included a wife killing her husband or a servant killing their master – then she would be burned at the stake.

"The master, John Hobson," she said, staring back into the past, "Foul bastard. I was a servant in his house. Sixteen and not yet plucked. He made the mistake of trying to pluck me whether I liked it or not. I did not, and in the struggle, I stabbed him in the neck," she looked at Andy with worry. He'd puffed his cheeks out at the thought of it. Had she shared too much?

"Got what was coming, didn't he," Andy said and she could see he was nettled by the thought of someone trying to take advantage of her – even if it was hundreds of years ago.

"So, they caught you, but then what?"

"It was common knowledge that I had The Gift, so his wife and son made up some nonsense about how I'd bewitched him and then bumped him off for his cash. They even hid some in my room. So next thing I know, I'm found guilty and tied to a stake with a cord round my neck. Even the executioners weren't totally sadistic, so the idea was, they'd set the fire, then strangle me with the cord before the flames got to me."

"But?"

"I wasn't going to stand there and let them kill me, so I kept putting the fire out. Every time they lit it, I cast a spell to put it out."

"That must've annoyed them," Andy said, imagining the scene.

"Oh yes! Drove 'em crazy. So, then they decided to forget the burning and just strangle me with the cord."

"But?"

"For some reason, the cord snapped," Bess smiled, "They tried three times with different cords, but it was no good. And by this time, the crowd were getting proper angry. There would've been a riot had it not been for a gentleman stepping forward to calm the mob. He told them that clearly it was the judgement of God that the verdict was wrong; that no witch had ever stopped the flames of a righteous burning and that my survival was divine intervention."

"And that worked?"

"Yes. He called out the judge to sign me over to his custody and then took me away in his carriage, much to the crowd's annoyance."

By now, they were away from London, beyond the Surrey Hills and halfway down the A22 to East Grinstead. Seeing the trees flash by as they passed reminded her of that coach ride to freedom, then she looked back at Andy.

"So come on, who was he?" he asked, glancing over at her.

"This is going to sound mad, but... it was Isaac Newton."

"You're winding me up!" Andy laughed.

"No, honest,"

"This is an elaborate piss-take!"

"No, really, it was Isaac Newton," Bess protested.

"All right, let's just say it was Isaac Newton – the father of modern physics, calculus, optics and the first person to describe how gravity works – what would he want with a sixteen-year-old convicted murderer and witch?"

"Ah, mister Clever Clogs, I can tell you exactly why he wanted to save me. And it was because of two things you left off your list..."

"What things?"

"He was also a great alchemist and occultist," and Bess gave him a 'stick that in your pipe and smoke it' look.

"Yeah, I grant you, he was into all that," Andy admitted.

"He'd heard of my case and wanted to see me, and when he saw me stop the flames and break the cord, he knew he needed me for his more esoteric work. So, he took me back to his house and I worked for him."

"Isaac Newton?" Andy said, shaking his head.

"Yes. Over the next ten years, I learned to read and write, learned mathematics, the sciences and the occult arts. And all that time I was working in the household and helping in his laboratory. Where I really came in useful was the occult side and the alchemy. His incredible imagination and intellect coupled with my Gift meant we made leaps forward in alchemy not seen for hundreds of years. Until finally, we thought we'd cracked the elixir of life."

"You are, aren't you?" Andy said, glancing across at her,

"You're winding me up!"

"I'm not, honest! Look, d'you want the answer to your question or not?"

Andy sighed. Every time he thought he had a handle on the new abnormal, some new weird shit was dumped on him.

"All right, go on."

"So, we'd made this stuff, but who was going to drink it? Well, I didn't think he should try it, just in case it was lethal. He was a great man and I was just a girl from Sheffield who'd cheated the executioner. By all accounts, I should've been dead ten years by then, so I volunteered. It was me or the dog, and I put my case better than the dog," and she winked at Andy, just to make him wonder if it was all bollocks.

Andy gave a dry chuckle and said,

"Don't tell me, the dog was Diamond."

"Yeah, that was the one – randy little git. Always trying to grab your leg... Anyway, I drank the mixture, collapsed and woke up five days later. But when I woke up, everything had changed. While I was in the coma, the dog knocked over a candle in the laboratory and all of Isaac's alchemical research was lost. Between that and looking like he might have killed me, it was all too much and he had a nervous breakdown. I was sent away during his recovery, so he wouldn't be reminded of what had happened, but it was never the same again. Losing all his research took the wind out of him and he turned away from alchemy. Over the previous year, I thought I'd fallen in love with the son of a local farmer, so I went off and got married. Didn't hear anything from Isaac for ten years."

Andy looked over at her. She didn't seem to be lying,

"So, the elixir worked?"

"No, that's the point. If it'd worked, I wouldn't have aged a day. As it is, I age one year per century. As far as Isaac was concerned, the experiment was a total failure."

"Except, by the time you look forty, it'll be a thousand years from now."

"Aye. That's why it's better than staying young through magic, because that can be unravelled like in Indiana Jones. But my cells have been altered to age very, very slowly. What you see is what you get."

Andy looked over at her, looked back at the road, slowed for the truck coming the other way, then looked at her again.

"I'm glad the experiment went wrong," he said at last.

"Why?"

"Because from where I'm sitting, you look amazing," Andy said watching the road ahead.

Elizabeth Russell felt a warm sensation in her heart. *He hasn't gone crazy or thrown you out of the car. Maybe this can really work?*

She smiled and looked over at him,

"Sorry this is so much all in one go... if it's any consolation, you're doing really well. The last man I said all this to went a bit mad. He recovered eventually, but you're doing loads better than him."

"That's good news... but I want to back up to the bit where you got married. What happened?"

"I had three children and endured domestic tedium for ten years with a man who was an idiot. Don't get me wrong, having kids was great, but my husband, David, was very dull. Until he finally did something interesting by dying of apoplexy at a brothel in Doncaster."

Andy wasn't sure how to react to the news that a man she'd loved enough to marry had died while cheating on her. Bess could see he was struggling to say something, so she continued,

"It was no loss. None of the children liked him anyway... but it's funny how Fate works. David was barely in the ground a month when who should turn up at my door but Isaac Newton – with a job offer."

"Doing what?"

"This," she replied, "Exactly what I'm doing now. You see, over those ten years, he'd become aware of a much wider world. Although he'd stopped practising alchemy, he had – what's that ridiculous phrase – 'deep-dived' into the occult. He had seen into the Great Beyond and made contact with occult masters from Tibet to Timbuktu. He realised the dangers we were facing from malevolent forces and asked if I would take charge of the defences."

"So, you've been doing this job since...?"

"1702,"

That certainly knocked his twenty years in the Met Police into a cocked hat! Andy whistled in respect, then asked,

"No offence, but why you? Why not one of these occult masters?"

"That's easy – because he knew me. Knew I was powerful, knew I could be trusted and when he saw I hadn't aged in ten years, that was the cherry on the cake. By this time, he was Master of the Mint, with influence right at the heart of government, so it was easy for him to set up the department. We started off as part of the Royal Mint and moved over into the Treasury in the 1850s."

"Incredible," Andy said as he drew to a halt at a red light. Between the driving and the revelations of their conversation, it was the first chance he'd had to relax on the journey.

"Bit of a mind fuck," Bess said, "But once you get your head round it, it all seems normal," and she patted his left thigh. He had nice thighs...

"Apart from your first marriage, have you...?"

"Six times in total, but one was purely for convenience and two were for professional purposes," she replied.

"What were the two for professional purposes?" Andy asked as he eased the Jag across the junction.

Bess told him about the Count D'ambrisio and his demonic cult.

"Sounds like a delightful bloke. What about the other – if you don't mind talking about it."

"Yeah, I'm fine. It was quite a long time ago... I had to marry an Uzbek Prince to gain access to the libraries of Samarkand. The operation was supposed to take a year, but I ended up stuck there for fifteen."

"Fifteen years!"

"Aye. I missed loads while I was out there. I could've gone to the premier of Beethoven's fourth piano concerto, with him on the piano, but no... I was stuck in the arse-end a' nowhere from seventeen ninety-five to eighteen ten. Bloody nightmare!"

"Was your mission a success?"

"The world's still here ain't it?" she said, pointing at the countryside.

"It was that serious?" Andy looked sceptical.

"Only time I've ever faced a genuine apocalyptic threat, but that's a very long story."

"Don't worry, I'm more interested in you. So, did you have other kids?"

"Yes," she said, and as she did, she shifted in her seat. She felt like there was an empty space inside her,

"I've had ten children in total, but none in the last hundred years. Obviously, they've all passed over, but I've got plenty of descendants knocking about the place. One of them's a good prospect for the department. Yeah, Kirk has a lot of potential," she said staring at nothing in particular.

Andy wanted to ask about the other marriages, but on the other hand, did he really want to know about her exes? Maybe one thing,

"Last question on this subject," he said, "When was your last serious boyfriend?"

"Nineteen thirties, but he went missing in action during Operation Jupiter in 1944."

"I'm sorry,"

"It's all right. Everybody lost someone during that bloody war, why should I be different? Since then, society's loosened up and I've been able to keep things bright and breezy. How about you? When did you last lose your heart?"

"About ten years ago. We went out a couple of years – longest relationship I've ever had. I think I could've married her, but she couldn't handle my job. I was trying to prove myself – doing long hours, working weekends... in the end she just walked out," Andy replied, keeping his eyes on the road.

"Her loss," Bess replied.

"Not really. She married a banker and lives in a great, bloody mansion out in West Byfleet. Got three kids, two dogs, indoor pool and a ski lodge in Meribel."

"And how do you know all that? Not keeping tabs on her are you?"

"Nah. We ended amicably and kept in touch. Cindy's been sending me her Christmas newsletter every year since her first kid was born."

They fell into a reflective silence as Andy powered the Jag onto the M23 and swept them down towards Brighton. He thought about her phrase 'lose your heart'. The truth was that he'd never felt this way about anyone else. Should he say that out loud? Would that sound weird and needy? He felt out of his comfort zone. He hadn't had to talk about his feelings since Cindy had left him, and even with her he'd never been that comfortable with it.

Don't overthink it. Just enjoy it, Andy thought to himself. He'd never been big on self-analysis, so why start now? Okay, so he'd discovered the world was much bigger than he'd ever suspected, but should that change the way he was in himself?

Fucked if I know, mate, he thought,

She likes you. Age isn't a problem. Result!

Yeah, that was the way to play it.

For her part, Elizabeth Russell was glad to have got her revelations over with. She'd never found it easy to tell this stuff to anyone she cared about – partly because their reactions could be so wildly different. Overall, Andy had taken it very well. Poor bloke! Since the clusterfuck of Krowos, he'd had a lot to try to process in a short space of time. Still, there was one thing that was alarming her just a smidge... the truth was that she'd never felt this way about anyone else. Not once in knocking on four hundred years. Should she say that out loud? Would that sound weird and overwhelming? Surely that would be too much pressure to put on their relationship.

Keep quiet on that, Bess. Just enjoy it.

But as she sat in the comfort of the car, looking out at the countryside stretching to the South Downs, she knew that what she had with Andy was unlike anything she'd experienced before.

Three hundred and fifty-seven years old and still finding new experiences... can't be bad...

Chapter Nine

Thar She Blows

As Andy turned down New Street in Petworth, a welcome sight met his eyes - there was The Star pub dead ahead.

"Park here," said Bess.

"But it's only one hour parking," he replied, pointing to the sign next to the free parking space.

"Don't worry, we can't get a ticket."

Andy's face took on a look of incredulity, but he did as instructed.

"We've got a dispensation across the country," she explained, "When a traffic warden inputs the licence number to give the ticket, they get an alert to leave well alone. What we do's hard enough without having to worry about bloody parking tickets."

Andy laughed and shook his head as he got out of the car – the more he learned about the department, the more he liked it,

"Hey!" he said as Bess started to lead the way to the pub,

"What?" she stopped and turned, allowing him to catch up with her. He said nothing, but simply took her in his arms and kissed her. They both felt the spark between them, and they lingered on the kiss.

"Been wanting to do that for the last hour," Andy said, "Now come on, I'm starving!"

Lunch was good, the beer even better and their easy conversation was best of all. Everything seemed bright and sunny as they discussed music, books and films. They had broadly similar tastes, although Bess wasn't as into grunge as Andy and he couldn't quite get her love of opera. They were enjoying the newness of their relationship and the 'getting to know you' bit. And now age was no longer an issue, there was nothing to hold them back. They felt liberated and at times their animated conversation bordered on the manic. They only had eyes for each other and their energy made their waiter smile to see it. He saw a lot of couples come in and always found it a little sad when one partner had that look, but the other one didn't. No, these two were besotted. No doubt there! Before they knew it, two hours had slipped by and when they stepped back out into the day, the brightness of the sun was blunted, and a golden late afternoon beckoned.

Andy fired up the Jag (ticket-free) and wound his way through the town before opening up the taps as they headed west towards the sun. They were running parallel to the steep ridge of the South Downs that were a soaring, verdant presence. Between the road and the Downs, the idyllic countryside of the South Downs National Park basked in the sunshine and they drove for twenty minutes in an easy silence, letting it all drift past. After they turned south onto the main road for Portsmouth, Bess asked,

"You ever been to the Isle of Wight?"

"Nah. When I was growing up, if we wanted to go to a beach we went to Southend. Now I'm a big boy, I go to the Canaries or the Med. Is it nice?"

"Yeah. Very pretty, miles of sandy beaches, great food, lots of interesting history. D'you like dinosaurs?"

"They're all right, I s'pose. I'm more interested in human history."

"Pity. The Island's full of fossils."

"Yeah, but apart from the people who've retired there, what about the dinosaurs?" Andy smiled.

"With gags like that, you'll fit in on the Isle of Wight. Oh, how they love their puns! Anything that rhymes with 'Isle' and 'Wight' is fair game. That's why I'm sure that obsidian butterfly came from The Island. It's bang on their sense of humour."

"Is that normal – to trap a demon in an object for a joke?" for all Andy knew, it was the sort of thing black magicians did all the time.

"No, absolutely not. I've never heard of anyone doing that. There's a lot of time, effort and danger involved with summoning a creature like a

Tzitzimitl. Unless the summoner is powerful and resolute, a spirit like that could tear them apart. And that's if they're lucky!"

"They can do worse than tear you apart?" Andy didn't like the sound of this.

"If you don't handle it right, a summoned demon could pluck your soul from your body and take it with them back to wherever they came from. And then you're looking at aeons of pain."

"As an Investigator, I won't have to summon anything will I?" Andy asked.

"No," Bess smiled, "We're in the business of sending things back where they belong, not bringing them here."

"Good," Andy was glad to hear it.

"Although you might be required to help with seances and the very occasional exorcism if we're short-handed."

"Looking forward to it already."

"But the point is, you'd have to be either very powerful or a total basket case to summon a Tzitzimitl as a practical joke," Elizabeth Russell said without the trace of a smile,

"Or there's the possibility that whoever did this is very powerful *and* completely off their trolley. In which case, this might not be such a relaxing trip."

"Wouldn't someone like that stand out?" Andy had seen plenty of violent men, and the ones who were genuinely crazy stood out like sore thumbs. They had an aura of instability around them.

"Not necessarily. Whoever did this is also very clever..." and Bess stared out of the window, thinking of the slow-release mechanism on the obsidian butterfly,

"They're clever enough to have done this without any of our people noticing..."

"Clever, powerful and probably barking. Sounds good for my first case," Andy suspected that this would be a baptism of fire.

"Which case would you rather crack – a stolen mobile phone or a serial killer?"

"The serial killer," Andy replied without hesitation.

"Exactly! This is more of a rush, it's more fascinating, something to really test you. And, be honest, that's what you loved about being a copper," and she fixed him with her direct gaze that saw through to his soul.

"Yeah, I fucking love it," Andy said with a grin.

Bess had to laugh. God, he was perfect for her.

"Andy, I can guarantee this will be two things – bloody and fun."

Half an hour later, they were parking next to a marina at Eastney, overlooking the mouth of Langstone harbour. Andy had thought they'd be heading towards the docks in Portsmouth, but Bess had directed him to the east side of the island.

"This looks swanky," he said as he grabbed their bags out of the boot of the Jag.

"Ever seen a marina that didn't?" she replied. It was a fair point. In Andy's limited experience, everyone who owned a boat seemed to have a bunch of cash to spare. He followed her across a metal bridge and onto the wooden walkway to which an expensive array of sailing and motorboats were moored. They took a right turn and followed the walkway to the very last berth, where a good-sized powerboat in white and dove grey with black highlights lay waiting for them.

"Looks nice," Andy said.

"Yeah, it's a Jenneau NC33. Quite comfy for a boat and it can go about thirty-five knots," Bess replied, stepping onto the boat and removing the black covering that enclosed the small seating area at the back.

"Is that fast?" Andy asked as he waited for her to finish.

"Fast enough," she said,

"Hang on, is that the name of the boat?" Andy pointed to a name written down the side.

"Aye."

"Thar She Blows?"

"Yeah."

Andy had to laugh. If anything pricked the potential pomposity of boating, it was a name like that.

"Thought that might tickle you," she said, taking her bag from him and then sliding back the door to the main saloon,

"You coming?"

Andy hesitated for a moment before stepping from the relative safety of the walkway to the back of the boat.

"It's funny, we didn't do much boating when I was growing up in West Ham," he said when he saw her look of mild amusement. In fact, the most he'd ever done was take the occasional water taxi up the Thames and one speed boat ride up to the Thames Barrier and back.

The boat was certainly nice to be on. The cream-coloured seating was stylish and the inside wasn't too cramped, with lots of windows and plenty of light.

"So, we've got everything you might need for a few nights out at sea – bathroom down below, a couple of bedrooms, storage and a big fridge... little hidden galley up here..." and she pulled up the surface on one side of the cabin to reveal a sink and double gas burner underneath,

"Oven down there and, of course, a beer fridge under the captain's seat," and she opened it to reveal a selection of bottled lagers and bitters.

"How good a swimmer are you?"

"Very. Been my main exercise since rugby."

"Great. Well, if you feel the need for a lifejacket, they're under there," and she pointed to one of the seats.

She then talked him through the boat's safety systems and how to alert other boats if they were in trouble, before showing him how to work the controls.

"That all seems pretty simple," he said.

"But you should leave the driving to me, because it's not as easy as going out and opening up the throttle. The Solent's a busy shipping channel and at low tide there are hidden sandbanks and rocks to catch the unwary. And if the wind's a north-easterly..." then she puffed out her cheeks and made a noise that indicated a north-easterly was not a good thing,

"Any road, I'm the one with the boat licence, so leave it to me unless it's an emergency."

"Fine by me. Do I have to call you cap'n?"

"Only if you want to be keelhauled," Bess smiled, "Now, go and untie us, then we'll be off."

Andy went out the back door and did so, then joined Bess inside as she eased the boat away from the mooring and steered them out of the sheltered water and into the main channel between Eastney and Hayling Island. She'd opened the door next to the driver's seat and a warm breeze blew through the cabin. By now the sun was in the west and the beaches of Hayling Island looked inviting in the warm light. Behind the beaches, the land was low and flat. A few wind-twisted trees stood testament to the direction of the prevailing wind, but most of the land behind the beach had been given over to a golf course. All that, with the scent of the sea, made it seem like they were off on a fun adventure. Andy was well outside his normal every day and he was loving it.

"Now comes the good bit," Bess said as they exited the narrow channel and she opened up the throttle. The boat responded and suddenly they were speeding across the Solent towards the Isle of Wight.

"We're going straight over there to Bembridge," she said, pointing, "Shouldn't take long at this rate."

Andy gave her a thumbs up, then sat back to enjoy the view.

They were aiming for the north-eastern tip of The Island, which stretched westward as far as the eye could see. In the distance, great hills loomed in the south, and it all looked green and lush. To the west lay the Solent, the stretch of water that separated the Isle of Wight from the mainland. That end of the Solent between Portsmouth and The Island was about four or five miles wide, but beyond their view past Cowes, the channel narrowed to about two miles and less at the western end. To their east, the Solent opened out into the English Channel where various ships were waiting to take their turn to come into the Solent. A lot of them were probably heading to the container port in Southampton. Andy thought it was funny that even ocean-going ships had to contend with traffic jams.

Then he noticed a fort out in the sea away to their right and dredged his memory for what it could be.

"Palmerstone's follies," he said at last, pleased with his ability to remember a fact that could only be helpful in a pub quiz.

"Oh yeah, the forts," Bess replied.

"Built in the mid eighteen-hundreds to protect Britain from a French threat that never happened," Andy began, but then remembered that Bess had been alive at the time,

"Although you can probably tell me more about them," he added.

"I'm no expert," she admitted, "I wasn't taking a great deal of interest in current affairs at the time. But I do know that the one over there is called Horse Sand Fort and the one at the mouth of Bembridge harbour is St Helen's Fort. We'll be going right past it, so you can have a look."

This appealed to the little boy in him. Little boys love forts and the prospect of one out in the middle of the sea was even cooler.

As they got closer to The Island, Andy noticed something slightly odd,

"I've never seen trees come right down to the beach before," he said. Unlike most British beaches, which have farmland or towns behind them, these beaches seemed wild, with the trees tumbling over each other to get to the sand.

"Yeah, they're lovely beaches here. Unspoiled," Bess replied, turning them towards the mouth of the harbour in the distance. Andy looked at the beach that ran from the harbour to a huge lifeboat launching station about a mile to the west. Yes, the trees really did seem to be trying to get into the sea and some had fallen forwards onto the beach. It was strange to see something so wild. Andy felt it was an indication that they were going to somewhere that was familiar, yet very different. This feeling only became stronger as they got closer. There was something uncanny about this place. He'd seen the lifeboat launch station from the other side of the Solent and, now that they were closer, he could see what a massive structure it was. A long pier on concrete columns that seemed to stand about fifty feet above the water level led to the great boathouse on the end. On the seaward side, a launch slide led down to the sea below. It must have been a major building project and told him one thing: these seas were dangerous enough to warrant a very serious lifeboat station.

And yet, looking out across the dancing water on that resplendent afternoon, it all looked very safe. Bess slowed as they approached the fort at the mouth of the harbour and it added to the sense of mystery. It was round and rose straight out of the water, with its lower skirts covered in barnacles,

"Does anyone live on it?" he asked.

"No. It's not linked to any utilities on The Island, so you'd have to do a lot of work to make it liveable. Although it does have an artesian well, so you could get water."

"Imagine living there," Andy said, his inner kid thinking it would be amazing.

Elizabeth Russell wasn't quite as enthusiastic. She'd met the previous owners... they hadn't been very nice.

Andy looked ahead at the harbour, which funnelled down to a narrow entrance and then turned west to what he presumed was a haven hidden behind the land. Beyond, the land looked flat until it hit a steep hill a couple of miles away,

"What's that up on the hill?" Andy asked, pointing to some sort of obelisk that overlooked the entire area.

"The Yarborough Monument on Culver Down. The Earl of Yarborough was the commodore of the Royal Yacht squadron over at Cowes and when he died, they built that for him. As a history buff, you'd like it up there. There's a Victorian fort and the remains of the First and Second World War gun emplacements. Nice pub, too."

"Sounds lovely," Andy said, but there was something about the hulking hill with its dark north face that he found unsettling. The whole lie of the land made him feel fragile and small, and the way the harbour was pulling them in towards a narrow point was like being lured into a trap.

"You all right?" Bess asked, picking up on his change of mood.

"Yeah, fine, just... I dunno. It's probably seasickness," and he shifted uneasily.

"You've got good instincts," Bess said, slowing to six knots and following the channel towards the entrance to the harbour itself,

"This is a very strange place. It has a different history to the rest of England – it's even had its own kings in the past. And it's been a place where things have happened out of sight of the rest of the country. There are a lot of restless spirits here, created by a combination of terrible events and isolation."

"Isolation? But you can see England right there," Andy protested.

"It's right there, but it's a world away. To the Islanders, everyone from over there are 'overners'. Whereas any Islander who has at least three generations on both sides of their family from The Island can call themselves a caulkhead. What you've got to remember is that people here love their individuality and freedom. They're happy to see the summer tourists, but they love getting their island back to themselves once the overners and DFLs have buggered off."

"DFLs?"

"People like us – down from London. Thing is, England is four miles that way, but there are people on this island who've never left it."

"Bollocks!" Andy laughed.

"Seriously. I met an old biddy from Niton on the south side of the island - ninety-six and had never been out of the village in her life. Said she didn't see the point because everything she needed was there."

"You're having me on!"

"No. And Halloween is bigger than Christmas here," Bess said seriously, "There are good reasons why it's known as Ghost Island and The Isle of Fright."

They were now at the end of the funnel, going through the narrow gap and turning right into the haven of Bembridge harbour. It was busy, with houseboats moored along the south side and little boats tied to buoys that seemed to have been randomly scattered around the harbour. Bess stuck to the marked channel and headed westward towards the marinas tucked away in the lee of the land. For someone who didn't seem comfortable with modern machinery, Andy thought she did a good job of parking the boat, and soon they were stepping onto the long wooden walkway and heading for dry land. Even though the boats were stylish, the boatyard at the end of the walkway was functional – a concrete car park with low industrial buildings on three sides.

"This is us," said Bess, when they reached a car covered in protective sheeting. Andy helped her take the cover off and was amused when they revealed a red Toyota Aygo with scrape marks down one side.

"I didn't expect that!" Andy said, while Bess folded up the sheeting and put it into a plastic storage box next to the parking bay.

"What?" she asked.

"After the Jag and the boat I was expecting something interesting like a TVR or an e-type. Not this," and he indicated the Aygo.

"It goes and it's just the right size for The Island," she replied, "Anyway, there's no point in having a fast car here – most of it's a forty zone and the parts where you can go fifty are few and far between."

"I'm just saying it's a bit of a come down," he said, catching the keys she threw to him.

When he opened the boot, he gagged. The wave of rotten flesh stench as the hatchback lifted was simultaneous with the sight of the broken body of a man haphazardly shoved into the boot. Before he could react, the eyes in the beaten face flashed open, a bloodied hand grasped his arm and the cracked mouth wheezed,

"Run! He'll kill you, just like he killed me!" then the eyes rolled back in their sockets and the beaten man gave a sigh that stank of rotten innards.

Andy yanked his arm away and the hand that had held him flopped across the lip of the car boot.

"Fuck me!" Andy cried, distancing himself from the body in the car.

"Oh, that is rank!" Elizabeth Russell said, shielding her mouth with her sleeve as she looked down at the battered body. Whoever the man was, he had been severely beaten. Both legs had been broken at the knees and were at odd angles to get the body into the car, and the face was a bloated mess of bruises and gashes.

Andy took his handkerchief out of his pocket, put it over his mouth and came back to have a closer look,

"No way he's just died!" he said.

"No. He's been dead in there a while," and Bess turned away, gagged, then composed herself, "Sorry. I've got an acute sense of smell - no help at all in this line of work."

"Sod the smell – he just grabbed me and spoke!" Andy was shaken to the core and his legs were wobbly,

"How the... did he do that?"

"Necromancy. But it takes a lot of skill to make someone this decomposed speak. That..." and she pointed to the body, "Is worrying."

"No shit!"

"Not for the obvious reasons. I'm not worried because this bloke's been murdered, or that he's been shoved in the back of my car, or even that powerful magic's been used to animate him... what's worrying is the reason it's been done..."

"To intimidate us?"

"No. To whoever did this, it's only a joke. It's a display of incredible skill and power, just to say, 'Welcome to the Isle of Wight, bitches!'."

Chapter Ten

The Four Gates Hotel

A peel of high-pitched laughter echoed through the vast candle-lit chamber. At one end of the room, Thomas Attrill leapt out of the armchair by the fireplace and clapped his hands excitedly,

"Downer!" he called shrilly as he walked across to a desk set against the bare stone wall,

"Downer!" he called again, and he made a 'tchuh' noise, then muttered, "Where could he be? Bloody layabout!" as he shifted some papers on his desk. Attrill was very tall and thin, with gangly limbs that moved with a restless energy as he searched for a particular piece of paper. He looked to be in his late thirties, but the flashes of grey hair at his temples and general presence hinted that he had more years behind him than it seemed,

"Aha!" his brown eyes lit up when he found what he was looking for. It was a piece of parchment covered in magical symbols,
"Downer!" he yelled again, before moving over to a five-foot-high iron candelabra to give him more light to read the parchment.

As he pored over the magical text, he fitted the scene perfectly. His blue velvet smoking jacket combined with a golden cravat were perfectly in keeping with the gothic surroundings – the windowless, candlelit hall; the vaulted ceiling with exposed beams and frescoes of demons indulging in all manner of disgusting acts with humans; the selection of scientific and magical devices ranged around the sides of the chamber; and the series of magic circles that had been painted along the middle of the floor, from a simple circle of protection at one end to the grand magic circle of Solomon up near the desk. The design of this last circle was identical to the one that King Solomon had drawn when he conjured and trapped seventy-two demons. And it was into the triangle just to the east of the circle that Thomas Attrill had summoned the Tzitzimitl a few months earlier. Without looking up from the parchment, he yelled,

"Down..."

"Yezzur, 'ere I be! Watten thee be wantin'?" said a sallow-faced man with black hair and hopeless eyes as he shambled in through the ornate door at the other end of the room.

"She's here!" said Attrill as he watched his faithful retainer walk slowly cross the room, avoiding the magic circles.

"Gurt! Zo yourn plan iz a comin' to fruit?" Downer replied, in the sort of thick Island accent that had all but disappeared by the early nineteen hundreds.

"Maybe..." said Attrill with a pensive look on his long, thin face,

"But she's brought someone with her. I wasn't expecting that. Usually, she comes alone," unlike his servant, Thomas Attrill spoke with a cultured English accent and had meticulously clear diction.

"Duzz zat leave your plan all of a hoogh?"

"No," Attrill exclaimed, replacing his pensive look with a toothy smile, "It'll add a dash of pepper to the proceedings! You should have seen the look on their faces when I warned them off – hilarious!" and his laughter at remembering the scene jangled around the stone walls.

"Zo, the spell from that there book a yourn worked then?"

"Like a charm – although I couldn't have done it without you," Attrill said, looking down at his servant who was more than a foot shorter than him.

"Thee bist too kind meyaster," Downer replied.

"Well, you're the one that beat him to death, after all. I can't re-animate a corpse without an actual corpse, now can I?"

Downer shook his head in the same, slow manner he'd crossed the great hall,

"What now?" Downer asked.

"Now we wait and see what they do. Will they find the trail, or will we have to prompt them?" and Attrill tapped a long, bony finger against his lips,

"Either way, we've got them like rats in a maze!" and he clapped his hands again,

"Oh, I haven't looked forward to anything this much in a long time," he exclaimed. If Downer shared his master's enthusiasm, there was no way of knowing it, because his hopeless expression didn't even flicker,

"We are now in a state of war, Downer! I need you to be ready to go at the drop of a hat, yes?"

"Yezzur," Downer said without emotion.

"Come on, man, give me a smile!" Attrill exclaimed, slapping Downer on the shoulder,

"This is the culmination of two years' work."

Downer tried hard to contort his facial muscles into something between a scowl and a leer.

"Urgh! On second thoughts, never try to smile in my presence again," Attrill said in horror,

"Right!" he cried, setting off for the door, "Time and tide wait for no man and we have a witch to trap!"

Downer set off after him, still with the unpleasant look on his face. He didn't like his master's sudden burst of energy. Just when it had looked like the master was slowing down, he'd had an idea which had filled the last two years of their lives. Downer sighed. Deep down, he wished it could all be over.

***

"Dead for at least five days," said the large man in the white coat as he examined the body in the back of the car,

"Although I need to get him back to the lab for a more accurate timing. Christ! He's ripe enough!" even with Vicks smeared under his nose, the scent was getting through to him.

Elizabeth Russell and Andy Harper were standing a couple of yards away, with John Fletcher, the Superintendent for The Island, at their side as they watched the medical examiner. They were within the confines of a blue tent that had been put up around the car, which was now lit by five powerful lamps.

"Anything else, Geoff?" Bess asked; she had worked closely with him before and got on well with him.

"He wasn't killed here," the medical examiner replied, turning to her. He had thick black hair and bushy eyebrows which he readily used to emphasise any salient points when he was speaking,

"These lacerations would have bled if he'd still been alive when he was folded in here," his right eyebrow arched,

"As it is, we have smears of blood, but no more. Like I say, these are only preliminary observations."

"Do you think this could be a flare up of our previous trouble?" asked Superintendent Fletcher, a small but powerfully built man in his late forties.

"Unlikely," Bess replied, "If it was *them* he'd be drained of his blood."

"Most of his blood's still in him," Geoff interjected.

"Are you *sure* it couldn't be *them*?" Fletcher had a worried look on his face.

"Ninety-nine percent. You've got to remember that those creatures can't resist feeding – especially if they've already done the hard work of incapacitating their victim. For them to leave a body full of blood would be like a wino leaving us a full bottle of Chateau Latour."

Superintendent Fletcher took off his hat and ran a hand through his thinning hair,

"I suppose that's good news," he said. His voice had a soft Hampshire burr to it,

"But that still leaves us with the question of who did it."

"It's linked to our case – no question about that," Bess replied, "I'm sorry, Fletch, but it looks like we've brought trouble with us."

They had already given Fletcher an outline of why they were there, and now he sighed, put on his hat and said,

"From what you say, it seems the trouble was already here but keeping a low profile. Whoever did this was here a few days ago..." and he looked long and hard at the mangled body in the back of the car, then at Elizabeth Russell and the bruiser she'd brought with her,

"Whatever help I can give you, it's yours," he said at last.

"Thanks," Bess smiled, "We'll try to be as low impact as possible. All we need right now is the identity of this man and access to his home and place of work as soon as you know it... and a car. I don't fancy driving in that ever again."

Half an hour later, Andy and Bess were in the back of a police car on the short drive to their hotel. Somewhere in the west, the sun was setting, but the shadows weren't thickening just yet as they drove across an area that looked like it might have once been a links golf course.

"This is St Helens Duver," she said, pronouncing the word to rhyme with 'lover'.

"Duver?" Andy asked.

"Don't look at me – it's a local word to describe... well, this," and she pointed out of the window. There were the backs of dunes on one side of the road and flat grassland giving way to marsh on the other. Then they turned inland and up a hill through farmland and woods. Houses appeared and, up ahead, Andy could see a village with a green.

"What the hell's that for?" Andy exclaimed as they passed a house that had a human effigy with a Donald Trump mask on its head propped on a chair in the front garden.

"Oh, that's an Island thing," she replied, "This time of year you'll see a lot of things like that dotted around the place," then she dropped her voice and said behind her hand,

"Last pagan stronghold in England," before continuing in her normal voice,

"First time I've ever seen one of Trump, mind you."

"Cheery," Andy said, "Really brightens the place up," but he gave her a WTF look, which made her smile.

Within a minute, they passed a house with another effigy, this time dressed in a tweed jacket and flat cap. The face was white – probably a sheet wrapped around a straw head – with crosses inked on in permanent marker for eyes, an inked oblong for a mouth, and a carrot for a nose. It had been posed so that it was furtively looking from behind a tree at anyone passing by.

"I'm sorry, but that's weird," Andy said.

"It's just a bit of fun."

This time he gave her a WTAF look.

Five houses later, there was an effigy dressed in a traditional teacher's gown and mortar board hat. Fair enough... but the fact that it had been posed with a cane raised above an effigy of child in a school uniform bent over for a beating...

"Seriously?" Andy exclaimed, pointing at the scene in the middle of the front lawn of the otherwise normal-looking house.

"Constable," Bess said to the driver, "Could you please explain all this to my overner friend who's down from London?"

"Just a bit of fun!" he said, smiling at Andy via the rearview mirror, "Loads of people do it. I had one of a burglar trying to get in me front window last year."

"See?" Bess smiled.

"Nice tradition," Andy said, wondering whether the next house would have a full-scale wicker man on display.

Five minutes later, they were taking their bags out of the back of the police car,

"...And your car will be delivered here later," the driver said out of his open window, "We'll leave the keys with reception."

"Thanks," said Bess, then the car pulled away.

They crunched across the driveway and up the wide stone stairs to the front of the Four Gates Hotel. Originally built as a baronial seat in the early seventeenth century, it had become a hotel during The Island's tourist boom in the early twentieth. It was an impressive example of Jacobean architecture, with diapered brickwork in red with black diamond shapes running from the ground up three stories to a stone balustraded parapet. A wide, central bay of sandy coloured stone served as a centrepiece around the arched main entrance. Andy was glad to see that the place was free of human effigies and was impressed by the great house,

"We're not staying in a Travelodge, then?"

"Sorry, they were all booked up," Bess smiled as they passed the fluted columns on either side of the entrance, then she led the way into the grand entrance hall. Their shoes clacked across the black and white flagstones, and ahead of them stood the most ridiculously over the top mantelpiece and fireplace surround that Andy had ever seen. Its stonework stretched five feet either side of the huge hearth and reached up fifteen feet towards the ceiling. It was an intricate display of different coloured marble and stone with pillars and friezes all topped off with a carving of a coat of arms. The unicorn and griffin on either side of the shield glowered down at Andy as if to say, 'How dare a commoner like *you* enter here!'. Dark wood panelling lined the other walls and, to their right, a wide staircase in dark wood and crimson carpet wound up and away to the first floor. As they went to the mahogany reception desk, Andy wondered how he could feel claustrophobic in such a large room.

Elizabeth Russell confidently smacked the brass ringer on the reception and the loud 'ting' seemed to hang in the air long after it should have. She looked at Andy and smiled,

"You'd better get used to this sort of nonsense," and she waved a hand at the opulent hall, "Because my operatives only stay in the best places."

Given that their work was fantastically dangerous, she felt it was only right that her colleagues should enjoy life while they had it.

"It's not shabby," Andy replied, looking up at the high, triple mullioned windows with their diamond shaped lead lights. Then he turned to look at the other side of the room and his smile faded. Coming through an archway near the stairs was a middle-aged man with the worst facial scarring he'd ever seen. It looked as though round chunks of the left side of his face had been ripped off and skin grafted over the gaps. Beneath his obvious wig, his left ear was missing, replaced with livid, over-taught skin and sections of his skin behind the ear and down the neck were grafted, too. What might have remained of his left eye was hidden by a black eye patch and the left corner of his mouth had been torn off and rebuilt. Meanwhile, the right side of his face had been badly burned and the grafted skin looked tight and uncomfortable. As he limped towards them, it was clear he'd lost his right leg and, instead of a left hand, he had a shining, silver hook.

"Bess!" he called out.

She turned and broke into a smile,

"Roddy! How lovely to see you!"

Andy wasn't sure he totally agreed with that sentiment, but he followed her as she met the man halfway across the room.

Elizabeth Russell gently placed her hands on his cheeks and kissed his lips, then hugged him tightly,

"It's been too long," she said, then let him go and stood back to look at him,

"How's it all going?"

"As well as can be expected... given where we are," he replied in a softened Scots accent, "And this is?" he asked, looking at Andy,

"This is the latest addition to our team – Andy Harper, meet Roderick Dalrymple."

They shook hands. Well, his remaining hand certainly had a strong grip!

"Good to meet you, Andy. Call me Roddy," he said, looking Andy over closely.

"Good to meet you, too," Andy replied.

"Roddy used to work with me, so we can be candid with him," said Bess.

"Unfortunately, I'm not the best recruiting advert for the Department of the Regulator," he said pointing at his leg and hook, "But I suppose I do get to live here."

"It's an incredible place," said Andy. He wanted to ask what the hell had happened to Roddy, but was too polite to just blurt out the question.

"The only trouble is, I've had the feeling like I'm being watched ever since the day I stepped off the ferry,"

"Still?" Elizabeth Russell gave him a piercing look.

"Aye, still after eleven years. I've told you before, Bess, there's something not right on The Island," and he looked behind him as if he expected to see something unpleasant descending the stairs.

"But you haven't found any evidence, have you?" Bess asked.

"No, no... you'd know about it right quick if I had. It's just a feeling..."

"Okay..."

"...A powerful, all-encompassing, twenty-four-seven feeling that something is terribly, terribly wrong," Roddy added.

Elizabeth Russell couldn't help but smile,

"But at least the weather's nice," she said.

"Don't try to play it down, Bess, you know it's true," Roddy held his ground, "That's one of the main reasons you don't like coming here. That's why you've got me and others to keep an eye on the place, because deep down there's something on The Island that disturbs you. And something near it that disturbs you even more."

Bess sighed deeply,

"Maybe..."

"Maybe!" Roddy laughed, then turned to Andy, "You know this is only the second time in a decade she's visited."

"That's because I'm sure you've got things covered," she said.

"And if you tell yourself that enough, you might even believe it's true," Roddy said and this time his words hit home.

Andy could feel a drop in the temperature, and the air between Bess and Roddy seemed charged as they looked at each other in silence.

"Ah, but don't mind me!" Roddy declared, dispelling the tension, "I'm just a crippled old curmudgeon, spinning yarns about baleful forces, when I should be happily welcoming an old friend to the best hotel on The Island. Now, don't worry about signing in and all that rubbish, I'll sort that. You're in suite number one. Here are your keys," and he handed them a key card each, "You in for dinner?"

"Yes, and I'd like you and Dan to join us. Could you give him a call for me?" Bess asked.

Roddy laughed,

"Same old Bess! You'd better watch it, Andy, before you know it, she'll have you taking and making all her calls."

"That won't happen," Bess insisted as Andy gave her a wary look – she had already given out his number to Superintendent Fletcher and the medical examiner,

"That's what I've got Oliver for… although while we're here, it would be good for Roddy and Dan to have your number."

"See?" Roddy exclaimed.

"So they can contact you, Andy," Bess said quickly, "Roddy's just stirring it, the little bugger!" and she wagged her finger at him.

"Tell you what," Roddy said, "Why don't you two get settled in, maybe show Andy around the place, then we can reconvene in the bar around seven-thirty?"

"Sounds like a plan," Bess replied.

"In the meantime, I'd better make that phone call for you," Roddy said as he headed towards the reception desk.

"Right, let's go!" Bess declared, picking up her case and starting up the stairs. As Andy had expected, the four-hundred-year-old staircase was very creaky. It was an effective intruder alarm, because there was no way anyone was getting up it silently. And, like the fireplace in the hall, even the stairs had some hilariously over the top Jacobean touches. The top of each newel post was adorned with an intricate wooden carving of some mythical creature. On one there was a unicorn, on the next, a dragon, on another a manticore – all standing nearly two feet high. Andy couldn't help but smile. When they reached the first-floor corridor, the darkness of the wood panelling on one side was balanced by the light flooding in through windows that ran the entire length of the other. The view was out over the driveway and the well-tended gardens that stretched to the main gates a few hundred yards away. Andy wondered about the source of the wealth that had built the house – slaves? Sugar? Probably a combination of the two.

"Here we are," said Bess, slotting her card into the reader on the door. It buzzed, clicked and then she was opening the door into what was a good-sized room, but nothing grand. Again, almost every inch of wall was covered in dark wooden panelling, and a vast four-poster bed with red curtains bunched with golden rope tiebacks filled one side of the room. However, it was the view that was the star attraction. There was a patio terrace down below them with wide stone steps leading down onto a vast terrace of lawns, split into separate areas by hedges with extravagant topiary. Another set of steps led to a sloping meadow with an avenue of poplars running straight down through it to the beach. Beyond, the sea shimmered with the last of the reddening sunset.

"Sorry about Roddy," Bess said as she started to unpack, "He's a little bit paranoid."

"Is that because of..." Andy pointed towards his face.

"Partly, yes."

"I'm surprised he's fronting a place like this," Andy suspected that little children wouldn't be fans of the odd man at the reception desk.

"Hmm? No, the punters can't see that. He's enchanted himself so that only certain people can see him as he is."

Andy nodded slowly as he processed the information, then said,

"Sorry, but I've got to know what happened to him."

"Get him going on single malt and he'll tell you the tale in remarkably gruesome detail, but the thumbnail is... we had a water demon causing a lot of trouble down in the west country, Roddy tried to banish it back from whence it came, it didn't want to go and tried to tear him to pieces with its tentacles. Roddy's last throw of the dice was to make some drums of petrol explode behind the creature. It took ninety percent of the blast, but he got badly burnt. Miracle he survived."

"He seems very sure that things aren't right here," Andy said.

"To be honest, I think he'd be like that wherever he was. He had a long, slow recovery that allowed him too much time to think about what'd happened. Now he sees potential enemies everywhere... but I still trust him. I would've had him back in the department, only he opted for early retirement. So, we reached a compromise and I put him in charge here."

"You know the owners?"

"We are the owners," Bess said and Andy's bewildered look amused her,

"I picked it up for a song in the eighteen-nineties. Obviously, it's worth tens of millions now, but it was very reasonable at the time."

Andy gave a raucous 'Ha!'

"Incredible. Every time I think today can't get more weird, it racks up a notch."

At that moment, Andy's phone rang, giving him a start,

"See? Bloody hell! Even the timing of phone calls is weird!" then he pulled his phone out of his pocket,

"Detective Sergeant..." Andy stopped himself, "I mean, Andy Harper here," he was still getting used to the idea that the police force was something he'd left behind.

"Hello Mister Harper, it's Geoff Armstrong – the M.E. for the Isle of Wight Police..."

"All right? What can I do for you?" Andy said, then mouthed 'It's Geoff,' at Bess. She stopped placing things in the wardrobe and turned her attention to Andy and the phone call.

Andy let the M.E. do the talking, keeping his interjections brief and to the point. Bess watched his face closely to gauge his reactions to what was being said. If it had been anyone but Andy, she'd already be in their mind and listening in to the conversation. However, her ability to do that on The Island was a bit erratic – and anyway, she'd made a promise to herself to keep out of Andy's mind as much as possible. She wanted their relationship to be real. No mind control. No reading his thoughts. She wanted to be surprised by him, not know what he was going to say before he said it. But when she saw the look of surprise on his face as he reacted to something Geoff had said, she wished she could have a little peak to know what it was.

"Right, thanks Geoff. Yeah, will do... speak tomorrow. Gu'night," and Andy clicked off his phone.

"Well?" she asked - not knowing was odd and she was impatient.

"You know how we've come down here to see the Crystal Guy," Andy said,

"Yes,"

"Guess who was in the back of our car..."

Chapter Eleven

A Night In

When Andy walked into the hotel bar at seven-thirty, he was unsurprised to see that it was a moodily lit symphony of dark wood panelling with a crimson carpet. Having spent the last half hour being shown around the impressive building, Andy was getting used to the heavy-handed use of wood panelling. Roddy was already there, leaning against the bar chatting to a fit looking man of about forty. The newcomer was dressed in khaki cargo trousers and a dusty sweatshirt, and had a shaggy head of tangled golden hair, which he kept having to sweep away from his face as he spoke.

"Dan!" Bess called and the two men at the bar broke into smiles as she marched over to them and hugged the blonde man, before dragging Roddy into the cuddle.

"The old team all together!" she said as Andy joined them.

After introductions, they got in four pints of a local beer – Goddards Ale of Wight - and settled down at a booth in the furthest corner. Elizabeth Russell got straight down to business, quickly explaining why they had come to The Island, and placing the pieces of the obsidian butterfly on the table,

"We have one lead: we know it was purchased from the Crystal Guy in Shanklin,"

"Oh yeah, I know him... what's his name?" Dan strained to remember,

"Reginald Dunseath," Andy said.

"Reg, that's it! So, you're going to see him?"

"Already have," said Bess, "Someone very kindly saved us a journey by beating him to death and putting him in the boot of my car."

"Oh God!" Dan's face fell, as if he was looking into a very unpleasant future, "You don't think it's a recurrence of the old problem, do you?"

"No," Bess replied.

"Well, that's a relief, because as far as I can tell, we've rooted out every last one of those blood-sucking bastards,"

Dan said in an upper-class accent that seemed at odds with his clothes.

"Are you saying you had vampires here?" asked Andy, but as soon as he said it, the other three reacted like they'd been stung,

"We don't use the V word," Bess explained, "Popular culture has romanticised it. You say 'vampire' and people think of gothic castles and elegant creatures of the night seducing men and women with erotic fantasies... the reality is, they're foul, stinking vermin that shouldn't even be here."

"They're about as erotic as a cockroach," Roddy growled.

"Only harder to get rid of," Dan added.

"Back in the late nineteen-fifties and early sixties, The Island had a really bad infestation," Bess explained, "And it was a popular tourist destination back then, so people were coming over, getting bitten and then going back to their homes and starting new nests. It was a total nightmare!" Bess's face set hard as she remembered it.

"My grandparents helped to eradicate the nests, although they both died in the process," Dan said.

"They were good friends," Bess declared, reaching over to squeeze Dan's hand, "And thanks to them, we cleared The Island and made it a much less attractive place for the little bleeders to come to."

"How?" Andy asked.

"There's a garlic farm," Roddy replied, "It's a huge tourist attraction and there are ads for it and signposts to it all round The Island... even ads for it on the ferries coming over. There's a vast selection of Garlic Farm products and they're in almost every food shop on The Island. This place has become a blood sucker's worst nightmare!"

"We've had a couple of flare ups since, but Dan's family has been doing a great job of flushing them out," Bess added.

"Yeah, after we lost nan and grandad, my parents took over and, now they're retired, I'm The Island's pest controller – I also build boats, hence the sawdust," Dan said, brushing some bits off his sweatshirt.

Andy took a long pull at his beer. So, he could add vampires to his list of bizarre information for the day. Talk about being thrown in at the deep end!

"Now your lead's come to a dead end, what are you going to do?" Roddy asked.

"My Investigator is going to investigate," said Bess.

"I've got access to his house and office," Andy explained, "I'll see what I can find. Unless he's picking stuff up under the table for cash in hand, he should have details of the obsidian butterfly somewhere in his records."

"And while he's doing that, guess what we're going to do tomorrow?" she said, looking at Dan with a cheeky glint in her eye.

"Oh goody!" Dan said, "A check of all the old nests."

"Yup! You never know, they might be at the bottom of this. Either way, it's about time I had a look."

"Six years, Bess! It's a long time to be away. Not scared, are you?" Dan said with a wink at Roddy.

At this, Elizabeth Russell pursed her lips and raised an eyebrow in a display of mock displeasure,

"You know I'm not."

"But things don't work like they should while you're here, do they?" Dan continued and, behind Bess's back, Roddy gave Dan a thumbs up – he wanted to hear what she would say when she couldn't brush off the questions as part of Roddy's paranoia.

"It's true," Bess admitted, looking at Andy,

"Among other things, when I'm here I completely lose my usual contact with people on the mainland, and my ability to make mind links with people here is patchy at best..."

"You make it sound like you don't have a mobile signal!" Roddy laughed.

"But we know the reason for it and it's not because of your mysterious feeling of being watched," Bess retorted.

"What is the reason?" Andy asked.

"Folk tales say that somewhere out to sea is the 'Other Place'. It's another island, hidden from mortal eyes, where all the old magic of the Isle of Wight resides. And when the Swaailen fog rolls in and covers The Island, that's a sign the 'Other Place' is near. It's a quaint old folk tale. The snag is... it's true. And every time I come here, the Swaailen rolls in and whatever is in the Other Place interferes with some of my powers."

Roddy gave a low, dry laugh,

"And it's not just that – they want her to join them. I don't want to imagine why, but I'm sure the result wouldn't be good."

"Which is why I try to stay off the Isle of Wight as much as possible," Bess concluded.

There was an awkward silence, which Elizabeth Russell finally burst,

"Well, now you've brought everyone down, Roderick, why don't you do something useful and get another round in?"

"I don't think I'm the right man for that, do you?" he replied, gently scratching his temple with the tip of his silver hook. There was a pause as the four of them looked at each other, then they laughed.

Dan got in the next round, and they followed it with an excellent dinner of grouse and venison, which seemed in keeping with the rich surroundings of the dining hall. Roddy and Dan were good company and the conversation jogged along. Andy thought it was good to meet some of Bess's friends and find out how they saw her. It was clear that both men respected her and would put their lives on the line for her, but were also quite happy to bring her down to earth. For her part, she took their jokes in good spirit and paid them back in kind. Although they could have talked all night, they decided to wind things up around ten. They had an early start, and a good night's sleep would make the next day a lot easier.

"I'll give you a morning call at half past five," said Roddy as they stood in entrance hall, "It's too early for the hotel breakfast, so just come to the kitchen and we'll see what we can get you."

"And shall I pick you up at half-six?" Dan asked.

"Perfect," Bess said, "Sunrise isn't until six forty-five, so we can start on the first location shortly after. Oh yes, I think we should have a fun day tomorrow!"

"One thing you'll learn pretty quickly, Andy, is her warped idea about what 'fun' is," Dan smiled, then he turned on his heel and walked away with a cheery,

"Nighty-night!" thrown over his shoulder.

When they got back to their room, Andy was feeling mentally tired. There was so much to process from the day! Would every day in this new job – this new life – be such a steep learning curve? All he wanted to do was flump on the bed and fall asleep, and yet, when Bess turned and smiled at him, he felt his tiredness falling away. There was something about her presence that made him feel... wonderful. He took her hand, then drew her close to him,

"You know, you really are very beautiful," he said, looking down at her face and drinking in every curve, line and detail. Up close, within the field of her aura, was like nothing he'd ever experienced. It made him feel disorientated, yet confident that it was where he ought to be. And she was looking up at him with wide eyes that seemed surprised at the power this man had over her. Andy bent his head and kissed her. Her soft lips responded to his and soon their kisses deepened as their hands explored. Then, just as his fingers started to unbutton her shirt, she disengaged, caught her breath and said,

"I do have a bit of bad news on the shagging front."

"What?"

Now wasn't the time for the whole truth about what had happened in America, but some of the truth would suffice,

"I'm afraid I've got the decorators in."

"Oh..." Andy was slightly surprised, "Sorry, I assumed that because you're..." he searched for the right words...

"Really, really old?" she suggested.

"I wouldn't put it like that, but yeah. I'd've thought that had all stopped."

"Sadly not," she said truthfully, "I'm ageing slowly and my menstrual cycle has slowed accordingly. I get twelve periods a century – one every eight years or so. It's just bad luck that I've got one this week. The long gap between them is nice, but on the down side, it could easily be two thousand years before I hit menopause."

Andy thought for a moment,

"Do they last longer than normal?"

"Thank God, no! That really would be a 'curse'. No, they last about a week, but even so, they don't warn you about this stuff in the alchemical handbooks. Anyway, menstruation aside..." and now she was fixing him with a predatory gaze as she eased up against him,

"I'm sure that there's plenty I can still do that will blow your... mind," and she kissed him with such desire that it made his entire body tingle. Then she pulled him over to the bed and made good on her promise.

Chapter Twelve

Swaailen

"I see you've brought the weather with you," Dan called through the open window of his battered Land Rover as he pulled up in front of Bess and Andy. They were standing in the porch outside the hotel, which had been enveloped in a swirling fog so dense that they couldn't see more than thirty yards down the driveway. The air was cool and had a damp scent of the cloud that had settled around them to steal the world beyond its grey shroud,

"Whatever is in the Other Place has a hard-on for you, Bess," Dan smiled,

"And a very good morning to you too, Dan!" Bess replied, then she turned to Andy,

"Right, this is me. I'll see you back here around six."

"All right. First one back gets the beers in," Andy replied.

"Sounds fair. C'mere..." and she pulled Andy in to give him a lingering kiss.

"Hey! Put him down - you don't know where he's been!" Dan called from the car.

"See you later," Bess said and her eyes seemed to burn with some internal flame against the background gloom, then she jogged down the steps and hopped into the Land Rover. Dan pulled away and soon the car had been swallowed by the fog so that the only evidence they had ever been there was the diminishing roar of the engine until that, too, faded into the cloud.

Andy stood for a few moments, staring into the fog, then blinked and looked down at the steps. Looking into the swirling cloud was disorientating - he'd have to be careful on his drive down the coast to Shanklin. He gave himself a shake and walked over to the anonymous blue Ford Focus that the local police had left for them in the night. He unlocked it and got in, placing the swordstick over on the back seat. Bess had insisted he should take it with him. Before they'd left the room, she'd checked that he had all his weapons,

"Don't think I'm mollycoddling you," she'd said, "You were doing a tough job before, but criminals know that if they harm a police officer, the law will come down on them hard. In this line of work, there is no law. It's just you and the tools you've got, up against things that might kill you as soon as look at you."

Now, as Andy put on his seatbelt, he could feel the Glock nestling under his left armpit. Silver bullets. That was his new reality – better get used to it. He started the car, put the address of the Crystal Guy's shop into the satnav and drove away from the house. There was a moment when Andy felt a degree of disquiet as the hotel disappeared into the fog behind him. All he could see in the rearview was the drive heading back into a grey bank of nothing, while ahead it led him towards an impenetrable wall of swirling fog. He couldn't even see the end of the drive. At that moment, he was in limbo – caught between safety and the unknown beyond.

"Sod it!" he said and planted his foot on the accelerator – he'd made the decision that this was his new life and it was time to roll the dice. Soon he was on the road where he'd seen the effigies in the front gardens on the way to the hotel. Last night there had been an end-of-summer vibe and yet still the effigies had been creepy. Today in the fog, the vibe was menacing and the sight of the effigies was downright unpleasant. The one peeping out from behind the tree in its front garden was the stuff of nightmares, as it seeped up through the fog when Andy approached, before seeping back into the cloud after Andy had driven past.

He drove through St Helens with its large village green. The fog made it difficult to get the lie of the land. Andy could see that the grassy area to his left started to slope down the hill, but then it was all lost in the cloud.

There must surely be more houses on the other side of the green, but he was damned if he could see them. Meanwhile, on the right side of the road were the pub, a post office and some pretty cottages. All were marred (in his opinion) by more of these effigies. Outside one otherwise delightful cottage, the effigy of a man in a broad-brimmed hat stood leaning on the front wall. The straw had been badly stuffed into the brown jacket, giving it a lumpy look, while the face that had been drawn onto the white material covering the head had thunderous eyebrows and jagged teeth. Meanwhile, the effigy that had been posed with a glass stuck to its hand at a table outside the pub could have looked quaint. It didn't. It was hunched over its drink with its head tilted to look over its shoulder at passers-by and the expression drawn onto its face was hostile. It was protecting its drink and would fight anyone who disturbed it. Andy was glad when he got through the village and the road wound down a hill between high hedges. He assumed there were fields on the other side of the hedges, but in the fog he couldn't be sure. For all he knew, the sea was just on the other side, or a cliff or an abyss into some screaming world of evil. He shook his head. It was incredible that this new level of existence into which he'd been thrown had been there all along.

As he passed a gate in one hedge, he could see that there was a field beyond. A scarecrow was standing in the field, lonely and just at the edge of his range of vision. Under a bowler hat, it too had a head that had been covered in white material. It must be some sort of local fashion. Andy was glad that he couldn't make out the details of its face, because if the things in the village looked disturbing, what dreadful expression would the farmer have given it to scare the crows? He drove on through the fog, up hill and down dale, following the satnav's instructions. He was now thoroughly disorientated and the gloom was such that the satnav in the car was running in night mode. Soon he was passing through the village of Brading where the houses and shops crowded around the narrow main street. He passed an ancient-looking pub called The Bugle Inn that inexplicably had a Herefordshire bull on the sign. As the road turned and widened, he noticed another effigy outside some sort of chapel. It looked like it was made completely from flowerpots and it was sitting amongst a colourful display of flowers in baskets. Even its face was a flowerpot, positioned so that the bottom of the pot faced out and the three drainage holes looked like two eyes and a mouth. On top of its 'head', another flowerpot was tipped at a jaunty angle as a hat. Finally, here was a figure that wasn't even faintly disturbing. In fact, it put a smile on Andy's face and served as an antidote to the others he'd seen.

It wasn't long before the smile was replaced by a look somewhere between bafflement and alarm. As the village thinned out, he could see a gaggle of effigies in a front garden that had been set up as an orchestra. There was a conductor with a baton, dressed in a black tailcoat. He was standing in front of a group of zombie musicians with papier mâché heads made to look like rotting corpses. Each had its own musical instrument, including a keyboard, a guitar and a tuba! Andy could hardly believe what he was seeing and looked in the rearview after he passed. He wished he hadn't. The conductor's face was drawn on with the evil eyes and jagged teeth of a jack-o-lantern and seemed to be watching him as he drove away before disappearing into the fog.

"What the fuck?" he said out loud, "Who would do that?"

The time and effort that someone had put in to create that disturbing little scene in their front garden worried Andy. What was the thinking behind it? They must have set out deliberately to make it as nightmarish as possible – and they'd succeeded – but why? It was still September. Halloween was over a month away. Why would they have that outside their house for so long?

Andy was still pondering this question when he drove through Sandown, which he might have described as 'shabby chic' had anyone remembered to add the 'chic'. Even without the fog, the houses and shops would have looked tired, but in the swirling gloom, the buildings looked exhausted. Like so many other English seaside towns, it had been booming once, but that time had passed. Why go to the Isle of Wight in the summer for a £200 round trip on the car ferry when you could fly to Majorca for fifty quid? It didn't help that where there should have been a view of the golden sand and glittering sea, all he could see was a bank of grey. It reminded him of the resorts his family had gone to when he was a kid: fun for children with a bucket and spade, plenty of chips and ice cream and a few rounds of crazy golf. Of course, Sandown had more to it than that – there was a well-known dinosaur museum, a big cat rescue centre-cum-zoo and the dubious charms of the National Poo Museum – but as he drove through, he couldn't help but feel uncheered by the dead, out-of-season mood of the place. On the plus side, the residents of Sandown hadn't gone in for filling the town with weird human effigies. That was nice. Andy made a mental note to come back when it was sunny.

Soon he was in Shanklin, which seemed to be more of a town and less of a resort than Sandown. He followed signs for parking, found a space in a central lot and parked up. On getting out, it was still cold and damp, so he buttoned up his mackintosh, put the swordstick into the boot of the car and went to find The Crystal Guy shop. He walked up the hill of the High Street with its narrow pavements. It had an interesting array of shops that catered for everyone from hardcore gamers to little old dears wanting a nice cup of tea. And there, wedged in between a nail bar and an antique shop, was The Crystal Guy. The metal shutters of the shopfront were down and had been nicely painted with a scene of a child holding a fairy in her hand as the fairy offered her a jewel. Andy liked that. Yes, it was a bit twee, but Mr. Dunseath had made an effort to make his shopfront look good and that was what counted. He took out the key he'd been given and went to the door next to the shutter. This was the entrance to the residence above the shop and also gave access to the shop itself. Andy slipped the key into the lock, took a deep breath and went inside.

The narrow hall ran about ten feet to the bottom of some very steep stairs. At this point, the space widened and the hall continued down the side of the stairs to a door at the end – that would be the way into the back of the shop. Andy thought about where to start. The personal stuff was most likely upstairs, but information pertinent to the business was probably in the back. He'd start there and head upstairs if he didn't have any luck. Reginald Dunseath, the man who had lived and worked there had been single and owned no pets, so Andy wasn't likely to be disturbed. The door opened into a backroom office which was mercifully neat, with a large filing cabinet behind the door. The place had a pleasant smell of expensive pipe tobacco, which permeated through to the storage room, kitchenette and the damp basement. Andy looked into the shop itself – lots of glass shelving to display the crystals, with a three-foot-high amethyst geode taking pride of place near the counter. He walked over to the counter and rummaged through the drawers. No, there was nothing here. He'd get back to the office and check out the filing cabinet.

"Gotcha!"

It was an hour and a half later, and Andy sat forward at the desk as he found the hand-written receipt he'd been looking for:

Stirling silver pill box with Blue John inlaid lid: £100
Soapstone carving of mermaid: £30
Stirling silver frog brooch with green aventurine eyes: £50
Lapis lazuli carved half-moon: £75
Obsidian carved butterfly: £75
Carnelian sphere (90mm diameter): £70
Total: £350
Paid to Thomas Attrill, Attrill Antiques, Unit 5, The Old Ropeworks, Brading. May 7th 2024.

There it was – the infamous obsidian butterfly, sold to the Crystal Guy by Thomas Attrill as part of a selection of curios. Two questions immediately occurred – did Attrill know that the obsidian butterfly contained a demon? And did the other trinkets also contain anything supernatural? That would be bad. Had they been sold, that could mean another five demons on the loose. Andy sat back in the chair and puffed out his cheeks. Demons! What-the-fuck? *Just remember, this is the new abnormal...* He jumped up and walked quickly through to the shop to see if any of the items were on the shelves. They weren't, but if they'd been sold, there'd be a record of the sales on the computer, with card details for any that hadn't been bought with cash. Andy smiled – one of the side-effects of the pandemic was that many shops had stopped taking cash, which made tracing payments much easier. He'd have to leave trawling through the computer records to the police, because he had no idea what the passwords were, but that was fine with him.

Andy went back to the office, photographed the receipt with his phone, then placed it neatly back into the folder. Okay, so now they had a lead. He looked around the office. He didn't much like it in there. Ever since he'd come in, he'd felt a vague prickling sensation at the back of his neck as if someone was watching him. Was Roddy's paranoia rubbing off on him? Maybe, but it was more likely the clammy gloom of the day getting to him. Outside the back window, the yard with the Crystal Guy's van in it was in perpetual twilight. Andy had the keys to the van, so he went out into the gloom and had a good look round inside it. Nothing useful. He wandered over to the wooden gates that led out to the back street. Locked. Andy stood and looked at the back of the building. There were two storeys above the shop and then a window under the eaves. Great! Only three more floors to check through. Hold on! Did that curtain move? In the eaves window, the thin net curtain seemed to have twitched, but did it? It could have been a trick of the light. After all, it was a grey curtain, behind a window reflecting grey, swirling clouds outside. Andy sighed. Only one way to find out...

As he re-entered the office, he felt for the gun under his jacket, but decided not to take it out just yet. He quietly opened the door through to the residential part of the building and slipped along to the bottom of the stairs, where he listened. Nothing but the muffled sounds of traffic from the High Street. He went up the stairs and was surprised at how steep and narrow they were, then he stopped at the top and listened again. Quiet as the... he decided not to finish that thought. The landing was thankfully more generous than the staircase and was painted in a warm white with antique drawings of seascapes hung at intervals. Straight ahead from the top of the stairs, an open door revealed the kitchen. Andy went inside and found that it opened out into an L-shaped kitchen/diner/living room which occupied the same footprint as the shop below and ran all the way to the front of the building. Reginald Dunseath had clearly done all his furniture shopping at antique markets, because the place was a mishmash of different styles and periods, but comfortable and homely for all that. Andy walked into the centre of the room. Well, there was nobody there and nowhere to hide. Onwards and upwards!

The honey-coloured carpet of the landing was thick and, incredibly for a building that must have been a hundred and fifty years old, none of the floorboards creaked as he walked to the foot of the next set of stairs. They were as narrow and as steeply raked as the first set and he pitied the removal men who would have to come and take out the dead man's bed and other furniture. He listened closely again, then went as lightly as he could up the stairs. As he got to the top, the last stair creaked horribly. Well, if anyone was there, they'd know he was on his way now! On this level, the bathroom occupied the same area as the kitchen below, but it didn't open into the rest of the space. Andy had a quick look inside. It had a nautical theme and the tiles and paintwork were in three tasteful shades of blue. He turned and looked down the landing. To the left of the bathroom, there was a back bedroom where the dining area was below. It was a good-sized guest room and Andy went in to check behind the door. All clear. He walked down the corridor to the next door and went into what was the dead man's bedroom. Again, the décor was a mixture of styles and periods. The bed was unmade and the closet door was open. There were various items of clothing on the bed, which gave Andy the impression that Mr. Dunseath had spent some time deciding what to wear before he left his house for the last time. Andy bent down and checked under the king-size bed – nothing but clutter.

He went out onto the landing and stood silently for a moment. There was that unpleasant prickling sensation again, as if someone was standing behind him watching. He glanced back into the bedroom. Nothing to see there. He gave himself a shake but felt the need to draw his pistol. Now he was at the foot of the last set of stairs. As so often happens with stairs leading to attic rooms, the expensive carpet stopped at the bottom, to be replaced by a tatty old runner in dark green. From where he was standing, he could see that the top of these stairs was different from the others. Where the others opened onto landings, these stairs were walled on both sides and ended in a closed door with barely two feet of landing separating it from the top step. Andy didn't like it. If there was someone in the top room, they could charge him when he was at the top of the stairs and he'd have no room for manoeuvre. Well, there was nothing that could be done about it, so he moved up the stairs and when he neared the top, he flattened himself to the left wall and slid up the last two steps. He reached out towards the door handle with his left hand, while staying flat against the wall and aiming the Glock towards the centre of the door with his right. He turned the handle and pushed. The door groaned as it opened, but what he could see of the uncarpeted room beyond looked empty.

Moving with surprising speed for a big man, he was in the room and scanning it with his gun,

"Oh great!" he said dryly as he looked around the room. It was a small, servant's quarters, but it had been given over to obsession. A desk was strewn with papers, news clippings and photographs, while above it, a large corkboard had photographs of people pinned to it along with notes about those pictured. Andy holstered the Glock and flicked on the light. There was a photograph of a man with a long, thin face under which was pinned a note:

'Thomas Attrill? Andrew Brett? Nathaniel Groves?'

Next to him was a photograph of a jaundiced looking man coming out of a supermarket:

'John Downer. Buried 1820?'

Andy didn't like the look of that. He liked the look of the next two pictures even less. One was Roddy, captured on the steps of the hotel, while the other was Dan standing next to a half-built boat. Under Roddy's picture it said,

'Roderick Dalrymple – witch?'
While Dan's read,
'Daniel Strickland – vampire hunter???'
Andy stroked his chin in thought,
"So, our Mr. Dunseath was something of an amateur sleuth..."
And good enough to have spotted Roddy and Dan.

The last photograph on the cork board was blurry and seemed to show someone in a grey hoody disappearing behind a church, under which a note read,

'The hooded man? Can he be real?'

Andy's heart sank. As if they didn't have enough weirdness to deal with, now there was the possibility of an 'unreal' hooded man running about the place! Andy photographed the cork board, then moved over to the desk and started sifting through the apparently random pieces of paper. It was then that he realised that underneath the clutter there was a map. He shifted the loose papers to reveal the map of the Isle of Wight. On it, three areas were circled in red. The first was the village of Godshill in the south-central part of the island. Next to the circle was written *'The Devil? Or a trickster?'*. The second circle was near the village of Newchurch and was accompanied by the words *'Knighton. Killed them all?'*. The third circle was in the area marked as marshland near Brading. Next to it were the words *'Wolverton. Hooded man. Killed them all?'*

Andy couldn't make head or tail of it yet, but it was clear that Reginald Dunseath had been investigating something before his death. Curious. What reason would a shop owner have to start following people and secretly photographing them? Andy realised the irony of this thought as he took a picture of the map with his phone. He walked around the room to get a feel of it and maybe get a feel of Dunseath. What had started this obsession? It was clear that his death was linked to whatever he was investigating, so what had he uncovered that had cost him his life? Could Roddy and Dan be involved somehow? Andy doubted it. No, his instincts told him that Attrill and Downer were at the heart of it. As he paced, he could see the bare boards were dusty beneath his feet, but in the moment that observation occurred to him, he stopped. Yes, the floor was dusty and clearly hadn't been cleaned in ages, so why was there a section of one of the boards near the window that looked so clean? Andy bent down and could feel that the board was loose. With a bit of careful prizing using his flick knife, the board came up. An A5 sized notebook had been shoved into the space between the floor and the ceiling of the room below. Andy picked it out, replaced the board and opened the book. As he skimmed though it, Dunseath's obsessions became clearer – the building of the church at Godshill, the disappearance of the population of Knighton and the destruction of the town of Wolverton.

Reading through the notes, Andy wondered if Dunseath had had mental health issues. The notes were fragmented, with no attempt to create a timeline and gave the impression that the man had never sat down to research his subjects properly, but just picked historical titbits up randomly. Only one thread seemed to run through it all – a figure in a grey, hooded cloak. He had apparently been pivotal in the demise of Wolverton, had possibly betrayed the population of Knighton to the Grim Reaper, and might have tricked the people of Godshill into building their church on top of a hill. The problem was, the notes were so disjointed and jumped from one subject to another, that it was impossible on first reading to separate the stories.

Added to this, it was clear that at some stage, history, legend, fantasy and reality had blurred in Dunseath's mind. As Andy got towards the end of the notes, the figure in the hooded cloak seemed to be stalking Dunseath in the present. And then, there was his disquiet about the trinkets he'd bought from Attrill:

'Did not sleep a wink last night. There is something very wrong in the house. I swear I heard voices and laughter in the darkness and was overcome with a terrible feeling of dread that lasted until the morning. When dawn came, I ran down to look at the little collection I bought from Attrill. In the light, they look pretty. Beguiling. Maybe I just had a bad night?'

But a week later, his suspicions had coalesced into a firm opinion:

'There is something cursed about the Attrill collection. I have not slept since they arrived. Every time I've tried to close my eyes I've seen unspeakable horrors. Last four days I've slept at a friend's house. Thank God! The rest has given me perspective. I shall sell everything in the collection for next to nothing. My sole aim is to rid myself of them. I would throw them away, but instinct tells me that doing so would release whatever is within them. God damn the man for tricking me! Just as God will surely damn me for being a fool.'

It all culminated on the final page,

'I will surely be damned for what I have unleashed upon the world. I was weak and a coward and I only thought about getting rid of them. I will surely pay for my cowardice with my soul. But I have one hope. All I can do now is feign ignorance and try to get more pieces from him to sell. I've set up a meeting for tomorrow and when I see him, I will send him back to hell with the knife of Amaranthus. That is if I live to see tomorrow. I have felt the presence of the man in the grey cloak. He seems to dog my every step, but I never quite see him. But I feel his anger and hatred. Oh God, his hatred is oppressive. I feel like he can come to kill me whenever he wants, but won't because he loves toying with me. He is my greatest fear, because if he comes for me before I can kill Attrill, then my soul will surely be damned forever. God have mercy on me for my sins.'

And then Andy heard the loud creak of the final step of the second flight of stairs.

Chapter Thirteen

The Horror In The Attic

Andy pulled the Glock from its holster as he heard the sound of someone heavy running fast along the upper corridor. By the time Andy had got to the door, a man in a hooded grey cloak was rounding the bottom of the stairs,

"Armed police!" Andy bellowed, levelling his gun at the onrushing man,

"Armed police!" he shouted again, but the man was halfway up the stairs and not stopping.

Andy pulled the trigger three times and the sound was overwhelming in the enclosed space. The bullets all hit the man in the chest from little more than a yard, but Andy had no time to move or think as the man charged into him, lifting him off his feet. Andy grunted from the impact, but even as he was falling backwards, he got in a good blow to the back of his assailant's head with the butt of his pistol. The pair crashed onto the bare boards and the wind was knocked out of Andy by the weight of the man on top of him, but he had to suck it up and fight as one of the hooded man's hands went for his throat while the other reached for his gun. Andy's free hand shot up to protect his throat just before the other man could get a grip and now everything was very messy as the two men struggled on the floor. His attacker was not only hooded, but masked with a featureless white face, made more disturbing by the dead, black eyes that stared out through the slits in the latex. As Andy fended off the hand going for his throat, he felt the other hand grip his wrist and slam it again and again onto the floorboards. Fuck! The short grip on the Glock 26 was slipping from his grasp…

The sound of the pistol skittering across the floor was instantly followed by the other hand going for his throat. Now Andy knew he was in trouble! The second hand got a grip and started to squeeze hard. Andy was scrabbling at it to get it off, but the man was too bloody strong and using his weight to keep Andy from bucking him off. Fuck! Everything was a jumbled mess of pain and those powerful hands were inexorably crushing the life out of him. Andy was flailing now and his punches were deflecting off the man's bunched shoulders as he pushed down with all his weight on Andy's neck. Then a final flash of inspiration… Andy's left hand went for his jacket pocket and the flick knife – no! He'd left it on the desk. But there was the heavy shape of the knuckle duster. As his face felt like it was about to burst, Andy slipped the metal onto his fist and swung at the side of his attacker's head. Although the blow wasn't hard, the effect was instant. The hooded man shrieked, loosening his hold enough for Andy to drag in a breath and simultaneously swing again.

This time his attacker was knocked sideways and Andy bucked with all this strength, clumsily pushing the man off him. Through a mist of pain, Andy hurled himself at his attacker, catching him in the midriff with another left. The man grunted and doubled up in agony. Andy didn't stop and threw punch after punch at any part of the man he could hit. Each shot got stronger as Andy dragged precious air into him, and now he was on top. The man's right hand reached up for his face, but fell limp when Andy punched the shoulder hard. With the right side of the man's head defenceless, Andy went berserk and punched the head and face again and again with mounting ferocity. There was the dull cracking of facial bones breaking under the latex mask and then the man went limp. Andy knelt above him, breathing hard and with his left fist drawn back at the ready, but the man was done. Andy looked across to where his gun had fallen and was disconcerted by how close the man's fingers were to it before he'd finally been knocked out. That could have got very messy! Andy shifted off the man and over to his gun, which he picked up and holstered. Then he got up and grabbed the flick knife from the table. If the bloke on the floor came to, Andy didn't want him to be able to arm himself. He looked down at the man in the grey hooded cloak and wondered how the hell he'd survived three shots to the chest at such close range. And, now that he wasn't being throttled by the fucker, he noticed that the man smelled bad – a mix of acrid BO and spoiled meat on a hot day.

Keeping his left fist at the ready, Andy moved back towards the man. Yes, there were the three gunshot holes in his shirt. What the hell? When he pulled the shirt open, he could see no Kevlar vest, just three neat, bloodless holes where the bullets had gone in.

"Who the fuck are you?" Andy rasped, then he reached down and pulled the latex mask aside.

"Jesus!" he recoiled at the writhing mass of maggots in the rotten, stinking face behind the mask,

"Fuck!"

That was the last straw. Andy scrambled backwards from the body, got to his feet, somehow had the wherewithal to grab Dunseath's notebook, and made a break for the stairs. On legs that had lost their strength, he half stumbled, half fell down the three flights of stairs before tumbling out into the street. How he didn't get run over was a miracle as he weaved across the street before slumping into a heap against the front of the shop opposite. He looked back at the open doorway and the staircase leading up to that horror in the attic. His heart and head were pounding and he was feeling sick from terror and the adrenalin flooding his limbs. Christ! Had that just happened? He could hardly believe it, but the pain in his throat and the knuckle duster carved with religious symbols on his left fist told him that this had been all too bloody real! He sat, staring at the staircase in the house and regaining his strength.

"Are you all right, dear?"

Andy looked up at an elderly lady with a walking stick in one hand and a plastic Tesco bag stuffed with biscuits and boxes of teabags in the other.

"Yeah, fine thanks, luv... sorry, do you want to come past?" and he pulled his legs up towards his chest so that she could get past him on the narrow pavement.

"Thanks," and she shuffled past him, "Are you sure you're all right?"

"Yeah, just had a bit of a shock," Andy said.

"My husband was the same after our last heating bill," she replied. Andy smiled up at her, she smiled back, then turned and went on her way. She didn't know it, but her ordinary enquiry about his well-being was just the sort of mundane grounding he needed. He was thinking clearly now. He'd have to call the police - no doubt about that - though he had no idea how he'd explain discharging a weapon. Damn! He'd left the spent shells up in the attic room... although maybe all that would be overlooked once they saw the rotten corpse? Christ! What a mess! And how would he explain it to Bess. His first time out on his own and he'd fucked it!

Before Andy could dwell too long on the whys and wherefores of what had just happened, he noticed thick smoke coming from the roof of Dunseath's apartment. How the hell...? He reached for his phone, dialled 999 and requested the fire service, but by the time he'd finished the call, the entire roof was aflame. Andy dragged himself to his feet and crossed the road. From the open doorway, he could hear the rushing and crackling of flames from up the stairs. He fleetingly thought about trying to retrieve the body, but that would be impossible. Should he dash in and get the computer? It would have a lot of useful info in it... then he realised that flames were also coming from behind the door that led from the lower corridor into the back office. How? How the hell had that caught fire? Unless the hooded man had set it... and then come up to the attic? That would be insane. But what other explanation was there? He looked up the stairs – flames were already licking the banister of the first-floor landing. But if the fire had started in the attic, how could it have spread downwards so quickly? And then, as he stood there thinking, the sound of high, jangling laughter seemed to come from somewhere above. It was like having ice cubes shoved down the back of his shirt and Andy stepped away from the building to look up at the top window. Nothing to see. He glanced around – no one other than ordinary passers-by. Had he really heard the laughter, or merely imagined it? The sound of sirens derailed his train of thought and a few moments later, a fire engine pulled up. The first fireman jumped down from the cab, shouting,

"Is anyone in the building?"

"No," Andy replied – well, not anyone alive, anyway, "I was just in there and it's empty."

The fireman gave him a thumbs up, then Andy stood back out of the way. Within a couple of minutes, they'd got everyone out of the buildings on either side of the shop and were getting to work with their hoses.

In spite of the skilful work of the fire crew, the building was gutted inside an hour. Everything Reginald Dunseath had built and owned was reduced to ash. And yet, the fire crew had somehow managed to save the buildings on either side of the blaze with hardly a scorch mark on them. Naturally, the police had also arrived to ensure public safety and keep the traffic moving. Andy was finishing his statement to a uniformed PC when one of the firemen approached them, taking off his helmet and wiping sweat from his forehead,

"Never seen anything like that before! Nothing seemed to stop the flames. And the heat was more like the chemical fire we had in Newport a few years back. But look at the houses either side – nothing! That's mental! You were in there, right?"

Andy nodded.

"Were there solvents or other chemicals stored in there?"

"No, nothing like that. It was an ordinary shop."

"Crazy!" the fireman said, shaking his head, "That is one to remember. God, I'd hate to be doing the clean-up on that'n," and he looked at the smouldering remains,

"Still, at least it happened out of season, eh?" he concluded.

The PC nodded,

"Could you imagine the chaos if this'd happened in July?"

"Christ! Don't go there!" the fireman exclaimed.

"Least this way the landlord'll be able to get things sorted by next summer," the PC added.

"Don't you bet on it! Remember that gutted pub in Sandown? Sat there best part of three years in a right state before they finally knocked it down. An' it was right at the entrance to the town like a big advert – welcome to Sandown, it's a shit hole."

"But it is!" the PC guffawed and he and the fireman had a good laugh until the PC noticed Andy wasn't laughing with them,

"Sorry sir, I know that seems unprofessional, but if you were from The Island, you'd understand we're not being rude, just being honest."

***

"One job!" Attrill screamed, "I give you one simple job and you can't even manage that!"

Downer stood in front of him, looking up with no hint of contrition on his jaundiced face. This wasn't the first time he'd had to put up with being torn off a strip. Now, Attrill was marching up and down in front of the fire in the great hall in full cry,

"Kill Elizabeth Russell's partner. I couldn't have been clearer. And yet here we are – he's still alive and you're... I don't even know what you are... useless! That's what!"

"Zorry, meyaster, but that there feller 'ad zummat that bamboozled me. I were doin' as I were told an' givin' 'im a right old bannicking when 'e gives me a clout zo 'ard as to wake up me anzestors!" Downer replied stolidly.

"Zummat?" Attrill sneered, "What sort of 'zummat'?"

"Zum zorta brass knuckle, I reckons," Downer said in a tone as close to thoughtful as he ever got.

"And now you've bungled it, what do you think's going to happen? Hmm?"

"I tries not to think too much, zir. I leaves all that to thee."

"I'll tell you what'll happen. Now you've tried to kill him – and failed dismally - she's not going to let him out of her sight. We won't get a better opportunity."

"If thee don't mind I speaking out of turn, meyaster, but why doesn't thee do it tha'zelf?"

"Because it's not my job, Downer. I think up the plans, you do the dirty work. And now I'm going to have to think up a new plan. So, go on, get out of my sight before I reconsider your position."

"Thank 'ee meyaster," Downer mumbled, then turned and walked inordinately slowly to the door at the far end of the room. Attrill was sure he moved that slowly just to annoy him.

When the infuriating little man was out of the room, Attrill was able to think... silver bullets and a brass knuckle that could floor a man who had magical protection. Elizabeth Russell's colleague was certainly serious! Attrill looked at the three bullets sitting on the desk that he'd dug out of Downer's chest. They gave him pause for thought. What else might they have with them? Attrill sighed and slumped into the armchair by the fire. Downer, for all his bumpkin idiocy, was right about one thing. Thirty short years ago, Attrill would have swooped in and destroyed them himself, but now he was feeling tired. So very tired! Every day he could feel his powers draining away. That was why he had to strain every last sinew to make the plan work. Fast! So far, it had. *She* had come to The Island and her presence had summoned the Other Place. Attrill could feel it out there in the fog. He grinned at some memory and it gave him the spark he needed. He leapt out of the chair, sloughing off his gloom. Yes! He wasn't finished yet and, Downer's ineptitude aside, the plan was falling into place. So, they would stick to their strategy and if the opportunity came to rid them of the witch's sidekick, they'd take it. Attrill strode over to the desk, poured himself a glass of wine from a decanter and drained it in one. Now it was time for the real fun to start!

Chapter Fourteen

Myths And Legends

"Well, that was unpleasant!" Elizabeth Russell announced as she swept into the hotel bar.

"Three pints of the Ale of Wight," Andy said to Roddy who was working the bar, then he got off his stool to greet Bess. She looked fatigued and had smears of dirt on her face and all over scarlet trouser suit, but she brightened on seeing him,

"Hey, gorgeous, how was your day?" she said, before taking him in a lingering embrace.

"Not bad. Got a lead, had a fight, burned down a shop. You?"

"Bloody awful!" she declared, before taking her pint and downing it in one. She gasped for breath, wiped her mouth with her sleeve and said,

"Thirsty work, vampire hunting! Another one of these, please."

Roddy laughed and re-filled the glass.

"You found some?" Andy asked.

"Just the one. In the fort you liked the look of as we entered the harbour."

"Ah..." this probably explained why she hadn't been quite as enthusiastic about the place as he'd been.

"Trouble with vampires is they live in filth and you always end up crawling through something nasty to get to the buggers. I'm going to have to get his suit dry cleaned – can you fix that Roddy?"

"Aye, but you know The Island – it won't be ready for tomorrow."

"That's okay, I've got options," Bess replied, taking a more measured pull on her second pint.

"Why don't you wear military fatigues like Dan, or leathers like that German vampire hunter?" Roddy asked and Bess made a show of nearly choking on her drink,

"No way, mate! Hans Gluck is a great vampire hunter – no doubt there – but he's the sort of bloke who'd wear lederhosen on his day off. He wears leather because it turns him on, not because it helps in hunting vampires. And as for Dan, he's not winning any prizes for sartorial elegance now, is he?"

"Yeah, but I bet his dry-cleaning bill's zero," Roddy said before having a glug of his own pint.

"My philosophy is, if you're going to do something, you'd may as well do it properly and in style," Bess smiled.

Not that there'd been anything particularly stylish about dispatching the vampire that afternoon. In truth, it had been a squalid affair. She and Dan had tied the boat to the rusted landing stage of the fort and used a creaking metal ladder to get onto the roof where there was an entry hatch. Once they'd climbed down inside, it was a case of working through the dank corridors and empty rooms. Of course, the vampire had ensconced itself in the deepest, dampest part of the fort. The moment they'd got down to the lowest level, Dan had pointed to his nose. Yes, there it was, the unmistakeable smell of decay and dead flesh. Fortunately, this time they hadn't had to squeeze their way through a crawl space, as they had in the abandoned cannery earlier in the afternoon. But when they'd got to the vampire's lair, it was a sorry sight. Judging from the dead rats littering the floor, it had been subsisting off rat blood. Bess and Dan's head torches swept the area and there was a hiss as his light hit something sticking out from under a soiled mattress in the corner. The glass fronts of their head torches were marked in black with the sign of the cross, so when their lights touched vampires, it stung. Not enough to do any serious damage, but enough to slow them down and keep them at bay. The ensuing struggle was short and, at the end, Bess had almost felt sorry for the creature. Almost. It had been painfully thin and its defence had been slow and feeble. When

Bess had cut off its head, it had been as much of a mercy killing as an act of pest control.

"It wasn't in here last week," Dan had said as he'd bagged the body to carry it back to the boat.

"Probably came off some passing ship and managed to hole up in here" Bess had replied, "But God knows why it's been living off rats."

"Maybe it mistimed getting off the boat and got burned by the sun coming in? Then had to wait it out while it regenerated."

"Whatever, it's history now," and with that, Bess had bagged the head and that had been the end of it.

Now Bess could finally wash the taste of vampire from her mouth and she took another long sip of her beer, then asked,

"So, you really burned down a shop?"

"Yeah," Andy admitted, "Though in my defence it wasn't on fire when I ran out of it."

"First time off the leash and he goes werewolf!" Bess laughed, winking at Roddy,

"Presumably it's all sorted with the powers that be?"

"Yeah, I did have a chat to Superintendent Fletcher. He wasn't too happy about it, but he was calm when I left him."

"So come on, what happened?" Bess asked and they listened intently as Andy told them his story, showing them the notebook and the photos he'd taken.

"Eurgh!" Bess exclaimed when he told them what was under the latex mask, "That's horrible."

"And it stank, too – you'd've hated it... and that was that. I ran out into the street and by the time I'd recovered, the place was on fire."

"It's a bit worrying that some rock shop owner managed to rumble you and Dan," Bess said.

"God knows how," Roddy replied, "I've hardly done any magic since I've been here, other than to make myself look pretty for the guests... but Dan does look like he might be a vampire hunter, so..."

"If Dunseath knew, it's likely that whoever killed him also knows," Andy said.

"But the main takeaway of Andy's morning is that we've probably got another five possessed trinkets and no way of tracking the buyers... that's a bit of a bugger," Elizabeth Russell mused. Yes, that could cause some serious problems,

"But there's no point in worrying about them until they release their demons. We need to focus on who made them."

Roddy leant in towards them and said,

"They know who we are, where we are, they're very powerful, they're good at covering their tracks and they've got a working copy of the Key of Solomon... can I re-retire and go somewhere nice, please?"

"You'd hate nice," Bess smiled, "Anyway, they don't know everything. They don't know that we've got Dunseath's notebook."

"Yeah, but I've been looking through it all afternoon and it's very disjointed. All we've really got is the fact that he thought that whatever happened at Godshill, Knighton and Wolverton were linked – possibly by a man in a grey hooded cloak."

"Like your Mr. Maggot Face," Bess said.

"Yeah."

"This is your patch, Roddy, know anything about these places?"

"It's my patch now, but with Knighton and Wolverton, you're talking about events that happened in the mid thirteen hundreds. And as for All Saints church in Godshill, that was also built in the mid thirteen hundreds, but it's not the building the legend is about," Roddy said.

"The legend?" Bess looked at him with a quizzical eye.

Roddy sighed,

"Do you really not know it, Bess?"

"No," she replied and when Roddy gave her an admonishing look, she continued,

"Look, I've got a lot of stuff to be across. Britain has been an island of legend and a conduit to the Great Beyond for thousands of years. I have to rely on experts around the country to help me, because I don't have the time to dig down to the granular level... and yes, I know that makes me sound like some middle management policy wonk, but it's true. So please, Roddy, as the expert, could you tell us the legend of Godshill church."

"Well, if you put it like that, okay," Roddy said with a twinkle in his eye,

"So, the hill of Godshill was an important pagan holy place from time immemorial right up to six hundred and eighty-six AD. That was when Arwald, the last pagan king of the Wihtwara was killed in battle and a very bloody Christianization of The Island took place. So, after a period of upheaval, the people in the neighbourhood of Godshill decided to build a church. They got all the stones together and laid them out in the shape of the church in a field at the bottom of the hill. So, imagine their surprise when they got up the next morning to find all the stones had been moved to the top of the hill," and Roddy looked first at Andy, then at Bess, who both seemed suitably impressed.

"Well, the people didn't want the church on the hill, so they took the stones back to the field below. But when they awoke the next morning, lo and behold, the stones were all back up the top of the hill, laid out in the shape of the church. So, they had to take them down the hill again. But once this had happened a number of times, they decided that it must be God's will that the church should be built on the hill, so that's where they built it. And that's where the new church is."

"The 'new' church, built in the mid thirteen hundreds?" Bess asked,

"Aye. The hill is Godshill and the field below where they'd intended the church to be built is known as Devil's Acre. But there's one little problem in all this as far as we're concerned..."

Andy and Bess were now leaning forward watching Roddy closely,

"There's no mention of a hooded figure in the Godshill legend. Just stones moving about in the night."

"Hmmph!" Bess was disappointed, "Maybe Dunseath got confused?"

"Unless he turned up some new information," said Andy, "But judging from his notes, that's unlikely."

"What about Knighton?" asked Bess.

"To be honest, I don't know that much about Knighton or Wolverton, beyond the fact that they're both lost villages."

Bess looked disappointed.

"But I do have a book on the history of The Island. I'm sure that's got something useful in there. I'll get it. Watch the bar... and I'll know if you've topped up your drinks!" he said as he disappeared into a corridor behind the bar.

"Why would he care about that?" Bess thought out loud, "We own the place. All this beer is ours by right!"

Andy smiled and then she turned all her attention to him, taking his left hand in hers,

"Are you all right with what happened today? Sounded intense."

"It was – just look what that bastard did to my neck," and he drew the collar of his shirt aside to reveal some nasty bruising.

"Ouch!" she said, assessing the damage, then she slipped off her barstool and moved in close to him,

"Let me kiss it better," and then she began to plant light kisses on his throat. He tilted his head back and closed his eyes – God, that felt good! The discomfort was melting away and now each kiss was becoming steadily more arousing. Bess slipped a hand up his thigh,

"Well, hello!" she whispered into his ear, "Good to see someone isn't tired," and then she bit his earlobe gently, "Once we've finished our drinks, why don't we go up and have a nice hot bath... see where it takes us?"

"Mmmm," he replied. That sounded like a plan... then a thought occurred,

"But what can I do for you, seeing as..." and he left it hanging.

"Don't worry," she said, easing back to look deep into his eyes, "There's more than one way to get into heaven," and her eyes told him she would take him there.

"Right, here's that book!" Roddy said as he came back in, "Oh – do you want me to come back later?"

"No, it's all right. We were just having a planning meeting," Bess replied, getting back onto her barstool.

"I don't want to know," Roddy said, "Here..." and he handed the book to Andy.

"Thanks, I'll give it a read later," he said.

"So, what's your next move? Professionally, not personally," Roddy added quickly.

"We pay Mister Thomas Attrill of Unit five, the Old Ropeworks in Brading a visit. And if it looks like he's our man, we grab him, bring him back here and sweat him until he tells us everything we want to know."

"You sure going at him head-on is the best idea?" Roddy thought it was a wee bit on the nose.

"I get the feeling that in this case time is of the essence. Do you know anything about him?" Bess asked.

"I've seen him a couple of times – Seaview regatta, Bembridge Street Fair, that sort of thing, but not to speak to. He's got a bit of a reputation among the yachties for raising sail with other men's women... but I don't know where he lives or anything useful."

"Thanks, you've been a great help!" Bess nodded, "That was just the sort of intel I was hoping for from someone who's been in post eleven years."

"You mean 'in retirement' for eleven years," Roddy pointed out.

Bess looked at him and said,

"Do any of us ever really retire?"

Roddy sighed,

"Just the ones who get retired permanently."

There was a moment's silence.

"Let's drink to them," Bess said and they touched glasses, then drank.

Chapter Fifteen

Mister Thomas Attrill

The thick fog still hadn't lifted by the time Andy and Bess pulled into the car park at Brading the following morning. They stepped out of the car into the damp air and Bess pulled the belt of her black trench coat tight.

"Don't forget your walking stick," she said as Andy was about to lock the car.

"Do I really need it? If I'm being honest, it makes me feel like a bit of a twat."

"Maybe, but if you'd used it yesterday instead of your gun, I reckon you'd've got away without a scratch. And today, we might be venturing into the lair of the beast. Better safe than sorry," she insisted.

"All right," he sighed, getting it out and locking the car.

"I think it makes you look dapper," and her smile broadened when she saw the grimace on his face elicited by the remark,

"Let's just go," he growled, shouldering the stick.

They walked through the town until they reached Quay Lane. It seemed like an odd name for a road in a town that was nearly two miles from the sea, but Andy knew that until the eighteen eighties, Brading had been a port. He'd stayed up long into the night reading the history of The Island and had discovered that the wetlands behind the town had been the shallow harbour of Brading Haven for hundreds of years. That was until the local landowner had decided to build an embankment across the mouth of the harbour. Since then, Bembridge had been the harbour and Brading had become an inland village for the first time in its history.

"This is it," he said. On one side of Quay Lane, raised up on a slight hill from the road there was a typical English village church. On the other side of the road was a building in the Tudor style with white painted bricks and black stained beams, leadlight windows and a thatched roof. A sign above a wide entrance way read 'The Old Ropeworks'. Elizabeth Russell turned to him and looked him in the eye,

"We need to be on our game, here. Like yesterday, anything could happen."

Andy didn't need to speak. The serious expression on his face was enough. She liked that. They walked through the cobbled entrance and into a courtyard where the owners had decided to lean into the Tudor vibe. Old barrels had been strategically placed in various corners for an olde worlde effect, while the courtyard had a balustraded balcony around the first floor that added to the feeling that they were standing in a very old building. It seemed that the place had become a haven for artists and artisans, and every shop was crammed with interesting items for the home from paintings and sculptures to curtains and soft furnishings.

After a couple of minutes of nosing about, they found Attrill Antiques. As with the other shops in the ancient building, its windows and door seemed slightly askew, which lent a quirky feel to the place. Andy had a look in the window – it looked like a bit of a jumble of old stuff, but it was warmly lit and seemed welcoming compared to the gloom outside. Elizabeth Russell led the way and opened the door, which jingled with a sprung bell. However, the inside was surprisingly cold and Andy drew his mackintosh closer about him when they stepped inside. The smell of musty upholstery, dusty books and old leather enveloped them, but there was a sour note somewhere in the scent of the place. They wandered slowly around the shop as tourists do, looking at the merchandise that Andy classified as 'expensive tat'. After a few moments, a miserable-looking man with a jaundiced complexion appeared from a backroom and gawped at them.

"Morning," Bess said with a smile, "Are you Mister Attrill?"

"No," the man replied. Such a loquacious fellow!

"Is Mister Attrill here?"

The man sighed as if he'd been asked to run a marathon,

"I'll zee if he be taking visitors," he said, then turned and shuffled into the back room.

Elizabeth Russell's nose twitched unhappily. The sillage of the man's odour was thoroughly repellent. She gave Andy a look and he nodded in reply. In the vernacular, the man was clearly a wrong 'un. There was now a tension in the room as they waited for Attrill. Andy tried to look at a selection of brass navigational instruments, but found his attention was drawn more to the door into the back room than on the overpriced gadgets on the table. Suddenly, a very tall, thin man burst into the shop through the front door with a,

"Hello, hello! I'm Thomas Attrill, how may I help you?"

Bess and Andy were both caught off-guard and swivelled towards him,

"Hello," said Bess, "We were hoping to talk to you about some pieces you sold to a friend of ours."

"Oh yes? Who was that? As you can see, I sell a lot of pieces, so the field is rather large."

Andy watched Attrill as he spoke. The man appeared to be open and friendly, but there was something about his long features that made it seem as though the bonhomie could be turned off in an instant.

"Reg Dunseath – he owns the Crystal Guy shop in Shanklin."

"Dunseath... Dunseath... Shanklin..."

Andy thought he was slightly overplaying the act of trying to remember.

"Some carved crystals..." Bess prompted. She wasn't buying it either and could see that there was something in the set of Attrill's mouth and eye that indicated they were more prone to sneering than laughing.

"Of course!" Attrill clapped his hands, "The Nettlestone house clearance... Downer! Fetch the acquisitions book!" he shouted towards the back room, from which a muffled,

"Yez, meyaster!" floated back.

"Yes, some poor old dear living alone in a rambling old Edwardian monstrosity... fell down the stairs and broke her neck, apparently. Pity..." Attrill's eyes showed none,

"Should've been in sheltered accommodation, but she didn't want to be parted from her collections. Anyway, I bid on the entire contents as a job lot and came out on top. Would you believe it, but her family couldn't even be bothered to come over from England to look at what she had!"

Andy found it interesting that he referred to England as if it were a foreign country.

"They were quite happy to sell everything she'd spent her life collecting without even checking it over. Hang on..." and he turned to shout towards the back room,

"Downer! This century please!" he bellowed, then to Bess and Andy, "Sorry he's very slow, but very strong," was there something in the look he gave Andy that held more meaning than just the words themselves?

"And strong's rather handy in our line... anyway, so I got all the house contents for a bit of a song, but as you'd expect, not all of it was quite our cup of tea... so I sold all the stuff that was outside our usual fare to specialists like your Mister Dunseath. Ah! Finally!" Attrill exclaimed as his world-weary helper came back into the room holding a big, leather-bound book.

Elizabeth Russell's eyes widened when she saw the book. Attrill noticed and said,

"I know, we should be doing everything on computer, but there's nothing quite like writing things down in a well-bound book."

"No," Bess agreed.

"Now, let me see... ah yes, here we are – the Blue John pill box, the soapstone mermaid, the frog brooch, the lapis lazuli moon, the carnelian sphere and the obsidian butterfly – God, did I really let them go for that little? Well, I suppose I was keen to shift them, but there were some lovely pieces there. The obsidian butterfly was exquisite!"

Elizabeth Russell didn't know it, but Attrill took great pleasure in the way her jaw had tightened when he mentioned the butterfly. Oh yes, this was excellent sport!

"But the long and the short of it is," Attrill continued merrily, "This little collection I sold Mister Dunseath was unusual for me. As you can see, we've got nothing else like it here," and his mouth turned down in commiseration at their wasted journey,

"But if you have any questions, I'm glad to try to answer them," and he flashed a somewhat unpleasant smile at them.

Andy regarded Attrill closely - he was certainly giving a bravura performance, but there was something about the way he'd been looking at Bess that was disturbing. Even as he'd been giving them the run-down of the items or admonishing Downer, his eyes had been appraising her as if she was a piece of furniture that he might acquire. Bess had noticed it, too, but kept her mask of friendly inquiry as she asked,

"Do you know where any of the pieces came from originally?"

"Not really, although I'm guessing the soapstone mermaid was Eskimo in origin, and the Blue John pill box is presumably from Derbyshire."

"Why'd you say that?" Andy asked.

Attrill turned and looked at him as if he was the stupidest mistake in all creation,

"Because there are only two places in the world that Blue John like that is used in ornamental crafting. One's in Derbyshire and the other's in China. I highly doubt her example was Chinese," Attrill looked down at Andy and wished he could throttle the life out of him there and then... but all in good time...

"I don't suppose you know where any of the pieces are now?" Bess asked. She was finding Attrill's performance quite fascinating.

"Goodness, no," he replied, "Once something's off my hands I don't keep track of it – otherwise I'd need dozens of those big books and Downer would spend half his time scribbling in them. And you wouldn't want that, eh Downer?"

This provided the other man with a spark of animation and he replied with feeling,

"No meyaster!"

"Sorry," Attrill said without feeling.

"Not to worry," Bess said brightly, "We thought it was a long shot. Sorry to have taken up your time. Thanks," and she started moving towards the door.

"My pleasure," Attrill replied as Andy opened the door and let Bess through.

"Bye!" Andy said, and then they were out.

Elizabeth Russell walked briskly back out to the road and stopped when she reached the pavement.

"What do you think?" she asked, pivoting to look at Andy.

"That's our man. No doubt."

"Why?"

"Gut instinct. And I have the horrible feeling that the other bloke tried to kill me yesterday. There was something very familiar about that smell. What do you think?" Andy asked.

"You're right. Attrill is clearly a practitioner of black magic and is probably a necromancer," Bess replied.

"Why?"

"Like you – gut instinct. When you're around people like that enough, you get to recognise them,"

Andy nodded – it was the same in police work,

"And there was the small detail that their big book is bound in human skin."

Andy looked shocked as Bess explained,

"Again, in this job I get to see a lot of books bound in human skin, so I can spot them a mile off. And call me crazy, but I think that man Downer is dead."

Andy nodded. It did sound crazy, but he agreed.

"So, what now?" he said.

"Let's end it right here. Get your knuckle duster and draw your sword – this is about to get unpleasant," and with that, she started to jog back towards the shop.

Andy slipped on the silver knuckle duster and drew the sword, then followed her. The jog turned into a sprint for the last ten yards, but when Bess got to the door, she stopped,

"Fuck me!"

Andy pulled up alongside her and stared. Where there had been a shop full of antiques only a few moments before, now there was an empty shop with a 'To Let' sticker across the glass of the door.

"We've been had!" she said bitterly as Andy quickly sheathed the sword and looked around to see if anyone had spotted them. Fortunately, not.

"Has that ever happened to you before?" he asked.

"What, you mean have I ever been duped into thinking an empty shop was full? No. That's a new one on me."

Andy was kind of glad that she'd been as fooled as him.

"Right! Let's sort this out," and she marched over to the nearest shop, which sold hand-crafted toiletries,

"Sorry to bother you," she said to the woman behind the counter, "But do you know what happened to Attrill Antiques?"

"They stopped trading here last April," she replied, "There was a pop-up kite shop there this summer – only cleared out last week. If you're interested in setting up a shop yourself, I could give you the number of the lettings manager."

"No, it's okay, thanks," Bess smiled and then they left.

"Dammit! This bloody island always messes with me!" she cursed as they walked back to the road,

"I should've realised it was all too convenient. And if this was anywhere else, I'd've sensed the illusion like that!" and she snapped her fingers.

"So, none of that really happened?" Andy asked.

"Yes and no. Yes, we have just had a conversation with the person who's been summoning demons and trapping them in trinkets... and no, because he wasn't there. Attrill, Downer, everything we saw, it was all projected there. We were in his illusion."

"Jesus!" Andy didn't like the feeling that thought gave him, "But it all felt so real!"

"That's because our Mister Attrill is bloody powerful. His illusion was quite stunning," she couldn't help but be impressed, but she also looked concerned.

"We were totally fooled... why didn't he just kill us?" Andy asked,

"Because he was somewhere else and when you're using that much energy to create such a complicated illusion, you can't do anything else. But he could've got someone to come in under the cover of the illusion and take us both out... and yet, he didn't. Why? That's what we need to work out," she said, heading back towards the car.

"You think he just wanted to suss us out?" Andy asked.

"That's my guess."

"I didn't like the way he was looking at you."

"Me neither. I once knew a man who made a living from binding books in human skin, and he looked at me the same way – like my body was something he could use," and then she gave a shudder.

"Sounds like you meet some lovely people in this game," Andy smiled and was glad to see it drew a smile from her, too.

"On the plus side, we've seen our quarry and got the measure of him. Now all we need to do is hunt him down and destroy him. What to do first?" she mused as they got back to the car. She looked around at the muffling gloom of the fog,

"What's the time?"

Andy glanced down at his watch,

"That can't be right," and he tapped it, then put it to his ear – it was working fine.

"Problem?"

"Just a sec'..." Andy took out his phone and looked at it,

"That can't be good..."

"What?" Bess said impatiently,

"It was about ten when we got to the shop and we were in there about fifteen, twenty minutes... but according to my watch and phone, it's now five to three in the afternoon."

***

Thomas Attrill's laughter rebounded off the stone walls of his great hall in a cheerless cacophony. Dressed in white ceremonial robes, with a wand in his right hand, he stepped out of the third largest of the magic circles on the floor and walked to the desk, laughing all the way.

"Ah! That was excellent!" he cried, pouring himself a large glass of wine from the decanter and taking a hefty gulp.

"They fell for it completely! I had them right in the palm of my hand. And *she* was incredible! Did you see her? Magnificent! So powerful and yet, I had her fooled! Shame I needed you here, otherwise you could've gone in and killed her sidekick. But such is life. And anyway, it was great sport!" and he turned to see if Downer was sharing his jollity. Of course he wasn't! Downer was still standing in the magic circle halfway down the hall. The white ceremonial robes made him look quite ridiculous and, standing motionless with his head bowed, he gave the impression of a carthorse that had been dressed up for a fair, but which knew it looked stupid.

"Oh, Downer..." Attrill sighed, "You're such a... downer! Go on, get away with you before you totally kill the mood."

"Yez meyaster," Downer said quietly, before turning and shambling away.

Downer's miserable reaction aside, it had been a very successful morning's work! Elizabeth Russell was everything he'd hoped for and more! And her body! What a physique she had! Yes... she was just what he needed. Imagine what he could achieve in a body like that... he took another gulp of wine, filled the glass and walked over to the chair by the fire, but by the time he got there, he was tired. He felt light-headed and sat down slowly.

Now reality was flooding in. Yes, the illusion had been a success, but look what it had taken out of him! He was suddenly exhausted. Wiped out. What would once have been a parlour trick for him had now left him shattered. Attrill's long face looked drawn and he had dark rings under his eyes. Perhaps this had been a mistake? It had been a dazzling display of his power, but now he hardly felt able to lift the glass to his lips. Attrill's eyes narrowed. Now he would rest, but tomorrow he would have to get busy. After all these years, he was suddenly in a race against time. It was alarming how he had fallen in ten short years from the master of all he surveyed to teetering on the brink. If it wasn't happening, he'd have never believed it.

"Ah! Forget it!" he said aloud, "Concentrate on what needs to be done," but he knew he had to wrap things up quickly. Just a last great effort and then the rewards! Yes... with a new lease on life, he could leave the Isle of Wight and explore new vistas. He stared into his potential future and smiled with a cruelty that made the expression unappealing.

From the door at the far end of the great hall, Downer was secretly watching. He could see the exhaustion. Yes, that trick had all but done for him. Mayhaps, in spite of his best efforts, the meyaster was too late? Now a smile stretched itself across Downer's face, and if Attrill had seen it, it would have chilled him to the bone.

Chapter Sixteen

Possessions

When the phone on his desk rang, Oliver Fernsby had the horrible feeling that Bishop FitzOsbern was going to be on the other end of the line,

"Office of the Regulator, Oliver Fernsby speaking..."

"This is Bishop FitzOsbern. I need to speak to the Regulator. Now!" the bishop shouted.

"I'm afraid that..."

"I said now, damn you!"

"But she isn't here," Oliver replied calmly.

"A likely story! Put me through to her right now. I want to give her a piece of my mind."

What mind? Was Oliver's gut reaction, but he avoided saying it,

"The Regulator is currently on the Isle of Wight. She's been there a couple of days."

"What the hell's she doing there? Taking a holiday?"

"No, she has a difficult case on The Island. Perhaps I can help?"

"I doubt it!" the bishop barked, "I've got five demonic possessions in different parts of the country at the same time and I think she knows exactly what's going on!"

"Five?" Oliver was genuinely shocked – to have five cases of simultaneous demonic possession was unheard of.

"Wouldn't surprise me if that satanic cabal she calls a department wasn't at the bottom of it."

Oliver had allowed the bishop to let off steam, but now it was becoming irksome. He therefore put on his most soothing voice as he said,

"Bishop, we are here to protect the nation from dangers such as satanic cabals. Why would we be responsible for five demonic possessions?"

"To make yourselves indispensable," the bishop replied. Although there was anger in there, his tone had already begun to calm as he continued, "You create a problem that only you can solve and then ride in on white chargers to save the day. It's a classic con job."

"I assure you we have done no such thing," Oliver replied in a tone so mellifluous that its calming effect was quite magical,

"Mmmm," FitzOsbern didn't sound convinced, but at least he was calm, "Nevertheless, I find it a bit convenient that there is a sudden rash of possessions where the demons aren't responding to our standard deliverance ceremony. It's like that one in America all over again. We're only making headway in one case. The other four seem impossible and after this phone call I'm going up to Leicester to personally take over a case because our man is in the hospital."

"I'm sorry to hear that. Will he be all right?"

"Yes, but he's got two broken legs and some horrific bitemarks on his arms. The point is, I need the Regulator's help..."

Ah, so that's why he's angry, Oliver thought.

"So, when will she be back?"

"I'm afraid I don't know. It's the tail end of the American possession case. We have a lead that the artifact used to contain the demon was from the Isle of Wight. Perhaps what she's investigating is linked to the other five possessions?"

FitzOsbern sighed impatiently,

"But presumably you've been in contact with her?"

"Not since she left."

"Are you saying she hasn't checked in on the department she supposedly runs for two days?" the bishop's voice was silky and dangerous.

Oliver kicked himself for saying too much, and replied,

"No, because if there was anything urgent, I would inform her."

"Well, you can inform her that her presence is required by the Archbishop of Canterbury. Here are the details of the cases," and he ran through his list of names, addresses and details from the possessions. When he'd finished, he added,

"I need you to contact her immediately."

"After this conversation," Oliver said.

"No, now while I'm on the line, I need to know that things will be taken in hand before I leave. You can put me on hold if you want."

"Well, I'll give it a try, but she might very well be incommunicado," Oliver said, but immediately regretted his honesty as the bishop replied,

"Ha! So much for you being able to inform her of anything urgent. Honestly, your department is hopeless!"

"I'll just put you on hold now, Bishop..."

Oliver pushed a button, then dialled Andy's number. After a couple of rings, it went to voicemail and Oliver left a message saying what had happened, to call him back and that Elizabeth Russell's presence was required by the archbishop. When he'd finished, he paused a moment to gather himself before reconnecting with the irate clergyman.

"Hello, Bishop FitzOsbern? I'm afraid that I couldn't speak to her directly, but I have left a message stating the urgency of your request."

"Dreadful!" the bishop muttered, "His Grace shall hear of this... right, I must go. Call my assistant the moment you're in contact with her. Now, some of us have souls to save," and he rang off.

Oliver stuck his tongue out at the phone. What a pompous twit! Suddenly Oliver had a lot of sympathy for his boss, given the fact that she had to meet that buffoon on a regular basis. But, buffoon or not, he was powerful and needed to be handled with care. Oliver hoped Andy wouldn't leave it too long to get back to him and that their trip to the Isle of Wight was bearing fruit.

***

By four-o-clock that afternoon, Andy, Bess and Roddy were sitting in comfy chairs taking tea in the enormous drawing room of the hotel. As with the rest of the place, it abounded with dark wood panelling and polished floorboards on which a couple of Persian rugs had been laid. A merry fire was crackling away in a hearth that was fully in keeping with the grand scale of the rest of the room. Elizabeth Russell stirred sugar into her cup of Earl Grey and stared out of the French windows that led onto the terrace. Where there should have been a delightful view down to the sea, all she could see was fog, fog and, oh yes, more fog. They had just finished telling Roddy about their morning with Mister Attrill and Downer.

"Odd fella, that Downer," Roddy said, "If I didn't know better, I'd say he was... dead."

"He does have a re-animated look about him," Bess mused.

"And he smells dead," Andy added.

"Yes, have you ever got that close to him, Roddy?"

"No."

"Don't. Or if you do, breathe through your mouth. He's not quite ripe, but..." and Bess made a gagging noise.

"Dunseath seemed to think he might have been buried in eighteen twenty."

At this, Elizabeth Russell gave a dry laugh as pieces fell into place in her mind,

"I know who he is," she said, "He's Molly Downer's dad."

While Roddy made a 'Tchoh!' sound and had an expression of 'Why didn't I figure that out?' on his face, Andy was still in the dark,

"Molly Downer?"

"The last official witch on the Isle of Wight. Died in the mid-eighteen hundreds. I met her once. She was very nice and certainly had The Gift, but the locals weren't pleasant to her, so she didn't go out much. Yes... if her dad also had The Gift, then bringing him back might be quite useful for someone like Attrill. He'd need a helper for conjuring demons and other ceremonial magic."

"Why not bring back Molly?" asked Roddy.

"Because she'd be too angry. You see, the locals believed that she had a hoard of treasure when she died. Obviously, the authorities were concerned that treasure hunters might come and dig up her coffin looking for it, so they publicly opened her coffin and stripped her naked to show there was no treasure to be had. Then they put her clothes back on and buried her. But if she'd been observing that from the Great Beyond – and I'm sure she would have been – that would've really pissed her off. Had Attrill brought her back, she might have gone on a vengeful killing spree. No, Attrill's a clever one. He wouldn't risk that, but he might bring back the next best person – her dad, John Downer."

"I thought you couldn't be arsed... I mean... couldn't find the time to learn the details of what happens in the regions?" Roddy said, giving her a sideways look.

"Yes, I'm a generalist, but if I've met someone, I keep track of them, especially if they're in the game," she replied.

Before Roddy could come back at her with some witticism, Andy's phone chirruped.

"Finally, a signal!" he exclaimed, "I've had nothing all day."

"Welcome to every day on the Isle of Wight, where the march of Progress has marched straight past and headed off somewhere else," Roddy smiled.

"It's a voice message from Oliver," Andy said, then put the phone to his ear and listened.

"Well?" Bess asked,

Andy looked around to see if anyone else was nearby, but no one was to be seen.

"Listen to this," he said and replayed the message on speaker. As Elizabeth Russell listened, her face became thunderous and, in spite of the crackling fire, the temperature in the room dropped noticeably. As he watched her, Roddy's broken mouth lifted at one corner in the closest he could get to a smile. He'd seen this sort of reaction many times before,

"What an unutterable cockwomble that man is!" she said with measured dislike,

"He and the archbishop seem to be labouring under the misapprehension that I work for them. That's if the archbishop is even involved, which I very much doubt. Either way, they'll have to wait until I'm done here. But at least he's told us something useful."

"What?" Roddy asked.

"That the other five artefacts have released their demons. Right, Andy, you're going to have to phone Oliver and relay exactly what I say to him..."

"Why don't you tell him yourself?"

"Because I hate those bloody things," she snapped.

Andy remained unperturbed and replied,

"If I put it on speaker, you can talk to him from there like he's in the room."

"Oh... yes, I suppose that would work," Bess regretted snapping, but she'd been riled.

"Okay, here we go..." Andy dialled the number and, as they waited, Roddy got up and closed the drawing room door.

"Andy, how are you? How's the Isle of Wight?" Oliver said,

"Yeah, all right, Oliver. You're on speaker and I've got Ms Russell here with me,"

At this, Bess gave Andy a bewildered look and mouthed 'Ms Russell?', to which he shook his head and mouthed 'Long story'.

"So, the bishop gave you a going over?" she said.

"Yes, he was in full cry - you'd have loved it. But it looks like we've got something of a situation here."

"So've we!" Bess replied, "We just met the man who conjured all those demons. His name's Thomas Attrill, he's clever, powerful and he's got home advantage."

Oliver wanted to ask what had happened, but knew that he needed to keep things brief.

"What now?" he asked.

"Now I've got to get my arse in gear, that's what now. I'm exactly where I need to be and I'm not leaving until we've got our man. And you can tell the bishop that, if he asks. First, get onto his team and tell them their exorcists need to look out for the following items..." and at this point, Bess indicated for Andy to read out the list of artefacts. He did so and then she continued,

"Those are the artefacts in which Attrill has trapped the demons. But warn them to be careful around them, because these artefacts have a mind of their own - if they know they've been spotted, they will try to escape. In the meantime, contact Jo, Quentin, Suzy, Martin and Hapgood. Brief them and put them on standby to be able to go and help the exorcists at the drop of a hat. I know it's not their usual line of work, but they all have experience, so they should be fine."

"Okay, got it," Oliver replied.

"We're going to track down Attrill, but he's a slippery one so it may take a while. Keep in close contact with Andy from now on and if you can't get through to him..."

"The mobile coverage down here's rubbish," Andy interjected,

"Yeah, if you can't get him, call Roddy at the hotel or Dan on his landline."

"Right. Consider it done," Oliver said.

"Good man! And sorry you had to put up with FitzOsbern," Bess said.

"Don't worry – all in a day's work."

"Thanks, Oliver. Bye!" and Bess indicated to Andy to end the call.

"So," Andy said once he'd turned off his phone, "What are we going to do now?"

"Tomorrow, you are going to investigate Knighton. See if you can dig up anything on the mysterious man in the grey hood - and his links to Attrill if there are any."

"What about you?"

"I'll get Dan to take me over to meet a man in Calbourne who might have Attrill's address. See, Attrill's been doing some very serious ceremonial magic, which needs a load of specialist equipment made of very specific materials, created at very specific times. This man in Calbourne is, as far as I know, the only person on The Island who supplies this stuff."

"What sort of stuff?" Andy asked.

"Everything from wands and swords to pens, ink and parchment. But none of these are simple. A spell might require parchment made from the skin of a virgin calf, slaughtered on a day ruled by a particular planet, at a time of day ruled by a specific planet, during a designated phase of the moon. And that calf must be killed by someone wearing ceremonial clothing, who has purified themselves using a prescribed ritual and then uses a consecrated weapon in a manner specified by the spell," Bess stopped to draw breath, then continued,

"As you can imagine, most of that doesn't fit modern animal welfare or health and safety standards. So, you need someone who has animals and is willing to break every law in the book to allow them to be ritualistically killed. Not only that, you need a blacksmith to make the weapons to kill the animal. *He* needs to understand that the weapons have to be made of particular metals, forged ritualistically on particular days and times. And then there's the small matter of making the parchment which, again, can only be made on special days and at special times dictated by the spell it's going to be used in."

"What she's saying," Roddy butted in, "Is that you can't just put on an old bedsheet and stand in a circle with an ordinary bit of paper and hope to conjure a demon."

"Exactly!" Bess cried, "Everything in a ritual takes a lot of time, effort and skill to produce, and there are few people who do it. So, first thing tomorrow, I'll pay a visit to Taran Sleeman and his brother, Uther."

Chapter Seventeen

The Farm In The Fog

"Have you had any dealings with them recently?" Bess asked Dan as the Land Rover bounced along the road to Calbourne the following morning.

"No. I stick to hunting vampires and leave ritual magic to thrill seeking nutters," Dan replied, "Anyway, they're an odd lot in that family. Not exactly chummy."

"They only came over from Cornwall in the eighteen-sixties, so they probably still feel like foreigners here. These two were boys the last time I saw them."

Dan chuckled,

"I think you'll find they've grown up a bit," and then he slowed as they entered the village.

In the fog, it looked mysterious as the houses seeped out of the gloom towards them. Most of them were built in a sandy-coloured stone with a mixture of tiled and thatched rooves. There was the occasional modern-built house, but overall the place could be described as 'quaint'. As they drove through the village from the north, they passed Winkle Street on their right, with its achingly pretty row of thatched cottages disappearing into the swirling mists. Bess could feel a tingle deep inside her. Calbourne had been a recognised settlement since the early seven hundreds, and she sensed the weight of that history. Now they were through most of the village, heading south towards the sea, and the high hedges on either side of the narrow road combined with the fog to give a hemmed-in feeling. Dan slowed, took a sharp turning up a driveway to their left and drove a few hundred yards along a track. It finally opened out into a large, concreted area with barns to the left and right, and a thatched farmhouse in front of them. A tractor and a Toyota pick-up were parked outside the left-hand barn and Dan pulled up so that his Land Rover blocked them both in.

"You wait here. I'll go and see what's what," Bess said as she hopped out of the vehicle.

"Actually, it might be better if I ghost about the place," Dan replied,

"Fair point. But don't get yourself into trouble."

"You know me, I'm Mister Careful."

Bess harrumphed at that idea, then headed for the house. She used the upturned horseshoe to knock on the nail-studded front door and waited. After about thirty seconds, a small, plump woman appeared at the door. From the flour on her pinny, she looked like she'd been called away from her baking. She looked up at Elizabeth Russell with some degree of wonder – who was this striking woman in the emerald-green trouser suit?

"Yes, can I help?" the woman asked.

"Good morning, very sorry to bother you, but I'm looking for Taran Sleeman, could you please tell me where I might find him?" Bess asked, gazing deep into the woman's eyes. She stood still, staring up into those mesmerizing violet eyes and her jaw slackened so that her mouth fell open,

"He's over in the processing barn," she replied.

"Thank you, and don't worry about me. You won't even know I'm here," Elizabeth Russell said, imbuing every word with a soothing tone,

"Now, go back, enjoy your baking and forget all about me," she smiled and the woman gently closed the door and did exactly as she'd been told.

Elizabeth Russell smiled to herself and walked over to the building the woman had indicated. It was an old wooden barn with great double-doors at either end for wagons to enter, and a human-sized door set into the middle of the side of it. Although the middle door looked old, the electronic locking system next to it looked anything but. She held her hand in front of the pad of numbered keys and concentrated. Would she be able to unlock it, or was the influence of the Other Place interfering with her ability to control electronics? After a moment, the lock clicked and she beamed as she opened the door. *Yeah! In your face, Other Place!* she thought to herself as she slipped inside. The door led into a big, white-tiled room in the centre of which was an enormous marble-topped table. A skinless goat was laid on the table, which was awash with the blood from its slit throat. On the far side of the room, with his back to the door, a big man in ceremonial robes was working on the goat's skin with a knife.

"About bloody time!" the man said without turning, "I need you to clean up this blood while I sort out this skin."

"Not sure I'm dressed for that," Elizabeth Russell replied and the man instantly swivelled to face her. Dan was right – Taran Sleeman had grown since she'd last seen him. He was broad shouldered with black hair and dark eyes that flashed with anger,

"I should've known from the Swaailen that you were here, witch!" he spat as he gripped his skinning knife more firmly.

"Really, Taran, is that any way to greet an old family friend?"

"You're no friend to me – or to my dad. I remember you coming sniffing round here when I was a nipper – never seed my dad so scared. And you looked the same then as you do now."

"Your dad looked scared because he'd gone wrong," she said, approaching the goat on the table, "And from the looks of it, you've followed in his footsteps."

"There's nothing wrong about skinning a goat," Taran countered.

"No, there's nothing wrong with skinning a goat, but I can see your aura, Taran. Black as pitch. What else have you been skinning?"

"That's between me and my customers!" Taran snapped, "You're not going to fit me up for skinning children like you did my dad."

"But he did skin children and made a small fortune doing it."

"I don't believe it!" Taran Sleeman looked defiant and hostile.

"Your grandfather was a good man – he believed it," she said, looking at the neat cut to the goat's throat and the perfect job of skinning that had been done. Taran certainly had talent...

"My grandfather went insane and murdered his own son. And it's all because of you, witch!" Sleeman was watching her closely, working out how best to get at her with the table in the way and the best place to stick her with his knife.

"I haven't come to rake up the past," Elizabeth Russell said, "All I want is information on one of your current clients. I take it you've been supplying Thomas Attrill..."

Sleeman's eyes narrowed. She took that as a 'yes'.

"Never heard of him," he replied.

Elizabeth Russell gave a shrug,

"Pity, because he'd be a very good customer. Do you still have your virgin aunt locked away in the house making all the ceremonial robes?"

"My aunt Alice can come and go as she pleases – not that it's any of your business."

"All right, Taran, I'm going to ask this question politely one more time. After that, I can guarantee you won't like the way I ask it: where can I find Thomas Attrill?"

Her eyes glittered as she noticed him tensing, ready to go for her. So! It would be the hard way...

"I don't know no Thomas Attrill and if I did, I wouldn't tell you, witch!" he shouted, "I'm beyond your power, see?" and he drew a pentacle on a necklace from the top of his robe.

That certainly caught her by surprise. Now was the time to attack! But even as he was starting to move, Elizabeth Russell disappeared from the other side of the table to materialise right in front of him, striking the knife from his hand. Before he could react, she'd grabbed his throat with one hand, his balls with the other and was crushing both. Sleeman gave a strangled groan as she twisted his testicles and he involuntarily bent his knees so that their eyes were now on the same level,

"Listen, you evil fucker, do you really think a trinket like that could stop me?" and her words were sharper than the blade of his skinning knife,

"Even with the Swaailen and the spirits of the Other Place trying to disrupt my powers, I could leave you in a straitjacket for the rest of your life,"

He was staring into those violet eyes and it was as if clouds were parting within them to reveal some terrible truth that no ordinary mind could comprehend.

"Put him down, less'n you want me to put you down!" a man shouted from the door.

Increasing her grip on both throat and balls, she turned her head to look at Uther Sleeman pointing a bolt-action rifle at her.

"I'm a crack shot and at this range I can blow your head right off," Uther said, but then froze as he felt the muzzle of a large calibre revolver press behind his ear.

"And just imagine what my fifty calibre Smith and Wesson Magnum would do to your head from this range!" Dan said in a friendly manner.

Uther Sleeman held his breath and waited to be told what to do.

"Lower it nice and slowly or this could all get very messy," Dan said, and Uther complied. Dan took the rifle with his free hand, winking at Bess and saying,

"Sorry about that. Do carry on."

Elizabeth Russell turned back to Taran and, with sparks of blue energy crackling around her, she stared through him and screamed,

"Tell me now!"

Her left hand became hot and wet as Taran Sleeman's bladder let go, then he choked out the words,

"We don't know where he is. When he wants something he sends Downer to tell us, and when they're ready Downer collects the orders. We don't know how to contact him. Uther followed him once, but lost him up near Culver down. And that's all we know – I swear on my children's lives."

Elizabeth Russell let the man go and he crumpled to the floor, coughing.

"See? That's all you needed to tell me. No need for any unpleasantness," and she walked over to a sink in the corner and washed her hands.

"Of course, the minute we leave, they'll try to let him know," Dan said,

"Only if they remember any of this... Get up!" she barked, grabbing Taran's ear and yanking him onto his knees. She looked into his eyes and said,

"You will remember nothing of this. We were never here. You pissed yourself because your prostate is inflamed. Get an appointment to see your GP. Now, go back to work. You will notice you've pissed yourself in ten minutes."

Taran Sleeman got up and did as he was told, picking his knife up from the floor and carrying on with the preparation of the goat skin.

Elizabeth Russell walked across the room to Uther, who had fear in his eyes,

"Hey, hey," she soothed, "No need to be afraid. This is the easy part," and then she fixed him with her terrible gaze,

"You will go back to whatever you were doing and not remember any of this."

Without a word, he turned, took his rifle from Dan and walked out of the door and over to the other barn.

"Right let's go," Bess said, but when they got outside, Dan grimaced,

"CCTV," and he pointed to cameras on both barns and the front of the house.

"No problem," she replied, before closing her eyes and concentrating. After a few seconds, she opened them,

"I fear they're going to need a new surveillance system," she smiled, then she looked up at the house. An elderly woman was looking out of a first-floor window and waving at them. Bess waved back.

"Hang on, doesn't that ruin everything?" Dan asked.

"No," Bess replied, leading the way to the car, "Aunt Alice won't tell. She was the one that wrote to me about what her brother was doing. She's a good person."

"Seems a shame to leave her here with them," Dan said, starting the car and turning it around.

"If we took her away it would probably kill her. And anyway, without her, where would people here and over in Portsmouth and Southampton get their ceremonial robes? Until I have concrete proof about Taran, he and his family are very useful. Come on, let's see what we can find at Culver Down," she said as their Range Rover disappeared into the fog, leaving the strange farm to its own devices.

Chapter Eighteen

Gallybaggers!

Andy had left the hotel at the same time as Dan and Bess, but while they had taken the road that would skirt around Ryde and take them through Newport to Calbourne, he had taken the familiar road to Brading. He was getting used to it now. Even the weird effigies leering out of the fog at him had taken on a certain familiarity. He wouldn't go so far as to say that he'd got used to them, but they didn't seem quite as malevolent as they had when he'd arrived. At a crossroads outside Brading, he took a right and, after a bit of wiggling, found himself going up a steep hill away from the town. Within a few minutes, the road levelled out and the usually high hedges on either side of the road had been cut down to a couple of feet – presumably to show off the magnificent views of The Island on both sides of the ridge. Today, his view was a shifting, grey blanket that threatened to smother him. He decided that after they'd finished the case, he would come back without Bess so that he could see The Island without the Swaailen fog covering everything.

Without the distraction of a picturesque vista, Andy was able to think about the place he was going to. According to the history he'd read, Knighton had been a hamlet up until the time of the Black Death in 1348. Then, so the story was told, the entire population of the settlement moved to the nearby village of Newchurch. All except one old man, who was so mean and unpopular, that the rest of the community left him where he was. Inevitably, a stranger in a hooded cloak came knocking on the old man's door. He knew at once that it was the Grim Reaper, come to take his soul, but the mean old man was cunning. He bargained with the hooded stranger – in exchange for his life, he would tell him where all his neighbours had gone. The stranger agreed and the mean old man directed him to Newchurch. Within a week, every last one of the former inhabitants of Knighton were dead, along with most of the population of Newchurch. The old man lived on in isolation, shunned by all, as word of his bargain with Death had spread across The Island. Andy shook his head. It sounded like bollocks to him, but in his new world of necromancers and illusion, could it be true? Perhaps. The question was, who was the hooded man? Was he connected to the maggot-faced nightmare in the hood that had already attacked him?

Soon he got to the turn for Knighton and was pleased to see that it was one of those rabbit hole roads – narrow, with a steep hill down and all overhung with trees. The fog gave it even more mystery and, as he plunged down into it, he wondered what he might find. There were at least two famous hauntings at Knighton and if ever there was a good day for looking for ghosts, this was it. Just before the road flattened out, a large pair of stone gates appeared in a gap in the trees to the left. Andy pulled over across the driveway and read the sign: 'Knighton Gorges. Strictly Private'. Aha! The first of his ghost stops. He got out of the car, this time being careful to take his walking stick, and wandered up to the gates. They seemed strangely out of place. The two stone gateposts stood at least nine feet high and were topped with ornamental carvings, but the gate itself was an ordinary wooden five bar farm gate. And instead of great walls on either side of the gate to keep the peasantry at bay, there was nothing but ordinary farm fencing designed to keep the sheep in.

The gate posts were all that remained of the great manor house that had burned down in 1820. Since then, fanciful stories had been spun about how the owner himself had done it to spite his daughter because she had married against his wishes. From Andy's reading of the book on local history, it seemed this was rather unlikely, as the man had provided generously for both his daughters in his will. He'd also gone to live on the mainland in Bath in 1818, but when did facts ever get in the way of a good folk story? Ever since, it was claimed that the house reappeared on New Year's Eve. Andy walked up to the gates and had a good look at them. Nothing ghostly there. He looked at the sheep grazing away in happy ignorance of the spooky legend about their home. Did they ever get the frights in the night? Unlikely. He sighed. Yes, this was atmospheric and all, but there was nothing there that might explain why Dunseath had been so concerned about it. Andy got back in the car and drove off to find the main area where the houses were. Maybe there'd be something there? Had he not been so focussed on the road ahead and thinking about where he might park, he might have looked in his rearview mirror and seen the figure in a grey, hooded cloak step out into the road behind him.

As it turned out, Knighton was a 'blink and you'd miss it' sort of place. He passed a side road that looked like there might be houses down it, then a couple of properties on one side of the road, three on the other, and the next thing he knew, he was into countryside again. Knighton was really just a small collection of houses. It didn't even have a pub! Andy muttered under his breath about this being a waste of time, then parked the car at the side of a farm track. He took his stick and walked back to where the houses were. The first one was an attractive house in sandy-coloured stone with a collection of well-kept outbuildings. Now he was on foot, he was able to see over the wall and into the front garden, where four figures had been arranged having a picnic under a weeping willow. For once, the effigies didn't look disturbing. It was Dorothy, the Tin Man, the Scarecrow and the Cowardly Lion from the Wizard of Oz, who had all been given happy looks on their faces. Even in the fog, they looked jolly and welcoming. Andy smiled – well, that was a first!

Just as he was turning away from them to continue his walk, he thought he saw a movement out of the corner of his eye. He stared into the fog further up the road, but there was nothing there. Probably just a trick of the interminable fog. He walked back down the road past two more very well-kept houses. Their gardens had a lot of mid-September colour in them, defying the dank weather conditions. As Andy walked on, he wondered whether he'd find anything here at all. He'd been hoping for a church, as they are so often the repository for local history, but there was nothing. Walking in the muffling fog, he could easily imagine that the place had been uninhabited for a long time after it was abandoned. He decided to walk down as far as the side road, take a look at whatever was there and then head back to base.

Just beyond Andy's vision, Downer hopped a gate into a field and slipped behind the hedge. Hunkered down in his grey, hooded cloak just inside the field of maize, he had a perfect view of the road, but was almost invisible. When Elizabeth Russell's helper walked past, Downer left it a few seconds and then followed him. Yes, now he could keep the man in his sights, knowing that his cloak perfectly camouflaged him in the swirling grey mass of cloud. His orders were to kill the man and, since the meyaster was still resting, Downer only had the remnants of his own magic to do it with. He wasn't happy. The pain of his previous encounter with the big bruiser was still fresh. He didn't want to engage the man in close combat again and he didn't have any long-range weapons, so what was he to do? He passed a field and could just make out a gallybagger keeping its lonely vigil. The gallybagger, known as a scarecrow by overners, gave Downer an idea and he grinned, displaying a decaying set of brown teeth. Yes, that would work! Now Downer left Andy to it, slipped into the field and approached the gallybagger.

Andy found that the side road led down to a big yard with some light industrial sheds on one side and cottages on the other. To the side of the furthest cottage, a track led over a stone bridge and Andy decided to see where it went. As he arrived at the bridge, he was greeted by a gargoyle perched on a stone post. It must have been some remnant of the old manor. Like the great gates, it was a memory of grandeur that hadn't yet been erased by progress. Andy walked over the bridge and along the track, following it for a few hundred yards. Across the fields, he could just see a scarecrow with its back to him, guarding its crops from unseen enemies.

Then, he walked through woodland and on to an area with two garages and a turning circle. Beyond lay some outbuildings and a farmhouse. He stopped. There was nothing to see here, and he couldn't very well go marching up to the front door of the farmhouse and ask them if they knew anything about the history of the area. He'd just have to chalk it up to experience. Having said all that, as an ex-copper, he could see that the place was perfect for all kinds of illegal activities. It was only twenty minutes from the nearest town, yet remote and far from prying eyes. Yes, you could grow a good crop of weed in those barns with the right setup - or store any manner of contraband. And who'd expect that in the middle of a holiday island catering to wrinkly retirees, yachties and parents with little kids?

As he turned his steps back towards the main road, he thought about the criminal potential of the Isle of Wight and wondered how much smuggling went on there. Letting the gears of his mind freewheel, he walked through the wood, back past the scarecrow with its grotesquely drawn face, and on towards the bridge. Yes, you could probably land anything on the south side of The Island with its long stretches of unspoiled beaches... Andy shivered. For some reason, he felt distinctly uncomfortable. Something wasn't right. What could it... the scarecrow. When he'd walked out, he could've sworn it was facing away from him. He remembered feeling relieved that he hadn't seen its face. He stopped, then jogged back to where he could get a view of it. When he reached the break in the hedge, he felt his stomach drop. The scarecrow was gone. It hadn't been swallowed up by the fog, because he could see its stand was still there, but the scarecrow itself was nowhere to be seen. Andy didn't like that. He didn't like that at all. He stared about into the fog for it, leaning over the hedge to get a good look into the field. And he was so focussed on looking, that he didn't register the rustling sound, like a bag of leaves being rhythmically shaken. It started quietly and inexorably got louder until he finally noticed it and turned.

Andy's cry was involuntary - the scarecrow was sprinting at him with a face of twisted hate. Andy instinctively braced himself with his left leg while crooking his right elbow up in front of his bowed head. The scarecrow slammed into the tip of his elbow and, being made mostly of straw, rebounded. However, Andy only got a moment's respite, as the scarecrow launched a frenzied attack, slashing and stabbing at him with its arms. Andy covered up like a boxer and, although the thing didn't have fists, the ends of its arms were a solid mass of hard straw tips, and a couple of glancing blows cut into his forehead. If he took one directly to the eye, he could be in real trouble. Andy stepped inside with a left hook to its midriff which sent the man of straw tottering backwards. Andy took the chance and slipped on the knuckle duster, praying it would work as well as it had before. The gallybagger went for him again and caught Andy painfully in the chest with the end of its stubby arm. He winced and swung his left with the knuckle duster. This time he caught it on the side of the head, but there was no spectacular result. The creature simply shook its head, fixed him with its evil glare and attacked, raining a welter of blows against Andy's torso.

Andy was pushed back, snagged his foot on a root and was trying to rebalance when the gallybagger leapt on him, knocking him backwards. It was on his chest, punching down at his face, trying to impale his mouth on the end of one of its arms. Andy caught one arm between his hands and held the end of it inches from his face. The scarecrow weighed next to nothing, but it was extraordinarily strong, pushing slowly towards his mouth. The musty smell of damp straw was choking and, as Andy strained to stop the twisted collection of straw ends, the gallybagger pushed its face close to his to look into his eyes. Andy yelled as he wrenched the scarecrow's arms sideways and headbutted it in the face before throwing it off him. He scrambled away and tried to keep it at bay with his stick, catching it with a couple of good blows, but it wasn't enough. The scarecrow wasn't tiring, but Andy knew that *he* would, and then he heard a disconcerting sound. From somewhere behind him, the 'leaves in a bag' sound was fast approaching. Andy had no time, but then a thought flashed. He drew the sword from the stick and slashed at the scarecrow in front of him, severing its right arm. The scarecrow dropped to the ground and Andy swivelled in time to slash at the other onrushing gallybagger. The sword caught it in the angle between its shoulder and neck, hacking deep into the top of its torso. That slowed it down. Andy pulled out the blade and swung at its neck, chopping its head off. The head – a semi-deflated football with a wicked leer painted on it – flew over the hedge into the field. The gallybagger's body keeled over backwards and lay still.

Andy turned back to the first scarecrow, which was trying to refit its severed arm.

"Oh no you don't!" Andy barked and set about chopping the thing to pieces. He stood for a moment over the mess of torn clothing and scattered straw. What the fuck? How the hell had these things come to life? Then a more useful question occurred – were there any more of them? And could he get back to his car before they found him? Andy glanced back at the headless scarecrow and was disturbed to see it had started to move and was feeling around for its head. Andy was caught between emotions. Was this funny, sad or terrifying?

"Sod it!" Andy said, deciding it was all three and that the safest thing was to hack the bastard up. After strewing the lane with its innards, Andy jogged back towards the houses. God, what if that bloody gargoyle at the end of the bridge came to life? Surely it would break his sword and that would be the end of him!

When he got to the bridge, Andy slowed and tried to see if the gargoyle was moving. It looked solid, but he didn't take any chances and sprinted past it. Once he was a good way into the yard beyond, he looked back – the gargoyle was still as stone. Thank God for that!

"Is anyone here?" Andy shouted as he walked up between the cottages and industrial units. There was no response and it was as if his call had been absorbed by the fog so that even if someone had been there, they wouldn't have heard him. Andy felt horribly alone as he jogged up to the road. He headed back towards the car, trying to think about what he'd seen coming into the village earlier. The side of the road with the great gates had been grazing land, so no chance of any scarecrows coming from there, but what about the other side of the road? Suddenly, the familiar sound of a straw man moving fast came to him and he turned to see another gallybagger running towards him along the road. It was a good fifty yards away and despite its disjointed movements, it was coming on fast. It was one of those ones with a white cloth face onto which a jack-o-lantern design had been drawn and it was the most unearthly thing Andy had ever seen. He knew he had to stand and face it, so he raised his sword and waited. Twenty yards, ten, five, wait for it... now! The slash of the blade caught it in the middle of its head, which collapsed into its shoulders. It stopped and flailed around, as Andy stood back and watched. Again, he chose his moment perfectly, this time cutting it off at the knees... if it had knees. The thing fell to the ground and Andy jumped up and down on it, swearing and cursing as he kicked the stuffing out of the old clothes until it was destroyed.

Andy ran on and while nothing more came from behind him, a nasty thought had occurred about what might be up ahead. Sure enough, as he rounded the bend before the last few houses in the village, the road was blocked. Dorothy, the Scarecrow, the Tin Man and the Cowardly Lion stood in a line across the road in front of him. Their cheery expressions hadn't changed, but they weren't there to picnic or follow the Yellow Brick Road. They were there to kill and, as soon as they saw Andy, they ran at him. Andy thought fast. If any of them got behind him, he was dead, so he dodged to the side of the road with the high hedge. It wasn't perfect, but it was the best he could do in the moment. Fortunately, it was so high and thick that even if there was a scarecrow on the other side, it couldn't get to him. Now his strategy would be tested as the Cowardly Lion defied his name and attacked first. It tried to stab him with the end of an arm, but Andy deflected it with the sword and swung it at the Cowardly Lion's chest. The tip of the blade tore through the costume and a few bits of straw bulged out. The Cowardly Lion looked down on what Andy had done and then stared at him. Its unchanging, friendly look was unnerving, because it gave Andy no indication of when it might... suddenly, it lunged at him. His sword met the slashing arm and the limb went spinning off, hitting the Tin Man in the face. He immediately stepped in to hit Andy with his axe and, for a moment, Andy thought he was done for. The axe blade struck Andy's shoulder, but it was only made of moulded tin foil. It must have been a disappointing result, but the Tin Man's merry expression didn't change, even as Andy hacked into it with three quick blows. Like its axe, the Tin Man's body was held together with tin foil, so once Andy had cut through it, the straw innards quickly spilled out and more of the foil tore as the thing tried to move. As the Tin Man stepped backwards, desperately trying to re-stuff itself, Dorothy and the Scarecrow launched a simultaneous attack.

Andy was sweating heavily now and he panted as he tried to fend off a welter of blows. Dorothy had a wicker basket attached to the end of one arm and caught Andy across the face with it. A bright explosion of pain was quickly followed by the sensation of his hair being pulled from behind. The worry that there might be a gallybagger grabbing him through the hedge flashed into his mind, but he had to focus on what was in front of him. He poked the Scarecrow in the face with the end of his walking stick while slashing at Dorothy's legs. Both strikes hit their marks. While the Scarecrow was only mildly inconvenienced by the poke in the face, Dorothy's left leg was hanging by a few strands of straw. Andy shoved her over, but took a hefty stab to his left side from the Scarecrow,

"Get off!" Andy screamed in fury and he used his bulk to muscle the Scarecrow back so that he could hack at him with the sword. It was a clumsy, but effective attack, which ended when Andy raised the sword high above his head and sliced down onto the Scarecrow's head. The blade hacked straight through, cutting the Scarecrow in two. Each half balanced for a moment, then fell.

Before Andy could enjoy his handywork, he felt the hair at the back of his head yanked hard and he cried out in pain as some of his hair was pulled out at the roots. He swung round, expecting to see Dorothy attacking him, but she was a couple of yards away trying to mend her leg. Andy's left hand went to the back of his head. What the hell was that? There was something made of straw gripping his hair. He got his hand under it and flung it off him, then turned to face his new foe,

"What the f..." Andy began as he saw a little dog made of straw running away into the fog.

"Yeah, you'd better run Toto, you little shit!" Andy shouted after it, then he turned on Dorothy, who had just fixed up her leg and was drawing back the basket for another attack. Andy lunged forward, pushing the tip of the blade clean through the middle of her chest. Now they were face to face. Dorothy tried to hit him with the basket, but the blow bounced ineffectually off his shoulder.

"Fuck off back to Kansas!" Andy said, grabbing her face with his free hand and ripping her head off. He threw it across the road and withdrew the blade. Dorothy instantly collapsed. Andy now turned back to the Tin Man and Cowardly Lion, which were trying to rebuild themselves for another attack. Andy calmly walked over to them and cut them to ribbons. As he looked down at the mess of straw and torn costumes, he noticed that the Tin Man didn't have a heart after all.

Andy jogged up the road towards the car and was pleased to find no more scarecrows blocking his way. He jumped in, locked the doors and quickly reversed back up to the main road, where he executed a passable jackhammer turn before speeding off through the remains of the Wizard of Oz characters. He hoped that Toto was still running down the road, because if it was, he'd run the little sod over. Annoyingly, it was nowhere to be seen and he was quickly through the village and powering past the great gates, up the hill and away to safety. Or so he thought. Behind him, holding Toto in his hands, Downer stood by the road muttering an incantation. It was a long journey back to St Helens and the fog could make the road treacherous. By the time Downer finished his incantation, he had ensured it would be positively lethal.

Chapter Nineteen

No Place Like Home

A few minutes later, Andy was barrelling along the ridge towards Brading. His eyes were wide and he was soaked in acrid fright-sweat as he tried to recover his wits. Even though he had got the better of the scarecrows, he was shaking with adrenalin. He took a corner a bit too fast and had to muscle the car to keep it out of the hedge.

"Calm, Andy! Calm!" he said to himself, "They were only animated scarecrows trying to kill you – what's so bad about that?"

Jesus H. Christ! *Only* animated scarecrows! And it was *only* the second attempt on his life in two days. He'd only come that close to serious injury five times in twenty years in the police. And that didn't even include the attack on Westminster Bridge in the summer. Yes, since he'd met Bess, he'd come close to being killed three times. He pictured Roddy in his mind – how long before Andy looked like him? Between his thoughts and the enclosing fog, Andy was only looking at the road straight ahead, so it was a jolting shock when something large slammed into the passenger side of the car, smashing the window. Andy swore loudly as the car skewed across the road and he corrected it with squealing tyres. He swore again when he looked into the rearview to see a scarecrow picking itself up and chasing after him. God, it was shifting! Andy felt an unpleasant flutter in his stomach as he watched its disjointed movements with their unnatural speed.

"Sod this!" he said, burying the accelerator. The Ford Focus kicked forward and, in a couple of seconds, the chasing scarecrow had been swallowed up by the fog. But now Andy had a different problem. He could see another one leaping over the hedge ahead of him. He reached across to the swordstick on the passenger seat, unsheathed it and held it in his left hand as he kept his foot pressed down on the accelerator, hoping that his sheer speed would be too much for it. It wasn't. Somehow the creature timed its leap to perfection and it was through the shattered window up to its waist and jabbing at him with the sharp ends of its arms. Andy took his foot off the gas as he tried to fend off the attack, but caught a painful blow to the temple and veered across the road. Thankfully, nothing was coming the other way, but now he was having to try to steer back to the left while fending off the scarecrow, which was working its way into the car. Andy thrust at it with the sword and was able to push it through the gallybagger's lower torso, pinning it back as he slowed the car to a stop. Now he could give the thing his full attention and he pushed his right hand past its flailing arms to grab the top of its head. He took a firm grip and shook it hard, wrenching the scarecrow left and right until the head came off. That took the wind out of its sails. He dropped the head into the passenger footwell and withdrew the sword so he could shove the body of the scarecrow back out of the window.

The scarecrow fell back, but at almost the same moment, the rear window shattered. Andy looked round to see the evil face of the scarecrow that had been chasing him, as it started trying to climb in the back.

"Fuck off!" Andy yelled, stamping on the accelerator. The sudden jolt knocked the scarecrow off and the car sped away. A quick look in the rearview and he could see the bugger was running after him again. Dammit! Then a movement down to his left caught his eye and he couldn't help but let out a startled exclamation – the head of the other scarecrow was rolling around the passenger footwell as if it was trying to throw itself at him. No! He wasn't going to have that, thank you! Andy took the sword and skewered the head,

"Stitch that!" he said and then turned his attention to getting off the ridge and back to safety as fast as he could.

But then a thought occurred – what if all he did was lead a horde of murderous scarecrows back to the hotel? He couldn't do that! But what could he do?

He was still trying to work it out when he drove into Brading. The roads were uncannily empty and, as he crested the hill going into the town, he cried,

"Oh, come on!"

There, standing across the road, were the effigies of the conductor and zombie orchestra, armed with their instruments. Even though he was now in a thirty zone, Andy floored it. With shattered passenger and rear windows, he didn't fancy the idea of one or more of those things getting into the car. The conductor was standing in the middle, with its baton ready as a stabbing weapon, but it never got the chance to use it. Andy hit the thing full-on with such force that its legs instantly detached and disappeared under the car, while its top half came over the bonnet. Andy had the vision of its white face with its drawn-on crosses for eyes and grinning mouth flattening against the windscreen and then it was gone. However, the band members took the chance to hurl their instruments at the car and the rear driver's side window smashed as the tuba slammed into it. Andy looked behind – great! Now he had the orchestra after him... although he took some pleasure in the fact that the only thing left of the glaring conductor was a puff of straw hanging in the air.

"Ha!" Andy shouted, then drove on, trying to be as fast as he could while being careful through the town. But really, he needn't have bothered. The place seemed to be empty – apparently, his was the only soul on the road.

Soon he had to slow for the dogleg into the main street and in that moment, the effigy made of flowerpots leapt from its hiding place and landed on the bonnet. Andy shied away backwards into his seat as he tried to shake the thing off, but he didn't even manage to change the jaunty angle of its flowerpot hat. It smashed a flowerpot fist into the windscreen, hammering a round impact point of weakened glass. Andy was trying to see past the flowerpot man, because there was a sharp turn coming, when the creature hit again and this time its flowerpot fist came through the windscreen. Andy stamped on the brakes and the flowerpot man was thrown off the front of the car, leaving the pot that had come through the windscreen stuck in the hole. Andy put his foot on the gas and was glad to hear the distinct sound of breaking pottery as he ran the thing over, although a glance behind him revealed the zombie orchestra still giving chase. Thankfully, that was it for Brading, because none of the other houses had the weird human effigies outside them. Now he was on a fast stretch of road and he dropped the hammer. The main road also brought him back to some semblance of normality, as other cars appeared for the first time in about fifteen minutes.

"Thank God!" he sighed as a perfectly ordinary Ford transit passed him, driven by a human being. He'd started to wonder whether he was the last person left on an island populated by scarecrows! As he drove, his mind was whirling. He couldn't bring this madness back to the hotel, so where could he go? Then he had a brainwave – the boat! He'd drive to the marina, get on the boat and drive it out into the harbour. There was no way these straw creatures would be able to catch him at sea. And, once he was safely on the boat, he could regroup and radio for help. He'd already looked at his phone and, of course, it had no bloody signal. Why would it? Why would technology ever work properly when it was most needed?

The only snag with the plan was that it would take him off the main road and back through St Helens, but it was the only way, so he gritted his teeth and took the turn, thinking about where he'd seen scarecrows on the way out. The first was one from a field on the hill leading up to the village. It tried to leap out of the hedge and through the passenger window, but this time, Andy was expecting it and dabbed his brakes as it made the leap. Instead of coming through the window, it sprawled across the bonnet, bumped off the windscreen and disappeared over the top of the car. One down... how many were there in St Helens? He'd find out in the next few, nightmarish minutes. The effigy outside the pub was standing by its table and as he sped past, it threw its pint glass. Andy swerved, but the glass came through the shattered passenger window and caught him on the top of the head. In a shower of glass, he jolted in his seat as his car caught the flank of one of the cars parked on the other side of the road. Andy swore and regained control, but had slowed enough to give the effigy from the cottage time to hop its fence and charge him. Andy turned the wheel hard to meet the scarecrow head-on and it crashed into the front of the car in an explosion of straw and feathers.

"Oh Christ!" Andy's fearful cry was an involuntary reaction to the sight of half a dozen scarecrows pelting up out of the fog from the unseen far side of the village green. God! Where were they coming from? All he could do was floor it and hope for the best. As he passed the junction with the road that led back to the hotel, he could see the schoolteacher and pupil with the carrot-nosed peeping Tom running down towards him. He just beat them before they could cut him off and now they joined the gaggle of leaping freaks hurtling in his wake. Andy glanced at them in the rearview, immediately wished he hadn't, flicked his eyes back to the road, and then there was Donald Trump! The effigy with the President's face was suddenly on the front of the car and trying to get through the hole in the glass. It punched through the flowerpot stuck in the hole, cracking the entire windscreen – one more hit and the whole lot would go! Andy took the sword and flicked the skewered head through the passenger window. Then, as the Trump effigy tried to push its head through the hole in the windscreen, Andy thrust the sword into its face. He withdrew the blade, pumped the brakes to throw Donald off, then ran him over. That was oddly satisfying! Then he was speeding down to the marina to get as much space between him and the chasing pack as he could.

He skidded to a halt in the parking area and leapt out of the car with the sword in his hand. He glanced back up the road – no sign of the chasers yet – then ran for the jetty, leaving the wrecked car in his wake. In less than a minute he was on the boat and had cast off. He got into the cabin and closed the door, then got the boat going. He'd watched Bess carefully when she'd driven it over, so was able to get away from the jetty and gingerly ease the boat into the channel. He drove slowly and was glad to find the controls were as easy as Bess had made them look when she'd been driving it.

“Right, just keep between the red and green buoys,” he said to himself. Not being a sailor, he had no idea which way the tide was going, but he did know that he had to stick to the navigable channel. As he made the turn out to sea through the narrow throat of the harbour, he could see the chasing scarecrows running towards the end of the spit of land on his left. When they got to the edge of the shore, they stopped and stood there glaring at him with their disturbing drawn-on faces as the schoolteacher effigy thrashed its cane through the air in frustration. Then, as Andy headed out of the harbour, they ran parallel with him along the shingle beach. Even though he was safe on the boat, their disjointed, flailing way of moving chilled him to the core.

Andy took out his phone and, by some miracle, he had a signal,

"Yes!" he said with a fist pump and hit Roddy's number,

"Roddy, it's Andy!"

"Hello, Andy, what can I do for you?" Roddy's voice was cutting in and out, so Andy made it brief,

"I'm in the boat heading out of Bembridge harbour. All the scarecrows on the island have gone mad and are trying to kill me. There's a bunch of them waiting on the shore right now."

"Okay, I'll sort something. Just stay somewhere in the vicinity and don't try sailing off to France, okay?"

"Right. My mobile signal's very patchy, but you can always get me on the boat's radio," Andy said.

"Okay, see you soon," Roddy said and disconnected.

That was a bit of luck! Andy suddenly felt that things might turn out all right.

He pressed on, following the twists and turns of the channel at a slow pace that the scarecrows could easily match on the shore. Peeping Tom with the carrot nose finally decided to try to swim out and get him, but the first wave that hit it swept it off its feet and then it was thrown about in the surf, unable to get back up. The others left it and soon it was broken to pieces in the waves.

"Serve you right!" Andy laughed. Now the immediate tension was over, he was feeling a bit giddy, but also cold and tired. He gave a racking yawn and aimed the boat to the left of the fort sitting at the mouth of the harbour. His plan was to swing around the fort and then keep chugging around it until help arrived. Yes, finally he could rela… hang on! Why were there stray whisps of straw on the floor? He looked at his clothes, yes, there was the odd bit of it stuck to him, and when he ran his hand through his hair there was some there, too. Maybe it had come in with him? Andy looked around the cabin more closely. Yes, what was on him might explain the bits between the door and the bridge, but there were whisps of straw down the stairs to the sleeping area.

"Oh shit!"

The door to the master cabin opened and a scarecrow with a Jason-style hockey mask for a face stepped through. Andy glanced over at the walking stick, which he'd absent-mindedly thrown onto the seating on the other side of the cabin. No way he could reach it and now the scarecrow was preparing to leap at him. Andy remembered the safety procedures Bess had told him about on the way over and quickly reached down for the flare gun. As he swung the gun up, the scarecrow leapt at him and he fired. The flare exploded in the scarecrow's chest, bathing the inside of the cabin in eerie red light and throwing the scarecrow backwards into the master bedroom.

"Yes!" Andy bellowed as a mixture of emotions engulfed him,

"Come back from that you arsehole!"

His triumph was short-lived. In seconds, the duvet on the bed was in flames. Andy swore long and loudly as he watched the burning scarecrow thrash around the bedroom, setting fire to the curtains and pillows so that inside thirty seconds, half the bedroom was in flames. Now what? He looked down at the fire extinguisher, but the flames were already way beyond what it could handle. Abandon ship! That was his only option. He could see that there was some exposed shingle right in front of the fort, so he turned the boat towards that. It wasn't far, but by the time he was close enough to jump ship, the master bedroom was a wall of flame. Andy grabbed the swordstick, got out to the back of the boat and leapt into the water. He was heavy in all his clothes, and he had to struggle to get back to the surface, but at least the water wasn't very cold. He breast stroked towards the fort as best he could with the stick in one hand until he finally felt something solid under his foot. As the boat ran into the rocks around the side of the fort, Andy squelched out of the water and slumped down on the yard of beach at the foot of the bastion. He looked across the water at the group of scarecrows on the beach. They were prowling in the hope of getting him when he finally came back to shore. Andy swore at them and flicked them a V sign. He might be cold and wet, but at least he was safe. And then the boat exploded.

Chapter Twenty

The Betrayal

When Downer entered the great hall, he knew he was in trouble.

"Useless!" Attrill screeched. He had clearly regained his energy, because he leapt out of his chair by the fire and covered half the room in a few long strides to confront the bungling imbecile. Downer stood impassively, waiting for the inevitable, with a mulish look on his sallow face.

"One man! That's all I want you to do – kill one man!" Attrill yelled,

"Is he a powerful mage, or a witch, or a man imbued with holy power? No! He's just some East End scumbag, but I see he's got the better of you again!"

"Is not my fault, meyaster, yon overner's got a sword..."

"Oh! He's got a sword! Well in that case, if he's got a sword then we'd may as well give up now and hand him the Island!"

"But..."

"But nothing! And what the hell are you doing with that ridiculous basket?" Attrill pointed at the covered basket Dorothy had been wielding earlier that day,

"Been out picking mushrooms, have we?"

"No, meyaster, I..."

"You're a blundering cretin and I'm not putting up with your incompetence anymore!"

And before Downer could reply, Attrill slashed at his throat with a knife that appeared out of nowhere.

Downer made a low gurgle as he tried to breathe through his severed trachea, then slumped to his knees, with very thick, dark blood pouring down his front. Attrill towered over him,

"See? That's what you get for being a hopeless buffoon. I don't know why I ever bothered with you – you useless, gormless waste of life!"

Attrill stepped back to avoid the widening pool of blood, and happily watched the final remnants of life seep out of his faithful retainer. At last, Downer fell over sideways and his face made a satisfying 'splut' as it hit the bloody stone floor.

"Now I've got to do everything myself!" Attrill complained. He wondered how best to eliminate Russell's helper. Getting rid of him was top priority. Although the gallybaggers hadn't managed it, Attrill had to hand it to Downer for style. Yes, that had been quite delicious to watch. In fact, he hadn't realized that Downer had that much magic left in him. He looked down at the body again. He still had that ridiculous basket in his hand like it was some sort of prize. What was that about? Then he noticed a movement under the cloth covering. Being careful to avoid treading in the blood, Attrill stepped over the pool, took the basket out of Downer's cold, dead hand and pulled the cloth aside.

"Crikey!" Attrill exclaimed. Inside was the straw Toto, looking up at him and wagging its tail,

"What are you doing in there?" Attrill asked, taking it out,

"Now really, why would Downer..." and then he noticed that straw Toto had a mouthful of something. He looked at it closely and then a sly smile spread across his face,

"Oh, that's good! If that's what I think it is, that's very good!"

Then he looked at Downer's body,

"Damn!"

Perhaps he had acted precipitately in killing his servant, especially if he had returned with such a prize. Well, now he'd have to reanimate him. Attrill looked at the time – he was lucky. In forty-five minutes, the time would be perfect, and he even had the right phase of the moon for it.

"I think fortune may be on our side, old chum!" he said to the body, then he turned to get his ceremonial robes on,

"And as for you, little fella," he said to the straw dog as he took the bundle of hair from its mouth, "You're now surplus to requirements," and he deftly punted Toto across the hall and into the big fireplace. The squeal that came from the straw dog writhing in the flames was so unpleasant that Attrill could do nothing but laugh. It was desperately trying to claw its way out of the flames, but it was impossible. After half a minute of thrashing about and squealing, it finally sank with a drawn out hiss as the flaring fire reduced it to ashes.

"Well done, Downer!" Attrill chuckled, "That was brilliant. I'll have to get him to do that again!" there was something about the way in which the eager little thing had been surprised at its treatment that gave him unalloyed pleasure. If it'd had a face, Attrill reckoned the expression on it would have been priceless!

An hour and a half later, Downer gulped in a huge breath of air and sat up. He was in the third of the magic circles, while Attrill stood in the fourth in full ceremonial dress with his wand held high. Downer looked about him and groaned. Here again! Would he never be free? Attrill concluded the rite to raise the dead and walked over to his servant,

"Sorry about that," he said, "You know how hot headed I can be."

Downer stood and felt his throat. Although everything was perfectly normal, it still hurt.

"Now, tell me," Attrill said, "Are these what I think they are?"

"They be the hairs off of that overner's head, meyaster," Downer said.

"Excellent! Well done, well done indeed!" Attrill said, slapping Downer on the shoulder, "Now, get yourself ready, we've got an important spell to cast."

"Wazzat, meyaster?" Downer looked up at his boss with barely concealed dislike.

"You'll like this... *we* aren't going to kill Russell's assistant – she is!" and Attrill was bursting with pride at his ingenuity. Downer was confused,

"Howzat, meyaster?"

"You'll see!" and Attrill's eyes were glittering at the thought of his plan, "This is going to be our best trick yet!"

***

It was late afternoon when Dan dropped Elizabeth Russell off at the Four Gates Hotel. Their trip up to Culver Down had yielded nothing except a strong feeling that there was something very wrong up there. With a three-hundred-foot-high chalk cliff and its exposed position, it was always a wild and woolly place. In the dense fog of the Swaailen, it had taken on a brooding feel, as if it had been willing the unwary to get too close to the cliff edge.

"Sorry that was a wasted journey," Elizabeth Russell said as she got out of the car.

"Not a problem," Dan smiled, "What time tomorrow?"

"I don't think we need you. I'll get Andy to take us over to Godshill and see what we can turn up there."

"All right, I'll stick to the day job," Dan said, "See you when I see you," and he waved as he pulled away.

It was only when he was gone that she noticed a lingering smell of burning in the air. Had Roddy been burning leaves? As she walked up the steps, there was straw everywhere. Curious.

"Ah! There you are!" Roddy cried as she walked into the entrance hall, "You've missed all the fun!"

"What fun?" she asked, walking up to the big fire and warming herself in front of it.

"Your boyfriend's had a spot of local difficulty," Roddy smiled, limping out from behind the reception desk, then he told her what Andy had told him about his day. When he got to the bit about the boat exploding, she exclaimed,

"The car *and* the boat!"

"Aye! Scuttled it on the rocks of St Helens fort."

Bess had to smile,

"I thought I was hiring an Investigator, but I've got myself a one-man wrecking crew!"

"He certainly is that!" Roddy laughed.

"So, what's with all the straw out the front?"

"Once he'd been rescued by the lifeboat and the police had brought him back here, some of his little gallybagger friends turned up for a chat. Don't worry, I had a meeting with them and explained that he'd had enough of 'em," Roddy held out his palm and a dancing flame appeared on it, flickering red and gold.

"Still got it, I see,"

"It's like sex. You never forget," Roddy said before closing his hand to extinguish the flame.

"Where is he now?"

"Up in your room. Said something about having a long soak in the tub. You know, there's room enough for two in there," and he gave her a wink.

"Yeah, we know," and she winked back.

"Same old Bess!" Roddy muttered as Bess jogged up the stairs.

"Hey there, sexy!" Bess said when she opened the door to the bathroom. The room was steamy and Andy was lying half-asleep in the gloriously hot water. He cocked an eye open and looked at her,

"All right? How was your day?"

"Not as expensive as yours!" she replied, going over to kiss his wet forehead. She licked her lips – salty!

"You heard, then?"

"Yeah. Still, what's two hundred grand between friends?"

"Yowch!"

"Not including the car. And to think, I let you drive the Jag! God knows what damage you could've done to it!"

Andy replied with a dry, "Ha, ha."

"Seriously, are you okay?" her tone softened and she dropped to her haunches to look at his face – it was exhausted.

"Getting there. Not sure I'll ever trust a scarecrow again."

"I know all this takes some getting used to, but…" she wanted to say that she felt he could handle it, but didn't want to sound patronising.

"It's all right. I'm still here. Not sure I could take this twenty-four-seven, mind you,"

"Don't worry, we usually have time between cases. Now, instead of you hogging the bath, how about I join you and I can tell you all about my day?"

"Works for me."

"Right. See you in a mo'," she said and went into the bedroom.

He was glad to see her. After the tornado of a day he'd had, he needed her. She was like a…

Suddenly he felt a horrible wrench as if someone was yanking him backwards by the throat. He thrashed in the water and tried to call out, but nothing came and then it was as if he was falling away from himself and the world, backwards down a deep well. Up above him in the distance, he could see the bathroom. He was getting up out of the water. What the hell? He was shouting from deep in the hole, but he couldn't be heard. He could see that he was walking towards the bathroom door, but he had no control over his limbs. Then a familiar voice came to him – Attrill's voice,

"Shut up and watch the show. Enjoy it, because it's the last thing you'll ever see. Ta ta!" and then Andy could see his hand reach out to the bathroom door, open it and walk into the bedroom.

"Oh, can't wait for me, eh?" Bess said as he came out of the bathroom. She'd taken off her jacket and shoes, and was unbuttoning her shirt as Andy walked straight at her. He grabbed her by the arm and pulled her to him to kiss her viciously. He was wet and soaking her shirt, and it wasn't warm enough for those sorts of shenanigans, so she pulled herself away,

"Woah there, stud! Save it for after the bath," she said, but as she looked into his eyes, her body tensed - she couldn't see Andy. This was…

Without a word, his hands went for her throat. She tried to evade, but he was too quick and now his big hands were squeezing hard. Normally, she'd kick the hell out of an attacker's balls, but this was her boyfriend's body, even if he wasn't controlling it. She quickly dug her fingernails hard into a couple of very painful pressure points on Andy's hands. His grip loosened involuntarily and she immediately dropped down so that his slippery hands lost her. Before he could react, she punched hard into the side of his right knee and, as it crumpled, she heaved upward under the left leg. He toppled over and she scrambled away. In another second, they were both back on their feet and facing each other.

"Dick move, Attrill!" Bess said, "Hoping I'd kill him to save myself?"

Andy's face contorted with rage,

"It's you or him," it was Andy's voice, but Attrill's thoughts, "I'm in here like a tic on a sheep and I'm not going to stop!" and he lunged across the room at her.

She stood her ground and, just as his hands were going for her again, each of them was caught by piece of curtain from the four-poster bed. The thick material wrapped around his wrists and his hands were pulled away from her. Then, with the muscles of his neck and shoulders tensing against the restraints, he was dragged backwards towards the bed.

In spite of his struggling, his hands were pulled back to the high posts of the bed, where the curtains tied them securely so that his arms were stretched out wide on either side of him. Elizabeth Russell went to approach him, but he kicked out at her. She made a tutting sound and said,

"Now then, Attrill, if we're not going to play nicely, we will have to be more securely restrained," and as she spoke, she clicked her fingers and the gold-coloured rope tiebacks that usually held the curtains in shape, whipped around Andy's ankles. They pulled his feet apart and tied them securely to the feet of the bed, so that Andy now resembled an angry version of the Vitruvian Man with arms and legs akimbo.

"That's better," she said, and she was enjoying the look of fury on his face at his plan being derailed.

"If you come any closer, I'll kill him!" Attrill said with Andy's voice.

"Don't be silly. We both know that if you could do that, you would've done it. Because this isn't about injuring me, it's about getting rid of him. You tried it on our first day and you tried it today. What scares you about my Investigator?" Now she was standing right in front of him looking into eyes that were no longer Andy's, but had a quick, devious look to them.

"I'm not going to tell you anything and I'm not going anywhere!" Attrill replied.

"Wrong on both counts," Elizabeth Russell said and her voice was suddenly hard,

"You've told me everything I need to know about you... and you're leaving right now," and she put a hand on either side of his face and pulled it downwards so she was staring into those devious eyes,

"Get out!" she screamed with such force that the great bed lifted six inches off the ground, then slammed back to the floor.

Andy's chin sank onto his chest and then he began drawing in gulps of air,

"What the hell was that?" he gasped after a few seconds.

"Your first possession," she replied, "You never forget your first."

"I'm so sorry," he said, "You must know I'd never try to..."

"It's okay. I knew it wasn't you. For starters, Attrill's a terrible kisser – that gave him away immediately."

"Even so, to lose control like that is..." he struggled to find the words, until he sighed, "It's bloody embarrassing," and he pulled against his restraints,

"You gonna let me down now?"

"I don't know," she said with a wicked smile, getting close and running a hand down his stomach, "I think you look good like this. I'm just glad I didn't have to kick you here," and she gently squeezed his balls,

"Not half as glad as I am," he replied, "Now, don't get me wrong, I'm happy to do this sort of thing if it turns you on, but right now I'm getting cold... and I've just been possessed by some toerag. So, be a love and let me get back into my nice bath... you can join me if you want."

"Sounds like fun. I'll let you go – although it is a turn on to have you at my mercy," she said as her hand toyed with him,

"But we don't want you catching a chill," and with a click of her fingers, his hands were released, then his feet.

"Ta."

He kissed her and padded back to the bathroom.

Ten minutes later, Bess was lying in the bath with Andy behind her, resting her head on his chest.

"When you said Attrill had told you everything you need to know about him, what did you mean?" Andy asked.

"He wants you dead. I'm still not sure exactly why, but he does. And he's clearly very powerful, so why doesn't he just kill you? First, he sends his servant to do it, then the scarecrows, then he possesses you and attacks me in the hope that I will kill you for him. That tells me two things: he's a showman. He loves a flourish and he enjoys tricking people. Getting me to kill you would have been a brilliant trick."

"Not for me," Andy said, stroking her arm,

"And the second thing it tells me is that he is unsure of himself. He is worried about his power and that's why he isn't daring to try to kill you directly or face me. I think that in the past he would have immediately killed us in some elaborate and entertaining way, but he doesn't have full command of his powers anymore."

"Any thoughts as to why?"

"Could be as simple as age. If he's very old, his powers might have suddenly waned. It happens."

"He doesn't look that old,"

"Neither do I," Bess replied. Andy looked over her shoulder and down at her perfectly toned body. No, she certainly didn't look a day over three hundred,

"So, what do we do?" Andy asked.

"Investigate. Find out what he's up to and then put an end to it. We can't have him releasing demons willy-nilly. First, we get ourselves a good night's sleep and tomorrow we see what's happening at Godshill," Bess replied, taking Andy's hands and holding them across her chest. He gently squeezed her to him and they lay together with the steam of the bath curling around them, enjoying the feeling of skin against skin.

***

The pop of a log in the fire snapped Thomas Attrill back into consciousness. He sat up painfully and realised that Elizabeth Russell's command had not only thrown him out of the Investigator's body, but thirty feet across the room from the circle of Solomon all the way to the fireplace. He looked down at his robes. They were covered in blood and, as he gently wiped his nose with his sleeve, he left a wide bloodstain on the white material. Well! She was even more powerful than he'd expected. He had to isolate her. And fast. He tried to get up, but immediately went dizzy. No... he'd sit there for a minute and then think about getting up. But when he did get up, he'd make the witch regret the way she'd thrown him out of her boyfriend.

Chapter Twenty-One

The Boy In Striped Pyjamas

When Chloe awoke, she was pleased to see sunshine framing the curtains. Yesterday had been gloomy and days like that made her a little sad. They made her think about what she was doing and whether it was the right thing. A couple of months ago, she had opened her father's eyes to the greater truth of existence in order to save their lives. Although that had worked – they were both still alive – he had been left in a permanent nightmare, because his mind hadn't been able to cope with the truth. Since that moment, she had used her blossoming psychic abilities to keep him calm. That had been her decision. She had also asked Elizabeth Russell to tell her family that both Ray and she were dead. Chloe didn't want to have to explain her powers and what she was doing with them to her grandparents. It would be best for them to have a clean break and mourn. Was this because she knew they would try to change her mind about looking after her father? Probably. From the outside, it would seem like a waste of her life, but to her it was what she needed. She was the one who had driven her father insane, so she should be the one to look after him. And this way, she could ensure that he was happy and that they could be happy together. Even if everything else was an illusion, the way Ray laughed with her was real. His love for her was real and so was hers for him. Who had the right to claim that their happiness wasn't real because it was based on a reality she was creating in his mind? Surely it was the right thing to do. Then along came gloomy days and Chloe would look out at the clouds and rain and wonder whether she was making a mistake.

She hopped out of bed and screwed up her eyes against the glare as she opened the curtains. Oh, that sun was already lovely and warm!

"Come on, Ray," she said, going to her father's bed and giving his arm a tug, "It's a beautiful day. We can't waste it lying about."

Ray came out of a dreamless sleep and smiled,

"Where's your mum?"

"Already gone to the shops. She's picking up croissants for breakfast."

"Vicky's one in a million," Ray said, pulling himself across the bed to his wheelchair. Of course, he didn't know it was a wheelchair. He thought he was simply getting out of bed and walking around normally. Chloe's ability to create a world where he didn't even realise he'd lost his legs or his wife was remarkable. Elizabeth Russell had told her so. The fact that Chloe could do it while taking lessons in honing her psychic skills - and even in her sleep - was nothing short of miraculous. Elizabeth Russell had told her that, too. Even so, Chloe didn't feel 'special'. This was simply how things were.

"Right, follow me!" she said brightly as she led the way out of their comfortable double room to the dining hall.

As they went, Ray had a cheery greeting for everyone and soon they were in the sunny dining room, looking out on the rolling farmland and woods.

"All right, nurse Taylor? Not working too hard?" Ray asked as one of the nurses passed their table.

"You know me, Ray," she replied, "Getting away with as little work as I can. How's your breakfast?"

"Lovely! My wife brought us croissants, but we just missed her,"

"Oh, that's bad luck," nurse Taylor said. She and all the other staff had been briefed to play along with what Ray said. Since he was such a happy patient, it was easy enough.

"It's all right. She'll be springing me out of here in a couple of days."

"Whatever will we do without you?" she asked.

"I dread to think!" Ray laughed. Nurse Taylor smiled and went on her way, leaving them to the rest of their breakfast. Chloe and Ray went back to chatting easily about what they were going to do later – this included watching The Lion King, playing some video games and going for a walk. A nice, easy day. But even as Ray was saying,

"Who knew that recovering from a car wreck could be so much fun?"

Chloe saw a boy in blue and white striped pyjamas at the other end of the dining hall. He had black hair and dark eyes which stared at her, unblinking. Chloe didn't like it. He was probably about five years old, but there was something wrong about the way he was standing. He didn't stand like a boy, but like a man. Like a hunter searching for something to kill. It was almost as if...

Gladys and Henry got up from their table, blocking Chloe's view. She stood up to meerkat in the direction she'd seen the boy, but he was gone.

"You all right?" Ray asked.

No. Seeing the boy had left her feeling cold and unsafe.

"Yeah," Chloe beamed, "Come on, let's get you to your physio, then we can play Mario Kart," and she allowed Ray to lead them onwards, with a cheery,

"I don't know why you're in such a hurry to get beaten, but ours not to reason why, ours but to do, and whup yo' ass in a go-kart."

Chloe smiled, but as they left, she looked again for the boy. He wasn't there. Was that better or worse?

When they came out of the physio room an hour later, Chloe could have sworn that there was a flash of white and blue at the end of the corridor as if someone had ducked away just as they'd swung into it. Then, as the morning progressed, she got a strange, prickling sensation at the back of her neck. Everywhere they went, she felt there was someone just outside her peripheral vision, watching her. And she wasn't entirely sure whether that the someone was friendly. Even though things seemed normal and nothing was out of the ordinary, the prickling feeling wouldn't go away. And then, while Ray was being helped in the loo by an attendant, and Chloe was alone in the corridor waiting, she felt a shiver run up the left side of her body. She turned and there was the boy, standing like a statue at the end of the corridor, staring at her. Chloe looked back at him. She didn't like his eyes. There was malice in them.

"Hello?" she said. The boy didn't answer but ran at her. Chloe didn't think, she bolted. Without a backwards glance, she was down the corridor and through the double-doors at the end.

She could hear his bare feet slapping on the hard floor behind her. Was she getting away from him? She was bigger than he was, but the sense of danger she was picking up from him made her want to avoid a fight. As she dodged her way through the dining room and out the other side, an image flashed through her mind of her strung up from a tree by her feet with all the skin peeled off her from her ankles to her neck. She put on a turn of speed, thinking ahead to the next corridor. Around the corner, there was a laundry chute set in the wall that went down into the hospital laundry. If she could get far enough ahead... she sprinted up the sunny corridor, avoiding old Alfred, who was standing talking to the wall and, as she ducked around the corner, she could see the boy was a good way off. She dived into the chute, slipped easily down it and was ejected into a big hopper full of sheets. She struggled to get out and tried not to think about what might be on some of those sheets, then nonchalantly walked past Trevor, who was loading attendants' uniforms into one of six huge washing machines.

"Morning, Trevor," Chloe said casually.

"Morning, Chloe. Been riding the chute again, have we?"

"Maybe..." Chloe smiled. She knew she wasn't supposed to do it, but she had been known to enjoy the occasional ride down the chute.

"How's Ray?" Trevor was chummy with Ray and sometimes played dominoes with him after his shift ended.

"Oh, he's fine... um... if you see a little boy in pyjamas, please don't tell him you saw me. It's a game."

"Don't worry, your secret's safe with me," he smiled and watched her carefully open the door to the corridor and scope things out before leaving. She waved and then was gone.

"Cute kid," Trevor muttered and went back to what he was doing.

Chloe worked her way back to where she'd left her father, hoping that she wouldn't round a corner and walk straight into the boy. Who was he? Where did he come from and why had he chased her? She couldn't work it out. All she knew was that he was out of place.

"Where did you go?" Ray asked, when she finally turned up.

"Back to the room. I wanted to make sure we had enough popcorn for the afternoon movie."

"And?"

"Don't worry – there's plenty."

"Okay, let's get into that sunshine," Ray said, "If I don't get my ten thousand steps, I won't be fit enough to be discharged back home," and he wheeled himself along the corridor with Chloe right behind him. The Woodlands Centre was surrounded by extensive grounds, with vast lawns that had been separated into different 'rooms' by mature planting of trees and shrubs. Down the hill, there was also a large, wooded area that had been left wild. A ten-foot-high perimeter wall, topped with razor wire, was primarily designed to keep people out, but it also meant that the staff could give patients the run of the place without worrying about them wandering off into the surrounding countryside. Chloe and Ray had been taking a daily walk around the place ever since he'd had the strength to wheel himself in his chair. Normally, this was a carefree time, but today Chloe was tense, keeping an eye open for the boy. After about fifteen minutes, she thought it might be best to head back, but when she turned to retrace their steps, she could see the boy standing about fifty yards away, blocking their path back. Chloe saw a flash in her mind's eye of the boy with a knife stepping up to her skinned body hanging by her ankles from a tree. He pushed the blade into her belly and her guts spilled out. Then the vision was gone. "Come on, let's get going!" she said to Ray and she hurried away from the boy, going along the path, which had high bushes on either side. Once they'd gone a few yards, there was no way the boy would have been able to see them from where he was standing, so Chloe started jogging. The path ahead forked, with one way heading back towards the main buildings and the other leading towards the woods. Chloe chose the path back, but as they turned the corner to head up the hill, there was the boy again.

"Let's go this way for a change," Chloe said, turning around and heading down the other path towards the woods.

"Hey, wait up!" Ray said. In his mind, he was walking after her, but in reality, he was struggling to turn the wheelchair around.

"Hurry up! How do you expect them to let you go home when you're so slow!" Chloe was trying to sound relaxed, but inside she was panicking. She trotted on down the path, trying to open up a psychic link to Bess, but it was as if she didn't exist. That was weird! Ever since that night in the summer, she'd been able to speak to Bess anytime, anywhere. This did not improve Chloe's state of anxiety. She turned back to encourage Ray to shift it and there was the boy, standing at the fork in the path, watching them. Chloe jogged on, with a,

"Come on Ray!" that was fraying with panic.

"I'm doing my best," he replied as the path turned down the hill. Once they were around the corner, a sunny lawn opened up on their left and the path ran around the bottom of it before circling back up the hill on the far side. Beyond the path, the woodland looked cool and dark despite the warm sunshine.

Once they were halfway around the bottom of the lawn, Chloe looked back to see exactly what she'd feared. The boy had just come around the top corner of the area and now there was nowhere to hide. Then the boy started to jog towards them with his arms held loosely at his sides. Chloe had to think fast. The boy wanted something from her, not Ray, so she'd take him out of the equation. As he pulled up next to her, he said,

"Why are we stopping?"

Chloe put her hand on his forehead and said,

"Sleep."

Ray immediately fell into a dreamless sleep and Chloe turned to sprint into the woods. She zig-zagged through the mix of oaks and beeches, then ducked behind a big oak. She flattened herself against it and tried to regulate her breathing as she listened for the sound of feet running through the underbrush.

There was nothing. Not the rustle of someone running, not the sound of birds singing, not even the whisper of breeze through the trees. As a city kid, even she knew that wasn't normal. The hairs on her exposed arms stood up and she felt a crawling sensation in her stomach. She was a long way from anyone and now she'd been chased into the dark woods. She didn't even have Bess to talk to. What should she do?

"You should be scared."

The quiet voice came from right behind her and Chloe leapt away from the tree as if she'd been stung. The boy was there and he put his fingers to his lips, then whispered,

"Be quiet. We don't want it to hear us."

Chloe froze but, as the boy approached, her mind was whirling through a hundred different courses of action.

"Sorry I chased you. I'm Billy. I need help," he whispered.

She looked at him carefully. Now he was up close, he looked more scared than dangerous, although there was still something about the way he held himself that she didn't trust. And the closer he came, the colder it got.

"What's wrong?" Chloe whispered back.

"There's a thing and it's in here with me and it says nasty things and it hurts me. And now a shouty man has come to my house and he's making the thing angry and it's hurting me more."

"Where are you from?"

"Leicester," and then he recited his home address with great pride that he could remember it.

"What's the thing?" Chloe whispered.

"I can't see it, but I know it's here. It throws me down a dark hole and makes me watch it do things with my body. I killed next door's cat. I bit through its neck. And it's always telling me it's going to eat my soul," and the boy looked like he was about to cry.

"It's all right, Billy. I know people who'll help. How did you get here?"

"I was running in the dark. I was trying to get away from it and the shouty man, but I couldn't see anything. Then I saw a light and ran to it and the light was you."

"Okay, Billy, I'll see if I can contact people to help us," Chloe said and then she concentrated hard to try to talk to Bess. No, still nothing. What was wrong? Then she thought of Oliver – if anybody knew what was happening, it would be him, but before she could make contact, the boy cried out,

"It's coming!" and he had a wild look in his eyes, "Run!"

Chloe took a step back, but Billy's hand shot out and grabbed her wrist. His hand was painfully cold.

"Stop!" Billy said, but now his voice was metallic, "Let me look at you..." and eyes that were no longer those of a young boy bored into her,

"Yes, you are preferable to this whelp. He has little power, but you... I could use *you* to hunt down men," Billy's face smiled at the thought of the chase and the ultimate cruelty he could inflict.

Chloe tried to pull her arm away, but the boy held her tight,

"There is a shaman here who is trying to rid the boy of me – he is a fool. He thinks his feeble magic has control over me! I am ancient! The spirit of the hunt! This 'Jesus' the shaman invokes cannot command me! And now I have found you, I can be free of the spell that entrapped me." Billy held Chloe's arm firmly, but instead of struggling, she immediately concentrated all her thought on saying the words of an incantation that Bess's friend Jo had taught her. Billy's face became vicious with anger,

"Cease your prattling, child! You cannot resist me!"

"Watch me!" Chloe hissed, then she spoke the words of a banishing spell.

"No! You little... I will make the boy suffer for your insolence. And when I have finished with him, I shall come for you!"

Chloe wasn't listening. She was repeating the words with all the strength she could muster. Then, as she shouted the last word, Billy vanished. Chloe slumped onto the leafy floor of the woodland with her chest heaving and sweat pouring down her face. Her heart was hammering inside her and she felt dizzy. She lay for a few moments with her eyes closed. Then she heard the screaming.

"Ray!" she gasped and she was up and running.

Fighting the thing in the boy had taken every ounce of her power and concentration, which meant that her father had been plunged back into real life. When she got back to the path where she'd left him, she found Ray had thrown himself out of his chair and was dragging himself across the grass, swearing, screaming and crying. Chloe put her hands to the sides of her head in horror. She hadn't allowed him to be like this since the night Krowos had attacked them. She'd forgotten how terrified he was without her. Crying, she ran over to him and placed her hands on his head,

"Peace!" she said firmly and Ray immediately stopped screaming,

"Oh, hey, Chloe. What are we doing out here on the grass?" he asked as if nothing had happened.

"I wanted to lie down and look at the passing clouds," she replied, wiping the tears from her eyes.

"Well get down here and let's do some cloud gazing," Ray said, then he turned to face the sky and enjoyed the warm sunshine as he put his hands behind his head.

Chloe lay down next to him and snuggled up to him.

"I love you," she said.

"I love you, too, beautiful girl," he said, kissing the top of her head, then he pointed at a cloud,

"Look, that one's just like a dog with floppy ears!"

After lunch, Chloe and Ray got comfy on the sofa in their room in front of The Lion King with a box of fresh popcorn.

"It's okay," Ray said conspiratorially, "It counts as one of your five-a-day."

Although Chloe was pretty sure it didn't, she helped herself to a handful. Then she started the DVD and, once she was sure Ray was happy, she stared through the TV and made contact with Oliver,

"Hi, Chloe, how are you doing today? Out enjoying the sun?" Oliver's voice sounded warm and soothing inside her head,

"I'm all right," she replied with her thoughts, "But there's something weird here today," and she told him about not being able to contact Bess, and about the little boy in the striped pyjamas.

"Okay," Oliver replied when she'd finished, "The reason you can't contact Ms Russell is because she's on the Isle of Wight. It always interferes with her abilities. I haven't spoken to her directly since she got there. The only way I can do it is by phone,"

"I bet she hates that!" even Chloe knew Bess couldn't stand telephones.

"It's driving her crazy!" and Chloe could feel the smile in Oliver's thoughts,

"As for your little boy..." and Oliver thought carefully, then asked,

"You said he's from Leicester?"

"Yeah,"

"Do you know his address?"

Chloe recited it back to him,

"Mystery solved," Oliver said proudly, "That is Billy Tanner. He is one of a number of cases of demonic possession that are related to Ms Russell's latest mission. And I think I know who the shouty man is,"

"Who?"

"That is Bishop FitzOsbern, who is an incredibly shouty man and who's currently up in Leicester trying to exorcise the demon from little Billy."

"It isn't working," Chloe said firmly, "Billy told me that it's only making the demon angrier and then it's hurting him. It says if the shouty man doesn't stop, it will eat Billy's soul."

"Right..." Oliver wasn't surprised that FitzOsbern was making a hash of it, "I've got Jo getting ready to go up there and sort things out..."

"No. I need to go," said Chloe, "Billy said he was running in the darkness until he found me. I'm his beacon of light. I must help him."

"I don't know if that's such a good idea, Chloe. You're very young and the demon is powerful. It would be better if Jo did it."

"Is she good at getting demons out of people?"

"Er..." Oliver wasn't sure what to say.

"She's only done it twice and she didn't enjoy it," Chloe was stating fact. She had seen it in Oliver's mind without even needing to look for it.

"Wow! That's impressive!" Oliver knew how hard it could be to read someone's thoughts at a distance.

"I'm sorry. I didn't mean to see your thought. It came to me."

"That's okay. And yes, of course you're right – she hates doing exorcisms. But even so, she's got a lot of experience in dealing with entities..."

"How about this," and Chloe sounded excited, "Why doesn't Jo come here and keep Ray calm and happy? She's so warm and kind. It's just what she'd love to do. And then you can take me up to Leicester and we can save Billy together. Bess won't mind."

Yes, Oliver's first thought was to wonder what his boss would think. How would she react if she found out that Oliver had sent a seven-year-old to exorcise a demon?

"You know it's the best thing to do," again, Chloe was stating fact – that was how Oliver felt, "And yes, I'm going to have to learn to control my mind reading skills," Chloe added.

Oliver couldn't help but laugh – she was reading him like a book. Of course, he could shut her out...

"But what would be the point of that?" Chloe finished his thought.

"Okay, you got me! I can't take any more," Oliver laughed, "I'll come and pick you up tomorrow and, yes, Jo will be relieved," he had read Chloe's thoughts and her worries about Jo's feelings,

"Oh! That is a bit weird, isn't it?" Chloe hadn't had anyone read her thoughts before.

"Yes, this is exactly how Andy feels when you do it to him," Oliver added, having seen that thought pop into her mind.

"Freaky!" Chloe squealed.

"It's all right, you'll get control of it soon. So, I'll contact Jo and reassign her to your dad. We'll be with you by eleven tomorrow morning... but only if you're sure – exorcisms can be very unpleasant and dangerous."

"I've got to do it. Just like I've got to look after Ray."

"Okay, we'll see you in the morning. And if Billy visits you again, let me know."

"Okay. Thanks for being there for me, Oliver,"

"My pleasure. Get a good night's sleep," Oliver replied and then he was gone.

Chloe reached out and took a handful of popcorn, then settled herself under Ray's left arm as Timon and Pumbaa launched into Hakuna Matata. 'No worries'. Sadly, Chloe wasn't the first seven-year-old to watch the scene and wish that they had no worries.

Chapter Twenty-Two

Godshill

While Chloe and Ray had been bathed in early Autumn sunshine, the fog on the Isle of Wight was keeping the island cocooned in an eerie twilight. When Andy and Bess stepped out of the hotel into the cool, swirling cloud, she said,

"Another glorious day on the Wight!"

"Is it really always like this when you're here?"

"Every time! Apart from the day when I arrive. When I get here, everything looks normal, but by the next morning, it's all foggy. There are some parts of The Island I've never seen properly."

They walked over to the replacement for the Ford Focus, which was another Ford Focus.

"Do you think you'll be able to keep it in one piece this time?" Bess asked as they got in.

"Depends on whether the rest of the scarecrows try to kill us," Andy replied, starting it up and pulling away into the bank of fog,

"If they leave us alone, I'd say there's an even chance I won't wreck it."

"I'm sure your confidence would warm the cockles of Superintendent Fletcher's heart," she said with a grin.

The drive up through St Helens and Brading was as murky and mysterious as on the previous days, but this time there was a difference.

"Wow! You really did a number on those scarecrows," Bess said, noticing that not one of the effigies that had been adorning either village was now on display.

"Bloody things!" Andy said with a shiver. He'd never look at a scarecrow the same way again. And, as they got to the other side of Brading, he was particularly pleased not to be faced by the ghastly musicians. All that was left to show they'd ever been in the front garden of one of the houses was a set of empty chairs and a music stand, where the conductor had once been placed. Good riddance! Andy took a right, and they were soon heading across country through high hedges until finally a pub hove into view.

"Ah, the Hare and Hounds! Not a bad pub," Bess said, "Greene King, so the beer's all right. I believe they've got the skull of the last man to be hanged on The Island somewhere in there. Bit of crime and punishment with your beer – should be right up your alley."

"Something to warm the cockles!" Andy smiled, then took the turn towards Merstone.

Within twenty minutes, they'd reached Godshill and parked up. It was chilly and the damp of the fog caught in Andy's chest as they walked along the main street. Even in the fog, the village had a chocolate-box beauty, with thatched houses at every turn. Well-tended front gardens and ancient walls tumbling with ivy and Virginia Creeper added to the feel of a place that passing time seemed to have missed. Andy was now getting used to having his stick and he carried it held up against his shoulder. Yesterday it had more than proved its worth, who knew what today might bring? Because they couldn't see the church on the hill, they had to follow signs to it, heading up a steep road and turning right.

"Wow! Now that's a postcard view!" Andy said as they got to the final approach to the church.

A steep driveway led up past a couple of big, thatched cottages, and a third cottage on the other side of the path at the top framed the entry into the churchyard beyond. Somewhere up there in the grey void stood the church.

"I don't like it," Elizabeth Russell replied.

"Too cutesy?"

"No, there's something off kilter here... dammit! If it wasn't for this Island messing with me, I'd be able to work out what the hell was wrong here!"

"Don't worry," Andy said, looking at her beautiful face, twisted with frustration, "We've got this."

"Well, if you put it like that... what are we waiting for?" and she strode up the hill.

As they got to the gap between the cottages, the square tower of the grey church loomed up out of the fog, and when they went through the gate, they entered a monochromatic world. There was the grey church, the grey headstones and the grey path winding through them. Even the grass, heavy with moisture, seemed grey in the dim light. As they walked to the entrance of the church, Bess was struck by how many of the gravestones were listing. They looked like they'd been randomly shoved in at any crazy angle.

"Must be movement on the hill," Andy said. He'd picked up on it, too.

"And these graves are all old," Bess replied. The lichen and faded words on the stones were testament to their antiquity.

"Probably generations of some families up here," Andy found it sobering that the graveyard probably saw the ending of more than one family line.

Bess squared her shoulders and put up the collar of her black trench coat, then walked away from the evidence of the inevitability of death and into the house of the life everlasting.

Like most old, English country churches, it was cold inside. The grey, flagstone floor, white-painted walls and stone arches offered little insulation. Above them, the vaulted ceiling showed off exposed wooden beams. The pews, pulpit and altar were understated, and few of the windows were of stained glass. Most of the colour was provided by the statues that were dotted around the church and the gold-coloured pipes of the organ. Almost straight ahead of them as they entered, a statue of the Virgin Mary looked down on them benevolently. On a crossbeam above them to their right, the crucified Jesus was flanked by two figures, whom Andy presumed were Mary Magdalene and the Virgin Mary. The overall impression was of a simple place of worship, created in the knowledge that no adornment devised by man could ever rival the divine.

"Don't be fooled," said Andy.

"By what?" Bess looked confused.

"By all this simplicity. Follow me," and he led her towards the altar and to an area on one side of the church that had been closed off with iron gates,

"See that on the wall?" and he pointed to a faded image on the wall of Jesus crucified on a lily branch,

"That would have been typical of the sort of thing that was painted all over the walls of this church – until the puritans had them all scrubbed off and painted over. They think this was saved by being hidden by the locals before the other paintings were scrubbed off."

"You really deep dived that history book, then," Bess smiled.

"I love a bit of history. And as far as I've read, this is the only surviving example of a lily cross in England. It signifies those days when Good Friday falls on the same day as the Feast of the Annunciation."

Bess looked at Andy with a raised eyebrow,

"Don't tell me you went to Sunday school."

"Oh, it's much worse than that – I was in the church choir from age seven. And it was very high church of England. You know, more Catholic than the Catholics..."

"Bells and smells?"

"Exactly. I did six years going to church three times a week. Ironically, a lot of it stuck - except the God bit."

Bess grinned. She was struggling to imagine the great hulking ex-copper as an angelic little chorister.

"I bet you looked divine in your cassock and rough," she said.

"Don't start!" he blushed at the thought of the photo of him in full regalia that still graced his mother's bedside table. Yes, that was one thing he hoped Bess would never see.

"You're certainly right about one thing," she said, "Looks can be deceptive."

"How?"

"I can feel conflicting presences here. This is a holy place of worship. I can feel the light... but there's something else. Something darker. And it's right here, but it isn't here. Am I making any sense at all?" her inability to be able to pinpoint things as she usually did was getting to her.

"Yeah, it makes sense. Remember, they weren't originally going to build the church here, because this hill had been used for pagan rituals. It was only after the nonsense of the stones being moved up and down the hill that they decided to build it up here. Maybe you're getting some residual feeling from that?"

"How long ago was it again?"

"I think you've got to go back to the seven hundreds for the last time this place was used for pagan worship," Andy replied.

"No, it's not that. What I'm feeling is happening now," and Bess started to walk around the whole of the church, trying to find the source of the conflict. Given the effects of the Swaailen and the proximity of the Other Place, this wasn't easy.

After nearly ten minutes of going from one part of the church to another like a sniffer dog with a heavy cold, Bess ended up right in the middle of the church, halfway between the altar at one end and the organ at the other.

"It's here. The conflict's right here..." she said, standing in one spot and turning all around,

"And yet, it's not here at all."

"Maybe there's a crypt beneath us?" Andy suggested.

"We haven't seen any signs of one... Oh, hang on! Why am I being so thick? Come on!" and she marched out of the church with Andy following her. Once they were in the churchyard, she turned and said,

"Apart from this stupid fog, what do you see?"

Andy puffed out his cheeks,

"Er... I dunno... some trees... a lot of old gravestones..."

"And what are they doing?"

"A lot of them look like they're falling over..."

"Exactly!" she cried, snapping her fingers, "You said there must be movement on the hill. What if it's not on the hill, but under it?"

"You think someone's been tunnelling under the churchyard?"

"And under the church."

"Why?"

"Because when the Christians took over the island, the pagans had to go underground. And here, I think they've done it literally. Okay, so we need to find how they're getting in there."

"That might not be easy. For all we know, the access point could be in the back garden of any of the houses around the churchyard," Andy replied.

"True, but let's exhaust the options in here before we go digging up people's rose beds."

Andy could tell by the look on her face that she wouldn't think twice about doing it.

"Okay," he said and then they got to it.

They scoured the grounds, looking at every grave marker there was. Although most of these were simple headstones, there were also graves marked with kerbs set into the ground around where the body would be. Some were plain, others had railings set into them. There were also low stone monuments some of which were flat, while others had gable tops. None of these looked as though they were being used as entrances to a subterranean passage.

"Maybe these chest tombs are a better bet," Elizabeth Russell said, pointing out a series of parallel tombs that were shaped like large chests. They took a good look all around them, but there were no signs that the grass was worn or that anything had been moved. Andy put his weight against the top of each one, but there was no play in any of them.

"Maybe it's that one with the railing around it," he suggested, pointing up the hill at another chest tomb. Annoyingly, closer inspection revealed nothing. Nearby, a cube pedestal with a fat obelisk on the top beckoned, but again there were no signs of any use.

"Should we split up to cover more..." Andy began, but Bess cut him off with a firm,

"Absolutely not! Firstly, because it's called safety in numbers for a reason, and secondly, because after destroying a car and a boat yesterday I'm not risking you blowing up the fourteenth century church the minute my back's turned."

"I'm never going to live that down, am I?"

"Never! Now come on, let's try the other side of the church."

They walked around the western end of the church and found more of the same. It was only when they'd worked their way around to the end of the church where the altar was that Andy spotted something interesting.

"See that old mausoleum over there?"

Bess looked across at the smallish mausoleum and nodded.

"Anything about it seem odd to you?"

Bess walked towards it across the dank grass, taking it in. It looked very old and, like so much in the churchyard, was listing somewhat. It was made of the same grey stone as the church and was built in the Gothic style. Yes, that was interesting...

"It's proper Gothic, not Gothic revival. So, it must be about the same age as the church. Might even pre-date this version," she said.

Andy nodded.

Bess looked at the black iron gates across the front of it and then she laughed.

"Got it?" Andy asked.

"Yeah. Medieval mausoleum, eighteenth or nineteenth century iron gates... brand, spanking new twenty-first century lock on them."

"Exactly!" said Andy with a grin.

The mausoleum was tucked away on the north-east side of the churchyard slightly down the hill and next to a large yew tree.

"That's indicative," Bess said, pointing to the yew,

"The yew's a magical tree. Very powerful... and looking at this one, I'd say it's the oldest thing here."

"And look how the grass is worn away around the entrance. Do you think that's all been done by tourists?" Andy asked.

"No," Bess replied.

Now they were up close and could see that the gates gave access to three steps down to the stone door of the mausoleum.

"Think you can open that padlock?" she asked.

"Reckon so," Andy smiled and pulled a set of lock picking tools from his coat pocket. Then, while Elizabeth Russell kept a watchful eye on the churchyard around them, Andy got to work on the lock. After a couple of minutes and only a small amount of swearing, there was a sharp click.

"Got it," Andy said, then opened the iron gate, "I would say 'ladies first', but in this situation I'm not sure it's appropriate," and he stepped down to the stone door.

The door had no lock and, once Andy had applied his shoulder to it and given it a good shove, it opened with the sound of stone grinding against stone.

"I'd better go first," Bess said, putting on the head torch she used for hunting vampires, "Give me the sword stick," she added.

Andy did so, then pulled the iron gates to and locked them in with the padlock,

"This'll make it harder for anyone to follow us in," he said, slipping the knuckle duster onto his left hand. Then he took out his Glock and a small torch.

"Push the door shut behind us," she said and led the way into the mausoleum. It wasn't a large space, and Andy was almost brushing the ceiling with the top of his head. Three stone tombs were set into recesses in the walls, while a large chest tomb dominated the centre of the space. They checked over the three tombs set into the walls first, so it was inevitable that the access to the tunnel below was under the chest tomb in the middle of the room.

"Always the last place you look," Andy muttered as he pushed the lid of the tomb aside. It was hinged and opened to reveal an empty tomb with an open manhole in its centre. A metal ladder led downwards and their torches revealed that it was about ten or fifteen feet before there was a passage below.

The smell of dank earth rose up from the hole and Elizabeth Russell took a deep breath of it.

"Well?" Andy asked.

"I can't smell vampires... but it might be worth texting Dan to let him know where we are, just in case things go south."

"You want me to text him now? *After* I've shut us into the stone building?"

"Yeah, what's the problem?"

"All this affects the signal... you know what, forget it," her blank look told Andy that if he said anything vaguely technical it would be meaningless to her. Remarkably, he did have a single bar on his phone, so he sent the text and copied in Roddy.

"Here we go... if it is vampires, aim for the head or the heart. Your bullets won't kill them, but it'll be like shoving a hornet in their shirt. Your knuckle duster will do them serious damage, and your silver knife to the heart will incapacitate them. Okay?" she searched Andy's face. It was set with grim determination,

"Let's do it," he said, then followed Bess down the hole.

The tunnel below was rough, with yew roots poking out through the walls here and there. It was cold and the smell of earth was overpowering as they crouched in the space that was barely five feet high.

"Still not very vampire-y," Bess said with relief. She'd had a bellyful of the blood-sucking buggers over the years and would be quite happy never to meet another one again.

She led them along the passage, which turned to the right. After a few yards, it turned again and the next stretch had a new tunnel branching off to the right halfway down it. Which way to go? Andy crouched and started scanning the floor with his torch,

"I reckon straight on – there are more footprints going this way than down there."

Bess liked that. Usually, she used her instincts and psychic powers to pick up on where she needed to go, but they were all on the fritz. Andy's talents of observation and understanding people were exactly what she needed. She patted his shoulder,

"Good call, come on..." and they followed the main tunnel. Three more branch tunnels joined it and at all of them, Andy was able to point them in the most used direction.

It was at the last of these junctions that Andy realised what had been bothering him about the tracks,

"It's children that come down here – all these footprints are small. Look..." and he shone his torch on one perfect shoe print, "Whoever left that can't be more than about eight or nine," then he looked up at Bess,

"Why would children be coming down here?"

"Not the first clue."

"They might have found a way in and come down here as a dare. Who knows, they might even have a den down here," Andy thought out loud.

Bess wasn't so sure. In her experience, children rarely went willingly down tunnels like these.

They continued on their way until, after a few more minutes, the tunnel entered a large, round space with a high enough roof for them to stand up in. A quick look around showed that this was definitely not a kids' den.

"Tell me that's not a pig's head," Andy said as his torch picked out something on the far side of the room that had been set on a stone table.

"Sorry, but that is a pig's head," Elizabeth Russell said as she approached, "And it's set on an altar."

Andy joined her and now their torches revealed pictures all around the head. They'd been drawn by children, some in pencil, some painted and some very crude ones in crayon. All of them showed a man in a grey hooded cloak doing lots of different things, but with one similarity – he was always playing tricks. In one, he was tripping up a teacher, who was falling face first towards a big pile of dog doings; in another, he had shaved the hair off half of a woman's head, while a little girl stood nearby with a speech bubble that read 'Mummy won't shout at me ever again!!!!'.

"Oh, this one's not good," said Bess, holding up a drawing of a car driving off a cliff while the man in the hood was watching and holding something that looked like a car part in his hand.

"Do you think these are what they want to happen, or..." Andy didn't like to entertain the notion that everything in the pictures had come to pass.

"Not sure," Bess replied, sifting through the collection of childish offerings that had been placed on or around the altar. There were packets of sweets and biscuits, toys and small items that had clearly been taken from their parents or older siblings. She looked up and, along a crude shelf cut into the earth above the altar, there was a collection of twig people.

"Well, thank goodness that's not creepy," she said.

"Where the hell did they get the pig's head?" Andy asked.

"Might've been brought by an adult... and it's fresh. Probably put here yesterday," Bess replied.

She stood away from the altar and trained her torch onto the middle of the floor,

"Uh-oh!" she said.

A perfectly detailed circle of Solomon had been laid out on the earth floor using pebbles that had presumably been picked up from beaches around the island.

"We must be right under the middle of the church," Bess said, "This is exactly why I was feeling that conflict. Up there you've got Jesus being crucified to save us all from sin and down here the most powerful magic circle of them all. The circle that King Solomon himself supposedly used to conjure and trap demons."

"Do you think the kids have been conjuring demons down here?" Andy couldn't believe it.

"No, but I'm sure somebody has been – most likely, the figure in the hooded cloak. I bet he's done it to show his power to the children. And I bet that some of the things in those drawings have happened."

"You think Attrill is the man in the cloak?" Andy asked.

"No,"

"You think Downer's been doing this?"

"No, Attrill is definitely the one in the cloak... but he isn't a man."

Chapter Twenty-Three

The Winning Trick

Roddy felt Thomas Attrill's arrival even before he entered the hotel. Standing behind the reception desk, he felt a sudden rise in the pressure of the air on his eardrums and a sense of oppression around him. Then the tall figure of Thomas Attrill strode into the great entrance hall.

"Ah, Mister Attrill, isn't it?" Roddy said as the gangly man approached him.

"Yes. I've seen you around," Attrill replied, "But never been introduced, mister...?"

"Call me Roddy."

"All right, I shall. Well, I must say, you've got a lovely place here, Roddy," Attrill said, stopping in the middle of the hall with his hands on his hips and taking it all in.

"Thank you," Roddy replied with a smile, but beneath the smile, he was coiling himself – something was wrong...

"So, how can I help you today?"

"You can die," Attrill said casually and, with a flick of his wrist a knife flew at Roddy's chest.

Roddy turned his body just in time and the knife planted itself into the panelling behind him. Before Attrill could attack again, Roddy reached out towards the crackling fire in the hearth and swept his hand at Attrill. A sheet of flame flared out from the hearth and Attrill leapt backwards to avoid it.

"Clever!" he said, patting out a small flame on the arm of his jacket. So, the former witch still had some considerable power... yes, he would have to be careful with this one. Attrill didn't want to expend too much precious energy on spells, because there was only one spell he wanted to cast that day. No, he'd have to be clever and draw the man out into a more traditional fight.

"Come out, come out, wherever you are," Attrill said, before running across the room and vaulting the reception desk. He was expecting to see Roddy crouched behind it, but he was nowhere to be seen.

"Oh, that's good," Attrill said, looking about the room for Roddy, "Yes, that's very good, but you can't hide forever," and he pulled his knife from where it had stuck into the wood panelling,

"I have a spell or two up my sleeve, which I think you will find impossible to resist."

From his vantage point near the top of the stairs, Roddy watched Attrill come out from behind the reception desk. Roddy had used an incantation to make him phase through space from behind the counter to the top of the stairs. Now he would use the same spell to catch Attrill out and end this quickly. Roddy watched and waited until his quarry had got into the perfect position and then he spoke the words of power. In an instant, Roddy had phased down into the hall and, before his opponent even knew what was happening, he'd swung his silver hook into the side of Attrill's neck. Attrill made an 'Oof' sound as Roddy withdrew the hook, then staggered backwards with a surprised look on his face as arterial blood jetted from the side of his neck. He stumbled and fell backwards onto the floor in front of the fire.

"Stitch that, you stuck-up bastard!" Roddy said and walked over to watch Attrill cough out his life blood as he lay on the hard flagstones.

***

"What do you mean he's not a man?" Andy couldn't follow what Bess was trying to say about Attrill.

"Just that. He's not a man," Bess replied, "You see, that's been one of the strange things about this case from the start – how could a man conjure, control and trap not just one, but half a dozen demons? And trap them with such power and subtlety as Attrill did. I've never heard of anyone doing anything like that before. No human has ever been powerful enough to do that. Therefore, the likelihood is, Attrill isn't human. If you want my opinion, he's what most people would call a god."

"No... what?" Andy couldn't believe it.

"Seriously, look around you – this is a shrine to a deity," Bess said, pointing at the simple altar dug out of the earth, "Look at the offerings they've given him. And unlike the god upstairs, this one actually does things. This one will play tricks on your enemies. And all he asks in return is belief and worship."

"But that doesn't mean he's a genuine god," Andy argued.

Bess smiled and shook her head,

"Gods and demons are just beings from other dimensions that have found a way into our world and have exploited human gullibility down the ages for their own ends. And if, along the way, people have credited them with creating the universe, they're hardly going to deny it. That's all a god is."

"Really?" Andy was disappointed.

"'Fraid so," Bess replied, "Mister Attrill could well be a god... and it makes sense in a way – that illusion he tricked us with was next level. Maybe if I hadn't been here with this fog fouling me up, I might have spotted it, but I doubt it. That is skill honed over a very long time. These creatures that get themselves into our world from the Great Beyond can live here thousands of years – even tens of thousands. Plenty of time to learn a trick or two."

"Hang on," said Andy, "I thought you said that he must be losing his powers. How can that happen if he's a god?"

"Because spirit is eternal, but ego isn't. The idea that when people die their souls go on forever with their personality experiencing the universe around them, just isn't true. Imagine going on and on forever as you. The likelihood is that after a few thousand years, you'd start getting bored - let alone after a few million years, or a few billion."

"I dunno, I could take up a hobby," Andy said,

"Yeah, like trashing cars and expensive boats," Bess raised an eyebrow. Yes, she wasn't going to let him live that down,

"The reality is that when people die, they pass into the Great Beyond and after a while, their souls get re-absorbed into the fabric of the universe. If they are good, they become part of the light, if they are evil, they become part of the churning mass of darkness. How long they stick around with their personality and ego depends on the will of the person, the circumstances of their death and a thousand other things. But that's just us. Out there in the Great Beyond, in the spaces between spaces, in other universes and the gaps in between, there are plenty of things that live a very, very long time."

"And Attrill's one of them..."

"Yes. I think he somehow worked his way into our world and has been here so long that he's finally starting to fade. Maybe this conjuring of other entities and trapping them in objects is some big final trick? Some grand flourish so that he goes out with a bang, not a whimper. I don't know... but he clearly can't trust his own powers."

"So, what do we do now?" Andy asked.

"Now we've got to tread very carefully. Attrill's abilities probably make mine look like the fumblings of a novice," and in the light of the torches, her face looked drawn with disquiet,

"We've got to put our heads together with Roddy and Dan. I might even need some re-enforcements from the mainland. Even at my best I've never gone toe to toe with a god. And right now, I'm not at my best. I must say, it's making my tummy get a bit watery! But first things first..." and she stood back from the circle on the floor,

"Gods draw power from belief, so we need to put a stop to this little set-up," and with that, she closed her eyes and held out her hand towards the magic circle. She recited a long incantation and, as she finished, all the stones dislodged themselves from the floor and rose up into the air a couple of feet. With a flick of her wrist, most of them shot across the room and buried themselves in the earth wall. However, a good number remained suspended in the air. Andy wanted to ask why, but worried that something might go wrong if he started talking. With another flick of her wrist, the rest of the stones flew across the room to embed themselves in the earth wall above the altar.

Andy shone his torch beam at the place they'd landed and said,

"That's a bit childish,"

The stones had embedded themselves to spell the words 'Fuck you, Attrill'.

"I think that about sums it up. Now, let's get out of here and I'll tidy things up as we go – give me some help here," she said as she scuffed the earth floor where the magic circle had been. Andy followed suit and, in a minute, there were no traces left of the magical symbols that had been dented into the floor by the pebbles.

"Good! And now those offerings can get knotted," and she took the pig's head on its platter and placed it where the centre of the circle had been. Then she swept up all the drawings, stick people, sweets and biscuits into her arms and dumped them around the pig's head.

"Right, I'll just close that other entrance..." and she pointed to another tunnel that entered the chamber in the corner opposite the entrance they'd used. She said a short incantation and then threw her hand downwards. The roof of the tunnel where it joined the chamber instantly collapsed so that the entrance was blocked. She took a lighter from her jacket pocket and put the flame to the paper and other offerings. Standing back from the flames, she held her hands out before her as if she was holding a ball of dough, and said an incantation in a language Andy didn't recognise. The flames intensified and the smell of roasting pork began to fill the room.

"Lovely! That should stop the darling children from enabling Attrill. Let's go!" Bess cried as the flames crackled away in the middle of the room. Once they were in the passage and a few yards clear, she stopped and pointed at the entrance to the chamber, repeated the incantation and at a wave of her hand the entrance collapsed.

"If I were being thorough," she said, "I'd collapse all the tunnels, not just the junctions, but I reckon if I did that, half the gravestones in the churchyard would be swallowed up."

"Collapsing the junctions should be enough to put off kids," Andy replied, working his way along the passage. As they followed their trail back to the mausoleum, Elizabeth Russell stopped to close off every branch passage,

"Clever of Attrill to get the kids onside," she said after she closed off the last one, "The belief of children can be very powerful. But it must annoy him to have to do it underground like this."

"Too right," Andy replied, "This crouching's doing my back in and he's taller than me."

Finally – thankfully – they got to the ladder and climbed up out of the tunnel. Then, before Andy closed the lid on the chest tomb, Bess collapsed the roof at the entrance to the tunnel. When they got out of the mausoleum and closed the stone door behind them, she stood and said the words of another spell.

"That should keep the little herberts out of there," she smiled and, just to really annoy Attrill's worshippers, once they were out and Andy had padlocked the iron gates shut, she took a tube of superglue from her coat and applied it to the opening of the barrel of the lock and around the points where the shackle joined the body of the padlock.

"No spell?" Andy asked.

"Sometimes it's easier to use glue," she replied, pocketing the tube, "You got any signal on your infernal device?"

"Yes, catch it while you can."

"Text Roddy and Dan. Tell them to meet us back at the hotel around six. We've got to get planning," she said, striding across the churchyard towards the exit.

Andy did as she asked and, as they walked back to the car, she expanded on the idea of Attrill being a god,

"For all we know, Attrill might have been worshipped there for thousands of years... oh, but no. No, that can't be possible..."

"Why not?"

"Because the original gods of the Isle of Wight have gone to the Other Place. Hmmm... but maybe... no, it couldn't be that, surely? But then again, maybe it really is that simple?"

Andy sighed. When Ray had been his boss, he had done this sort of externalisation of his internal monologue, too. And he often hadn't made much sense either.

"You going to share your workings?" he asked, when they got to the car.

"Hmmm? Oh, yes – sorry! In a world of my own... okay," she said, getting in,

"When Britain was invaded by the Angles, the Saxons and the Jutes from the early four-hundreds onwards, they brought their gods with them... we're going back to the hotel, by the way,"

"All right," Andy said, starting the car and pulling out of the car park,

"And while the Saxons and the Angles merrily took over the south and east of England, it was the Jutes that came to the Isle of Wight. They displaced the Romano-Britons..."

"By killing most of them," Andy interjected,

"Yes, and they brought their gods with them. And if Attrill's one of those gods, then that hill might have been his place of worship since four hundred and fifty AD."

"Until the Saxons arrived in six-eighty-six, as Roddy told us, and massacred most of the Jutes to replace their gods with Christianity," Andy said.

"Yes, I always think that massacring the locals is the best way to preach the gospel of peace and love," Bess smiled thinly,

"But in this case they might have missed our Mister Attrill, who's been ploughing his lonely furrow ever since as the last pagan god on the Isle of Wight..." at this point, Bess trailed off and looked around them,

"Hang on, where are we?"

"On the road back to the Hare and Hounds," Andy replied.

"It's funny, we've been going uphill quite a long time, but I don't remember going down such a long hill on the way in," Bess said and, now she mentioned it, Andy had to admit that nothing seemed familiar. He glanced over at the sat nav.

"The car thinks we're somewhere between Merstone and the Hare and Hounds."

"The car's wrong," Bess said as they came around a right-hand curve and the road steepened sharply, "We never went down anything this steep. It's this stupid, bloody fog! Makes it impossible to work out where you are."

"Yeah, but the fog shouldn't be affecting the sat nav," Andy didn't like the creeping sensation he was getting up his spine. On the way to Godshill, despite the fog, he'd been able to see that they'd driven through fields of crops. There had been farmhouses, hedges, signs of human activity, but looking out of the car now, there were no hedges. The sides of the road were grassy with the occasional gorse bush or tangle of bramble, but otherwise nothing. There was no sign of human interference. And the higher they went, the denser the fog became, so that soon they could barely see ten feet either side of the road.

"I don't like this," he said.

"Me neither... stop!" Bess pointed excitedly at something near the roadside.

Andy braked and Bess hopped out of the car. Andy turned it off and got out, too. Leaning on the roof of the car, he watched as Bess ran over to a bush.

"What the hell?" she exclaimed.

"What is it?" Andy called. Bess looked up from the thing she'd been investigating and then returned to the car, staring into the fog all around them as she came. Andy strained to see what she was looking for, but could only see the fog rolling in and thicker curls of cloud blowing across the road with the scent of the sea in its folds.

"Well?" Andy said as she got back.

"Into the car, quick!"

Andy didn't hesitate to do it.

"Drive straight on. There should be a turning point up ahead. Turn around and get us off this hill."

He followed the instruction and, when they were moving, he asked,

"What's the problem?"

"We're on Saint Boniface Down."

"And why's that a problem?" Andy asked as he turned the car around in an area of rough gravel at the side of the road.

"Because we left Godshill heading north, and Saint Boniface Down is on the south side of the Island right above Bonchurch and Ventnor."

"Maybe I took a wrong turn?" Andy said, peering through the fog to see which way the road was heading.

"No, you'd have to take about twenty wrong turns to end up on this Down coming from Godshill. Plus, the only way to get up here by car is by going through the northern part of Ventnor first."

"But we haven't been through a town."

"Exactly!" she replied and for the first time, Andy saw Bess look unnerved,

"You see, the Swaailen isn't just fog. It has its own enchantments," she explained, "When the Swaailen rolls in, they say that the hills on The Island move."

"Hills can't move!" Andy snorted, "That's just prattle from ignorant locals getting lost in the fog," the rationality of his old life was kicking back at the deluge of magic and mystery.

"I wish! The reality is, we were driving north and now we're on a hill that's usually three miles south of Godshill. And the sat nav says we're north of Godshill right now."

Andy said nothing. His mind was trying to cope with the insanity of it all. Hills that moved! It was crazy! And yet, she was right. She had known where the turning space was and the sat nav was merrily showing their position north of Godshill.

"That's why we need to get off this hill," she said, "Before we turn a corner and find ourselves plunging off a cliff into the sea."

"Okay, I'll be very careful," Andy said, changing into second gear to control them as they went down the steepest part of the slope. They could only see twenty feet in front of them and the swirling grey of the fog was starting to play tricks with his vision.

"The question is, what's happening elsewhere? Attrill is a god and we've been prodding at him like kids with a wasp's nest. While we're blundering about up here, what the hell's he up to?"

Now Andy had slowed to a crawl as the fog got thicker and thicker.

"Christ on a bike!" he cursed, staring at the smothering fog. For all he knew, the road really did stop at a cliff thirty feet ahead of them. And now another thought came to him. A thought of a mass of homicidal scarecrows with nightmarish, drawn-on faces emerging from the fog to kill them. They were isolated and vulnerable – it was the perfect moment for an attack. Andy flinched as a gorse bush loomed up out of the grey.

"Don't lose it! Stay frosty!" Bess said.

"You stay frosty!" Andy snapped back.

"Ha!" she exploded with laughter, "Yeah, don't take any shit from me."

"I won't, because you're just as scared as I am," he replied without taking his concentration off the road for a second.

"I am!" she laughed, "And I don't know why I'm laughing, because between you and me, I'm shit-scared!"

"Join the club," he said and he, too, was teetering on the brink of hysterical laughter,

"Fucking hills that move! You don't get this in south bloody London!" Andy couldn't help laughing at the absurdity.

And now they were both laughing in spite of the enclosing fog, the possibility of sudden death and the myriad terrors that their minds were conjuring. They were laughing so much that when the slope started to lessen, neither of them noticed it. It was only when it started levelling out that they realised there were hedges around them again.

"Thank the Lord for that!" Bess sighed, regaining control of herself, "I thought we were going to be stuck up there forever."

"I wonder where we are now?" Andy was having trouble orienting himself.

The road, which had been two lanes was now a single track with passing places.

"Could be almost anywhere on The Island," Bess said, peering into the fog, but it was still too thick to give her any idea about the lie of the land. All she had to go on was that the road had a lot of twists and turns and was going over rolling countryside. It was only when a red brick building loomed up on their left with a sign which read 'We Love Yurts' that she exclaimed,

"I've got it! We're on Burnt House Road about halfway between Newport and the Hare and Hounds. I remember that sign... which means we're currently a few miles northwest of Godshill."

"But the hill we were just on is usually three miles south of it?"

"Yeah... I tell you, I've seen some weird stuff, but there's nothing quite like the Swaailen to give me the heebie-jeebies. It is freaky!" she said, then rested her head back on the seat and sighed deeply. At least they were sa...

"Shit!" Andy cried as they rounded a corner to find a man standing in the middle of the road. Andy slammed on the brakes but couldn't swerve because of the bank on one side and the hedge on the other. There was a thump as he caught the man just under the hips, then a bang and crack as he was thrown into the windscreen before tumbling over the top of the car.

"No!" Andy shouted as the car skidded to a halt, then he was scrambling out and running towards the broken figure on the road. From the angles of the legs and arms, Andy didn't need a doctor to tell him that the man he'd hit had multiple broken bones.

"Roddy!" Bess screamed, dashing over to the body, then she was gently raising the head and Roddy's heavily scarred face was looking up into hers.

"Don't worry," she said, "I can save you!" and she started to speak the words of an incantation, when Roddy whispered,

"You can't,"

"I can, you know I can. Now keep quiet."

"No," and he coughed up something reddish-black and treacly. She wiped it away with her sleeve,

"Oh no..." she said, and her voice was heavy with sorrow.

"I'm sorry," Andy said, standing slightly back with a shellshocked look on his face.

"It's alright... I'm already dead. Look down there," and Roddy's eyes flicked towards his chest. Bess gently pulled open his shirt, revealing multiple stab wounds,

"Attrill came around... I thought I'd killed him, but as you can see, I was very wrong."

"He re-animated you. Why?" although Bess thought she knew.

"It's a gag," Roddy whispered, "It's always a gag with Attrill. Wanted you to think you'd killed me. He's a trickster... but I've played a trick on him. Saw into his mind when I hooked him. I guess even gods have their lives flash before their eyes... that's what he is..."

"Yes, we just came from a shrine to him in Godshill."

"He's the one behind it all – Knighton, Godshill and Wolverton... all him and more, but listen..." Roddy coughed again and Bess could feel him fading, so she laid a hand on his forehead and concentrated all her power into keeping him conscious.

"There's something he fears in the well at Wolverton," Roddy said with his strength ebbing away, "He betrayed the town... all but one were massacred. The survivor discovered Urian's secret and hid it in the well, which he cursed, so it will always be hidden from *him*."

"Attrill?"

"Yes, Urian... Attrill... the hooded man... all the same. Find the well. He thinks it will be his undoing... I've got to go."

Elizabeth Russell had tears in her eyes as she whispered,

"I'm sorry I got you into this. You deserved a happy retirement."

"Don't worry. I'll make a nuisance of myself on the other side for a good while yet. Sorry I couldn't kill him."

"How were you to know he was a god?"

"He's not a god, he's... an... arsehole!" Roddy drew out the last words and then slumped backwards.

Elizabeth Russell held him in her arms for a few moments, then laid him flat and stood up. She flicked away her tears and, half-crying and half-laughing, she said,

"I wish I'd had a bet on Roddy's last word being 'arsehole'," then she went to Andy and fell into his arms. He held her tightly as her shoulders shook with her tears.

She felt it was all her fault, that if she'd been more on her game nothing would have happened to him. If anyone had deserved a few more years of life it was him, but she was sure he was right – he would make a nuisance of himself for a while in the Great Beyond. She gave Andy an extra hard squeeze and then broke off, wiping away her tears,

"Right, we'd better get moving. We've got a god to kill. But first, have you got a signal?"

Andy checked his phone and nodded,

"Text the word 'kumquat' to Dan."

"Kumquat?"

"Yes. That's the signal to drop everything and get out. It's bad enough Attrill killing Roddy, but Dan's got a young family. If anything happened to them, I'd never forgive myself."

"Done!" said Andy, "And should I call this in?"

Bess sighed,

"Yes... it's gonna take some explaining, mind you. And Fletch isn't going to be happy when he sees what you've done to the car."

"That weren't my fault, he materialised in front of us," Andy argued.

"You all right after that? Wasn't pleasant," and she fixed him with a keen eye.

"I'll be fine. Compared with everything else this week, running a man over is refreshingly ordinary... even if it turns out he was already dead."

"Good man!" and she winked at him. Then, as he put the car's hazard lights on and made the necessary phone calls, she took a travel rug out of the back of the car and laid it over Roddy. She looked down at the broken body of a man who'd been her friend for thirty years. She knew that his journey wasn't over and that right now he was out there making the transition to a purely spiritual existence, but she felt a pang in her chest. She should have come to see him more often while he'd been on The Island. She should have braved the pull towards the Other Place and hung out with her old friend. Her longevity sometimes made her forget how precious time is – especially time spent with friends in the here and now. Yes, she would see his spirit and talk, and laugh with him again, but he would always be of another place. Spirits had a very different agenda to the living and, as a living being, she found there was always a feeling of being out of kilter when interacting with them. They were free from the shackles of their bodies and looked back on life as a lesser state, but she didn't agree. Yes, life was a brief melding of two very different forms – body and soul - but whatever spirits said afterwards, she knew that life was greater than the sum of its parts. That combination of body and soul, that brief burst of flame that we call life, is spectacular. Standing above Roddy, Elizabeth Russell thought she would do well to remember that. Then she looked up the narrow road with its high hedges as it disappeared into the fog. Somewhere out there, she could sense Attrill laughing at them. Her eyes flared in the dim light. She would enjoy making Attrill regret what he'd done to Roddy.

Chapter Twenty-Four

Wolverton

As the Four Gates Hotel crept up out of the fog, Elizabeth Russell knew she was about to be put on the naughty step. Two police cars and a van were parked outside the front door and Superintendent Fletcher was walking out of the building in animated conversation with a uniformed officer.

"Here we go!" she said as Andy parked the car.

"Low impact!" Superintendent Fletcher cried with his palms upturned as he strode towards them across the gravel.

"I'm really sorry, Fletch..." she began, but then he spotted the damage to the car,

"Oh, come on, Bess! Are you trying to wreck my vehicle budget?"

"That's not me, that's my Investigator – although given his track record so far, I might have to rename him 'The Destroyer'," then she caught Andy's eye - he didn't look pleased she'd thrown him under the bus, but he'd get over it.

"Seriously, what are you two doing?" Fletcher lamented, looking at the cracked windscreen and dented frame.

"Don't worry, my department will cough up for everything before the end of the month," she said and as the Superintendent looked her in the eyes, he calmed,

"Well, that will help, I suppose... but do you know what's been going on here? We've got a wrecked lobby full of blood, no bodies and some very wealthy, very freaked out guests."

Elizabeth Russell sighed,

"You haven't heard, then?"

Fletcher's face told her he hadn't.

"We found Roddy out on Burnt House Road. He's dead. I'm guessing quite a lot of that blood is his."

"Oh..." Fletcher looked down at the ground, "That is bad news. Roddy was one of the good guys."

"Yes. Yes, he was," and she felt a tear bulge in the corner of her right eye, which she flicked away – she would have none of that, not now,

"The rest of that blood is Thomas Attrill's,"

"Attrill's? So where's his body?"

"That's the million-dollar question which I and my Investigator are going to try to answer tomorrow. I know you've got enough on your plate with regular crime, but we've got a situation here. Attrill is extremely dangerous and not to be approached – same goes for his sidekick, Downer."

"Do I need to warn the public?"

"No, they're only a danger to us and our close associates. I've already had to tell Dan to get off The Island. With any luck, he's already well away."

"And you're absolutely positive that they're not a threat to the general public?"

"Yes," she replied as Fletcher searched her face for truth.

"Good," Fletcher said, satisfied, "God, it's non-stop every time you visit!"

"That's why I don't come very often," she smiled.

"Okay, so I'll call off the medical examiner and his team... are you going to stay here tonight?"

Bess shot Andy a questioning glance. He shrugged – like he knew what the hell was going on!

"Yeah, we are," she said to Fletcher.

"All the guests have buggered off – you know what rich people are like when there's any kind of trouble. The staff are still here, but with Roddy gone..."

"Don't worry, he had a good deputy. I'll just promote him, give the staff a couple of days off and then reset after that."

"Sorry, yes – I forgot you own the place..." and now he smiled as if a weight had been lifted, "Well, that's all sorted... although, I guess you'll be wanting a new car?"

"Yes please. And some climbing ropes and other climbing stuff."

"Climbing stuff?"

"I don't know. Stuff that would allow me to go down a well or climb the cliff at Culver Down."

"I don't want to know," Fletcher said, raising his hand, "We've got a couple of climbing enthusiasts in the department, so I'll get them on it. Your 'climbing stuff' will be in the boot of the car. Any chance we'll get it back in one piece?"

"Ask him," Bess smiled, pointing a thumb over her shoulder at Andy,

"I'll do my best," he said, but he could tell that the Superintendent didn't expect to see the car again.

"Right! We'll be off, then," Fletcher said and then, with genuine warmth, added, "Good luck tomorrow. I hope you chase down Attrill and nail him to the wall."

"That's what we do," Elizabeth Russell said, and the from the set of her jaw, Fletcher was very glad he wasn't in Attrill's shoes.

Four hours later, after showering, changing and packing their bags, Bess and Andy were in the vast reception area of the hotel. All signs of blood had been cleaned and the remains of the reception area, which had been destroyed in the fight between Roddy and Attrill, had been cleared away into the furthest corner. Two deep armchairs had been brought from the drawing room and placed in front of the great fireplace. Now that there were no staff on the premises, Bess had locked up the rest of the hotel and wanted to stay in the heart of the place rather than up in their room. Lit by the dancing flames of the fire, they each had a tray on their lap and were eating a venison risotto the chef had knocked up for them before he'd left. Between that, an extensive cheeseboard on the table and the bottle of zinfandel they were sharing, they were well set up for the evening.

"Okay, what do you know about Wolverton?" Bess asked.

"Only what I've read in the history of The Island," Andy replied,

"Well, that's more than I know. Come on, spill."

"All right, just let me think... so, Wolverton was a manor of Bembridge Isle in the medieval period on the southern side of Brading Haven. That's when Culver Down and Bembridge were cut off from the rest of The Island. There was a settlement on the south side of the haven, and ships that could navigate the shallow harbour could dock there. It had a church, but no one's really sure what it was called. Could've been Saint Urie, Saint Uryth, Saint Turien, or Saint Urian,"

"Oh!" Bess exclaimed, "Like Roddy said."

"Yeah. The only problem is, there isn't a Saint Urian. The other three are saints..."

"Uriel is the archangel of wisdom – is that Saint Urie?" Bess interjected,

"Yes. Then Uryth was an English saint from Devon, Turien was a French Bishop who became a saint, but Urian is no one. But I'll get to that in a bit. Anyway, so they had their little church and the settlement was fortunate enough to have a well that gave very pure water. Apparently, it was perfect for long voyages at sea, because it didn't go stale. It was even claimed to have curative properties. So, everything was fine in Wolverton until thirteen forty, when the French raided the town, burned it to the ground and massacred all but one of the inhabitants. Apparently, the only building left standing was the church, but even that didn't survive the Reformation. So, by fifteen fifty, nothing was left of Wolverton except a single old ruin. Now it's all lost somewhere under Centurion's Copse."

"Centurian's Copse?"

"The Romans subjugated the Isle of Wight sometime around fifty AD, and there are various sites of Roman villas, including the famous one at Brading. It seems that down the years, the name Saint Urian got turned into Centurion. Especially once the Victorians got hold of it. They were mad about the Romans... although you probably know that first-hand."

"Sadly, yes. It was a strange time. They did like to compare their empire with the Romans. I couldn't see the allure of it myself. The Romans were a brutal lot."

Andy leaned across to the table and cut himself a few large pieces of cheese, refilled his wine glass and then sat back to continue. Before he did, Bess got up, chucked a big log onto the fire and stirred it up with a poker. Now the flames were crackling away merrily as the accompaniment to Andy's story.

"All that I've said so far is as close to historical fact as people have managed to get. Everything from here is legend that's been woven into the history so closely that it's hard to tell the fact from fiction... so, Wolverton was a trading settlement and ships arrived from all over Europe and the Mediterranean. It prospered enough to afford gold and silver for the church and life was about as good as it could be in the thirteen hundreds. Among the colourful merchants, one man kept returning to the town to trade items. He didn't appear to be as prosperous as some of the other merchants, but he had beautiful things to trade and gave people good advice. He was also a purveyor of potions for the sick, people with unrequited love or any one of a hundred different problems. This made him a popular figure about the place. And what's more, he didn't even want much money for his goods. Sometimes he would trade them for favours," and at this point, Andy took a swig of his wine.

"What favours?" Bess asked. Andy looked at her and thought that in the dancing light of the fire, she was the most beautiful woman he'd ever seen.

"You look incredible," he said.

"You don't look half bad yourself... what favours?"

"This is where it gets interesting. This merchant would give an item to someone and then a while later he'd tell them to play a trick on a person of his choosing. And if they didn't want to, he'd threaten them with terrible consequences for going back on the bargain they'd struck."

"The plot thickens!"

"And not only that, unlike all the other merchants, who came to the town either off their boats or from Brading, this merchant always came from Culver Down."

By now, the night had thickened around them. Outside, the muffling fog seemed to have cut the hotel off from the rest of the world, and inside, the great hall was lit only by the fire. Beyond its flickering light, the darkness closed them in, so that their world had become flame, shadow and the story of the lost town of Wolverton.

"Of course, after a while, the locals started to wonder about the merchant, and people tried to follow him to find out where he went. Every time, he led them high up to the Culver cliff, but the moment they looked away or got distracted, the merchant would vanish. The locals wondered if he was some sort of wizard, but no one dared to confront him. Then a change came over the town. As the gossip about the mysterious merchant increased, the luck of the town began to turn for the worse. Trade slowed, crops withered and neighbours quarrelled. The one thing they still had was their holy well near the church. Its waters were still the purest in England and the sick were still coming to be cured by them. However, there was an old legend about the well, which claimed that if the holy water was ever polluted with human blood, then calamity would befall Wolverton and that Culver's Ness would fall into the sea."

"Culver's Ness?"

"A ness is a headland, so I presume in those days there was one sticking out from the Culver cliffs," Andy replied, "So, as far as the villagers were concerned, as long as their well was safe, they were sure that good times would return. But one day, the merchant came to town claiming that he'd had a vision. He said he'd seen a man in grey hooded cloak who was coming to Wolverton to poison the well. He warned the locals that they must be vigilant, and that their recent bad luck was as nothing compared to what would happen if the hooded stranger were to succeed in his evil plan."

"I bet that put the wind up them," Elizabeth Russell could just imagine the effect on simple villagers of that sort of news.

"It did and, sure enough, not long afterwards a foreign ship arrived. From it emerged a man in a grey cloak and in his hand, he held a strange plant. No one recognised the plant, and that put the cat among the pigeons. Here was the man in the grey hooded cloak, just as the merchant had described, and he was carrying some unknown plant straight towards their holy well. As he passed through the town, a crowd gathered and armed themselves with rocks. When they caught up with him, they saw him kneeling over the well. They didn't hesitate and started throwing their rocks at him before he could carry out his plan. A few of the rocks hit him in the head and that was the end of that. He fell dead next to the well with the poisonous plant still in his hand. The well had been saved... except it hadn't. Blood from one of his head wounds ran to the edge of the well and dropped into it."

Andy took a sip of his wine and continued,

"The moment the blood hit the water, there was a terrible crack like thunder and the earth shook under their feet. Culver's Ness had collapsed into the sea. And as the aftershock rocked the town, the priest ran out of the church in time to see some of the town's buildings collapsing. When he saw the dead man at the side of the well, the priest went to him and found a letter of introduction from the Archbishop of Nicosia in Cyprus. The man the villagers had killed was a pilgrim, and the plant he was carrying was a holy relic from the Garden of Gethsemane with which he was going to bless the famous well. At this, the villagers were dismayed and the recriminations began, but then, cutting through the noise, they could hear the sound of laughter. They turned and saw the merchant standing on the hill laughing at them, but before they could do anything, a cry went up from the dock – French raiders were landing. Mayhem ensued as French soldiers stormed the town and every man, woman and child was killed – except one. A boy from the village had been picking blackberries on Culver Down and saw the merchant walking back from the Wolverton laughing to himself. Unaware of what was happening in the village, the boy decided to follow him. Where everyone else had failed, the boy saw the merchant enter a cave in the cliff and, when he ran over to it, the merchant invited him in. He found a grand hall filled with gold and silver, and with a long table laden with food. The merchant sat the boy down and told him to tuck in. However, the boy said grace before touching the food. As soon as he uttered the prayer, the entire cavern was consumed by fire and the boy suddenly found himself standing in the midst of the smoking ruins of Wolverton - the sole survivor. By the time people came to help from

Bembridge and Brading, the only building left standing was the church of Saint Urian, but no trace of the well could be found. Hearing the boy's story, they all agreed that the merchant must surely have been a demon. As a result of his experience, the boy chose to lead the life of a religious hermit, taking residence in the remains of the empty cave in the cliff. And that's the story of the lost village of Wolverton."

Andy sat back in his armchair and only the crackle of the fire saved them from being enveloped by silence. They sat for a couple of minutes without talking, then Elizabeth Russell said,

"Roddy said the survivor discovered Urian's secret and hid it in the well. He then cursed the well so that Urian could never discover it."

"But if it was already lost, how could he hide it?" Andy asked.

"It was only lost by the time the people from Bembridge arrived. Maybe the boy discovered something in the cave and cursed the well as soon as he materialised in the town? Remember, this is his story. There was nobody else left to tell it, so he could make up whatever he wanted to throw Urian off the scent," and now Elizabeth Russell's face broke into a smile,

"So, all we have to do is find the well that's been lost for eight hundred years."

"I don't know why you're smiling. It sounds impossible. If Attrill can't find it and your radar's being scrambled by the Swaailen, how are we going to find it?"

"*We* aren't – you are," she said with a mischievous curl of her eyebrow.

"Me? Are you drunk? How much of that wine have you had?"

"I'm not drunk, or mad. You're going to find it, because you're my Investigator."

"Just because you gave me that title, it doesn't mean I have some magical power to find things out," Andy said.

"True," she replied, "The title doesn't give you the power to find things out. It's the power you have to find things out that made me give you the title."

"What do you mean?"

"I mean that unbeknownst to you, you have the uncanny ability to see the truth in things."

"Nah. I'm just a well-trained copper," he shook his head.

"Yes, you are that, but you're more. The first time I saw you, I watched you walk through part of an entity that you couldn't see. Everybody else on the street walked through it without a flicker, but you flinched. In fact, you stopped and shook yourself like you'd got an ice cube down the back of your shirt."

"Really?" Andy could hardly believe it.

"Oh yeah," and now Elizabeth Russell slipped from her chair and moved over to him. She knelt between his knees as he sat in the chair and placed her hands on his thighs,

"Now, tell me," she said, looking up at him with her beguiling gaze, "On every case you've worked, you've always been the one to turn up the vital bit of evidence – true?"

Andy thought about it. He did always seem to be in the room when a case was cracked... but that wasn't evidence of some supernatural power. Had he always found the key to every case?

"I dunno... sounds a bit far-fetched."

"Everything I've been doing for the last three hundred years has been far-fetched," she replied, running her hands gently up his powerful thighs,

"What word popped into your head the first time you saw Attrill?" she asked.

"Bent," he replied, trying to keep his breathing regular as she stroked her hands up and down his thighs.

"And you were right. I'm willing to bet you've always been able to..." and now she put on an exaggerated cockney accent, "...spot a wrong 'un."

"Yeah, I have," he said, looking into her eyes. She knew exactly what effect her supple hands were having on him. What was her game?

"No game," she said, sliding up to straddle his left leg and running her hand up his arm to his neck to stroke it.

"Hang on - you said you weren't going to read my thoughts,"

"I didn't. That was just an educated guess. The reason I'm saying this is because with a bit of training, you can fully unlock your gift, but right now I need you to trust your instincts. We have to find that well tomorrow and you need to be able to listen to the little voice in your head, however crazy it might sound. You need to tune into it and let it guide you. That's all."

Elizabeth Russell leant in and kissed him. The feel and smell of her were arousing. He wanted her, wanted to possess that body and thrill her soul, but...

"I don't think now's the time," he said reluctantly.

"And *that* is the voice you need to be listening out for tomorrow," she whispered into his ear before playfully biting the lobe and sitting back on his leg.

"What, you mean all this prick teasing has only been to get me to listen to my instincts?"

"Of course," she said, in a businesslike manner, "There are a number of ways to get someone into the right state of mind to tap into their instincts – hypnotism, deep relaxation and so on... but I thought this way would be the most fun," and she winked at him impishly.

"So, you were never intending to..."

"Hell, no. Here? Now? With a god potentially out to kill us? That would be foolhardy – which is exactly what you thought when you listened to that little voice."

She wasn't wrong. Even though his desire for her was off the scale, his instinct was that any sort of lovemaking would have been madness.

"I suspect that when you say 'this is the most fun' way to do it, you mean it's the most fun for you," he said.

"Well, yes, I did get a kick out of seeing your desire for me, but you've got to admit that was quite pleasant."

"Yeah... but you have a bit of a sadistic streak in you, don't you?"

"That's for you to investigate when we get home," she said and gave him a kiss on the end of his nose,

"You know what my instinct is now?"

Bess shrugged.

"To put you across my knee..."

"Anyway..." she said, hopping off him before he could actualise his instinct, "You need to get some rest. Tomorrow will be tough."

"I'm sure," he growled, but there was a smile playing around the edges of his mouth. Elizabeth Russell found it very sexy. He was clearly thinking about ways in which he could give her a taste of her own medicine. And she very much looked forward to finding out what they might be.

Once they had cleared away the dinner things and got some thick blankets to see them through the night in the chairs, they settled themselves in front of the fire.

"How do you want to do this?" Andy asked, consulting his watch – it was almost eleven, "I could sleep until three, while you keep watch, then you could sleep until seven or eight."

"I'll keep watch all night," Bess replied.

"That's not fair on you, though..." Andy began, but she held up a hand to silence him,

"It's fine. Thanks to various techniques I've learned, I can go a week without sleep if I have to. A night is nothing."

"Oh, well... only if you're sure."

"Yeah, it's fine. Anyway, it gives me a chance to watch you sleep."

"Nothing creepy there!" Andy said,

"Seriously, you can tell a lot about a person by watching them sleep."

"And how exactly am I going to fall asleep, knowing you're watching and judging me?"

"If you find it difficult, I can always help. It would be very easy to help you fall sleep," she said, looking into his eyes. Suddenly, his eyelids felt heavy.

"Well, I suppose you could try, but..."

"So very easy to help you fall into a deep and dreamless sleep..." she said quietly.

Andy wanted to reply, but it all seemed like too much effort. Much better to keep his eyes and mouth shut. Elizabeth Russell smiled to herself as she leaned across to tuck his hand under his blanket. He was like an

English Mastiff curled up on its master's favourite chair. He might be asleep, but he had a presence and strength that made her feel safe – even though she was the one on guard.

Yes, this one's a keeper, she thought to herself and then put another log on the fire before settling back for her lonely vigil.

Chapter Twenty-Five

The Exorcism Of Billy Tanner

Oliver and Chloe had a very pleasant drive from London to Leicester. It was sunny and warm, and England looked ready to slip happily into Keats' autumn season of mists and mellow fruitfulness. Chloe had left her father in the capable and caring hands of Jo, who was small, round and bustling, with a pair of spectacles on a cord around her neck. She had taken over so smoothly that Ray never noticed, and he'd waved Chloe off as if she'd been going to school. This was good. Chloe could concentrate on the job in hand without worrying about her father for a moment. Oliver took the opportunity of the journey north to teach Chloe how to better control her mindreading abilities. Like any muscle, it was simply a matter of training and he showed her some exercises. He was very pleased to find that she didn't just have talent, but that she was fascinated by how everything worked.

Yes, he thought to himself as they drove past Newport Pagnell, *with this ability and attitude, she could be very powerful.*

"As powerful as you or Bess?" Chloe's thought intruded into his mind.

"Hey, nosy!" he said out loud, "Okay, try reading my thoughts now."

Chloe tried, but it was as if Oliver had simply vanished. Physically, he was still sitting next to her, driving the car up the motorway, but his mind was nowhere to be found.

"Wow!" Chloe said excitedly, "That's amazing! Where have you gone?"

"Oh, I'm still here," and this time, Oliver's voice was in her head.

Chloe tried to latch on to the voice in her head to find a way into Oliver's mind, but as soon as he'd spoken, he seemed to have disappeared again.

"That's so cool!" Chloe squealed aloud! "Show me how you did it."

"Not today. It's very complicated and requires time and calm. And those are two things we don't have right now. Sorry," Oliver could feel her disappointment, but then she displayed her greatest quality – she put it behind her and turned her attention to the now,

"Can you tell me anything about the boy?"

Oliver smiled at her maturity and replied,

"Billy Tanner's five years old. His mum, Jade, is a part-time hair-dresser, and his dad is called Ryan and he's a plumber. They went down to the Isle of Wight for a week in June, where Ryan picked up a silver box with a Blue John inlaid lid for Jade's birthday. Unfortunately, that box contained a spirit, which we think is Hurna Antuwahha. It's a demon referred to in Hittite history from over a thousand years BC – the hunter of humans."

"It said that it wanted to use me to hunt men."

"That sounds about right. I spoke to one of Bishop FitzOsbern's team yesterday and it appears that Hurna Antuwahha is very angry that people no longer fear it. So, you can imagine how annoyed it is that there's a Christian bishop trying to extricate it from the boy it's possessed."

"It's come from the darkness," Chloe said, "When it touched me, I could feel its anger… and its fear."

Oliver glanced across at Chloe, who was staring with a gaze that was seeing something far beyond the countryside around them,

"Its fear?" he asked.

"Yes. Before being trapped in the box, it was slowly being dragged into a great darkness. It was afraid it would lose itself."

"But now it's here, it's going to cling on with all its might," Oliver said, "Maybe this is too dangerous for you."

Demons were savage enough at the best of times, but if this one was desperate…

"No," Chloe said simply, "I made a promise to Billy. I'm going to keep it."

When they reached it, Billy's house was an identikit red-brick semi, typical of the estate of houses around it. The tiny front garden was paved and a low fence separated it from the chaos of litter and weeds next door. As Oliver pulled the car up and parked behind what he assumed was the bishop's Bentley, he said,

"The next-door neighbours are currently being put up at the Premier Inn at Oadby, at the Church's expense. Apparently, they were complaining about the screaming and shouting, so Bishop FitzOsbern cast them out. Makes sense - if you can't cast out the spirit, you'd may as well get rid of the neighbours."

They got out of the car and Oliver went to the boot and took something from it, which he slipped into his jacket pocket, then they walked over to the house. It all seemed very ordinary. Oliver rang the doorbell and they waited. He could feel that Chloe was nervous, but there was also determination in her. After a long pause, the door was answered by a youngish priest,

"Oliver Fernsby?" he asked,

"Hi... Jeremy Salter?"

"Yes, good to finally put a face to the name," the priest said, shaking Oliver's hand. Although they had spoken on the phone many times to organise the schedules of their respective bosses, they had never actually met. However, when he saw Chloe, he looked troubled,

"Oh! Who's this?"

"Chloe!" cried a voice from a room at the back of the house and a moment later, Billy ran along the narrow hall from the kitchen to the front door. Chloe slipped past Jeremy and was immediately given a big hug by Billy,

"Thank you! Thank you for coming!" the little boy said, and he had tears in his eyes,

"It's okay, Billy. We're here to help," Chloe said, hugging him, "I almost didn't recognise you without your PJ's," she smiled as she looked at Billy standing there in jeans and a Leicester City football shirt.

"What on earth is this?" the words were cold and hard.

Chloe looked down the hall and there, filling the doorway to the kitchen, stood Bishop FitzOsbern. He walked towards them with unnerving speed, sweeping down the narrow hallway with his purple robes billowing.

"You never said anything about this," he said, pointing at Chloe as if she was an inappropriate item, rather than a little girl.

"I said I was bringing someone with me who had specialist skills and would be able to help in Billy's safe deliverance," Oliver replied calmly. However, even his sweet tones could not stop the bishop's face from colouring with anger.

"Children, go into the front room," he said with barely controlled rage.

Chloe looked up at the intimidating hulk of purple robes and purpling face. Although she was not cowed by him, she could feel that Billy was terrified,

"Come on, Billy, why don't you show me your room?" she knew that he felt safest in there.

"Okay," he said and, holding Chloe's hand, he led her up the stairs.

"Jeremy, go with them," FitzOsbern ordered, and his subordinate immediately complied. As soon as the bedroom door closed, FitzOsbern rounded on Oliver,

"How dare you! How dare you bring a child to a deliverance! Of all the stupid, dangerous..."

"Is there a problem?" the woman's voice was small, but perfectly timed to cut in as the bishop paused to think of more adjectives to throw at Oliver. The bishop stepped to the side and there in the hall were Ryan and Jane Tanner. Both looked exhausted and frightened.

"The problem is that this gentleman has brought a child to the house," the bishop replied,

"As you know, I advised against your agreeing to his joining us in the first place. It is not recommended that the ministering priest should be joined by anyone except another priest of his choosing as support. This is a safety precaution. The fewer people exposed to the entity, the better. Another adult in the house gives the entity another target, but to bring a child into the house is reckless beyond belief, because children are so much more vulnerable. I am very disappointed in you, Oliver," and the look FitzOsbern delivered was a slap in the face.

"But we agreed to it," Jade said, "When Mister Fernsby told us about the girl – Chloe, isn't it?"

Oliver nodded,

"And that she could help us, then of course we were willing to take the chance. The last two days have been very hard on Billy, and he said he wanted Chloe to come."

Bishop FitzOsbern turned on her, and she and Ryan shrank back from him as he said with controlled contempt,

"Yes, but you have no experience of the lies and subterfuges of demons. Did it not occur to you that the demon might have manipulated Billy to say that?"

"Yeah, but it was during one of his normal phases. He said he'd dreamt of the girl and was sure she could help," Ryan said, stepping forward even though he was head and shoulders smaller than the bishop and found the man quite scary.

"You can't be sure he was in a 'normal' phase. Demons are sly and masters of mimicry. That might have been the demon requesting the chance for another soul to corrupt," FitzOsbern hated how ignorant people had become in the secular age,

"No, I'm sorry, but the girl has to go. We can't take the risk," and there was a bullish finality in his words.

Ryan stepped back and Jade took his hand – how could they argue with a bishop?

"Sorry," Jade said like a child who'd broken something expensive.

Oliver looked at the couple and it was clear that they were not only scared of the demon possessing their child, but also scared of FitzOsbern.

The man clearly used the same bullying tactics on demon and human alike. That was probably how he'd risen so far. Oliver knew that this sort of borderline psychopath always did well in everything from business to politics to medicine. So! Now he had the bishop, the box and the demon to deal with...

"Where is the box you bought on the Isle of Wight?" Oliver asked, turning all his warmth towards Ryan and Jade.

"Didn't you hear me? Get rid of the girl," FitzOsbern stood between Oliver and the Tanners.

"Yes, I heard you, but right now we need to destroy that box," Oliver said quietly, "Where is it?"

"Is this the ridiculous notion that Jeremy was blethering about last night - that somehow the box controls the demon?"

"It's not a notion, it's a fact and you would do well to lower your voice, because I don't want to alert it to the danger it's in."

"Alert the box?" FitzOsbern exploded in consternation, "I knew it! I knew your lot would try to turn this into a three-ring circus. Well I'm not having it," and he loomed over Oliver with his fists clenched, "Get out now!"

A high-pitched scream from upstairs prevented Oliver's reply.

"Billy!" Jade cried and she started for the stairs. Before he knew it, Bishop FitzOsbern had been left flat-footed as Oliver leapt up the stairs just ahead of Jade and Ryan Tanner.

Oliver vaguely heard the bishop roar,

"Fernsby!" but his focus was upstairs. He was up there in a few bounds and pulling a claw hammer from his jacket pocket. He threw the door of the bedroom open and saw Chloe standing in one corner, protecting Billy who was on the floor behind her. In the opposite corner, Jeremy Salter was on his knees with his hands held behind his back by black tentacles coming from the silver-blue box hanging in the air behind him. Another tentacle was wrapped around his throat, strangling the life out of him.

"Kids! Out!" Oliver cried, putting himself between them and the box as another black tentacle whipped out towards them.

Chloe heaved Billy up and they scrambled out into the hall, where Jade swept her son into her arms and started crying.

Oliver slammed the door with a flick of his wrist and attacked the box.

"The door's jammed!" Ryan shouted as he tried to get into his son's room to help.

"Run!" Oliver's cry from within was muffled, but they followed the order and bundled down the stairs.

"What's going on?" FitzOsbern demanded as they all but fell into the tiny downstairs hall.

"The box is trying to kill Jeremy," Chloe said.

"The box!"

"I think the demon is loose. We have to protect Billy," she continued, leading Jade, who was still holding Billy, into the small but comfortable front room. FitzOsbern followed them and snapped at Ryan,

"You! Get my things from the kitchen!"

Ryan, whose mind was scrambled by the stress and lack of sleep obeyed without hesitation.

"And as for you, I want you out of here right now," the bishop shouted, glowering down at Chloe.

"She's mine!"

Chloe and the bishop both turned to the sofa, where Billy was crouched with a murderous look on his face. Beneath him, his mother lay unconscious.

"First I shall devour the boy's soul and then I shall take her body!" he snarled in the metallic voice Chloe had heard in the woods.

FitzOsbern stepped forward and made the sign of the cross, at which Billy laughed,

"Your signs and sigils have no power over me!" then, as Ryan approached with the bishop's holy water, wafers, oil and bible, the door slammed in his face with such force the whole room shook.

"Let's see what you do without your trinkets!" Billy hissed.

"In the beginning was the Word," FitzOsbern said with power, "And the Word was with God, and the Word *was* God. The same was in the beginning with God..."

However, Billy merely grinned and crawled sideways across the sofa. Chloe backed around so that the bishop was between her and the boy. Her heart and mind were both racing. What should she do? What *could* she do? She had the feeling that this was where she needed to be, but didn't know anything beyond that.

"All things were made by him..." FitzOsbern declared,

"No they weren't!" Billy spat,

"And without him was not any thing made that was made. In him was life; and the life was the light of men."

"I witnessed Ephron sell the cave of Machpelah to Abraham. Your words cannot bind me."

"And the light shineth in darkness; and the darkness comprehended it not."

"But the darkness shall smother the light," Billy replied, plunging the room into an eerie twilight as if he had drawn a heavy curtain across the window.

And that was the moment Chloe knew what to do.

"There was a man sent from God whose name was John," the bishop said firmly, but before he could continue, Chloe stepped between him and Billy,

"Hurna Antuwahha! Leave this boy!" she ordered with a forceful voice she barely recognised as her own.

"What are you doing? Get back!" FitzOsbern commanded, grabbing her arm and pulling her away,

"I will kill the boy and devour your soul!" Billy growled, gathering himself to leap at her.

"Let me go!" Chloe shouted at FitzOsbern, "Can't you see your words aren't working?" but his hand had her wrist in an iron grip and he was yanking her backwards,

"Get back and shut up!" he shouted.

"Why won't you listen?" Chloe demanded.

"The same came for a witness, to bear witness of the Light, that all men through him might believe," FitzOsbern declared, throwing Chloe behind him and turning on Billy, who chuckled.

"He was not that Light, but was sent to bear witness of that light..."

"Enough!" the demon roared and the force of it send FitzOsbern tumbling backwards. Billy stood up from the sofa and approached Chloe with a hunter's supple movements,

"You should have listened to the shaman, child. Now you are mine..."

Chloe got to her feet and faced him down.

"Hurna Antuwahha! I banish you to the void!"

"You do not have the power!" he sneered, "You're a child. Compared to me, you're the blink of an eye."

From where he'd fallen, FitzOsbern watched in dazed horror as light seemed to gather around the girl.

"You are the prey – I am the hunter," Billy said, "I have existed for aeons!"

An unnatural roar from the floor above split the air and the whole house jolted, shattering every window. In Billy's bedroom, Oliver sank to his knees. He was drenched in sweat and had the hammer in his right hand. On the floor in front of him were the shattered remnants of the silver and blue pill box – now there was no more refuge for the demon. Oliver drew in a big gulp of air and reached over to the body of Jeremy Salter. He still had a pulse, but he'd need medical help fast. Throughout his fight with the box, Oliver had been in mental contact with Chloe and now he said,

"Box is gone – do it now!" then he fumbled for his phone to call an ambulance.

In the sitting room, Billy paused and doubt flickered across his demon-twisted face.

"Nowhere to hide," Chloe said, "Not even in the dark," and now she was glowing blue-white in the gloom cast by the demon. Billy snarled and leapt at her, but in that same moment, light burst out of Chloe's fingers, catching Billy in mid-air and holding him there in a ball of light.

"No!" he screamed and, with thrashing limbs and straining muscles that threatened to burst Billy's veins, the demon tried to break free from the light.

Now, repeating the words that Oliver was putting into her mind, Chloe recited an incantation.

"Please, no! You're hurting me..." the plaintive voice of the young boy begged, "Don't say these words. They're going to kill me."

"Listen to him, girl!" bishop FitzOsbern shouted, "You don't know what you're doing. This is heresy."

Chloe kept going, trying to ignore the demon and the bishop as both of them tried to make her stop.

"The demon won't let me live if you finish the spell," Billy wheedled,

"This witchcraft is going to kill the boy!" FitzOsbern cried,

"The demon has gone now. I feel normal. Please let me down, this hurts so much!"

"You have to stop! You must not fight evil with evil!"

Suddenly, as Chloe came to the last lines of the incantation, Billy's voice changed again. It was so deep and powerful that Chloe could feel it in her bones and see her shirt quiver from the vibrations of it,

"If you try to rip me out of the boy, he will be torn apart. You do not have the power! You are nothing!"

Chloe ploughed on, even though her legs were starting to buckle. She was sweating and each breath was becoming harder, as if all the air was being sucked out of the room. Every word was now a supreme effort of will and, with each one, Billy strained and shouted abuse at her. As she forced her way to the end of the incantation, inky darkness was forming around the boy until she spoke the final word. Chloe and the bishop felt more than heard the boom that followed the last word. It was like being hit by a powerful wave and droplets of blood oozed from their eyes and noses. Billy's body fell from the ball of light and crumpled on the floor below. As the bishop wiped blood from his eyes, he could have sworn he saw a black shape within the ball of light – like a man with a jackal's head.

"This cannot be! You are too young, too weak. You do not have the power!" the low voice bellowed.

Bishop FitzOsbern watched in terror - blinding light was filling Chloe's eyes and mouth as she said,

"You are old, but you haven't learned – I don't need to be powerful, all I need is to channel the eternal power of light!"

Then Chloe opened her mouth wide and her scream burst with the light of a supernova as blinding bolts shot from her eyes and mouth with the sound of burning cosmic fire. The demon, held in the ball of energy, was hit by the full blast of the light from Chloe and roared with pain. Now the entire house was shaking apart as the demon collapsed in on itself, its limbs folding into a single black point in the centre of the light. With a painfully loud 'snap', the white light flared and was gone. The demonic gloom vanished and the light of the sunny day flooded in. Chloe staggered back,

"Billy..." she mumbled and fell to the floor, unconscious.

***

"Chloe! Chloe!"

It was the warmth of Oliver's voice that brought her back from oblivion and her eyes fluttered open to see his friendly face smiling down at her.

"Billy!" she gasped, trying to move, but failing.

"He's all right. A few bruises, but nothing serious."

"Did it work?"

"Yeah, just a bit!" Oliver smiled, "I don't know what you did, but it certainly scared the heck out of Bishop FitzOsbern!" he whispered, "I was expecting him to tear me off a strip the moment I came downstairs, but he was as meek as a lamb – even made me a cup of tea! Speaking of, do you want one?"

"Yes please," Chloe said weakly.

"Want me to help you sit up?" he asked. She nodded and he helped her up. She was on the sofa in what was left of the Tanner's front room. A wide crack ran through the centre of the ceiling, the window was gone, the TV smashed, the door shattered and the walls cracked.

"How's Billy's mum?"

"She's with the paramedics. Took a blow to the head, but should be fine."

"Did I really do all this?"

"Most of it, but you can't take all the credit, Hurna Antuwahha did his fair share before you kicked him out. Hang on, Ryan!" Oliver called as he spotted Billy's dad pass the door,

"Yeah?" Ryan looked tired, but happy,

"One more tea here, please."

"No trouble. Is she all right?"

Oliver gave him a thumbs up, and he went off to the kitchen.

"Must have been pretty spectacular!" Oliver was impressed by the shambles around him and wished he could have seen it.

"I can't remember what happened," Chloe said. She had impressions of the last moments and a feeling of utter joy, but didn't remember details.

"You opened a direct link to the powers of goodness and light... and they did the rest. Not wanting to make you big-headed, but you are very special – not many people can do that. Not like you just did, anyway."

"But I couldn't have done it without you," Chloe said.

"I just gave you the words. You did the rest."

"So, the power of light is stronger than darkness?"

"No. One day, you'll see for yourself exactly how it works and, if you're lucky, your hair won't turn white. But what I can tell you is this – the powers of darkness are also the powers of chaos, of pain, humiliation, lies, betrayal and a hundred other unpleasant traits. Dark entities can be unbelievably strong, but because they are all treacherous and chaotic by nature, they can't focus their collective power. Whereas beings of light and goodness can. So, yes, the demon here today was more powerful than we were, but you were able to call on a collective power such as it had never seen in all the thousands of years it existed."

"Did I kill it?" Chloe asked.

"No, but it sounds like its time was almost up. You said you felt it was afraid of being dragged into the darkness, well, after this Hurna Antuwahha's essence will probably be re-absorbed into the whirlpool of evil out there in the Great Beyond. Whether good or evil, nothing lives forever. At some point our essence returns to its source."

"Tea," said Ryan coming back into the room with a couple of steaming mugs,

"I didn't know how you like it, so I just made it strong and sweet," he smiled.

"That's just how I like it, thanks," Chloe said, gratefully taking her mug. She took a sip. Perfect! Then she and Oliver sat in apparent silence as they drank.

Outside, on the strip of paving that passed for a front garden, Bishop FitzOsbern stood and looked at them as they sat on the sofa with their backs to him. What he had seen earlier had scared the hell out of him - he freely admitted it. He'd thought he was watching pure evil at work. Now he wasn't so sure. The girl had a power that was unnatural, but that didn't mean it couldn't be directed towards goodness by the Church. Perhaps there was a way he could bring her into the fold? What he had seen was surely beyond anything Elizabeth Russell could manage. If he could get the girl on his side, then perhaps she could finish Russell for him? Yes... if he played this right, Elizabeth Russell would be history... it was a pity the girl was a mulatto, but he could overlook that. He would work with the tools he had...

"Excuse me, sir, but your assistant has come round and was asking for you,"

FitzOsbern turned and looked down at the paramedic,

"Yes, yes of course – thank you," he said and walked towards the ambulance.

Sitting on the sofa, Chloe and Oliver couldn't help but overhear the bishop's thoughts. Even when thinking to himself, he was shouty.

"What's a mulatto?" Chloe asked.

"It's an old term for being half black and half white. Sorry you had to hear that," Oliver replied.

Chloe frowned. Having grown up in an ethnically diverse neighbourhood and gone to a school that reflected that, she'd never had anyone say that the colour of her skin was a problem before.

"What a horrible thing to say. Is he always like that?" Chloe asked.

"Yup!"

"Must get tiring if you have to work with him," she said.

"Yup!" and Oliver took a long sip of his strong, sweet tea.

Chapter Twenty-Six

A Stroll In Centurion's Copse

It was around nine in the morning when Andy and Bess heard the sound of cars coming up the hotel driveway. They had already been up for a couple of hours and had eaten a breakfast of kedgeree and sausages, which had been left for them by the chef. They walked out into the dank gloom of the interminable fog as an unmarked Ford Focus pulled up in front of the steps, closely followed by a squad car. The driver of the Focus was in uniform and got out with a cheery,

"Lovely morning! One car, as requested," and he scrunched across the gravel to hand the keys to Andy.

"Thanks."

"Is the climbing equipment..."

"In the back, yes," said the officer, "And the chief says please could you return it all, because it belongs to a couple of the lads."

"Tell your chief he can act like a piece of rope..." Elizabeth Russell said,

"Eh?" the police officer looked confused,

"...and get knotted," she finished.

The officer stood for a moment as it sank in and then burst into laughter,

"I might get demoted, but I'll tell him," he said, heading to the other car,

"Good luck!"

And with that he got in and his partner deliberately spun the wheels, so the car spat gravel as it sped off into the fog.

After a quick check of the stuff in the boot, they put in their bags. Bess locked up the front door of the hotel, turned on the alarm system and then they, too, disappeared into the grey bank of cloud.

"Brading, then?" Andy said.

"Aye," Bess replied. Earlier they had looked at a map to see the best way to get to Centurion's Copse. There were three easy ways, but only two had parking. Had it been a sunny day, they'd have driven over to Bembridge windmill. From the hill, they would have been able to look down upon the area that had once been Brading Haven, but which was now the Brading Marshes nature reserve. From the high vantage point, they would have been able to see exactly where Wolverton would once have been and then walk to it down the hill, skirting the northern edge of Bembridge airport on the way. However, that route was much longer and not worth the extra effort on a foggy day. Instead, they went to Brading itself and soon they were parking in the same car park they'd used previously.

Once he'd got the climbing equipment out of the car, Andy looked around and breathed deeply. He was starting to get used to the chill, damp scent of low cloud. He slipped into the loop of the climbing ropes so that he could carry them slung diagonally across his chest, locked the car and nodded to Bess. She was carrying the spade they would need, which wasn't the best accessory for her outfit of red trouser suit and beautifully tailored black trench coat. The combo made her look like a well-dressed gangster off to bury a body.

"Let's go, then," she sounded subdued, businesslike, and they didn't speak until they walked past the building where Attrill had conjured his illusory shop.

"This all seems horribly familiar," Andy said.

"Mmm. We need to be on our guard. I get the feeling that there won't be any illusions today. Things might get a bit too real for our liking," she replied as they headed down Quay Lane, past the church. Andy looked over at the churchyard with its drunken headstones lolling at odd angles in the long grass and wondered whether, like Godshill, there was a shrine to Attrill somewhere under it. They continued down the narrow road and, with the visibility down to about twenty yards, the houses seemed to come up out of the fog to take a look at the strangers.

"There's still so much colour in the gardens," Bess said as they walked past a front garden that was a riot of late summer blooms, "All seems a bit incongruous with the cold and the fog."

Andy nodded. None of it felt right. The weather was telling him it was winter, but all the plants seemed convinced that they were still in a long, sunny September.

The houses petered out, so that they were walking down the narrow road with high hedges tumbling with greenery on either side and blank walls of grey ahead and behind them. They walked past a break in the hedge on the left, where an apron of concrete disappeared into the gloom. Was there the shadow of a building somewhere just beyond their sight? It was hard to tell. The only sounds were the rustle of their clothes and their shoes on the tarmac, with the occasional call of a bird. When they crossed a bridge over a single-track railway line, Andy asked,

"Know where that goes?"

Bess shrugged,

"Could be the line from Ryde to Sandown, but I wouldn't bet my house on it."

As they continued on their way past a couple of farm gates and a facility used by Southern Water, there was still nothing to see. Everything had been swallowed up in the fog. Then, when the trees at the sides of the road began to arch over it, turning it into a tunnel, Andy had to say something,

"I think I'm getting claustrophobia."

"Yeah, it's a bit smothering," Bess replied, "But on the plus side, we'll soon be out on the marshes... in this," and she raised a hand to the fog.

"You're not selling it to me," Andy said.

Ahead of them, the road ended at a house, but two paths forked either side of it. They took the right one through a wooden gate and followed the narrow path until, after a couple of hundred yards, they were out in the wetland. The path was raised up about six feet higher than the reeds and grasses of the marsh and would have afforded them a lovely view across the flat land on a good day. This wasn't a good day. The feelings of claustrophobia Andy had had on the road soon became much worse. Once they had crossed a river – Andy presumed it was the Eastern Yar - the tangled hedges on either side of the path formed a tunnel of intertwined branches above their heads.

"So, this is what it's like to be a sodding rabbit," Andy said with annoyance. He hated this hemmed-in feeling and wanted to kick against it.

Elizabeth Russell was feeling twitchy, too. She'd never been to that place and it had a menacing energy to it. She felt that they were walking towards something that didn't want visitors, and the feeling was becoming more intense with every step.

"I'd draw that sword if I were you," she said.

Andy didn't need to be told twice, though as he continued with the sword in hand, he wondered about the reaction of any ramblers or dog walkers who might cross their path. It would be disconcerting to see a man with a sword blundering out of the fog towards them. Having said that, who would want to walk their dog in such an odd place on a day like that?

In a few minutes, they reached the edge of the woodland that was Centurion's Copse. There the path split. The left fork would take them along what would have been the shoreline of Wolverton, while the right fork plunged up into where the heart of the village would have been.

"Listen," said Bess.

Andy did so but couldn't hear anything.

"Nothing," he replied.

"Not even a bird," she said.

Each path was a tunnel through the tangled trees and bushes. The area between the paths was a jungle of dense undergrowth and mature oak, ash and hazel trees. It was dark under the trees and the fog seeped up through them, binding them together so that after about ten yards there was nothing to see but an impenetrable wall of murk.

"Is it me, or is it much colder here?" Andy asked. Bess nodded,

"This is a place of desolation," she said, then realised that wasn't the cheeriest thing to say,

"Sorry – didn't mean to demoralize us. But this is uncanny. These trees are all wrong."

"How so?"

"Oak, ash and hazel are important trees in magic. They are healing and protective... but these have become corrupted. There is something here that has curdled the ground and filled the trees with malice," and then she thought about the story Andy had told about the destruction of Wolverton,

"Of course, they've grown up feeding on the blood and ashes of a massacre," she said, "Hardly surprising they're not right."

"They say that dogs won't come here at night. Maybe they're picking up on it," Andy said - although, if truth be told, he couldn't feel it as keenly as Bess. He just felt that generalised feeling of claustrophobia and the desire to get away.

"Which way?" Bess asked.

Well, here was some pressure. He was the Investigator and everything was resting on him to find what they needed, but what did he know about locating wells? He needed to put those thoughts aside and allow his instincts to guide him.

"Left," he said after a pause, "I doubt the well is down here, but I want to get the lie of the land."

"After you, sir," she replied and followed Andy into the gloom.

To a Londoner like Andy, the silence was bizarre. No birdsong, no traffic noise, and there wasn't a breath of wind, so even the leaves on the trees were silent. In London, there was a constant, background roar. The city was always alive with noise, but here... nothing. They walked along the path, which was just inside the treeline at the edge of the marsh and it didn't take long for Andy to spot the line of the old sea wall. It was covered in ivy and brambles, but some of the ancient stones along the top were still visible. He stopped to look over the edge. There was a four-foot drop down into a tangle of undergrowth that might itself be two or three feet deep. The woodland undergrowth stretched a pace or two out from the wall and then marsh plants took over. The mature trees were all rooted on the landward side of the wall - an intriguing reminder that until the 1880s, the sea would have been lapping at it. A few young hazels were trying to venture out beyond the wall, but they would never get far into the reeds, which stretched away into the fogbank.

"Looks like the sea wall," he said, "I'm guessing boats would have docked along here, so there were probably a couple of warehouses over here," and he walked to the other side of the path and looked into the chaos of the woodland.

Without a machete, it was an impenetrable confusion of underbrush and trees. The ground clearly fell away, which meant that in a couple of steps, he'd be up to his thighs in the undergrowth. All this made it impossible to see what might have been there.

"The only way to really see what it might have been like would be to clear the woodland," he said, then continued walking along the path. He was looking around and thinking about the most logical place to sink a well. Not too close to the sea, surely? Wouldn't there be a chance of saltwater seeping through to the well if it was too close? In which case, it would have to be a couple of hundred yards from the shoreline. Wouldn't it also depend on the depth of the water table and how seawater seepage affected it? But how could he know what that was without seeing the results of a geological survey? Andy stopped and peered into the tangle on the landward side of the path.

"It's not down here," he said. His gut was telling him so, and in the absence of a degree in geology, that was all he had to go on.

"Shall we go back, or...?" Bess said,

"Keep going," he replied and led the way.

After a few minutes, the path split again, with one branch continuing along the old shoreline, while the other led up the hill into the heart of the wood.

"Up here," he said, and they walked up the tunnel through the trees towards the ever-present wall of fog. On one side of them, unhappy-looking trees were reaching up out of stagnant pools of black water.

"We need to get higher. They couldn't have a well of famously pure water near this," Andy said. There was the faint smell of rotted leaves rising from the pools and he didn't like it. Elizabeth Russell watched him carefully. It always interested her when people used skills she didn't have. And seeing someone consciously using those skills for the first time was even better. *Yes, ignore your rational mind and listen for the tiny voice somewhere in the background behind your internal monologue. That's the way to do it.*

"Okay," he said as they reached another parting of the ways. They had the choice of going further up the hill or turning right and heading back towards Brading.

"Wait here," and he jogged up the path about fifty yards. Bess watched as he dropped to his haunches and looked at the path itself. Once he was satisfied, he jogged back,

"The edge of the path up there is clearly part of the foundations of a building. There's also a small stream running down the hill."

"You think that could lead us to the well?"

"No. I'd say the well's more likely to be back towards Brading. Do you know what's up the hill?" he asked.

"It's Culver Down."

"Yeah, of course – that's where the mysterious merchant went. Who knows, maybe he walked right past that old building. And it's chalk up there, isn't it?"

"Yes. The cliffs facing the sea are chalk about three hundred feet high."

"Probably why the water in the well was so pure, if it filtered through hundreds of feet of chalk..." then he tailed off. Another thought had knocked all questions of water tables out of his head.

"I've been such an idiot!" he said, and there was a new excitement in his voice,

"I've been trying to find the well, even though I know sod all about them. You know what I should've been looking for?"

"What?"

"The church!"

She thought for a moment as he looked at her expectantly to see if she could put the pieces together, too,

"Because... of course! The holy well was next to the church," and she looked pleased with herself.

"Yes."

"But I don't see how that helps us."

"It helps us, because while I know nothing about wells, I know quite a lot about medieval towns."

"Really?" And she arched an eyebrow, "I'm surprised that didn't come out on any of our dates."

"Not something I tend share on a date. Talking about my interest in history doesn't usually trigger the passionate animal instincts in a woman. Or, if I was that way inclined, in a bloke."

"So, animal instincts aside, where would the church be?"

"In this part of the Isle of Wight, historical precedent would put it down by the water. St Mary's in Brading is a good example – look at this..."

Andy took out his phone, which thankfully had a signal, and searched online for a minute. Then he held it up for Bess to look at,

"This is an engraving of Bembridge windmill from when Brading Haven was still a harbour. Straight across the water at Brading, you can see the church. Anything strike you about it?"

She looked at the phone,

"It's quite close to the water."

"Exactly! One of the reasons for blocking Brading Haven off in the eighteen-eighties was because the sea was crashing onto the church during storms. Over in St Helen's the original church was right next to the beach. Trouble was, the sea was undermining it by the sixteen hundreds. So they put up a new church a mile inland. Part of the original eight hundred year old church tower is left next to the beach, and it's painted white to act as a marker for ships. Here's the thing - the churches in Brading and St Helens were standing when St Urian's church stood right here in Wolverton.

These were communities that relied on the sea. They worshipped near the water, and I think that's where we need to be," Andy said, walking along the new path,

"This should take us round the top of the village and back down to that first fork," he continued, and Bess was struck once more by how he reminded her of an English mastiff on the hunt.

They hurried along the path, but while Andy was focussed on finding the church, Bess was taking in their surroundings. The air of menace was increasing and the trees were more twisted.

"I'm not saying it's going to be down by the dock... in fact, I don't think it's in there at all," he said, indicating the tangled mass between them and the marsh. Bess was happy about that, because she didn't trust any of the trees in there. Then, when they were within twenty yards of the place where they'd taken the path along the old sea wall, Andy stopped and turned away from the woodland. He was looking past some hazels and out towards the grassland beyond.

"I was reading in that history book that the ruin of St Urian's was clearly visible in the mid sixteen hundreds. But some of the oaks in the main wood must be five or six hundred years old. Be hard to see a chapel if it was surrounded by oak trees. But if it was just outside the wood, you'd be able to see it from Brading, from up on Culver Down behind us, maybe even from Sandown. Swap." Andy said, holding out the now sheathed sword stick to exchange it for the spade. Bess handed it to him and then he fought his way off the path and through the underbrush and hazels out to the grass beyond. He began to pace around looking at the ground, then occasionally looking up to orientate himself between where he thought Culver Down, Brading and Sandown might be. As Bess watched, she was impressed at how well he was leaning into his instinctive side. However, as she stood there with her back to the woodland, she began to get a familiar prickling sensation at the back of her neck. She unsheathed the sword and turned in a single movement, ready to defend herself. The trees and shrubs stood, unmoving and unmoved by her. Just down the path, towards their earlier entry point, a tree caught her eye. She walked down to it and stood, regarding it suspiciously. It was a huge oak, whose trunk was hidden under a mass of ivy. She'd always thought that the trunk of a tree was like a face – that was where you could see its character. This tree's face was hidden by the mask of ivy. What was it trying to hide? Long, twisted branches extended in pairs from either side of the trunk so that it reminded her of a great stag beetle standing upright with the underside of its abdomen facing her. The impression was completed by two great branches reaching skywards like stag beetle antlers. But it was more than just the look of the tree that bothered her. It seemed belligerent.

"I don't like the look of this tree," she called over her shoulder.

Andy wasn't sure what he was supposed to do with that,

"Don't hug it, then," he called back, looking at the ground carefully. Was there a shadow of a geometrical shape in the way the grasses grew? He looked more closely. Surely it couldn't be... but why not? Looking at a section of the grass, he could see that some of it was higher than the rest. He looked along the line of higher grass. Maybe it was wishful thinking, maybe he was imagining it, but he thought he could see a clear shape in the grass. It looked like the footprint of a church. Yes, the rounded bulge at the eastern end would have been where the altar was placed. Then the straight lines of the north and south walls heading westward, with square bulges a third of the way down to make the cross shape, and then the main entrance would be at the western end. Andy jogged along to where the line of higher grass delineated the western end of what he thought was the church. Yes! He looked in amazement – it was as if he was seeing the church standing there.

"I've found the church!" He cried, barely containing his excitement.

"Excellent!" Bess called back without taking her eyes off the treacherous looking oak tree,

"What about the well?"

Ah! The well... Andy thought about the story of how the priest came running out of his church to see the pilgrim lying dead next to the well. So, the likelihood was that the well was near the west end of the church. He walked into the area of grass where he thought the church had been and strode towards the western entrance, then over the line of slightly higher grass. Now he was 'out' of the church. Off in the fog to his right was where the haven would have been. In the story, the pilgrim came straight from his ship and walked to the well, followed by the villagers. He would have walked along path by the sea wall and then come up to the church. Andy felt that the well must be somewhere close to the front of the church, but on the seaward side. He walked slowly through the long grass looking for... that was it! Until their arrival and the fog rolling in, September had been dry and much of the long grass was browned by the sun, but here was a patch of lush grass. Grass that clearly had its own additional source of water. He hurried over to it and started digging.

"Found something?" Bess called.

"Maybe," he called back. As he'd suspected, the earth there was damp, unlike the hard ground all around it. This made the digging easier, but even so, it didn't take long before he was sweating. He pulled off his coat and laid it on the ground a distance away to avoid getting earth on it, then he was back to work, pushing the spade into the ground and lifting it away to the sound of tearing grass roots. The smell of earth filled his nostrils as he started by digging out the top layer with the grass and roots. Once he'd taken the top layer off a six-foot square section, he stood back and looked at his work, panting.

"I'll buy you a nice pint later," Bess called.

"I'll hold you to that," he replied, then bent to his task once more.

The work was dirty and laborious, and after an hour of digging, Andy was starting to wonder whether his instincts were worth listening to. A large pile of earth had built up next to the hole and he hoped the farmer didn't swing by, because he didn't know what he'd give as the explanation for digging up his pasture. Meanwhile, Elizabeth Russell had made herself useful by tethering the climbing rope to a pair of hazel trees at the edge of the field. Unlike the trees that seemed to be consumed with hate on the inside of the path, the hazels were a pair of ordinary trees. Perhaps they were growing on ground where no blood had been spilled during the massacre? Whatever the case, she was happy to use them and was sure they would hold the weight of anyone going down the well. After nearly two hours of hard graft, Andy's shovel struck something hard.

"This could be it," he called to Bess, who walked over to see him digging around a square stone. In five minutes, he'd revealed a number of stones set next to each other in a curved formation. Another twenty minutes and a ring of stones were clear to see.

"There's a lid on here," Andy said, digging away inside the centre of the ring with his hands,

"Feels like metal."

"Want a hand?" Bess asked.

Andy looked over his shoulder at her in her pristine red trouser suit and black trench coat,

"No, it's okay," he said, "You'll ruin your outfit. Mine's already messy," and he continued to dig away with his hands. He concentrated on the very centre of the circle and, just as he'd hoped, he found an anchor point in the top of it. After this, he used the spade around the inside edge of the brickwork to try to prize the lid away from the stone.

"Chuck us the end of that rope,"

Bess did so and he threaded it through the central anchor point, then tied it on before stepping out of the hole he'd created.

"What a mucky pup!" Bess said as he walked towards her with his face, hands and clothes covered in dirt.

"Want to give me a hand pulling this lid off?" he asked, offering her the rope.

"How romantic!" she said, then smiled and took the rope.

"Okay... One, two, three!"

They heaved on the rope with little effect.

"Maybe if you use the spade to prize it up as I pull?" Andy suggested.

"You're the boss," she replied and jumped into the hole to put the edge of the spade into the thin gap between the lid and the stone.

Andy counted them in again, then pulled on the rope with all his strength.

"Yeah, it's coming!" Bess said as she leaned into prizing off the lid and then, as Andy dug his heels in and put all his weight into it, the lid moved,

"Don't stop now! Come on!" she exhorted and, with a final effort, the lid came free, lifted up and then thudded down onto the earth next to the well.

Andy fell back and lay on the damp ground, puffing.

"Nice one!" Bess said, then put on her head torch to have a look down,

"Hard to see much from here," she said, then picked up a stone and dropped it in. The was a pause of about three seconds until a distant splash.

"I guess it's about a hundred and fifty feet deep," she said as Andy got up to join her.

"Right, off you go," he said.

"Hmm?" she looked confused.

"I'll lower you down the well."

"Oh no, I'm not going down there," she said, "You're going down the well."

"Me? But you're smaller – it'll be easier for you to go down and easier for me to hold your weight," Andy said.

"But what if we come under attack? Who's better placed to fend off – say – an angry god? You or me?" she asked, looking at him with her very direct gaze.

"You, I suppose," he conceded.

"And you suppose right! Which means you're going down the well. Anyway, you're already dirty, so it makes sense. Here..." she said, handing him her head torch.

"Thanks!" Andy said, adjusting the size and putting it on, before untying the rope from the lid of the well.

Soon, he'd got himself into the harness and sorted the rope so that he could abseil down the well.

"You've done this sort of thing before?" Bess asked.

"I'm more than just a pretty face. I used to date a climber and you know what it's like – you try to share your partner's passions."

Bess nodded – that was exactly how she'd got into problems with Count Hermes D'ambrisio, only his passions had been human sacrifice and conjuring demons.

Andy walked over to where Bess had tied the rope to the hazel tree and checked it over. Yes, that was good. He went back to the edge of the well, got himself over the lip and trusted to his equipment as he leant back and let himself down. Now they were at their most vulnerable. Elizabeth Russell took the sword and stood with her back to the well to keep a watch for anything coming at them out of the fog.

Chapter Twenty-Seven

The Well Of Fears

Inside the well, the cold immediately seeped through to Andy's bones so that his fingers were aching after only a few seconds. He lowered himself slowly, ensuring that he got a good look all the way around the walls as he went. The stone lining glistened under the light of his torch, but there seemed to be nothing to see. The well was narrow enough that if he wanted to, he could hold himself up by bracing his feet against one side and his shoulders against the other, and he stopped for thirty seconds to test his ability to hold himself. Yes, that was good. If the rope snapped, he'd be able to stay wedged for a while. But not forever. That wasn't a good thought!

"Don't think like that, Andy!" he said to himself,

"Everything will be fine..."

"You all right down there?" Bess called.

"Yeah. All good!" he called back, although, as he looked up at the receding opening of light above him, his stomach fluttered.

He thought about how the well had been cursed after the blood of the stranger had tainted it. The unnatural cold and the dank smell with its sour note certainly gave him a feeling that he was descending into a place that was accursed.

Andy looked straight down but could still not see the water below him. He continued his careful progress until he was down about fifty feet, and then he saw the writing. It was carved into the rock walls and had remained there, unweathered, for hundreds of years.

"Got something!" he called up, but there was no response. Presumably, Bess couldn't hear him because of his depth. He twisted himself around to find where the writing started, looking through his breath which was billowing in the cold and damp. Before reading a word, he took out his phone and filmed all of what was written on the walls. Only when he was satisfied that he had a record of it did he put his phone away, climb back up a few feet and start reading:

Here be the testimant of Tom Attrill, the last soul of Woolverton in Binbridge Isle.

Andy was surprised. This couldn't be the Thomas Attrill that they'd met, could it?

When the grate disastre came I was but a yong boy of twelve. Now the number of my yeers be twenty. But though I be full in manhood and a lusty bacheler I niver wif shal take lest the curse of Woolverton be upon oure children. Alle oure woes be layde at the feet of Urian. Devyl, lyar and crulle trikstyre. Yet still he remayneth in the Wight in ful controlle of magicke as blak as his heart.

So, after manipulating the destruction of Wolverton, Urian had even stolen the name of the last survivor to use as his alias in the present day. It was like sticking two fingers up at the dead – it fitted Urian's character perfectly. Andy steadied himself in the narrow tunnel of the well and continued reading through the white clouds of his breath,

But I knowe his Nature and how his strengthe maye be taked awaye. I have not the powere to do the deed that must be done, but I will here write how. Go thee to the Othere Place and there entreatie the Gods to returne to the Wight, that with theyre strengthe ye maye caste Urian to hell as the Devyl he be. Now I shal hide this well and go to Culver cliff for al tyme to preye for the soules of the lost and anye otheres that maye yet be cursed by Urian the Trikstyre.

It seemed like good news – there was a way of defeating Urian. All they needed to do was go to the Other Place and get their help, although Bess had seemed wary of what might be there. After he'd finished reading, Andy checked that there was nothing else written, then watched back the film of the text. Yes, he could make it all out. So, that was it! Job done!

"I'm coming up!" he shouted. No reply.

"Bess! You there?" he yelled and the silence that followed chilled him more deeply than the cold of the well. Something was wrong. He looked up. There was no circle of light above him. The mouth of the well had been blocked off.

***

Bess had been looking and listening for anything that might come at them out of the fog while Andy was down the well. Then, at the moment he reached the inscription, a dreadful creaking sound cut through the muffling gloom. Bess turned towards where the sound came from. Another loud creak was quickly followed by another. Something big was moving and Elizabeth Russell had an unpleasant dropping feeling in her stomach. She knew what the noise was. It had been inevitable since she'd seen that evil-looking oak and now she'd have to face it. She dropped the sheath of the sword stick by the well, took a couple of deep breaths to steady herself, then ran into the woodland just before Andy called out,

"Got something!"

As she ran into the copse, there was cracking, creaking and what sounded like a low groan. Something that shouldn't be moving was moving and finding it painful. She ran down the path and, sure enough, the huge oak was leaning forwards to try to stand on its six branches. The only problem was, it was still rooted and now it was using its strength to pull its roots out of the ground with a dull, tearing sound. Finally, it was able to crash forwards onto its six leg-like branches as it slowly pulled the last of its roots out of the ground.

"Fuck a duck!" Bess gasped as the tree snapped its two antler-like top branches together and turned towards her. Now it really did look like a leafy, seventy-foot long stag beetle. It swung its antlers from side to side as if it was gauging how they worked and then it took a step forward. Something was wrong – it was off-balance. She watched as it shook great clods of earth off the roots at its back end. It took another creaking step and this time it didn't have a problem. Now all the problems were Elizabeth Russell's. She thought quickly. The main thing was to make sure it didn't get to the hazel tree and the rope holding Andy halfway down the well. She ran deeper into the copse to keep the fight away from the well and was speaking the words of an incantation as she went. The tree turned to follow her and smashed its way through the other trees as it chased her down in a few strides. She could feel its huge presence right behind her and her breaths were coming in short gulps as if she'd been doused in freezing water. She skidded to a halt and turned to face it.

"Hold it!" she shouted with the sword in her left hand and her right arm cocked and ready to throw something.

The tree stopped and swung its antlers at her, making her jump backwards to avoid being swept aside. In reply, she threw something from her right hand. A ball of flame exploded against the head of the tree and it reared up in pain, then crashed back to the ground, shaking its head violently to put out the flames. It started to move towards Bess again and she made a show of creating a ball of flame in her hand, which she pulled back ready to throw. The tree stopped in its tracks. It understood the significance of that arm, ready to throw another fireball. As some of its leaves were still smouldering, it didn't seem to want to risk another explosion.

"That's right – be a sensible tree. Go back to where you were," Elizabeth Russell said as she stood her ground. The problem was, she was so busy looking up at what was towering above her, that she didn't notice the ivy stems slithering from the trunk of the tree along the ground towards her.

"Go on! Go back!" she said firmly as if she were talking to a stubborn dog,

"I don't want to hurt..." but her sentence ended in a startled cry, as the ivy stem whipped around her ankle and yanked her leg out from under her. It dragged her across the ground by her left ankle and amidst the blur of discomfort, the smell of earth and the sight of the underside of the oak, Bess had the presence of mind to throw her fireball. This one exploded on its exposed underbelly. The tree leaped into the air, then landed with a boom and was charging off through the woodland. Elizabeth Russell barely had time to think about her next move as she was dragged off through the underbrush by the incensed creature. Now her senses were overwhelmed by the kaleidoscope of multiple sharp pains as she was scratched and battered against the ground, brambles and other trees. Then she was airborne as she was jerked over the path near the edge of the marsh, before slamming into the ground and having the wind knocked out of her. Next thing she knew, she was wrenched over the edge of the sea wall and into the marsh.

She hit the sodden ground with a 'splutch' and was immediately soaked in stinking water. Thankfully, the tree stopped running and she came to a halt, gasping for breath amidst the reeds. She had to concentrate hard to force herself to start breathing again and managed to sit up. About twenty yards away, just inside the wall of fog, the tree was extinguishing the flames beneath it by wallowing in the marsh. Bess knew she had seconds before it was moving again, so she slashed with the sword at the ivy attaching her to the tree. Yes, that worked, but the tree must have felt something, because it turned and lowered its head towards her and snapped its antler-like branches together. She scrambled to her feet, bleeding, disorientated, panting and trying to work out what to do next. It was like going toe to toe with a dinosaur! She'd studied self-defence with some of the greatest practitioners of the fighting arts, but at no point had they covered how to fight an angry, highly mobile tree. Unfortunately, she was going to have to fight it to keep it away from that well.

She prepared another fireball, but this time the sodden tree wasn't cowed. It charged her and it was only when she tried to evade it that she realised her feet had been sucked into the mud. Her attempt to leap to her right failed and she slumped sideways. She instinctively put her right hand down to stop her fall and the fireball in her hand was snuffed out. And now she saw the antler-like branches sweeping towards her. Even with the protective spell she'd cast as she'd run into the woodland, the impact of the branch into her left flank snapped a couple of her ribs and she was flung like a toy thirty yards through the air. Fortunately, the reeds and marshy ground softened her landing, but the fall left her gasping and confused as she spat out muddy water. The sharp pain in her left ribs made trying to restart her breathing even harder as she clumsily flapped about in the mud. She let out a low moan as she struggled to get back to her feet, concentrating hard on simply making herself breathe again. Once she was breathing, she gingerly felt under her jacket... yes, those ribs were bust all right. But it wasn't the state of her ribs that worried her most, it was the fact that she couldn't see or hear the tree. That meant that it was heading for...

"Andy!" she gasped and started running clumsily back towards dry land. With each step, pain and anger flared inside her, so that by the time she clambered up over the old sea wall, her face was set with fury.

In the well, Andy tried not to panic. Someone had sealed the top of the well, so it would be a matter of moments before they cut his rope. He immediately braced himself across the well so that the only thing holding him up was the pressure between his feet and shoulders. A moment later, the slashed rope fell down on him.

"Lucky escape!" he breathed, then looked up to the blocked off mouth of the well. Although it was further than the head torch was designed for, Andy could just make out the thing that was sealing the well. Weird! It looked like the root system of a tree. Andy looked at it harder. Was it... no, that couldn't be... he blinked and looked again – the roots seemed to be growing downwards towards him. Andy looked away, then looked back. Yes, they were definitely coming towards him. Not quickly, but the sight had the uncanny quality of time-lapse photography, and the roots were filling the entire well as they moved inexorably towards him. Watching them became steadily more disturbing, as they seemed to be blindly questing in the darkness for him. What would they do when they reached him?

The thought gave him a queasy feeling. Andy started to shift himself further down the well, but it was tricky and now there was no safety rope, he knew that any mistake would be the end of him. He glanced back up at the oncoming roots. Yes, they were moving faster than him. What could he do? Could he use his gun? No. Its only probable effect would be to deafen him. The knuckle duster would be no use, so that just left the flick knife. He drew it from his pocket and flicked it open. The silver glinted under the light of the head torch. It was better than nothing, but really, what was he going to do – prune the roots to death? All he could do was watch and wait as the roots stretched down towards him, bringing with them the musty smell of earth. Andy had a flashback to his father's funeral. It had been winter and as the ten-year-old Andy had picked up a handful of earth to throw it onto the coffin in the grave, the same strong smell of earth had overcome him. To Andy, that was the smell of death and it was getting closer with every passing moment.

As the roots closed in on him over the next two minutes, Andy was struck by the apparent intelligence of the way they moved. It wasn't random. And there was something about the way the roots expanded and grew thicker behind the flexible, questing tips that sickened him. What would they do when they got to his body? Would they slip around him or try to push through him like the fabled bamboo torture of southeast Asia? And what would they do when they got to his face? He tried not to picture them searching out his ear canals and then sliding into them. Oh God! He couldn't stand the thought of it or of how they might slowly puncture his eyeballs. He moved himself further down, but it was no use, they were still coming towards him with a disconcerting inevitability. Yards away... he could see the tangled mass of stems behind the questing shoots... feet away... he could hear the sound of the stems rubbing against each other and the faint sound of unfurling as the shoots grew towards him, and now he tried to slash at the roots with the knife, but to no effect... inches away... and all he could see, hear and smell was the root system that now clogged fifty feet of the well above him... it was like being buried alive with the lid of the coffin slowly breaking in on him from the weight of earth above. Then the inevitable happened - the first, questing root touched his leg. He recoiled as best he could, but the root slipped down between his thighs. Now he was up close, he was horrified by how fast the roots were growing. He could feel that first root was halfway past his thigh in a few seconds, and then another root touched him on the top of his head. Then there was another, and another, and then his body was crawling with roots exploring, probing. He stabbed upwards with the knife, but his hand was entangled in the roots and held fast as he felt the knife prized from his grasp. Then came the sound of snapping metal. So much for the silver knife! Andy wanted to scream but was terrified that if he opened his mouth, roots would go down his throat and burrow into his lungs.

None of the roots had tried to penetrate him so far. Instead, they had slipped around him and he realised that he was no longer holding his weight – they were. They had wrapped themselves around him and under him, so that he was held fast. That was when he saw the thicker root coming down towards him. Now that they had him firmly braced, it would be easier to push through him. The thick root slipped downwards until it was resting on his solar plexus. Andy watched it with horror, hardly breathing as its hard tip started to slowly apply pressure. When Andy had been impaled with an iron railing earlier in the summer, it had been sudden and unexpected. The time between the impact on his back and the metal rod bursting through his chest was a fraction of a second. Andy had the feeling this was going to be slow and painful. There was cunning in the way the roots were moving, an unpleasant intelligence that made him want to scream. Then came the pressure – the insistent building of pressure on a single spot. Like the tip of a blunt pencil pushing down... now the pain was building, the pain of pressure and of skin being stretched. Slowly, the pressure would stretch the skin until it couldn't stretch any more and then the tip of the root would slip through the split in his skin and start to push down through his sinews. Andy gulped as two more roots positioned themselves in front of his eyeballs.

Elizabeth Russell sprinted along the path by the sea wall, ignoring the pain in her side. That pain would be nothing next to what she'd feel if she lost Andy. She ran straight towards the well, knowing that the tree would be going for him. When she got to the edge of the woodland, her heart dropped. The oak had already positioned itself on top of the well and was facing her and ready to keep her away. She stepped out of the woods and her furious eyes were like two violet flames lighting up the gloom of the fog. As she stood, staring at the tree, the temperature plummeted and the light seemed to be sucked away. The oak took a swing at her, but her fury gave her perfect clarity and precision. She swayed beneath the slashing branch and when she came up, she lifted her hands to the sky and shouted words of power in Old Norse. The air instantly crackled and there was the heavy scent of ozone as Elizabeth Russell screamed,

"Drep!"

An explosion of lightning flashed white in the darkness and the ear-splitting sound of the super-heated air suddenly expanding caused the hazel trees to shake. In a split second, a smouldering stump and blasted branches strewn around a radius of forty yards was all that remained of the oak.

"Yeah? Want some more, yer fucker?" she shouted, striding towards the stump. She was now in the frenzy between anger and insanity that came in the wake of conjuring lightning, and she took the sword and set about hacking up the remains of the tree, swearing and cursing as she did. After about thirty seconds, she began to return to her senses and stopped attacking the dead tree. She lifted her face to the sky and let out a scream to flush the residual energy of the spell out of her system.

"Fuck me, that's a rush!" she exclaimed. It had been a long time since she'd conjured lightning and she'd forgotten just how awesome it made her feel. She felt like she could do anything, but she also knew that feeling would only last about half an hour and then she'd be done for the day.

In the well, Andy had been holding onto the big root to try to stop it from impaling him when the blast of lightning had destroyed the tree above ground. It was just as well he was holding on, because the moment the tree exploded, all the roots that were holding him went limp. Now he was hanging on for dear life from the one root. He swung his feet up and, after some scrabbling, managed to wedge himself across the inside of the well with his feet and shoulders. This would give him some respite, but how long would it take to remove all the roots above him? And what if Bess was injured – or dead? What if there was no rescue? No! He couldn't think that way. Those thoughts were the killers. He thought his situation through. He was happily wedged in the well about a third of the way down, but he'd only be able to hold himself for twenty or thirty minutes before fatigue set in. He could try to work his way to the bottom of the well and float in the water, but if it was freezing cold, how long would it be before it killed him? He looked up into the tangle of roots and had an idea. He pulled up the length of rope that had been cut earlier and threaded it through the roots. After threading it through a couple of dozen loops of root, he tied it off and shortened the length through the descender. Then, holding onto the big root just in case, he allowed the rope threaded through the roots to take his weight. At first, it creaked in an unsettling way, but it held fast. Okay, that would allow him to conserve his energy until it was needed... but there was still the problem of being stuck fifty feet down the well, which was blocked by a huge bung of roots. Andy hung with the stifling smell of earth and roots filling his senses. He swore loudly and fluently for about thirty seconds, then became still to conserve his strength.

At the top of the well, Elizabeth Russell was working out what to do. She tried to make a mind connection with Andy, but couldn't find him,

"Bloody Swaailen!" he cursed. She really hated the effect it had on her – and people wondered why she was so reluctant to visit The Island! So, speaking to him directly was out... or was it? There was one other option... but no – things weren't *that* desperate were they? She grimaced at the realization that things were, indeed, *that* desperate. With some degree of contempt, she reached into her coat pocket and pulled out an ancient flip phone that would have been out of fashion a decade before smartphones took over the planet. She opened it up and turned it on. If she got a signal, she might be able to phone Andy. She waited for the antediluvian device to start up and looked carefully at it when it was ready. No signal. Good old Isle of Wight!

"Ah well, can't say I didn't try," she said with some relief as she turned the infernal thing off again and put it away. Well, she'd simply have to get the rescue started and muddle through without letting Andy know the plan, which had formulated while she'd been faffing about with the phone.

First thing was to get rid of the stump, which was about seven feet high and about eight feet in diameter. Fortunately, the stump was smouldering and hot, and she was still crackling with energy from the lightning. She muttered an incantation and concentrated all her power on the glowing embers in the heart of the tree. Suddenly, flames flared from the embers and in a matter of moments, she harnessed and intensified the flames until they were white hot. She stood back, continuing to talk to the flames, exhorting them to burn hotter and directing them with her hands to any parts of the stump that needed to be burned away. Within ten minutes, the whole stump had been consumed. When the flames revealed the root system beneath, she ceased encouraging the fire. She allowed it to burn unaided for a couple of minutes, then focussed her intent and clapped her hands. The flames vanished, revealing the great knot of roots that were clogging the well. Bess didn't like it. For all she knew, Andy was already dead at the bottom, or had been strangled to death by the roots. She shook her head as if to dispel the thought and got to work. She picked up the hollow sheath of the sword stick and hurried down to the marsh, where she filled the sheath with water. She took it back to the top of the well and held the heavy silver ring on her right little finger over the top of the sheath. She felt for the catch and opened the face of the ring. Inset into the ring was a compartment full of blue powder, which she tipped carefully into the sheath full of water. The surface fizzed and she was careful not to breathe in the vapour rising from it, before drizzling the mixture over the roots until there was nothing left in the scabbard. After a minute, the roots began to turn black, wither and disintegrate. There! It was done. Nothing to do now but hope and pray that the man she loved was safe and sound.

Andy was still suspended from the bundle of roots above him, vaguely contemplating turning off his head torch to save the battery, when the rope holding him gave slightly. He only slipped a few inches, but that was enough to see him quickly brace himself against the sides of the well. What the hell? Once settled, he calmed his breathing and listened. There was something happening above him. He could hear a distant hissing fizz - like a lit dynamite fuse. It was quiet at first, slowly becoming more distinct as it seemed to get closer. Now some sort of ash was falling onto him and he shielded his eyes. He was looking towards his feet when the trailing roots around his legs suddenly turned black and disintegrated.

"Andy!"

It was Bess's voice. She sounded relieved.

"All right, darlin!" Andy shouted back in his best approximation of a leery builder calling out at a passing woman.

"You okay?"

"Been better," he called back, "Got any more rope up there? I'm wedged in here, but I can't hold it forever."

"Don't go anywhere!" she called, then disappeared, returning about half a minute later with another length of rope, the end of which she threw down to him.

Once he'd got it through his descender, he started to haul his way back up the well and Elizabeth Russell watched nervously as he made his slow progress up to the surface.

Finally, Andy heaved himself up and out of the top of the well and dropped, panting, to his knees. He was a mess and bathed in sweat,

"Fuck me, that's a killer!" he gasped, then looked up at Bess. She wasn't looking too clever either. Her clothes were ragged, she was soaked and covered in mud and, now that the effects of summoning the lightning were subsiding, she was looking exhausted,

"What the hell happened to you?" he asked, gathering his strength to stand up.

"Got attacked by that tree I didn't like the look of," she replied.

"Were those its roots down the well?"

"Yeah. You didn't breathe in any of the ash from them did you? I had to use a plant killer on them and it's not that great for people, either."

"No, I'm fine," he said, standing up, "C'mere!" and he opened his arms.

"Careful, I've got two broken ribs," she said as she limped into his embrace. They held each other gently for a while and then kissed.

"Your lips feel tired," he said.

"I've been having a helluva time up here – but what about you? Did you find...?"

"Yeah," he smiled, "And I filmed it on my phone, so you can see exactly what it said."

This news injected her with renewed energy,

"Great. You can tell me while we're putting the lid back on that well and covering it up."

"Do what?" Andy exclaimed.

"We don't want some sheep or rambler to fall down the well, do we?"

At that point, Andy frankly couldn't have given two shits if a flock of sheep and a scout troop fell down the well, but he sighed and said,

"All right... where's the spade?"

Chapter Twenty-Eight

The Hag Stone

An hour later, Andy and Bess stood back to admire their work. Yes, the field was still messy with bits of blasted tree, but the well was covered. The grass on the top was clumsily put back in place, but it would do.

"One last thing," Bess said, then she mumbled an incantation as she walked around the well three times. When she was done, Andy gave her a questioning glance,

"A little cloaking spell. This patch will look exactly like the rest of the field to anyone – even Attrill, or Urian, or whatever he's called. And besides, I've sealed the lid in place with a spell which makes it impossible to open without my permission."

"Come on, let's get you back to the hotel," Andy said. She was looking done in. He'd already told her that the only way to defeat Urian was by going to the Other Place, and he'd seen the news physically take the wind out of her sails. Now, she was barely able to hold herself up as they walked away from the scene of their fight. After about fifty yards, Bess turned back to look at where they'd come from, but it was lost in the fog. She smiled ruefully,

"This stupid fog is a curse and a blessing. It hampers my abilities, but without it, everyone in Brading and Bembridge would've been able to see that bloody tree rampaging about the marsh. That would've taken a bit of explaining!"

And with that, they limped their way back to the car in silence.

Back at the hotel, they went up to their room and Andy ran the bath. He came back into the bedroom to see Bess naked from the waist up. She was standing in front of the mirror with her left arm raised in the air, while she spoke the words of an incantation and laid her right hand onto the purple bruising that covered most of the area between her armpit and her hip.

"Jesus!" he said.

"Bloody tree!" she muttered once she'd finished her spell, "Bugger really caught me. I'm lucky it didn't take my head off..." and then a thought occurred to her – was it lucky? In that moment, the tree could easily have killed her. She'd been stuck in the mud, but instead of skewering her or battering her to a pulp, it had flicked her aside. Weird...

"Could you check me all over for thorns?" she asked.

"Yeah, I'll do that," he replied, "But I hope you're not expecting anything else out of me, 'cos I'm knackered."

"Don't worry – just a thorn check, please," she said, stepping out of her ruined trousers and taking off her underwear. Andy undressed, too, and sat naked on the edge of the bed to run his eye and hands over all the parts of her body that she couldn't see. There were a few bramble thorns embedded in her back and he used her tweezers to get them out.

"The rest looks clear to me," he said, standing up and starting to go to the bathroom.

"Hey!" she said, grabbing his arm and gently pulling him to her, "Kiss me."

He looked down at her. Even after being battered by a tree, she looked amazing, and her lips were too inviting to refuse her request. He bent his head and they kissed, softly at first and then deeply. Their bodies were pressed into each other and the skin-to-skin contact was exhilarating. It was almost as if they were one, joined on a level far deeper than the physical. Andy felt a bloom of golden heat in his chest as if she had shared some part of her with him. Bess felt it, too, and the moment gave her a sense of sublime joy. When they finally disengaged, they were both breathless.

"I'd better turn off the bath," Andy said and walked through to the bathroom. Bess smiled and put her hand to her chest. It was still warm from the glowing moment they'd shared. Was there any better feeling in the world than this?

"Bath's ready," he called and she went to join him.

She eased into the water, wincing as she did.

"You sure you shouldn't go to the doctor with that?" he asked.

"No. It'll be fine in the morning. The spell just takes time to knit everything back together," then she let out a long sigh as she relaxed back into the hot water.

***

"Downner!" Thomas Attrill screeched. He was standing by the fire in his grand hall, pouring the last of a bottle of 1982 Margaux into his glass. Suspended in the air in front of him was a circle about two feet across. Projected within the circle, Elizabeth Russell and Andy Harper were limping away from Centurion's Copse. Attrill watched them with a sour look on his face, then dispelled the circle with a peeved flick of his hand.

"Meyaster?" Downer said as he shuffled into the hall through a door near the fireplace.

"Over here, please," Attrill said with a smile.

Downer walked reluctantly to where he'd been directed. He knew that Attrill was at his most dangerous when he was being polite.

"Excellent. And could you raise your left arm, please?"

Downer didn't even question it and did as he was asked. Attrill stepped up to him.

"Thanks," he smiled, but the glint in his eye...

Suddenly, Downer was doubled over from the vicious right hook into his exposed ribs. Attrill looked pleased – the dull crack indicated that he'd fractured something in there.

"Wazzat for?" Downer groaned.

"So you can share her pain," he replied, "I knew I shouldn't have entrusted you with enchanting that tree..." and Attrill stared into the middle distance,

"But I was feeling so very tired that day... Anyway, your bloody tree damn near killed my witch."

"I did my best, meyaster. Not my doing that I ain'ts as skilled as thee," Downer grumbled.

"Not only almost killed my witch, but roundly didn't bloody kill her assistant! And to cap it all, I watched them find the well, but now she's put a spell on it and the damned thing's disappeared."

"Oh dear," said Downer without emotion, "Will ye be going to the hotel tonight to kill he yerzelf?"

"No, I need to save my energy. You, however, will keep a close watch on them,"

Downer looked unhappy about the prospect, but said nothing as Attrill continued,

"As soon as she leaves him alone for any length of time, I want him dead – you understand?"

"Yez, meyaster," Downer nodded.

"I cannot impress upon you enough how important it is to kill him. While he's alive, there's a slim chance our plan could fail. Get him out of the picture and we're almost home and dry."

Downer nodded again.

"Good. Now, get me another bottle of the Margaux '82."

Downer turned and walked away. Watching him go, Attrill thought about how close he was to achieving his goal. Once he'd done it, his first act would be to put Downer out of his misery in the most painful way possible. Attrill smiled. Yes, that would be a fun way to start his new life!

***

Neither Bess nor Andy was surprised to find that they fell asleep in the bath. Andy floated back to consciousness, looked around the steamy room with its low, golden lighting and realised what had happened,

"Hey," he whispered,

"Wha...?" Bess jerked into wakefulness, splashing water over the side.

"We fell asleep."

"Damn."

"Why damn? We needed it," Andy said, stroking her right shoulder. It was getting cold.

"With me asleep, Attrill could have come and killed us both."

"But he didn't. Why don't you let some water out and put more hot in?"

Bess did so and tried to wake herself, but found it difficult. The short sleep had been blissful and her body wanted more. Once the bath was hot again, she slumped back against him and lowered herself deeper into the water.

"Oh, that's so good!" the arms of Morpheus were open and all she wanted to do was fall into them,

"But I mustn't sleep," she mumbled.

"Why not?"

"Got to protect us," and now she was barely awake. Her eyelids were so heavy!

"Tonight, I'll keep guard while you sleep. After what happened today, I think you need it more," Andy whispered, slipping a hand across her stomach and gently stroking the area between her navel and mons veneris.

Her only reply was a low "Mmmm," and then he could feel her slipping into sleep.

Andy was as good as his word and stayed awake as the water unwound their tired muscles. In the end, he had to wake her up before the water cooled off. They got out, dried off and dressed, then went downstairs to get some food. There was a wide variety of cold cuts, pies and salady stuff, and they were able to make a good meal of it. It was only just past eight in the evening, but once they'd finished dinner, they went to the big armchairs in the entrance hall, which Bess continued to insist was the safest place for them to sleep. While Andy cleared the grate and built a new fire, Bess got comfy in her chair and soon the hall was filled with the dancing light of the flames.

"You sleep until three and if anything happens before that, I'll wake you," Andy said.

"But how will you stay awake," Bess asked blearily. Now she was in a comfy chair, she wasn't able to keep her eyes open.

"Don't worry, I've got a few old copper's tricks up my sleeve," Andy said and kissed her on the forehead. She was asleep by the time he'd sat in his armchair. He smiled - she was cute when she was asleep. Although as far as he was concerned, she always looked cute – even when she was bedraggled after being dragged through a marsh. He reached into his pocket and took out a small pill box, tipped a little white pill into his hand and downed it with some water. The speed should keep him awake and focussed through the night and, if it didn't, he'd take another.

As Bess slept, Andy kept himself busy by tending the fire, taking his Glock to pieces and reassembling it, and then trawling the internet on his phone for more information on the Jutes. Three-o-clock came and went, and it was just after seven when Bess finally stirred,

"It's light," she said, looking out through the window, where the fog was still wrapped around the hotel.

"Yeah. I thought it would be best to let you sleep. How're you feeling?"

"Rejuvenated!" she said, stretching hard, "I guess I needed that! Conjuring lightning really takes it out of me."

"Well I never!" Andy said with a smile, "I would not have expected that."

"Alright Mister Sarcastic... but thanks for letting me sleep. How are you holding up?"

"Fucking golden!" he replied. He'd taken a second pill around six and he was buzzing,

"So, what's the plan?" he asked.

"Breakfast; re-watch that video you took of the inscription; walk on the beach until the shops open; buy a wetsuit; hire a kayak and then I'll go to the Other Place."

"You've really thought it through!" Andy laughed, "Not quite sure how the walk on the beach fits into it, but I'm up for it."

"Well," she replied, slinking over to him to get under his blanket,

"The romantic walk on the beach is the most important part," and she gave him a lingering kiss.

It was about half-past-eight when they arrived in the Bembridge lifeboat station car park. Unsurprisingly, given the inclement weather, the car park was not full of tourist vehicles. Andy got out of the car and wandered over to the end of the long pier that stretched out to the launching station. The pier led off into the fog, but the end was hidden in the gloom. Since he'd seen the station on their way in, he imagined it was usually a pretty spectacular sight from where he was standing.

"Come on," Bess called, "We can access the beach down here," and he followed her across the grass of the overspill car park to a small gap in the gorse hedge. A short, steep path led down to the pebbly beach, which scrunched loudly under their feet as they stepped down onto it. Looking at the breakers and the high tide mark, Elizabeth Russell could tell that the tide was about halfway.

"D'you think the tide's coming in or going out?" she asked.

"I'm a Londoner, not Bear Grylls!" Andy replied as he scrunched along the shingle.

"I'll ask at the kayak hire place," she said, looking out to sea. The water beyond the breakers was calm. Not much wind, either. That was good.

The beach itself had a wild feel to it. The pebbles were strewn with driftwood that had been smoothed by sand, stone and waves, and twisted into fantastic shapes. Meanwhile, on the landward side, the ground rose in a cliff of about seven feet high, topped by brambles and gorse bushes. Nothing was tidy or curated about it. There were places where the sea had taken bites out of the golden cliff with its topping of brown soil, and roots straggled out of the bitemarks. And even though there was the occasional wooden groin built out into the sea, it was as if this beach was untamed and could swallow all signs of human activity whenever it pleased. After they'd walked a couple of minutes, Andy said,

"So... why are we...?"

"Know what a hag stone is?" she asked.

"Not a clue. I remind you again that I am a Londoner."

"It's a stone with a hole all the way through the middle."

"What, from natural erosion?"

"Aye. And this beach is good for them. All we need to do is walk along and find a couple of nice ones. Preferably blood red flint."

"Alright..." Andy had no idea what that looked like, but assumed that it did exactly what it said on the tin and was a flint that was blood red.

"Dare I ask why?" Andy was now scanning the pebbles ahead as they walked.

"Today, I'm going to the Other Place. I know almost nothing about it other than the fact the Old Gods are supposed to be there, that time is different there and that it's very hard to get back from. There are stories of sailors getting caught in the Swaailen and ending up in the Other Place. Only some of them return. In the case of one fisherman, he came back five years after he disappeared."

"And the hag stones?"

"Aha!" Bess exclaimed, bending down to pick up a stone, "This is the sort of thing we're looking for," and she held up the pebble, which had a hole through one end of it.

"It's not blood red flint, but it'll do in a pinch," and she looked at Andy through the hole, "Hello, handsome!" she smiled, then pocketed the stone.

They walked on in silence for about ten yards, then Andy said,

"Got one!" and he picked it up. Yes, there was a hole through the stone with a bit of gravel wedged in it.

"Nice try, but we need them clear of bits."

Andy started to try to prize the bit of gravel out, but she intervened,

"That's not allowed."

"What?"

"Interfering with the stone. For a hag stone to give you its full power, it must have a hole all the way through it with no human intervention of any kind."

"All right... lots of rules for these hag stones. Anything else I should know?"

"Not really," she said breezily and continued to walk on.

After five more minutes, Andy said,

"Right, I've got a good 'un here."

"Oh yes – that is perfect!" Bess said happily as he held up a red stone about half the size of an egg, with a clean hole right through the middle.

"Yeah, you've hit the jackpot there. If I can find one half as good as that, we're in business."

It took another fifteen minutes and a few rejected stones before she found one that fitted the bill.

"Oh yes!" she said proudly, "This is excellent. Look!"

Andy looked at the stone which had the glossy sheen of flint, but in a deep red.

"It looks great..." he began, but she interrupted,

"Get yours out, so we can see them together."

Andy did so and he had to admit that they made a good pair.

"Now, bear with me," she said, standing in front of him and entwining the hand she was holding her stone in around his,

"Kiss me and tell me that you love me," she said.

"Easiest thing in the world," he replied before pulling her close and kissing her deeply. Then he looked down into her glittering, violet eyes and said,

"I love you," and as he said it, she could feel it was true. Bess smiled, then pulled him to her and put all her affection into a lingering kiss.

"I love you," she said, looking up into his face, and there was such open vulnerability in that look that he felt a pang in his heart. He gulped. No one had ever given themselves to him like that before. This was like no other feeling he'd ever had and, before he could think about it, he said,

"I love you," and in those three words he conveyed that his body and soul were hers, that he would fight for her, die for her, that he would be forever faithful to her, that if she disappeared, he would wait for her, that he would be her rock and anchor, and that nothing could ever break that bond in this or any other world. They were looking into each other's eyes and the world around them blurred into emptiness. They were all that existed. She leant up and kissed him again. And now their pact was sealed.

Elizabeth Russell stood back and couldn't help but laugh with nervous energy. Andy laughed too.

"What just happened?" he asked.

"Something rare and magical beyond words," she whispered.

Yes, Andy thought that pretty much summed it up.

"C'mon, let's get to the shop," she said, taking his hand and leading him back up the beach.

"Seriously, though, what's so special about these stones?"

"Yeah, I was going to tell you earlier – if you're going to the Other Place and you want to come back, you need to take a hag stone with you and leave at least one here on The Island. They anchor your soul to this place so that you can always find your way back. That's for normal people, but I'm not a normal person,"

"You can say that again!"

"Thanks. I suspect that I'm going to be in a lot of danger when I go to the Other Place. For whatever reason, they have been calling to me from the very first time I came here in the mid-seventeen hundreds. I doubt they're going to make it easy for me to leave. That's why I need you and your stone. When the time comes, I'll need you to look through your stone and call my name. That will bring me back."

"How will I know when it's the right time?" Andy didn't like the idea that her safety was relying on any psychic powers on his part.

"Don't worry. You'll know."

Andy looked dubious, but Bess seemed sure of it.

After the beach, they drove over to Shanklin, left the car in the station car park and walked to a nearby surf shop. The surf dude behind the counter was a bit surprised when the striking-looking woman in a purple trouser suit walked through the door, but when it became clear that she was there to buy, not browse, he gave her his fullest attention.

"I need a shorty wetsuit," Bess said, "A pair of wetsuit boots; a kayak; a paddle; a seat for the kayak; a buoyancy aid; a set of wheels for the kayak; a little dry bag I can hang inside my wetsuit; a hooded towel robe; a baseball cap, a bikini and a really great looking pair of shades," if she was potentially disappearing off the face of the earth, she was going out in style.

The surf dude ran a hand through his long, curly hair and said,

"Okay, you'll have to run over some of that again, but yeah we've got it all," and his voice had an Island burr to it with the faltering delivery that only smoking copious amounts of weed seems to create,

"Let's start with the boots – what size and do you want round toe or split toe?"

"Round toe, size six, please," she replied so fast that it threw the surf dude. He wasn't used to people knowing what they wanted.

"Right... um... right," he stammered as he looked about for a suitable pair.

"Oh, and Colin..." she said,

"How did you know..."

"Your name tag," Bess pointed to his chest,

"Oh yeah... yeah, right..."

"Colin – just chill. There's no hurry. Take it easy," and her voice was so calm that he felt a warm, fuzzy feeling seep through him. He sighed,

"I'll get those boots," and he wandered into the back of the shop.

Andy smiled at Bess and mimicked smoking a spliff – Colin was clearly higher than the average kite. Bess smiled back and sat down to take off her shoes while she awaited Colin's return.

The next forty-five minutes were a surf-shop version of the shopping scene from Pretty Woman. Although she didn't try on the bikini, when it came to the wetsuit, Bess insisted on trying it. Andy couldn't help but catch his breath when she emerged from the changing booth,

"I don't know how you do it!" he said.

"Do what?" she asked, looking at herself in the mirror.

"Look so incredible in a wetsuit. Almost no one looks good in a wetsuit. If I wear a wetsuit, I look like a pregnant seal, but you look like you just stepped out of a surf catalogue."

"What can I say? I've got a fantastic body," she said, then turned to Colin, whose mouth was somewhat agape,

"I'll take it."

"Righto," he mumbled.

"In fact, I'll wear it and the bikini, so if you could take the tags off, that would be great," Bess said.

"No problem," he said in a daze that for once wasn't THC-induced.

They finally emerged from the shop with Andy pulling the kayak on its wheels onto the pavement. Most of the kit was piled onto the body of the kayak, except the paddle, which Bess was carrying.

"I'll stay here while you put my clothes and the towel robe in the car and then we'll go to the sea."

"Gotcha!" Andy said and took the things in his arms. He returned shortly and then led the way with the Kayak down the road towards the sea.

"I thought you were going to hire one of these," he said.

"I was, but then I thought about how dangerous this journey could be. I wouldn't want to lose someone else's kayak."

It made sense, although Andy did feel a bit of a tit trundling a kayak down what seemed to all intents and purposes an ordinary road in the middle of a town. They followed the road straight down the hill and across a couple of crossroads. Andy noticed the name of the road had changed and pointed to the sign,

"Hope Road," he said.

"I guess that's what you'd call a good sign," she smiled. Although it seemed like nothing, she'd always found that the more the little positives you could accumulate, the better your luck became.

Now, most of the houses on the road were bed and breakfast places or hotels, whose front gardens were planted with palms and other succulents. They seemed out of place in the fog. Finally, the road snaked steeply down to the beach and Andy took the wheels off the kayak to drag it across the sand to the edge of the sea. Colin the surf dude had told them that the tide was on the way out – another little positive to add to the collection. Elizabeth Russell checked through all the things she'd need, then placed her hag stone into the little dry bag, hung it around her neck and slipped it inside her wetsuit.

"Where's your stone?" she asked.

"Right here," he said, taking it out of his pocket.

"Good... could you check my zip?" and she turned so that he could do it.

"All fine," he said, patting her behind... God, she looked incredible in that wetsuit!

"Yeah, I do," she said, turning to look at him.

"I thought you said you wouldn't read my mind..."

"Sorry, force of habit. Plus, this is quite a moment," she said, "Now, there's just one thing I need to do to you..."

"Hardly the place, is it?" he replied,

"One track mind," she said, shaking her head, "No, you need a cloaking spell. I'm guessing the second I'm out of sight, Downer or Attrill will pop up and try to kill you. And we can't have that now, can we?"

"No," Andy agreed with that wholeheartedly!

She closed her eyes and spoke the words of the spell, then bent down, took a handful of sand and threw it up into the air above him.

"Don't brush it off," she said, "Not for a few minutes, anyway. That will protect you indefinitely. Your enemies now cannot see you. And if you're in a car, they won't see that, either. Once I go, you need to drive to Old Blackgang Road car park near St Catherine's. Park up and get some sleep, then take the path down to Rocken End beach and wait for me there."

"Old Blackgang Road car park... got it."

"Get some snacks and plenty of water on the way. If I'm not back in a day, check into any hotel nearby and stay there until you feel the need to call me back. Then go down to that beach."

"Why that beach?"

"Because it's hard enough to get to on a beautiful day, so on days like this no one ever goes there. I will be drawn to your hag stone, and since I don't know what shape I'm going to be in when I get back, I think it's best not to have an audience."

"Gotcha."

"Best be off, then," she said, then she tilted up her baseball cap and leant up to kiss him. They lingered on it, then pulled themselves away. Bess took hold of the handle at the front of the kayak and led it through the gentle waves.

"How's the water?"

"Nice. Not even cold," she replied and then, once she was past the point where the waves were breaking, she got into the kayak.

"Good luck!" Andy called as she started to paddle into the fog. She looked briefly over her shoulder,

"Tally-ho!" she called, and disappeared into the cloud. Andy immediately turned and walked back to the car. He could feel the speed starting to wane and he wanted to get provisions and over to the car park before he was floored.

From his vantage point about thirty yards away, Downer swore quietly to himself. He had watched the witch and her lummox go down to the beach, but she must have cast a spell. One moment the big bruiser had been there, but then the witch had thrown some sand over him and he'd instantly disappeared. Now she had paddled into the fog. Downer hurried to the beach. Perhaps the thug was still there? Maybe he was leaving footprints? However, when he got down onto the sand, there was a curious thing. In the damp sand just up from the waves, there were two sets of footprints. They arrived next to each other, then stood around and muddled together, then one set led into the sea. However, while the other set seemed to have arrived, they appeared never to have left. Downer swore again. The meyaster would most prob'ly kill him for this failure. As he shuffled away from the beach, he wished the meyaster would kill him and leave him dead this time.

As Andy Harper had walked up the three steps from the beach to the pavement, he'd seen Downer walking straight towards him. Andy's first instinct was to put on the knuckle duster, ready for another round, but then he realised that Downer hadn't seen him. Downer's eyes were fixed on a point near the shore and he walked within inches of Andy as if he wasn't there. Andy wasn't sure whether to laugh or take a swing at the man. In the end, he contented himself with staying near the exit to the beach and watching Downer as he investigated the place where Bess had said goodbye. After a while, Downer gave up and shuffled back up the beach to the road. Again, he passed within inches of Andy without noticing him. He thought about following Downer. Andy was invisible, so why shouldn't he follow Downer to see where he and Attrill had their base of operations? He started to go after him, but then a wave of tiredness hit him. The speed was tailing off. Andy had to make a quick choice – do exactly as Bess had asked him, or use his own initiative and follow Downer...

Chapter Twenty-Nine

The Other Place

Once the beach was swallowed up by the fog somewhere behind her, Elizabeth Russell had little way to tell which direction she was going. There was no wind and the sea was gently swelling around her, without any wave crests. She stopped paddling for a moment and thrust the paddle straight down over one side of the kayak to see if she could touch the bottom. No. She took it out and paddled onward. Well, she was out of her depth and the silence around her told her that she was nowhere near the shore. She kayaked for about half an hour in what she thought was a straight line, but which could have been round and around in circles. The sea had a strangely viscose consistency, more like molten glass than water. It swelled around her in a lazy way and the kayak slipped through it easily. Looking at the water was strangely hypnotic and she had to blink to keep focus. Everything around her was grey and the silence was only broken by her paddle in the water. Odd. Not a single seabird. Not a distant plane or the mournful sound of a ship's horn in the fog. She had struck out from Shanklin beach heading southeast, which meant that there was nothing between her and France for about a hundred miles. She wasn't paddling hard, so if she was still going in a straight line, she was probably only about a mile from shore. Only a mile, but already a world away.

After another hour, she paused for a drink and to rest her hands, which were taking it in turns to go numb. Hang on... was that a sound? There seemed to be the faintest noise. She paddled forward a bit and then stopped to listen again... yes, there it was – a faint voice calling her name. She paddled towards the sound and over the next few minutes, the indistinct voice lured her forward. As she went, she noticed that the fog around her was thinning. It was thinning and everything was getting brighter until she finally emerged from the fog into glittering sunshine. Ahead of her, for what looked like a couple of miles, there was the dazzling sea, and above her the endless blue of the sky and the warm sun. She took her shades out of a compartment in the floor of the kayak and put them on. Now she wasn't blinded by the light, she could see that a fog bank stretched across the entire horizon ahead of her. She looked over her shoulder and the sight was quite unsettling. She had emerged from the bank of fog surrounding the Isle of Wight, and it filled the entire world at her back. Now she was out of it, the voice she'd been following was louder and she could make out... Chloe!

"Chloe, is that you?" she thought.

"Bess!" Chloe's voice replied in Bess's head, "Where have you been?"

"On the Isle of Wight," Bess replied.

"Oliver said that going there messes with your powers,"

"That's an understatement!"

"So, are you back?"

"No," and Bess explained what she was doing, concluding,

"My guess is that the Other Place is hidden by the fog bank in front of me."

"That sounds horrible," Chloe said - she didn't like the idea of being alone on the sea, "Are there sharks?"

Bess laughed. Although Chloe was grown up in lots of ways, the fact was, that she was still a young kid and thought like one.

"Yes, of course there are sharks out here – porbeagle sharks, for starters."

"Do they eat people?"

"Not that I know of, but they can grow about ten feet long, so I wouldn't want to fight one. Anyway, enough about me, how are you doing?"

Chloe told her about Billy Tanner, the demon and the bishop, including what he'd thought about using Chloe against her.

"Oh, he is a so and so!" Bess said when she'd finished, "But he's only a problem if we allow him to be. Still, that doesn't take away from what you did – that's incredible. I could never have taken on a demon when I was your age!" there was no doubt in her mind that Chloe was a prodigy.

"Yeah, but it wasn't me it was... you know, the other beings out there... they were the ones who..." Chloe struggled to express the experience of how she had channelled the power of light from the Great Beyond,

"Yes, I know who you mean," Bess said, "You have a very rare gift to be able to channel them like that. Even I can't do it quite like that. But how are you now?"

"Still a bit shaky," Chloe replied. She'd slept the whole of the next day and, if truth be told, she was still feeling tired.

"Doing something like that is exhausting. What you're feeling is perfectly normal."

"That's sort of what Oliver said,"

"Ah, yes! Oliver!" Bess called.

"Oh, hello," Oliver's smooth tones joined them, "Are you off the Wight?"

Bess brought him up to speed, then pressed him for information about the exorcism and what was going on.

"I managed to destroy the artefact in which the demon Hurna Antuwahha had been trapped – that was... unpleasant," he said, remembering how the thing had tried to stab him in the eyes,

"Yeah, they're tricky little buggers," Bess replied, "But then, Attrill is a god, so it's hardly surprising."

"But here's the thing – although FitzOsbern is a bit of a dick, he's training his people well. The soapstone mermaid and the lapis lazuli half-moon have been destroyed and the demons exorcised."

"That's good news. And it only leaves us the silver frog and the carnelian sphere."

"Hapgood's gone to give support on the frog – the demon's from Central America and isn't responding to anything the deliverance minister has to offer,"

"Good choice," Bess knew Hapgood had travelled widely through the Americas, so he was perfect,

"And Suzy's dealing with the sphere. I think that'll be the knotty one. Seems that your Mister Attrill has summoned something with no previous history here..."

"Fuck-a-doodle-do!" Bess exploded, "Trust him to find something weird. I bet he had a good laugh when he trapped that one."

"Yeah, you can tell it's not used to people from what it did to the priest," Oliver said, "It made all his hair fall out and gave him an appendectomy."

"What?"

"I know, it's so random!" Oliver laughed, "Goodness knows what it'll do when it gets used to being here."

"Well, Suzy should be fine. She's as weird as they come, and she loves a puzzle."

"What help can we give you?" Chloe asked.

"None, I reckon," Bess replied, looking at the bank of fog she was heading towards, "I think that the moment I'm back in the fog, I'm on my own again."

Chloe didn't like the sound of that.

"Hey, don't worry," Bess soothed, reading her thoughts, "This is what I do."

"But I want to help!" Chloe insisted.

"You've already helped more than you should have," Bess replied.

"Sorry," Oliver said – he knew he'd cop it for letting Chloe go with him.

"No, I'm not cross," Bess said, "You did the right thing. Left to FitzOsbern, Billy would probably be dead by now, but Chloe is still young."

"Not too young to kick ass!" Chloe exclaimed.

"Yeah, you certainly did that, but you're still learning. What you've done is amazing, but it's more than enough."

"Okay," Chloe replied, but being young and inexperienced, she wasn't able to shield her thoughts from Oliver and Bess, who both immediately knew that she was going to try her darnedest to do something to help, whatever they might say. Bess chuckled – Chloe really was a peach!

Over the next hour, Bess, Chloe and Oliver chatted and, in the glorious sunshine, Bess was rather enjoying herself. However, all good things...

"I think you're about to lose me," she said, looking up at the looming bank of fog.

"Good luck," Oliver said, "Any other instructions?"

"No. I've micro-managed enough for one day."

"Okay, I'll catch you on the other side," Oliver said and disappeared from Bess's mind.

"You all right?" she asked, as Chloe had gone a bit quiet.

"I'm scared," Chloe replied.

"Oh, you'll be all right."

"Not for me, for you!" and Chloe's voice inside Bess's head was close to tears,

"I can't lose you! I can't!"

"Hey, hey, it's okay. I'm going to be fine."

"You don't know that. I've lost Vicky and the thought of losing you..." and now Chloe started to cry.

"But you still see your mum and if anything happens, you'll see me, too."

"It's not the same, though, is it?" Chloe could talk to her mum, but she couldn't do the one thing she was so desperate to do – give her a hug. That's all she wanted – to feel her mum wrap her up in a big hug. To be held in her arms again, to feel that warmth and safety and to feel the love flow from Vicky to her. Since her loss, only Bess had hugged her like that, and now even the slightest chance of losing that was terrifying for her.

"I know," Bess replied, feeling Chloe's fears, "It isn't the same. All we can do is trust to hope and send me positive thoughts. Visualize my success and that will help more than you can imagine."

"All right," Chloe sniffled. She wasn't sure she totally believed it, but she'd do what Bess suggested.

"Are you back at Woodlands?"

"Yeah," Chloe replied.

"Jo still there?"

"Yeah, she's busy with dad right now, which takes all her energy – it's harder for anyone but me,"

"Having the personal link makes all the difference..." and now Elizabeth Russell started to talk more urgently as she realised that although she'd stopped paddling, she was heading fairly quickly into the fog bank,

"Listen, tell Jo that I need her to stay with you and help,"

"But I'm all right, I can handle dad now I'm back," Chloe replied,

"Please, I need Jo to stay with you. Not for you, but for me,"

"How will that help you?" Chloe asked. There was silence.

"Bess? Bess!" Chloe cried, but it was no use. She was gone.

Elizabeth Russell was alone in the fog. This fog bank was thicker than the one around The Island, and she could only see to the end of the kayak. She wasn't paddling, but was slipping through the water as if she was being pulled along.

"Fine by me," she said to herself, laying the paddle across the kayak and taking a long drink of water. This fog was colder than the other and the lack of visibility was disorientating. She couldn't really tell if she was moving forwards, backwards or sideways. Looking out into the fog was like being struck with grey blindness. All she could see was greyness, nothing else. It was only when she looked down or forward that the yellow of the kayak and the colours of her wetsuit and paddle burst in to remind her that she could still see. The way she was moving was... odd. And it went beyond her not having to paddle to move. No, she reckoned that the strange feeling was because she wasn't simply moving through physical space. She was moving sideways through time and in the spaces between space to whatever dimension the Other Place occupied.

After some minutes, there was something new. At first, it was merely a hint that there was something out in the grey. Slowly, it developed into an approaching constant. It was white noise. Indefinable without context. Elizabeth Russell closed her eyes and listened to it, imagining all the things it could be until the realization dawned. It was rushing water! Somewhere out of her sight, a lot of water was falling, and she was heading straight towards it. She took up the paddle and put the right-hand end into the water and pulled it around in a wide arc towards the back of the kayak, turning her around. Then she paddled hard away from the sound. Although she was trying to get to the Other Place, she had no idea whether this was the right way. Maybe she'd gone off course and was heading towards some fiendish trap to end the quest of the unworthy? She paddled with all her strength, but realised after a minute that it was no use. She was still heading for the rising noise and moving even faster than before. Using the paddle to steer, she turned the kayak around again. If she was about to plunge off some bloody cliff, she was damn well going to do it facing the danger.

As she sped towards the noise, she had an idea. She could try to dispel the fog ahead of her. She centred herself and then spoke the words of power. No effect. Ah, but wait – there was something... the sound of distant laughter that shimmered like silver wind chimes.

"Yeah, ha-ha," she said dryly. They should try doing this for the first time and see how many laughs they had. Smug bastards. Then, just as she was thinking about how she might make the unseen voices regret that laughter, the noise of water got suddenly louder and she cried out as a wall of water appeared right in front of her. She didn't even have time to swear as the front of the kayak hit the wall, but, instead of being pushed under by the falling water, the nose flew upwards, swiftly followed by the rest of the kayak. Now she was holding on for dear life as the kayak shot upwards at ninety degrees, riding on what seemed to be a reverse waterfall. As she held on, she chanced a look over her shoulder and was disconcerted to see she was already at least a hundred feet above the sea and rising rapidly. She looked ahead, but it was a blank, grey nothing. She was losing her bearings and all sense of time, so she started counting,

"One elephant, two elephant..." just to give her some kind of idea of how long she was on the waterfall.

Thirty-nine elephants later, the waterfall levelled out and the kayak was thrown into the air by its momentum. A second later, it splashed down hard and her teeth clacked together,

"Argh! Son of a..." she began, but stopped. The fog was gone and now she could see that she was on a river flowing through green water meadows that stretched out on either side of her. In the distance, there were forests and hills and, straight ahead, the towers and spires of a great silver castle rose up, and the river was flowing directly to it. Bess took off her shades – there was an eerie twilight, which shifted the shapes of things. Some reeds at the water's edge looked at one moment like reeds, the next moment like bars on a prison cell, the next like spears thrust into the ground, ready to be picked up and thrown. Were those trees in the distance, or a host of lost souls standing and awaiting her arrival? Bess looked around to try to get some sort of bearing. The sky was cloudless, yet opaque, and there was no sun, no moon and no stars. She realised that there was also no sound. Gone was the rushing of water. Now there was nothing. Not a bird, or breath of wind. She clicked her fingers. Yes, she could hear that. If anything, knowing that there could be noise, but that there was none made the silence of the world around her more disturbing. And all the while, the river carried her towards the silver castle, or was it a white sepulchre? Or was it a sleeping dragon?

Bess didn't like this dreamlike place. She had to rail against it, so she put one blade of the paddle into the water to direct the kayak towards the bank. It had no effect. She tried paddling towards the bank, but no matter what she did, the kayak stayed in the middle of the river. What the hell? It was taking her to the silver castle whether she liked it or not. She looked over the side into the water. It was clear and deep. Maybe she could slip out of the kayak and swim to the bank? She didn't like the way the river was taking her to the citadel. She wanted to get there on her own terms. Bess put her hand into the water but immediately pulled it out – it was freezing! She swore to herself as she shook the water from her hand and tried to warm it up again. The pain was startling. She'd never felt liquid water that cold before. It felt like it was far below freezing, and yet it wasn't solid. How that worked, she didn't know, but she did know that if she jumped in it, she'd be in a world of pain. She nursed her frozen hand, massaging it until life flowed back into it as the twilight world slipped silently past her. She now had the distinct feeling of being observed. Shadowy shapes flitted at the edges of her vision, but when she tried to catch sight of them, nothing was there except the water meadows, which were beginning to transition into forest.

Soon the trees were thick and crowding around the river, so that their roots were entwined into the banks. All the trees were deciduous, but all were stripped of their leaves. As she looked into the bare forest, Elizabeth Russell could see great oaks, elms, beech and ash spreading out across the land. Nearer the river, willows, elder, rowan and alder stood like guards, ensuring that no one could access the forest from the water. The forest was colder and darker than the meadows and she felt that it was an ancient, unfriendly place. Every tree was twisted by age and long-held grudges, and their branches reached out towards her with a hunger. She could feel their desire for her life-force. She looked at the forest floor and realised there were no leaves. These trees had clearly been without the renewal of bud or leaf for so long that some of them had forgotten what it was like to wear their green summer finery. How long had they been trapped in this Other Place of shadow and forgetfulness? If the coming of Christianity had exiled them to this parallel world, then they would have stood here for thirteen hundred years. If the coming of the Romans and their massacre of the druids had been the trigger for the exile, then it would have been nearly two thousand years. Plenty of time for anger to fester into hatred and evil. The trees watching her slip past desired nothing more than revenge on those that had banished them to this dismal place.

Elizabeth Russell mastered her rising panic and breathed carefully. It was unsettling to feel the trees staring at her naked soul with such longing. And the trees were not alone. The flitting shadows had followed her into the forest and were using the trees as hiding places whenever she tried to catch them in full view. She would need to protect herself against whatever lay ahead, so she started to speak the words of an incantation but although she was saying the words, no sounds were coming out of her mouth. She coughed, smacked her chest and tried again, but no sound came from her. Silver laughter filled the forest. The trees and shadows were amused by the witch trying to weave her magic in their realm.

"Get stuffed!" she said out loud and was surprised that she could hear it,

"So, it's just the magic that can't be spoken," she said, looking around at the forest,

"Very clever," and the sour note in her voice was not lost on those watching her and laughing at her.

The question for her was whether her inability to cast spells was something that the inhabitants had created to protect them from intruders, or whether this place robbed everything that entered it of the power to weave magic. She hoped it was the former, but suspected it was the latter. If the beings there still had the power to protect themselves from magic, then perhaps with her help, they could return to the Isle of Wight and destroy Attrill. However, if the Other Place had taken their magic away, then she wondered how they would be able to help her at all.

With the river speeding her along, she was soon within sight of the silver castle. Again, it changed before her eyes. It was a castle. Blink. It was an ivory sepulchre. Blink. It was a great, white dragon, sleeping with smoke rising from its nostrils. However, what didn't change was the area in front of the castle. There, the river simply stopped. It didn't feed into a lake or sea, it didn't disappear off the edge of the world in a waterfall, it ran towards a point where the land blocked its progress and that was it. Like the end of a canal. There was a landing stage from which she'd be able to disembark, and then there was a grassy area about two hundred yards wide and a hundred yards deep to where it met the castle walls. The forest loomed around the sides of the grassy clearing like spectators waiting for a gladiatorial combat to begin. Between the landing stage and the castle, in the middle of the clearing, stood a single great oak - the sole guardian of the castle. Did it take long for her to reach the landing stage, or did an aeon pass? In that Other Place beyond time, she couldn't tell. All she knew was that she had gone from the state of sweeping down the river, to the state of arriving at the landing stage. She grasped a rope and hauled herself out of the kayak, took off her buoyancy aid and left it on the dock, then walked from the landing stage and out across the grass towards the tree.

As she walked through the silence, she saw that hundreds of shadows were moving among the trees that crowded around the vast lawn. Whatever was about to happen would have an audience. She wished she was wearing something more substantial and stylish than the shorty wetsuit, but there was nothing to be done about that now. She examined the oak tree as she approached – its trunk was gnarled and ravaged by time and weather. The tree looked as if it had once channelled great power. It was some sort of conduit, possibly between a source of power and the shadows moving in the forest. However, it seemed to have hardened through lack of use. Was it angry that it was no longer fulfilling its purpose? Elizabeth Russell couldn't tell, but she made sure to stop at the point where she was beyond the reach of its branches. Suddenly, a single, trumpet note cut through the air. It was so loud and piercing that even with her hands clapped over her ears, she felt her legs buckle so that she fell to her knees in agony. The note held, unwavering, and the pain it caused was a golden vice squeezing her head. She opened her mouth to scream and as she did, the castle turned into a sepulchre whose twenty-foot-high ivory doors swung apart. The grey shape of a woman in flowing robes floated out through the doors, which closed behind her as she glided over the lawn. Elizabeth Russell struggled to focus on her approach through the veil of pain, but soon she was looking up at the spectral form before her.

The trumpet note stopped and Elizabeth Russell lurched forward onto her hands and knees, gasping for breath.

"It is right that you kneel before me," the spectre's voice was hard and cold,

"I am the queen of Ynys Wyth and the Mistress of Death. This is my husband, The Life Giver," she said, pointing to the knotted oak,

"Tell me your name, witch, and why you dare disturb us."

Elizabeth Russell raised her eyes,

"Please forgive me, great queen. I am Elizabeth Russell and I have come to seek aid in banishing the being that has usurped your place in the physical realm."

At this, the spectre stretched out her open hand, which she squeezed closed. Elizabeth Russell gasped in pain as her arms were pinned to the sides of her torso as if she was being crushed, and then she was raised into the air as the spectral queen approached her to look into her eyes.

"So, you finally come to us Elizabeth Russell. After centuries of ignoring our calls, you come as the agent of the master of lies!" and the grip around Elizabeth Russell tightened, squeezing the air from her.

"No," she choked out, "I have come to find out how to destroy him."

"Then you are a fool," the spectre replied, "We cannot destroy him. We are the victims of his trickery. He came to our land with the conquering people from across the sea. He was one of their gods and offered us gifts of friendship. Had we known his nature, we would never have accepted. The gifts were a trap. When we took them, we fell into this parallel place, cursed to watch him rule the world that was once ours. Powerless. Forgotten. Here we are caught in stasis, shadows of our former selves."

Held in the air in the crushing grip of an invisible hand, Elizabeth Russell didn't understand. The message written on the wall of the well had said that only the spirits of the Other Place would be able to cast Urian into hell.

"When he came to me in a dream to tell me that he would send a powerful witch to release us, I did not believe him. I certainly did not expect him to send you," the spectral queen said, with her long hair waving slowly about her head as if it was under water, "And yet, here you are. And you are even more powerful than we ever hoped."

There was a greediness in her black eyes that Elizabeth Russell didn't like one bit. She had a horrible, sinking feeling that Attrill had played her.

"By harnessing your power, we can come back to the world," the queen said.

"But what will he get out of your return?" Bess gasped.

"Your body. That was all he wanted in exchange for our release," the spectral queen waved her hand and Bess gently drifted towards the tree,

"First, we shall strip you of your power; then we shall strip you of your soul and leave your body to him; then we shall return home."

Elizabeth Russell felt something sharp at her back, slicing up through the wetsuit from the top of her buttocks to her neck. The back of the wetsuit was spread apart to reveal her bare flesh, as the branches of the great oak wrapped around her arms and pulled her to its trunk. She felt the rough bark digging painfully into the exposed skin of her back. And even as her arms were pulled back around the trunk so that she was held tightly against the bark, her mind was racing. She'd been played all right. That nonsense at the well and the inscription from Tom Attrill had been devised to trick her into coming here of her own accord. She'd clearly been right that Urian's time was almost up and that soon he'd be reabsorbed by the great forces of the universe. Now he wanted to extend his time by taking her body – it would give him at least six thousand more years. The existential problem for her was that her soul would have to be stripped from her body to do it.

Elizabeth Russell involuntarily let out a groan of pain as her arms were pulled back to the point where her sinews were straining to keep her shoulders from dislocating. She gritted her teeth as the bark of the knotted old tree trunk pierced the flesh of her back. She could feel her blood dripping from the wounds and a horrible sensation that the old tree was being revivified by the sweet taste of her. The spectral queen glided down to hover in front of her face, which was already bathed in pain-sweat,

"Fight it," the queen said, "Your struggle will increase the power you yield tenfold. With it, we might even be strong enough to hunt down the master of lies."

Elizabeth Russell began to call out Andy's name, but the 'A' became a drawn-out scream as the real agony began.

Chapter Thirty

Dilemmas

Andy Harper awoke with a start. He was in the passenger seat of the Ford Focus, which he'd parked in the Old Blackgang Road car park. He blinked and stretched out his body as best he could in the cramped car. He'd pushed down the back of the seat as far as it would go and now he pulled on the handle to get it more upright. His mouth was dry and he had that out-of-place feeling that comes after certain drugs. As he sipped some water from a bottle, he checked his watch - about four in the afternoon. He'd slept for three and half hours and, although he wasn't quite feeling refreshed, he felt it had done him good. He was very glad that he hadn't tried to follow Downer, because his body might have crashed out at any time. Instead, he'd followed Bess's instructions and bought drinks and snacks. The trip to the Co Op in Shanklin hadn't been glamorous, but as well as the crisps, sandwiches, chocolate and bottles of water, he'd been able to buy a Thermos flask, fill it with fresh coffee from Costa and top it up with rum. After that, he'd headed to the car park and got some sleep. Now he was awake and feeling distinctly unsettled. It was as if he'd been jolted from his dream by a hard prod in the back. Was this the signal for him to act? He got out of the car. With the heavy fog, he could only see about twenty yards beyond the stoney car park. At the seaward end, there was a gate into the fields, which he presumed ran down to the beach. He pulled out his hag stone and looked through it into the fog. No, it didn't feel right to call her name. Not yet. However, he did feel a pull towards the sea.

Once he'd gathered the bag of snacks and drinks, the bag with the towelling robe and Bess's clothes, and his trusty walking stick, he followed the narrow dirt path out of the car park, hoping it would take him down to the beach. What he could see of the land around the path seemed to be grazed, probably by sheep, given the steep terrain. The nibbled grass was interspersed with ragwort and gorse, which caught on his jacket when the path led through a thicket of the evil stuff. Andy swore as the prickles went straight through the jacket into his skin, but he continued on the path as it steepened. The one thing he didn't want to do in the fog was leave the path, even if it meant the occasional prickle, because he knew from looking at the map that there were cliffs here. Blundering off the edge would not be useful at all. The path seemed to have been made by a drunkard, as it weaved around the land, sometimes veering sharply downwards, sometimes taking him back up the hill. Eventually, he could hear waves on the beach somewhere ahead of him and then there was a final scramble down a steep slope where the path had been gouged into the earth by running water, and he was stumbling onto the beach.

The tide had turned and was coming in. Andy looked along the beach to check the high tide line, was satisfied that he wouldn't drown if it came in all the way, and started walking east along the beach. The map he'd consulted earlier had shown that the eastern end of the beach ended in a mess of rocks and landslip detritus, so no one would be entering it from that end, ensuring privacy. As he scrunched along, he was struck by the oddness of the beach. It wasn't sand, but it wasn't pebbles. It was a sort of rounded gravel, unlike any beach he'd ever been on.

"Full of surprises," he muttered to himself as he thought about the Isle of Wight. He'd always assumed it was just like the rest of the south coast, but no. It was unique. Its history, land and outlook were similar, but at the same time very different from England. Was it really part of England at all? He wasn't so sure. In ancient times, Britain had been a legendary island at the edge of the world. A place of magic and mystery. Progress might have hidden much of that magic, but he was quickly discovering that it was still there. All you had to do was cut through the hustle and bustle of modern life and you could find magic. Ancient, brooding and waiting to be tapped by those who dared. And there were some places, like the Isle of Wight, where the magic woven into the land seemed more obvious. He wondered whether Anglesey was the same.

Eventually, the end of the beach emerged through the fog. Rather than going all the way to the end, Andy stopped. Yes, this was a good place. He could see one end of the beach, the low cliff behind him and the sea. In the world of swirling grey cloud, he at least had some sense of place. He walked up to the cliff, laid down the stuff he'd brought so it was above the tide line and then went a little way off to take a leak against the cliff. Before letting go, he had a good look around – he didn't want to get caught out by an attack mid-stream. Satisfied that he was safe for the moment, he let go and couldn't help sighing. Was there any greater simple pleasure than relief? And yet it was the sort of everyday feeling that's so easily taken for granted and only missed when age or illness take it away. With the act completed, he walked down to the water and watched the waves breaking on the beach. They had the boisterous quality of an incoming tide announcing to the land that the sea was coming back and it would take some of the beach with it. Andy felt in his pocket and took out the hag stone again. He looked through it, but still didn't feel the urge to call out her name. He wondered how Bess was getting on and found himself praying to any powers that might listen to deliver her safely back into his arms.

***

In the hills of Surrey, in that strange wild area between the city and the great encircling motorway of the M25, Chloe didn't know what to do with herself. She was sitting on the sunny patio with Jo and her dad, who was bent over a thousand-piece jigsaw puzzle.

"Bess is in trouble. I can feel it," Chloe said quietly so that Ray couldn't hear it.

"Bess is always in some sort of trouble," Jo smiled, "You just have to get used to it," and she put a chubby arm around Chloe to give her a squeeze. She had only known the girl a few weeks, but already there was nothing she wouldn't do for her. When Jo thought about what that child had been through, it brought a lump to her throat.

"I don't know how I could get used to feeling like this," Chloe replied. She was feeling a sense of panic that was a squeezing sensation in her chest. She wanted to do so many things at once that she was caught in helpless indecision.

"Can you look after Ray? I've got to move," Chloe said.

"Of course," Jo beamed, "Although it's going to be hard work sitting here in the sun with a cuppa," she said, dunking a hobnob into her tea.

"Thanks," Chloe said and, as Jo took over the creation of her dad's reality, she got up and calmly walked to the end of the terrace.

"Where's she off to?" asked Ray.

"I think she's gone to find a friend," Jo replied, then leant across the jigsaw and picked up a piece,

"Ooh, this one goes here," she said, completing a window in one of the fishermen's cottages in the scene of Port Isaac in Cornwall.

As soon as Chloe was around the corner of the building, she started running. She didn't know why, but she had to run – anything to shake the horrible feeling of having too many options to choose from. She ran down through the sunny gardens until, a little breathless, she stopped at a secluded bench, which had high rhododendrons behind it. The position was a suntrap, and she sat on the bench with her eyes closed and her face pointing up at the sun. The brightness made the inside of her eyelids glow golden. What could she do? She was still finding her way with her powers and didn't know what might be possible. She tried to talk to Bess, but there was nothing out there. As when she'd been on the Isle of Wight, it was as if Bess had dropped off the face of the earth. Yes! That was it! Bess *had* dropped off the face of the earth. The Other Place wasn't physically on the planet at all. It wasn't even in the same dimension as the physical world. So, Chloe searching for her on earth was a waste of time.

She slowed her breathing and used a technique Jo had taught her to calm her mind. Instead of seeking Bess out, she would relax and open herself to what was calling to her.

She could feel a constant, shifting soundscape like a shallow stream running over stones. Everything was a wash of indistinct sound. Then she concentrated on something nearby,

"This looks like a lobster pot to me," it was Jo's voice,

"Yeah and it's got to go somewhere down here by the shore, but there's a shedload of shore," Ray replied.

Chloe took her focus away from them and their voices receded into the wash of sound. So, it wasn't running water, but the sound of millions of voices tripping over and around each other. All Chloe needed to do was pull out the ones that seemed relevant to her. She visualised the jumble of sounds as a stream running through woodland with dappled sunlight on the water, while she stood at the edge of the stream with a fishing line in her hand. Occasionally, there was a flash of silver in the stream and she would toss her line at it, then draw it out,

"I'm going to do for her..." it was FitzOsbern, "God, why can't we go back to hanging them. It was so much simpler," was he talking to himself, or were these just very loud thoughts? It was hard to tell with him. She let him go and surveyed the stream again. A flash of silver caught her attention,

"No, there's no way to contact her," it was Oliver,

"Surprise surprise – she's in grave danger, no way of helping and nothing to do but worry. That's just the way she likes it," said the voice of a woman Chloe didn't recognise. The woman paused and seemed to address Chloe directly,

"Can I help you, love?"

"Er..." Chloe panicked, "I, er... sorry..."

"Hi Chloe, don't worry, this is my good friend and colleague Hester," Oliver said.

"Sorry, I didn't mean to interrupt. I was just..." just what? Chloe didn't have the words to explain what she was doing.

"Just trying to tune in?" Hester said, "Don't worry, love, we all do it. But if you don't want to be noticed, it's better to go to whoever you want to listen to, not draw them to you."

"Oh, thanks," Chloe replied, though she wasn't sure how she'd do that when she was fishing them out of the stream.

"That's easy," Hester said and her voice was kindly, "Hover over to them and get down close."

"How did you...?" Chloe began.

"Hester is a consummate mind-reader," Oliver laughed, "That's why she's perfect for the Office of the Regulator."

"But I'd be making a lot more money if I'd become a gossip columnist," and Chloe could hear the smile in her voice.

"I'm sorry I bothered you," Chloe said.

"No bother at all. It's nice to finally almost meet you," Hester replied, "And remember what I said about how not to be noticed. Some people can be quite unpleasant if they catch you. And by unpleasant, I mean dangerous. All right?"

"All right," Chloe replied, "And I am sorry,"

"Don't worry," said Oliver, "See you very soon, okay?"

"Yeah..." and Chloe let them go.

Over the next half-hour, Chloe practised finding and listening to people without using the fishing line. She'd spot a flash of silver in the stream and then rise up into the air and float over to it, flying towards the point like Superman just above the water. Then she'd concentrate on the spot and listen carefully. It was thrilling to have the power to tune in to so many conversations and even thought processes. Chloe wondered whether everyone with psychic abilities could do it. Maybe. Hester, Oliver and Jo could, so maybe it wasn't so special, but to do it for the first time was amazing and each time she listened in to one of the millions of conversations in the stream, she had a goofy grin on her face. She wanted to laugh out loud, but didn't know if that would give her away to the people she was listening to. It gave her such a feeling of joy and power that she could barely contain herself. Eventually, she had to pull away from the stream so she could laugh. She stood by the stream and laughed hard, with no inhibitions. The sound was vibrant and fizzing with the overflowing energy of what she'd been doing. Was this why witches always cackled in films and TV shows? Was laughter the only way to release the energy to stop them exploding from exultation? She didn't know. All she knew was that the laughter made her feel calmer. With her eyes still closed to the physical world, she let out a long, satisfied sigh - this was amazing!

Once she'd calmed down from the excitement, she went back to visualising the stream. Before, she'd only noticed flashes of silver, but now she realised that there were lots of different colours flashing in the tumbling waters. She was tempted to investigate all the colours, but one spot kept tugging at her. It was a red fleck that she couldn't ignore, so she flew slowly over to it. When she got there, she felt an unexpected shiver. There was something bad here. She instinctively knew she would have to be very careful and not get noticed. She imagined herself being as calm and invisible as still air, then concentrated on the red fleck.

"Idiot!" a man shouted, followed by a dull thump and a groan of pain from another man.

"Useless..."

Thump.

"Moronic..."

Thump.

"Good-for-nothing..."

Thump.

"Scumbag!"

There was a nightmarish snap, followed by a howl of pain from the other man.

"I don't need enemies when I've got you bungling every order I give you! All you had to do was keep an eye on the man, but you can't even do that!" the man's voice was high and vicious.

"Sorry, meyaster," came the pained voice of the other man, "It was yon witch. She casted an enchantment on he. Theys were on the beach and her throwed sand over he's head and he disappeared. Then her gets in a boat and goes into the fog."

"That's a bonus, anyway," said the posh man, "She's taken the bait. Soon it'll be goodbye Elizabeth Russell, hello Olivia Attrill!"

Chloe had to stop herself from reacting. This was the man Bess had been looking for! She focussed all her attention on them. Maybe she'd hear something that would help her find Bess.

"Who be Olivia Attrill meyaster?"

"Well... me, of course! Once I take over her body, that's who I'll be. Keep up, Downer! God, is there anything going on between your ears?" Attrill was exasperated by the stupidity of the man,

"But my perfectly laid out plan is put at risk by you losing that big thug of hers."

Chloe smiled – that would be Andy. So, he'd given them the slip...

"If he becomes a problem, I'm not going to kill you..."

"Thank ye meyaster,"

"...No, I'm going to keep you alive for as long as I can so I can torture you whenever I want."

At this, the other man made an unhappy sound.

"Finding that man is our top priority," Attrill continued, "She could use him to find her way back, or he could find her body washed up..."

"And he has the sword. Powerful strong it be. Strong enough to be the undoing of my gallybagger spell."

"So, not really very strong at all," Attrill felt his cutting tone was probably about as dangerous as the sword Downer was so exercised about,

"You were clucking like a wet hen about the dangers of the knife of Amaranthus that Dunseath had, but look where it got him. Now, stop fussing over nothing and come on, we've got some serious spell casting to do if we're going to find the boyfriend..."

The one who called himself Attrill then issued a complicated list of instructions before things went quiet. However, Chloe remained where she was. She wasn't about to lose track of the man Bess had been looking for. At the edges of her mind, she could hear the slightest murmuring, but she couldn't latch onto any distinct sounds. She had the feeling that they were his thoughts as he prepared for the ceremony that he hoped would reveal Andy to him. Chloe put all her will into visualising whatever was happening where the man was, until slowly, incredibly, a bubble formed on the surface of the water. Inside the bubble, she could see a tall man with long arms and legs moving purposefully around a big room with a set of intricate circles drawn on the floor. This was like nothing she'd ever imagined! She was using the power of her mind to see through space and spy on someone. She could feel the urge to laugh coming on her again, but she resisted it. She didn't want to break off and stop watching, just in case she couldn't find him again. So, she kept herself calm and watched as he and then the other, smaller man gathered everything they needed for the ritual, before each of them went away in turn. When they returned, they were wearing white robes and entered the second largest of the circles. Chloe watched in fascination as they performed the ritual, speaking in a language she didn't recognise. She watched the way they moved and the way everything they did was done with purposeful concentration. Although she was young and inexperienced, she could feel that what they were doing was powerful and that there was no way she should let them see her or feel her presence. These were dangerous men and she instinctively knew that if they found her out, they'd kill her. But she had to keep watching. If there was any way she could find something to help Bess, the danger would be worth it.

Chapter Thirty-One

Soul Stripper

Elizabeth Russell's chin slumped to her chest and, through bleary eyes, she watched her sweat dripping from her face onto the ground below. Her breathing was laboured, as her arms were still pinned behind her and the bark of the huge oak tree was embedded in the flesh of her back. Finally, the intense pain had stopped, but only because the tree had drained her of all her power.

"Good..." the voice of the queen drifted through the haze of semi-consciousness. Elizabeth Russell wanted to focus, but she felt weak and the sweet relief of oblivion beckoned. It would be so easy to let herself go and fall into the darkness - to finally rest! After three hundred years, she deserved to rest. Annoyingly, there was something deep within her that wouldn't let her go. The indefatigable desire to keep living was dragging her back from the precipice.

Gotta keep going, she thought, *Get it together... breathe...*

And with each new breath, she drew life back into her.

Had she been able to lift her head, she'd have seen that the forest around her had begun to change. Where the trees had been barren, with lifeless branches piercing upwards to the sky, now the branches had buds. The great oak truly was the Life Giver. His deep roots were entwined with every living thing in the forest and beyond, so that as he had drawn Elizabeth Russell's power from her, he had shared it with all the life in the Other Place. Now her power was stimulating Spring in the Other Place for the first time in over a thousand years. Even the spectral queen was full of colour. No longer a grey shade, she was as solid as flesh and resplendent in robes of red, gold and green. She hovered in the air, her long, black hair lustrous, her eyes aflame and her red lips parted in ecstasy. She exhaled a drawn-out, luxurious "Yes!" as every fibre of her being tingled with life.

"We live," she said, softly stepping onto the grass in front of Elizabeth Russell,

"We live!" she screamed, raising her arms towards the sky.

The sound jolted Bess and she looked up at the terrible sight of the queen stalking towards her with her red eyes fixed upon the sacrificial victim,

"But you..." said the queen, taking a fistful of Bess's hair and pulling her head up so she could look into her eyes,

"You have given us life. Now we will give you death."

She reached down and picked up a small, dead branch that had fallen from the oak. It was long and thin, with many twigs fanning out from one end. As she held it, the twigs lost their rigidity and flopped down so that it resembled a cat o'nine tails. The queen swished it and the sound of each tail cutting through the air chilled Bess.

"A branch from the Life-Giver in the hands of the Mistress of Death will flay the soul from your body like grain from a bushel of wheat. Release her!" the queen ordered, and the branches holding Bess against the trunk of the tree instantly let her go.

Elizabeth Russell fell onto her hands and knees. Her back was such a bloody mess of scrapes and puncture wounds that it seemed unlikely the scourge could do any more damage. However, as she waited with her arms shaking, trying to hold herself up, she knew that the damage to come would be spiritual. And the pain to come would make her current suffering seem like a sweet memory.

The queen looked down at her on all fours with her head bowed – nothing more than an animal, waiting for the cut of the sacrificial blade. She had no pity and she would give no quarter, but as she drew her hand back for the first blow, the victim spoke,

"You don't have to do this."

In spite of the punishment, the voice was undaunted and now the victim looked up at her with a pain-streaked face,

"You have what you need to return home. You owe Urian nothing. If you do this, it is your choice."

The queen looked down at her with contempt,

"You have ignored our calls for hundreds of years. Such insolence must be punished. Your sacrifice will serve as notice to the universe that we have returned!" and then she lowered her voice so that her next words were intimate,

"More than that, I desire your sacrifice..."

The cat o'nine tails slashed across Elizabeth Russell's back and pain engulfed her. The agony wasn't focussed in one place but exploded in every part of her at once. Her scream was shrill and quickly followed by another and another as the queen thrashed her with rising fury. Elizabeth Russell was now caught in a whirlwind of torment and with each blow, she could feel her soul being torn away from her flesh, leaving her as nothing more than a single, exposed nerve. But in the core of her being, her will focussed her thoughts. Her magic was gone, her soul was being stripped from her body, but she was damned if it was going to end like this. As long as she drew breath, she would fight. Even as she screamed with each fresh slash of the scourge, her will was gathering her strength.

There was cruel delight on the queen's face as she drew the scourge back to continue the thrashing, but this time, the blow didn't strike home. She had just started bringing the scourge down, when Elizabeth Russell sprang at her, catching the hand holding the cat o'nine tails. The simultaneous punch to the queen's solar plexus forced the wind out of her, and her hand involuntarily dropped the weapon. Bess shoved the queen backwards, grabbed the cat o'nine tails and shouted,

"Andy!"

***

Andy was pacing restlessly up and down the beach. The weird gravelly sand scrunched under his feet as he fretted about his role in the drama taking place out there in the fog. His right hand, firmly shoved into his pocket, turned the hag stone over and over as he walked. How would he know when to call her name? What if he did something wrong? What if the hag stone didn't work? What if...?

Suddenly, without thinking about it, Andy took the stone out of his pocket, looked through the hole and bellowed her name out into the fog.

"That's torn it!" he said in surprise. Why had he done that? He didn't know. He didn't even remember having any thought that he should do it – he just did it. And now what? Would Bess fall out of the sky, or come kayaking out of the fog, or what? Andy stood still, listening... just the waves breaking on the beach and dragging the gravelly shingle back down towards the water. He looked down at the hag stone in his hand. Had it worked? Should he try it again? Now that his mind was back in charge, it didn't know what to do. In the end, he decided to put the stone back in his pocket and continue to walk up and down the beach. Minutes passed. It was excruciating! The same thought kept coming to him – had he got it wrong? What had possessed him to suddenly call her name out of the blue? Maybe she'd been wrong about him? Maybe he wasn't imbued with any kind of psychic gift?

He stopped walking and listened again. Somewhere in the regular sound of the waves, there was an irregular splashing. He ran along to where it seemed to be from and peered into the fog. Yes. There it was again... and this time, there was a cough. He called her name, didn't get a response and called it again. Still nothing. He took off his jacket, pulled the Glock from the holster under his armpit and slipped it into one of the jacket pockets, then threw his phone and car key fob onto it. In a moment, he was wading into the sea. Bess had been right – it was a lot warmer than he'd expected. He called her name again, but even though he was now out far enough to be up to his chest in water, he still couldn't see her in the fog.

"Andy..." the voice sounded fragile, but it was definitely her,

"Bess!" he shouted, wading out further and looking around for any sign of her. Was that...? Yes! A flash of white hair about twenty yards over to the right. Andy launched into a splashy crawl, trying not to lose sight of the flash of white, and then he was with her,

"Okay, I've got you! You're all right," he spluttered through the water,

"Come on, let me take you," and he manoeuvred her into the classic lifesaving position before striking back for shore. As they went, she was groaning in pain, but it was only when they got into shallower water and he was able to stand that he realised she was bleeding. He changed his grip so that his hands were under her arms as he pulled her up towards the breakers.

"D'you think you can walk?"

"Back's messed up," she mumbled.

"Right, I'm going to turn you over, get you up and help you onto the beach, yeah?"

"Yeah."

When Andy turned her over, he winced. Her back *was* a mess. What the hell had happened out there? There wasn't time to worry – he needed to get her out of the water and into that towelling robe ASAP. He gently got her arm around his neck and she stumbled out of the sea with him. He helped her a few yards up the beach from the waves, then carefully set her down. Jesus! She was like a block of ice!

"Don't fall backwards, I'm getting the robe," and he sprinted to where he'd left the gear. He was quickly back and helping to get her arms out of the wetsuit. This was complicated by the cat o'nine tails which she was gripping so firmly in her left hand that he had to prize her fingers from it. Finally, he got it out of her hand, then rolled the wetsuit down to her waist, so that they could get her top half as dry and warm as possible. Once he'd pulled the wetsuit down, he looked at her back again. Now she was out of the water, he could see that at least the wounds weren't bleeding freely. He sacrificed her shirt from the bag of clothes to soak up as much of the blood as possible before easing the towelling robe over her head. She sucked in air through her teeth as the material brushed against the exposed flesh of her back,

"Sorry," he said, then the robe was on and he was pressing it against her arms and the front of her torso to get her dry.

"Here, drink this," he said, pouring her a coffee and rum. She reached out her hands, but they were shaking with cold, so he brought the cup to her lips.

"Oh..." she groaned gratefully.

"Rum and coffee," he said.

She looked up into his eyes,

"F-f-fucking star!" she shivered.

"Just drink. You can thank me later," he said, bringing the cup back to her lips.

As she drank, she thought that if they got out of this alive, she'd thank him all night, every night for a week.

***

"Got her!" Attrill cried in triumph, stepping out of the magic circle,

"Go to Rocken End beach and bring her to me. If her man is with her, bring him, too."

"Why meyaster? I should kill he right there."

"No. I want that pleasure. Once I'm in her body, I'm going to take that sword of his push and it right down his throat. The last experience of his life will be the woman he loves killing him in a very painful way – it'll be hilarious!" and Attrill let out a piercing shriek of a laugh,

"Now go, go! And don't balls it up!"

"Right, meyaster," Downer said, then shuffled away.

"Pick up the pace!" Attrill barked and Downer was stung into a walk that was almost brisk, right up to the point when he was out of the room, when he went back to his usual half-dead shuffle.

"Right!" Attrill said to himself, "I'd better get myself ready for their arrival. Got to look the part... Oh yes, this is going to be sublime!" he clapped his hands in excitement and left the room through the door near the fireplace.

Watching it all, Chloe was overflowing with anxiety. She wanted to get away from the scene and call Jo for help, but she couldn't leave her place above the stream. If she wasn't able to find them again and anything bad happened because she wasn't there to help... no! She couldn't leave, even if it started going dark. She thought about trying to follow the tall man, but decided to stay looking at the big room. She needed to calm down, and looking at the empty scene would give her thinking time. At least Bess was back from the Other Place and Andy was with her, so that was good. Could she warn them that the other man was coming? Chloe searched for Bess, but as she did, she saw the bubble in the stream fading,

"No, no, no!" she said and she turned her concentration back to the bubble, sighing with relief when the picture of the big room became clear again. Okay, so she couldn't keep that link going and try to contact someone else at the same time, but what else could she do to help? What if the other man brought them back and all she could do was watch them torture and kill Andy and Bess? No! That wasn't going to happen. She wouldn't let it.

Chloe looked at the room carefully. What if there was a way she could do more than hear and see it? Maybe if she concentrated really hard, she could somehow get in there? When Hester had warned her that some people didn't like to be spied on, Chloe had got the feeling that there might be some way they could reach out and hurt her through the link. If they could do that, then why couldn't she reach in? She slowed her breathing and concentrated on the scene below her, then reached out her forefinger and gently pressed it against the bubble. She did it with infinite care, because she didn't want to burst it. Fortunately, it wasn't like a soap bubble. It didn't burst at the slightest touch, but as she investigated with her finger, she found there was apparently no way into the bubble either. Once the softly softly approach had failed, Chloe betrayed the impatience of her age by giving the bubble a good old prod to see what would happen. Again, the bubble didn't burst. The image was bent out of shape by the pressure of her finger, but nothing more. Physically, it was no use trying to get in there and she pulled her finger away. Maybe she'd be able to slip in by visualising herself in the room? She focussed her thought, trying to see herself in the great hall, trying to imagine what it was like to be in there in the hope of manifesting herself into the room. Of course, being a child, she wasn't thinking through the consequences of success. And she certainly didn't think of the probability that her sudden appearance in the hall of a man who was a murderous lunatic would only make matters a lot worse.

***

Cell by cell, life was coming back to Elizabeth Russell. The hot coffee and rum (into which she'd insisted Andy put more rum) was having the desired effect and now she could feel her hands and feet. Meanwhile, Andy had taken off his wet shirt and holster, dried himself on a corner of her robe, and gone over to where his jacket was lying on the beach. He put it on as he came back to her, then picked up the cat o'nine tails. Even exhausted and in pain, Bess found the jacket without a shirt look amusing, especially coupled with what he was now carrying,

"You look like a particularly cheap strippergram," she said, raising half a smile.

"Thanks. So, what is this, an S&M toy?"

"Something like that. The queen of the Other Place was using it to flay my soul out of me."

"For real?" Andy looked shocked.

"Uh-huh. And people wonder why I've been avoiding the Isle of Wight!" Bess grimaced, then put her anger and pain to one side and concentrated on the practical,

"Can you fit it in a pocket? I wouldn't want that falling into the wrong hands."

After some manoeuvring, he managed to get it into an inside pocket without it being obvious he had anything in it.

"Good. Give us a hand," she said and he was glad to feel that her hands were no longer blocks of ice when he heaved her off the shingle. Bess hissed and winced with one eye closed as pain radiated from her raw back.

"Help me out of this wetsuit. It's making me cold sitting in the damp."

Andy did as asked and, though he tried to be gentle, the wetsuit required some manhandling, which caused Bess more pain.

"Sorry!" he said as he peeled the last bit of the wetsuit from her left leg.

"It's okay," she replied, though from the way she wobbled and collapsed on her bum on the sand, it was obvious nothing was okay.

"Want to tell me what happened out there?" he asked as he eased off each of her sodden diving boots.

"Only if you give me another coffee and there's a beef sandwich in the snack bag."

Andy laughed and said,

"Good job I pay attention to your lunch orders," as he reached into the bag, "Co Op's finest steak and balsamic onion sandwich."

Once Bess had downed another cup of coffee and munched her way through half the sandwich, she told him about the fun and frolics she'd had in the Other Place.

"So, are they on their way here?"

"Least of our problems," she sighed, "I've got so little magic left in me, I couldn't pull off a card trick, we've got no idea where Attrill is and even if we did, there's no way I can tackle him..."

"That's handy!" Downer's voice sounded happy as he stepped out of the fog.

Andy immediately reached for his gun,

"Don't!" Downer ordered, training a sawn-off shotgun at them. Andy slowly took his hand away from his pocket.

Downer shambled along the beach to join them,

"A'right?" he said, "Nice trip to the Other Place?" and he gave Bess an unpleasant grin. She looked at him with tired eyes and offered him a two-fingered reply.

"An' the same ter' thee, missy. Must be a aggravation to have less power than I," Downer then turned to Andy, walked round behind him and pressed the barrels of the shotgun into the base of his spine,

"How's about thee takes out yourn gun 'n drops it on the ground?"

Andy complied. When it was done, Downer prodded him with the shotgun,

"Go join she," and keeping the shotgun trained on them, Downer picked up the Glock and pocketed it,

"Where be yourn sword?" Downer asked.

"Over by our stuff," Andy replied, indicating the pile of things further up the beach. Downer trudged over to the pile without even glancing back at them. The witch was spent and without his gun or sword, the man was no threat.

Downer came back with the sword at his usual, slow pace, then stood looking at them.

"In't this a nice party! Shame to ruin it, but we gots to be a goin'," and he approached them.

"So, thee take he's hand," he said to Bess. Without getting up, she reached and took Andy's hand.

"And thee take I's hand," he said to Andy as he pushed the barrels of the shotgun against Andy's stomach. Andy held out his hand and Downer took it with his free one. Downer's hand was clammy, cold and he smelled of spoiled meat.

"An' if either of thee acts up, yourn man gets a new hole in he," and Downer looked pointedly at Bess, who rolled her eyes,

"Just get on with it," she sighed.

"Here we go!" then Downer spoke the words of an incantation that even Elizabeth Russell didn't recognise and, with a snap, they were gone.

Chapter Thirty-Two

Trapped

In the blink of an eye, they reappeared in the third magic circle in Attrill's great hall. The moment they materialised, Downer let go of Andy's hand and scuttled back, keeping them covered with the shotgun.

"Excellent work! Downer, you've surpassed yourself," Attrill declared and at the sound of his voice, Andy and Bess turned. As he had hoped, he was an arresting sight, standing in front of the big fire in a suit of Prussian blue. The jacket had a high collar and was covered in gold embroidery, which Bess noted was a set of magical symbols. A thin smile played across her lips - if Attrill was to be the one who finally did for her, at least he had style.

"Welcome," he said, striding towards them with ebullient bonhomie,

"Of course, by now you'll have realised, Ms Russell, that my original plan has failed. The queen of Ynys Wyth was supposed to kill you and leave me your body, but you know what? I think it might be more of a laugh this way."

Andy fixed him with a hostile look, while Elizabeth Russell could barely lift her head.

"Here be the sword," said Downer, taking the sword stick from under his arm and offering it to Attrill.

"I'll look at it later," he said, waving Downer away. He couldn't care less about inanimate objects – he had an audience and he wanted to entertain,

"I presume you realise how much trouble I've gone to in order to get you here?" he directed the statement at Elizabeth Russell, who looked spent and murmured,

"Summoning six demons and setting them on innocent people seems excessive. An email would have been quite adequate."

"Adequate, but not entertaining – and you'd have arrived full of beans. Between you and me, I haven't been myself lately. I couldn't risk taking you on while you were at full strength. No, this has been enjoyable - apart from Downer's COMPLETE FAILURE, to kill your colleague here," the uncontrollable scream at his servant mid-sentence shattered his carefully crafted illusion of affability. However, he immediately switched back to Mister Congeniality as he gave a satisfied sigh,

"Aah... I've led you such a merry dance!"

Andy couldn't think of a single moment of merriment.

"Did you enjoy my antique shop?" he asked, hoping for more of a response than Elizabeth Russell's,

"Very impressive," which she mumbled without raising her head.

"Yes, it was rather elegant. However, you have Downer to thank for the gallybaggers. As you'd expect from a bumpkin like him, they were a tad agricultural, and they failed to kill your man, but they were good for a laugh. The only thing that really worried me, was that you might not fall for the gag with the well. I only etched the inscription last week, so ageing it was vital. Was it too over the top? I thought it was right on the cusp..."

Elizabeth Russell said nothing and didn't look up, while her lumbering idiot was still staring at him with murderous intent. The audience were not playing their part and it was beginning to annoy Attrill. However, he pressed on,

"And the negotiations with the queen of the Other Place... well, you know first-hand how annoyed she is with me. Yes, she took a bit of persuading. She came round in the end – even said that if I held up my side of the bargain, they'd forgive me for tricking them into the Other Place. All nonsense, of course – she'll be coming to tear me a new one the first chance she gets, but don't worry about me – I'll be long gone by then."

"You're quite the trickster," Bess muttered.

"Guilty as charged! I do like a good gag. Godshill Church was fun – watching those idiots lugging stones down the hill every day for a week..." and Attrill chuckled as he remembered their fear and exhaustion, "But tricking the people of Wolverton into bringing about their own destruction was particularly satisfying."

"And I s'pose betraying the population of Knighton to the Grim Reaper gave you a laugh, too!" Andy was finding Attrill's arrogance wearing.

“Ah, the dullard speaks," Attrill said, looking at Andy with contempt, "Sorry, but I can't take credit for Knighton. Nothing supernatural there, just the Black Death. Although the way people blamed that poor old bloke for surviving was rather amusing... anyway, I don't want to talk to you, because *you* are tedious. Downer, get him out of here.”

“I'm not going anywhere,” Andy said, subtly shifting his weight so he was ready for a fight.

“Oh, that's priceless!” Attrill laughed, “The idiot thinks he can protect you. What you don't seem to understand, my neanderthal friend, is that you're in my world now. All I need to do is squeeze...” and he reached out a hand towards Andy, then gripped thin air. Andy immediately clutched at his heart as a searing pain crushed his chest and, in a moment, he was on his knees.

“Leave him alone,” Elizabeth Russell said weakly. Even with Attrill attacking Andy, she didn't have the strength to raise her head.

“Hmph!” Attrill was disappointed in her. He'd been hoping for more fight. The queen must have done more damage to her than he'd realised.

“Just go with Downer,” he said, releasing Andy, who slumped forward, but growled,

“Fuck off!”

“Maybe I'm not giving you the right motivation,” Attrill said, turning towards Bess and reaching out his hand, “I'm sure that after what the queen did to her, even the slightest pressure on her back will...” and as his fingers started to close in the air, Bess let out a cry of pain.

“All right!” Andy shouted. Attrill dropped his hand and Bess's shoulders slumped as the pain stopped.

"I'll go. But I'll be back for you, Bess. That's a promise," and he gave her hand a reassuring squeeze. A look of confusion flickered across his face, which was missed by both Attrill and Downer, who now came over and prodded him towards the door by the fireplace with the shotgun.

"No need for that. I'm going," Andy said, but as he started across the room, Attrill stopped him,

"Hang on, what's this?" and he pointed at something black tucked inside Andy's jacket.

"Something I picked up on the beach," Andy tried to sound breezy, but Attrill's hand was already reaching in.

When he pulled out the cat o'nine tails, Attrill was delighted,

"Oh, you're not serious – is this really a whip made from a branch of that old bugger the Life Giver?" and then realisation dawned on him,

"Ah! His queen used this on you, didn't she? No wonder you're so quiet," now Attrill went up to Elizabeth Russell and roughly took her face in his hand to make her look at him as he said,

"What she did to you with this is just the start. I'm going to enjoy finishing the job," but her eyes seemed too dazed to take in the significance of his words.

"Right, get him out of here!" Attrill barked, annoyed that his audience was too broken to appreciate his genius,

"I'll be up to deal with him later," he said to Downer with a wink. His faithful servant nodded and pushed Andy towards the door. Attrill wanted to wait until they'd gone before speaking to the witch again, but Downer was so damned slow that before they'd got to the door, he'd lost patience and said,

"Anyway, where were we? Oh yes – the small matter of flaying the soul out of you... right, let's get this big robe off you... have a look at what I'm going to be living in for the next few thousand years," and he roughly pulled the towelling robe up and over Elizabeth Russell's head so that she was left in nothing but the bikini she'd been wearing under the wetsuit. Andy's last sight of Bess was her standing exposed before Attrill's greedy gaze, then Downer shoved him through the door and into a short corridor that ended in a spiral staircase.

Andy ground his teeth and frantically tried to think about what he could do. The shotgun prodding into his back reminded him that his options were limited while Downer had the gun. They went up the stairs, which ended in a heavy door studded with iron. Maybe this could give him some opportunity? The stairs were steep and narrow – if the door was locked, Downer would have to squeeze past Andy to open it. That would be his most vulnerable moment. Failing that, if Andy could get through the door first, maybe he could slam it on Downer as he came through. It would be high-risk and the results wouldn't be pretty, but if either opportunity presented themselves... Andy's muscles tensed.

"Open!" said Downer, and the door swung open before Andy got to it. Then, as Andy reached the threshold, Downer gave him an almighty shove into the room so that he was propelled a good yard forward, stumbling to stop himself from falling over. He recovered, only to see that Downer was safely through the door and had him covered with the shotgun. So much for his clever plans!

The room was large and not quite round – had Andy taken the time to work it out, he'd have found that it was a pentagon – with five doors set in its bare stone walls. It was lit by a pillar of yellowy-orange flame which rose up in the centre of the room without a chimney above or any apparent combustible material at its base.

"What's that?" Andy asked. Downer ignored the question, motioning to an armchair by the wall to the right of the flames,

"Sit," he said.

Andy complied but immediately wished he hadn't. The seat was low and squashy, which would make it difficult for him to get out of it quickly. Downer gave him a nasty smile. He knew he was safe from a sudden attack and moved to the other side of the room, where he placed the shotgun on a similar armchair to the one Andy was stuck in. Downer walked back to the pillar of flame and drew the sword. He looked at the blade, holding it up towards the flames. The silver runes inlaid on one side of the blade glittered in the flickering light. Andy noticed the look of joy on Downer's face. Whatever he saw in that blade, he liked it. He turned it over and said to himself,

"Et lux per tenebras secabit... but will it? Why don't we see?"

He ran the sword into the flames and his eyes widened as they instantly dimmed and sputtered. He withdrew the blade and the flames flared a couple of times, then became a solid pillar once more.

"Well, well, well! Thee'd do well to mark old Downer's words, meyaster. Now *I* holds a secret!" and he seemed very pleased with himself.

Sitting in the squishy chair, Andy also had a secret, one that he had almost betrayed in the hall had his captors been paying closer attention to him. When he'd squeezed Bess's hand before he'd left her, she'd squeezed his hand back... and damn near crushed it.

Meanwhile, Attrill was circling Bess, who was standing looking fragile in the bikini.

"You know, I'm not quite sure I trust you... remember the way you restrained me when I tried to kill you in the bedroom?"

Loops of vine grew out of the floor and bound her ankles, and a moment later cords whipped around her wrists and pulled them above her head, stretching her uncomfortably.

"Yes, that's much better," Attrill grinned, "And it will make it so much easier to beat the soul out of you."

"No!" the cry was high and childlike, and it didn't come from Elizabeth Russell.

"Who's that?" Attrill demanded, spinning around. He scanned the room, but no one was there. Then he looked up towards the ceiling,

"So, we've got a nosy child spying on us!"

"Leave her alone!" Chloe's voice echoed around the chamber.

"You're in no position to give orders, young lady. I can see you!"

At the other end of the psychic link, Chloe was gripped by fear as she hovered above the stream, looking into the bubble that showed her the hall where Attrill and Bess were standing. She wished she'd kept quiet. Hester had warned her about not being noticed, but she hadn't been able to stop herself shouting. Now Attrill was looking up at her as if he was trying to gauge distances.

"Run!" Bess yelled and the order made Chloe pull back from the bubble just in time as Attrill leapt up and his hand burst through the bubble to grab for her. Chloe screamed and opened her eyes, breaking the link. It was early evening and the bench in the hospital grounds was now in shadow. Chloe sprinted up the hill to find Jo. She didn't dare look behind her in case she saw Attrill loping after her with those long arms outstretched to drag her into his world. She didn't stop until she tumbled into her father's room, where Jo was helping Ray put on his cardigan before going to dinner.

"You all right?" Ray asked and she ran into his arms, crying. Jo put a hand on Chloe's shoulder as she spluttered,

"I fell asleep on the lawn and had a bad dream," and then, in between sobs, she described how she'd dreamed she could see other places and that an evil man had tried to grab her.

"Hey, hey, it's all right, you're safe now," Ray cuddled her and kissed her tear-streaked cheeks.

"I'm sure once you've woken up, all links between here and the dream world are broken and that you're perfectly safe," Jo added with a knowing look that reassured Chloe, although Jo would have to have a serious word with her later about the dangers of creating psychic links.

"I'm sorry," said Chloe, drying her eyes, "I didn't mean to worry you, but it all seemed so real. My friend was in terrible trouble."

Jo understood exactly what Chloe was trying to say, but couldn't give much comfort on that score,

"Sometimes things happen that are beyond our control. We have to be strong and face whatever tomorrow might bring," Jo said and she gave Chloe's shoulder a gentle squeeze.

"Yeah, you're all right now and that's what's important," Ray said, "Now give me another hug."

Chloe snuggled into her father's arms and held him tight, hoping upon hope that Bess would be okay.

Chapter Thirty-Three

A Time To Die

In the great hall, Attrill looked annoyed,

"I almost had her! Little sneak! Still, it doesn't matter. I saw exactly where she is. I'll pay her a visit in the very near future. She's so powerful for one so young – I shall enjoy her."

"Don't bet on it," Elizabeth Russell's voice sounded exhausted, "She exorcised your Hittite demon single-handed. You might find her too much for you, Urian."

Attrill chuckled at the name,

"My goodness, no one's called me Urian for over six hundred years. I'd almost forgotten him."

"Almost forgotten your own name?"

"But is that my name?" Attrill's eyes were impish as he looked at Bess,

"Even my own kind never knew my true name. Safer that way. While everyone revered my cousin Tronki as the god of thunder, I gave different names to different people. Meant that I could never be forced to appear by magicians invoking my 'true' name. If I ever did appear, it was by my own volition. I was never bound by the magician. The looks on their faces when they realised too late that they had no control over me..." and he let out a long but mirthless laugh.

"What about the children worshipping you here – what do they call you?"

"The Thin Man. Yes, I shall miss the children of The Island. Good kids. They've kept me going for the past thirty years. When your stock in trade is playing unpleasant tricks, children are a natural audience – they have such a delightful vicious streak! Anyway, enough about me – what about you?" Attrill said, casting an appraising eye over her,

"Well, the tattoos are a surprise, but I'm sure I can live with them," Attrill said, looking at the patterns that covered almost every inch of her body. Had he been well-versed in world religions, he would have recognised that each pattern was a different religious symbol, with some of them stretching back into pre-history. A scholar would have seen a comprehensive set of defensive and offensive symbols of power, which included the heavy silver rings on her fingers. Attrill was no scholar.

"Yes, you have a wonderful body – so strong and supple. I could have a lot of fun in there! This body has served me well, but I can't say that it's ever driven anyone wild with desire. Occupational hazard of being a jester. Ever seen a really handsome comedian?"

Attrill awaited a response, but none was forthcoming. Her head had slumped in exhaustion.

"No, of course you haven't. We're a different breed to the Thors, Odins or Apollos of this world. But in your body, I'll be able to experience what it's like to be a Venus or Freyja," and he rubbed his hands together in glee,

"I've never been picky between men and women. Always happy to give it or take it," and now he stopped to muse, "Nothing quite like a big man taking you hard, is there?" and he lifted her chin,

"Like your neanderthal. Once he's pounded you and spent his last ounce of strength, I'll bet you could keep going. Of course you could..."

Attrill let her head slump and continued to talk about his sexual exploits, giving his opinions on desire, but Elizabeth Russell wasn't listening. Ever since Downer had cast the spell that had brought them to Attrill's home, she had been changed. Yes, the tree had sucked the magic out of her, but the moment she'd arrived at Attrill's, her starved body had started to absorb the magical energy of the place like a sponge. And the longer Attrill burbled on, the stronger she was becoming. What made her want to laugh was the fact that the less she reacted to him, the more he talked and the more magical energy she could soak up. And she needed everything she could get! So, she was happy to let him ogle her. And besides, he was right – she was awesome! His unwitting positive reinforcement of her magnificence was only tipping the balance further in her favour. Attrill was behind her now, clucking about the damage done to her back by the tree,

"That must've hurt!" he said without sympathy, "And it still hurts, doesn't it?" and he brushed the cat o'nine tails very gently across her back. The pained hiss it elicited from her brought a grin to his face.

"It's still going to be painful once I've beaten your soul out of there, isn't it? I haven't been in real pain for a long time, so the next few days are going to be pretty unpleasant."

"I'm weeping for you," Bess murmured, unable to resist commenting.

"Thank you... but no pain, no gain!" Attrill laughed, "And anyway, it looks like these wounds are already beginning to heal. Do you heal quickly?" he asked, coming around to the front of her.

She nodded as if even doing that was a great effort.

"Oh, that's good news. I bet you don't really scar much, either, do you?"

She slowly shook her head.

"Great! Otherwise, it would be like buying a new car with a big dent in it."

Bess decided that remark deserved a kick in the nuts, but held back. If she could have another few minutes...

"And what about... women's things?" and his lip curled in distaste at the thought of fallopian tubes and all the other female gubbins,

"They all still working?"

Elizabeth Russell didn't dignify the question with a reply. The recent loss of her pregnancy at the hands of a demon who had been conjured by the arsehole in front of her, made her anger flare. Oh yes, she was going to kick him so hard, he'd be gargling his own testicles.

"I suppose I'll soon find out. It's going to be an interesting learning curve."

Attrill chuckled, not in a pleasant way.

"I've just had a delicious idea..." Attrill slipped in close to her and softly ran his fingers from her throat, through the valley between her breasts, down her stomach to her navel.

"I'm going to try before I buy. Give you a good seeing to as a road test. I'll be able to experience what all my future lovers will enjoy. Isn't that hilarious?" Attrill was gleeful as he moved to stand in front of her,

"If I screw you and then become you, I'll have literally fucked myself!"

To his surprise, Elizabeth Russell looked up at him and her violet eyes were glowing,

"You've already done that, mate!" and she kicked upwards with all her strength. Attrill hadn't noticed that when he had tried to catch Chloe, Bess had snapped the vine holding her right ankle. Now her foot thumped between Attrill's legs and she felt something soft squash between the flat of her foot and his pubic bone. His shriek was satisfyingly piercing. As he doubled over, she snapped the vine holding her left ankle and the cords holding her wrists. He coughed uncontrollably as he stumbled away from her, but she wasn't about to let him off the hook.

Her left fist smashed into his right temple and, as she'd hoped, the ring with the mark of Aegishjalmr, the Viking helm of awe and terror sent him reeling. She didn't give him the chance to regroup and followed it up with her right knee into his ribs. His yelp of pain and the crack of his rib was proof that the tattooed symbol of the Asian sky God Tengri was also a weapon against him. Her follow-up right hook caught him a glancing blow on his chin, but if the ring with the Celtic triquetra had had any power to harm him, even that glancing shot would have floored him. As it was, it only had the effect of an ordinary punch. The fact that there wasn't an explosion of pain in his face gave him the moment he needed to gather his wits. As Elizabeth Russell stepped in to deliver another left, he swatted at her with the cat o'nine tails. Her shriek filled the hall as the lashes of the scourge electrified every cell in her body. But if he thought the agony of the blow would drive her off, he was very wrong.

"Fucker!" she screamed and fell upon him like a cat, biting, clawing and punching as she sought to grab hold of the hand that held the nightmarish weapon.

Attrill fended her off as best he could, but she was able to grasp the wrist with the scourge, even as he grabbed hold of her other wrist. Now they were locked together, using their strength and balance to try to gain advantage. She had another go at slamming her right knee into him, but he was wise to the danger it posed and he used his long reach to keep his body away from it. Both were breathing hard, grunting and sweating as they grappled in the centre of the great hall, when Downer's voice broke into their world of pain,

"Thee bist needing to look at he's blade, meyaster."

Attrill and Elizabeth Russell both glanced across in confusion as Downer shuffled towards them with Andy's sword held out in front of him. Couldn't he see they were busy?

"Sod off!" Attrill hissed, quickly shifting his weight as Bess tried to use the distraction to her advantage. They were back to stalemate as Downer arrived, holding the blade up for Attrill to examine.

"The runes, meyaster!"

Attrill glanced, then put all his attention back on Elizabeth Russell, but she could see the fear in his eyes. Yes, there was something there that he recognised, something from his youth that he clearly hadn't forgotten.

"Be it the spell of undoing, meyaster?" Downer asked in a way that made it clear he already knew exactly what the spell was.

"No!" Attrill grunted, "Do something useful and stab her with it."

Bess suddenly had a horrible dropping feeling in her stomach. If Downer wanted to, he could run her through and that would be the end of that. She tried to manoeuvre herself so that Attrill was between her and Downer, but Attrill wouldn't let her.

"No, meyaster. I wants to see how it be on thee," and, to Attrill's staring horror, Downer slowly pushed the tip of the blade towards his master's face.

"No! What are you doing, you idiot! Don't..." and then Attrill screamed as the blade ran across his right cheek. Every millimetre of skin that it touched instantly decayed, revealing the muscles and sinews of his jaw and opening a gaping wound. His involuntary recoil pulled Elizabeth Russell off balance and he was able to use her momentum to throw her across the room. Swearing and clutching his mangled cheek, Attrill lashed out at Downer with the cat o'nine tails, catching his 'faithful' servant across the shoulder. Downer squealed and backed off, leaving Attrill free to slash at Elizabeth Russell as she leapt at him for another attack.

The lashes caught her across the face and chest, sending her crashing to the ground, and then Attrill lashed her again where she lay. Just as he was about to hit her again, a shotgun blast sent him spinning away from her.

"Schhiit!" he said through his ruined cheek as he saw Andy walking fast across the room with the shotgun trained on him.

"Go near her again and I'll blow your head off!" Andy shouted. Attrill positioned himself so that he could more or less see all of his assailants. Downer darted in with the sword, but failed to hit home and Attrill slashed at him with the cat o'nine to keep him at bay. Attrill wanted to make a pithy comment, but one side of his mouth was a painful gaping wound of bloody gums and grinning teeth. Instead, he decided to even up the odds. As Elizabeth Russell began to move again, he slashed the scourge across her exposed back. The shotgun roared and the impact threw Attrill backwards, but to Andy's disquiet, he recovered himself, then looked down at the mess the shotgun blast had made of his jacket.

"Ny schuit ish ruined!" Attrill exclaimed, unable to pronounce 'm' or 's' clearly.

He looked at Andy with venom and decided that he'd kill the annoying neanderthal right now. But first... Attrill gave Andy a wink, then dealt three quick slashes across Elizabeth Russell's back. Her screams split the air and Attrill was glad to see the attack was too much for Andy to bear. The moronic thug bellowed and turned the shotgun to wield it as a club. Oh, this would almost too easy! Andy ran forward, swinging the shotgun, but

Attrill batted it off with his arm, then caught Andy across the chest with a backhanded swipe. Andy was thrown off his feet and backwards a few yards, tumbling across the stone floor. Attrill was moving in to finish Andy off, when Downer slashed at him again with the sword. Attrill screamed as the blade opened up a decaying wound in his left side just under his ribs. He quickly scrambled back from the blade, slurring his words through his decayed cheek as he shouted at Downer,

"What d'you schink you're doing you little schhiit?" and he slashed at Downer with the cat o'nine.

"I be payin' meyaster back," Downer replied, keeping low to avoid the scourge, "I never wanted to serve thee. I med a ben at peace in me grave, but no! Thee bringed me back to life over 'n over agin! Thee bist a highty tighty cagmag overner an' I gonna gee thee a good basten!" and he lunged at Attrill, who dodged the thrust and countered with the cat o'nine, which caught Downer full in the face. The lightning strike of pain threw the sword from Downer's hand, sending it clattering across the floor.

Attrill cried in triumph and instantly fell upon his servant, grasping him by the throat and pulling him upright. Attrill looked into Downer's dazed face and shook him,

"Wake uff!" he yelled. He wanted Downer to be fully conscious when he took his life for the last time.

With Attrill busy attacking Downer, Andy grabbed a heavy silver candlestick from a table and launched himself at the man. All of Andy's weight and momentum were behind the candlestick, which caught Attrill just behind his right eye socket. The horrible crunch sent a spurt of blood and part of Attrill's eye showering across Downer, but Attrill didn't make a sound. He simply turned his ruined face to look at Andy, then winked his good eye, dropped the cat o'nine and took Andy by the throat. Andy choked and tried to hit him with the candlestick again, but Attrill's long arms meant that all he could strike was his shoulder. Attrill increased his grip and lifted both men off the ground. Andy dropped the candlestick as everything started to go blurry.

Attrill had so much to say – especially to that backstabbing little traitor Downer – but with his face mangled beyond recognition, it would all sound like gibberish. He'd cut to the chase, kill the bastards and resurrect them later to give them a proper talking to and torture them at his leisure.

"Now you die!" he lisped and the glint in his remaining eye was the last thing Downer saw before Attrill snapped his neck. Time for the Neanderthal...

Through an oxygen-starved blur, Andy knew he was done. Attrill turned his face towards him and looked him in the eye, but his expression of triumphant glee suddenly became startled. Attrill's breath was forced from him as Andy watched the sword blade emerge from his solar plexus,

"Now *you* die!" Elizabeth Russell panted, collapsing back onto the floor behind him. Attrill dropped Andy to grasp the tip of the blade with both hands. He stared down at the spell of undoing, glowing silver in the Elder Futhark runes of the sword. Andy looked up to see Attrill's hands turn into rotten flesh and his lower jaw come loose even as he tried to say something. A moment later, his decayed legs snapped below the knees, unable to support the weight of the rotting body. Attrill collapsed straight down, then slowly fell forward onto Downer with the hilt of the sword sticking out of his back.

Now the entire hall started to shake. Andy scrambled over to Bess, who was sitting staring at the result of her final attack.

"That seemed to work," she said with a weak smile.

"We've got to get out of here!" Andy shouted as the whole room seemed to twist and plaster fell from the ceiling around them.

"Where to?" Bess sighed. They had no idea how to get out and she was too exhausted to try running about like a headless chicken.

"Just hold me and hope," she said, and glowed inside as Andy put a protective arm around her.

A loud rumble had started and, as objects fell off the furniture and walls, even the bodies in front of them seemed to be moving with the vibration.

"Oh bollocks!" Bess sighed as she realised Downer wasn't moving because the room was shaking,

"Trouble!" she shouted, pointing at Downer, who was now lifting himself onto his hands and knees.

Andy leapt up, saw the cat o'nine on the floor and grabbed it before standing on what was left of Attrill and pulling the sword out of his back. As Downer got shakily to his feet, Andy stood between him and Bess with the sword and cat o'nine ready for another fight.

With the room shuddering and collapsing around them, Downer turned and faced Andy and Bess. His head was at a horrible angle and it seemed to be hampering his movements. Downer grabbed the sides of his head and yanked it up and to the left. Even with the increasing rumble and shattering destruction around them, they could hear the 'crack' of Downer's neck going back into place. He shook his head side to side to check it was right, then moved towards Bess. Andy slashed at him with the sword and he recoiled.

"Okay, let's call it a draw," and this time there was no trace of a local accent. He pointed at Bess and shouted,

"I'll see you somewhen, Elizabeth Russell!"

He clapped his hands and was gone. There was a cataclysmic crash, then darkness engulfed them as the world collapsed.

Chapter Thirty-Four

Tears For The Dead

Elizabeth Russell knew she must still be alive, because she was coughing. She opened her eyes, but they seemed to be gummed up - all she could see was a sort of white soup. She breathed in but was instantly racked by a spasm of coughing. She sat up, choking and hacking until the spasm passed, then rubbed her eyes. No, they weren't gummed up – she was engulfed in a whiteish cloud of thick dust. She struggled to her feet and bent over double with another fit of coughing. When she finally stood upright, she realised that sunlight was filtering through the dust. Andy! she looked around her and a couple of yards away there was an Andy-sized shape on the floor, covered with what looked like lumps of chalk. She hobbled to him and turned him over. He was alive and breathing. Thankfully, a warm breeze was blowing and the dust was clearing. Now she could see that the roof of the great hall was gone, along with one end of the room, leaving only the end with the fireplace. From the way the wind was blowing, she got the impression that they were high up. She looked down at her bare arms and legs – they were plastered in white stuff. Okay, so they were alive and relatively safe for now, so she concentrated on reviving Andy. She was too drained to try any magic, so had to resort to gently slapping his cheeks to bring him round.

After a minute without success, Bess bent down to kiss him. She'd hoped that it might jumpstart him like a fairytale princess, but nothing happened.

"Andy!" she yelled into his ear as she gave his cheek a hard pinch. That galvanised him and he jerked into wakefulness,

"Attrill!" he croaked, then had a coughing fit.

"Awake now?" she asked when he'd finished coughing and sat up.

"We're not dead, then?"

"No," and she gave him a big kiss on his stubbly cheek.

As Andy got up, he found that everything hurt.

"What the hell?"

Now that the dust was clearing, they could see that they were hundreds of feet above the sea, which was shimmering in the evening sun. They walked slowly towards the light and in the distance to their right, they could see a shallow crescent of coastline which ended in a high hill and cliffs.

"Sandown and Shanklin," Bess said, pointing down at the long beach, "That means we're somewhere up Culver cliff – explains all this chalk," and she coughed again as she waved away the clouds of dust.

Andy looked up and behind them. Sure enough, the chalk cliff rose above them by at least another fifty feet. He groaned as his head swam from looking up and he tottered. Bess grasped his arm and held him,

"If you think it's high up there, you probably don't want to look over the edge." She had, and reckoned they were a couple of hundred feet above the crashing waves below.

"It's all right," Andy said and he had a look, "Bloody hell! Did you see the huge chunk of cliff that's down there?"

Bess took another look and exclaimed,

"How did I miss that?"

There was a great block of white cliff, with its grassy top at forty-five degrees, lying down below.

"I hope the rest of the cliff's stable," Andy said, and both of them instinctively stepped back from the edge.

Once she thought she was a safe distance back, Elizabeth Russell turned her face towards the setting sun and sighed,

"That's nice!"

"All that fog's gone. Does that mean the Other Place has gone, too?" Andy asked.

"Oh crap!" her shoulders slumped at the thought of the queen and her minions coming after them,

"We've got to find the sword and that whip thingy," she said, going over to where Andy had lain. She vaguely remembered he was the last to have them.

It only took a minute or two of sifting amidst the fallen plaster and chalk to find them.

"Be nice if we had the stick part of the sword stick," Bess said.

"I saw it as I came in. Downer left it on the chair by the fire."

Andy walked over to the chair, which was a chalky mess, and picked it out.

"So, what happened with you and Downer?" Bess asked, handing him the sword, which he sheathed. Andy told her about the room with the strange flaming column and what Downer had done with the sword,

"And then he says to me 'stay there' and walked out of the room. Left the shotgun on the chair and everything."

"Must've had enough of Attrill's bullshit," Bess mused, "I guess he'll finally get to rest in peace now that Attrill's running around in his body."

"So, that definitely wasn't Downer who escaped?"

"Sadly not," she said bitterly. She hated loose ends – especially when those loose ends threatened to return.

"I'll have to add Attrill to the long list of things that want to kill me," she muttered. She was exhausted, in a lot of pain from her back and would merrily kill for a cold pint.

"Practical question: how the hell are we going to get down from here?" Andy asked.

Bess shrugged,

"Got a phone signal?"

Andy fished around in his pocket and turned his phone on.

"It's a miracle!"

"Dial 999 and ask for the coastguard. Tell 'em we're stuck up Culver cliff. Now, if you don't mind, I've got to sit down," and Bess limped over to one of the armchairs by the now extinguished fire, cleared the debris from it and curled up. She was asleep inside ten seconds.

Andy made the call and had to work hard to convince them that he wasn't a crank, and that he was, indeed, stuck about two hundred feet up Culver cliff. Once that was done, he hunted about for the towelling robe, found it in a corner and laid it over Bess to keep her warm until the rescue helicopter arrived. Standing alone in the wreck of Attrill's lair, Andy noticed that the floor was no longer flagstones inlaid with magic circles, but was roughly carved out of the chalk. And the furniture, far from being opulent, all looked like second hand tat from a junk shop. Had the whole thing been an illusion, like the shop in Brading? Had Attrill ever lived there? Or had he been an illusion, too? Andy shook his head. No, Attrill had been real, all right. Exactly *what* he was... well, that was something he'd leave to Bess to figure out. He looked down at her, curled up asleep in the chair, and felt a wave of love and protective feelings.

"I hope this job isn't like this every week," he said out loud, then he perched on the arm of the chair and waited there until the rescue helicopter arrived.

Andy had never heard of Lee-On-Solent, didn't know it was only ten miles from where he was sitting, and certainly didn't know it was the main helicopter base for the Coastguard on the south coast. So, he was surprised to hear the clatter of the helicopter within twenty minutes of his call. Soon, Bess and he had been winched aboard with the help of the very calm and efficient team, and then they were flying back to the mainland. Bess, who was now wrapped in a silver blanket, stared down at the Isle of Wight as they flew over it. How could somewhere that looked so pretty always cause her so much stress?

"You all right?" Andy shouted, cutting through the din of the helicopter.

"Glad to be off that sodding island!" Bess replied, then she turned to one of the crew,

"Got any beer?"

He shook his head sadly.

"I'm knocking a star off my TripAdvisor review for that!" she said. The man smiled. It was always a good day when the people they rescued could talk after their ordeal.

Soon, they were at the rescue base, being checked over by two paramedics in the back of an ambulance by the landing pad. Andy had nothing more than a few cuts and bruises, although the man checking him over was curious as to why he had bruising around his throat. However, when the other paramedic took a look at Bess and saw her back, he called his colleague over.

"What d'you reckon?" he asked as they looked at her back, then at each other. They both knew there was no way that damage had been caused by a fall down a cliff. It looked more like torture. Maybe the man had done it to her?

"You need to get these wounds properly cleaned, disinfected and dressed. We can't do that here. We'd better get you to a hospital," said the smaller man with sandy hair.

"No need," Bess replied, then turned to one of the helicopter crew,

"You got showers here?"

"Yeah."

"Can we use them and borrow some towels?"

The man hesitated and looked at the paramedics. They didn't look sure, but he replied,

"I guess so. Give me a couple of minutes and I'll sort something out," and he hurried off to the main building. Bess turned to the paramedics,

"And presumably you've got everything we need to clean and treat these," she said pointing to her back.

"Yeah, but..."

"So why block up A&E with someone like me? The doctors aren't going to do anything about that, are they?"

The paramedics looked at each other – she had a point...

"No," said Bess, "They'll think I'm a time waster. So, let's just get it over and done with here. I'll get him to wash me down," she indicated Andy,

"Then you can have a good look at me and bandage me up to your heart's content. Deal?"

Five minutes later, Bess and Andy were in the women's changing room, with its old-fashioned communal showers.

"Right," said Bess, arranging the towels on a bench, "You're going to have to come in with me, but don't get any ideas, 'cos I'm knackered."

"Don't worry," Andy replied, "I'm barely awake myself."

Now that the adrenaline of the fight and rescue was wearing off, Andy was shattered. Although, as Bess stripped off the bikini, he couldn't help one or two lustful thoughts. She picked up the dispenser of antiseptic soap, which they'd borrowed from the kitchen, and limped over to the showers. The layer of chalk caked onto her back stretched her injured skin as she moved, giving her some quite piquant sensations. She turned on the shower and stood next to the cascading water while she got the temperature right. As Andy joined her, she said,

"Right, this is going to hurt a lot, but you've got to get all this gunk off me, okay?"

"Don't worry. I've been a first responder at more than enough crash sites. I'm not squeamish about other people's pain."

"Just give me a while to get used to the water, then get on with it," she said, handing him the soap dispenser.

She eased under the water and it was like needles all over her back. In between ragged breaths, she put her knuckle into her mouth and bit down on it. Andy gave her time, then said,

"Ready yet?"

"Bit longer," she gasped – that water was really sodding painful! She concentrated, eased her breathing, tried to get used to the discomfort and then signalled for Andy to start. Rather than going straight for her back, he decided to clean the chalk from the rest of her first, soaping down her arms, face, hair and the front of her torso, before moving down to her legs. Bess thought that once she'd recovered, this sort of treatment would be rather pleasurable, but at that moment, she was experiencing it through a cloak of pain. Finally, the rest of her was chalk free. All that was left was her back.

"I'll start at the top and work my way down," Andy said. Bess nodded and put the knuckle of her right forefinger into her mouth.

Even though he was being gentle, the effect of the soap and the pressure of his hand was excruciating and she couldn't help but groan.

"Sorry," he said, but he didn't stop. He calmly continued doing what had to be done. Soon her legs began to shake from the agony,

"Want a break?" he asked.

"No, keep going," she panted. She was at the heart of a maelstrom of pain. With her eyes screwed tight, all she could see were images of what had happened over the past couple of weeks, from her first meeting with Bishop FitzOsbern, to the exorcism in Delaware, to Roddy dying. Swirling throughout them were her memories of the Other Place and Attrill's leering face. But one thing kept coming to the fore - the Tzitzimitl that had possessed poor Aggie Thompson. It kept rising up through the pain to not only taunt her about her inability to protect the life that had been forming inside her, but also to accuse her of cowardice for not telling Andy. As Bess struggled to stop herself blacking out, the Tzitzimitl was screaming that Bess deserved to suffer for her inadequacy and her deceit. Andy's child was dead because of her, and she was scared to tell him. She was scared to admit that the Tzitzimitl had given her the chance to walk away, but she hadn't taken it. Instead, she'd fought the demon in full knowledge she was pregnant, and the Tzitzimitl had ripped the life from her because she wasn't strong enough to stop it. How could she admit that to the 'great love of her life'? And, in spite of the screaming storm of agony engulfing her, Bess could hear the sly voice of the Tzitzimitl whispering into her ear that if she told him the truth, their relationship would never be the same again... if he stayed at all.

Bess was standing under the cascading water with her forehead pressed against the tiles and her shoulders shaking as the unrelenting pain forced the tears from her. The demon was right – it was all her own fault! And now the Tzitzimitl kept adding its poisonous thoughts to the agony gripping her.

You left it so long without telling him – how will Andy react? He won't be able to trust you anymore. Or maybe he'll think you didn't trust him enough to tell him? Either way, your relationship will go sour. And you haven't been together long. Less than three months and you're already ensnaring him with the complications of a baby. And even worse – the loss of one. Men hate that.

The demon said it as if it was fact.

Men hate to think about 'women's troubles'. It makes them feel useless. It shuts them out. And then what do they do? They leave. They leave and they find someone less troublesome. That's the truth. That's why you can't tell him. But if you keep silent, you will have to live with your secret knowledge – even as it slowly eats away at your insides. Tell him or keep silent – both options will ruin what you had.

And now the Tzitzimitl's laughter added to the deafening chaos in Elizabeth Russell's head.

Take this pain – you deserve every moment of it!

Then, amidst the scouring torture and the piercing knowledge of her wretched failures, Bess saw a vision of Andy. It was the moment on the beach when they had found their hag stones. She saw their kiss and heard him say 'I love you' in a way she'd never heard before. That moment had been real. What the demon had said were lies wrapped up in fear and pain. Bess could tell Andy. Everything would be all right.

"I've got to tell you something," she said through gritted teeth.

"What?" Andy asked, concentrating on cleaning the chalk from a nasty puncture wound.

"You know that Aztec fertility deity I exorcised in America..."

"Yeah?" Andy remembered when she'd told him about it only a few days ago – now it seemed like a strange dream from another lifetime.

"Well... it took something from me... from us."

"Us?"

"I didn't know it, but when I went to America I was pregnant," she waited, concentrating hard to hear his reaction amidst the screeching tumult of pain,

"Oh, Bess," and the tenderness of the way he said it cut through everything.

"When I was fighting it, the demon told me I was pregnant. Offered me the chance to walk away with our girl alive inside me... but I refused. I thought I could save the old woman and exorcise the demon without it doing me any harm... but it took our girl from me," and now she turned to look up at him,

"I'm so, so sorry!"

"Come 'ere," he said, opening his arms to her and stepping in to join her under the shower.

She clutched him to her, while he placed an arm gently across the back of her shoulders just above where the lacerations started, and held her. He kissed the top of her head.

"You did your best. That's all anyone can do. You're amazing. I'm just sorry you had to go through that alone." Andy had no experience with any of his former partners of miscarriage or loss, but he knew his mother had had two miscarriages. After his father's death, he and his mother had become very close and talked about anything and everything. She had told him about the siblings he might have had, and one thing had stuck firmly in his memory – she'd said that losing a pregnancy or a baby was the loneliest place in the world. Only the mother could know the true depth of the sorrow. Even other women who'd been through the same trauma couldn't truly know another woman's grief. Andy would never be able to feel Bess's pain, but he could love her and be there for her unconditionally. He wanted to envelope her in his arms and hold her tight, but her wounds wouldn't let him. Instead, he bent his head down to her ear,

"I love you and I'm always here for you if you need me."

She released her grip on him so she could look him in the eye,

"It's at least eight years before we get another chance," she said.

"That's eight years for me to get my head round it."

"You'll be fifty."

"Charlie Chaplin was over seventy when he had his last kid."

"I'm sorry I didn't tell you before."

Andy looked surprised,

"That's all right. It's not like we've had any convenient moments since you got back. Anyhow, this is about you, not me. How are you?" it was hard for him to tell, because she was clearly in a lot of physical pain.

"Better for telling you... but my back..." and she trailed off as her face screwed up in agony.

"We should get this finished, then," he said, and she reluctantly nodded. Then, just as she was about to turn towards the wall, she reached up behind his neck and eased him down to kiss her. Even in all the pain, that felt good.

"Okay," she said, taking a couple of deep breaths, "Get on with it and don't take it personally when I swear at you."

Twenty minutes later, they emerged from the changing room and the paramedics saw to her back. First, they gave her an injection for the pain, then, as they did their work, she held Andy's hand, crushing it from time to time when the discomfort got too much. Even though the rest of the shower had been agony, once she had told Andy the truth, she'd found the torment somehow cathartic. The pain and the cascading water had cleansed her of her toxic feelings, so that now she could look forward. By the time the paramedics had finished, the cacophony of suffering had been dulled by the effects of the injection. As she was gingerly easing into a big HM Coastguard hoodie, one of the rescue team appeared, looking confused.

"There's a bloke in an enormous Rolls Royce out the front. He says he's come to pick you up."

"Good! Oliver's come up trumps," said Bess. With the pain dimmed, she sounded more like herself.

"When did you...?" Andy began.

"Soon as we were in the helicopter," she replied, "I've got everyone on the lookout for Attrill – or rather Downer... I'll explain at the pub," then she turned to thank the paramedics before asking the rescue crew member to take them to their car. As they hobbled through Solent airport and out into the evening sunshine, she asked,

"Got any Fuller's pubs round here?"

"Yeah. The Wyvern's about eight hundred yards that way," he said, pointing off to their left.

"Thank heavens for that!"

Although getting into the huge car was a painful and slow process, it was worth it, because within five minutes they were sitting at a table outside The Wyvern, with a view across the airport and pints of ESB in hand.

"That's gorgeous!" Bess sighed after her first big mouthful.

Andy took a couple of glugs of his and closed his eyes in blissful contemplation.

"So, you spoke to Oliver?" he said at last.

"And Jo, and Chloe, and Hester, and Suzy, and Hapgood," Bess replied, "Attrill gave Chloe a bit of a scare and said something about going after her, so I'm going to get her more protection."

"What a tosspot!" Andy wasn't a fan.

"True! But on the plus side, his last two demons have been exorcised without any casualties. And as of now, I've got the whole Department and all our contacts looking out for him. If he so much as tries to pull a rabbit out of a hat, we'll be on him like a ton of bricks," and she punctuated that happy thought with another mouthful of beer.

"So, what now?"

"Finish these. Back to mine. Sleep for a week. Sound like a plan?"

Andy said nothing, but simply raised his glass to her. In the last, golden rays of a warm September evening, that sounded like the best plan he'd ever heard.

THE END.

Afterword

Please review this book!

Reviews make a huge difference to the success of a book, so if you enjoyed The Wolverton Demons, please consider leaving a review on Amazon or your favourite book review site. I'd very much appreciate it.

If you want to see what I'm up to, then you can find me on Facebook

I try to keep news about what I'm having for lunch (with pictures) to an absolute minimum, but if I'm having something incredible, I do reserve the right to post it.

Or, if Facebook isn't your scene, you could throw yourself into the abyss of chaos that is my website VJNash.com

There, if you are brave enough, you can sign up for my newsletter. It's free, I don't harvest or share your data and it's crammed with exclusive info on what's coming up and access to the occasional short story.

Made in United States
Orlando, FL
24 April 2026

80797003R00217